Readers love
K.C. Wells

First

"For those who love a sweeping romantic gesture, the ending is a romance reader's dream that is sweet, sweet, and sweet. A recommended read of two truly opposite characters who find love in the city despite the odds."
—Joyfully Jay

"I've always been a fan of K.C. Wells and this book continues her works that make her books must reads for me."
—GGR Review

"I highly recommend *First* by K.C. Wells to anyone who loves to read a great MM love story."
—Rainbow Gold Reviews

Make Me Soar

"I had very high expectations for this book and I have not been disappointed."
—Three Books Over the Rainbow

"This is one of my top favorite stories of the series as the author uncovers the layers of Dorian's personality and of Alan's past and the relationship that most influenced his life."
—Hearts on Fire Reviews

"The sexy times are plentiful once they get started and they are hot as ever so be prepared!"
—Gay Book Reviews

By K.C. Wells

A Bond of Three
Debt
First
Love Lessons Learned
Waiting For You

COLLARS & CUFFS
An Unlocked Heart
Trusting Thomas
With Parker Williams: Someone to Keep Me
A Dance with Domination
With Parker Williams: Damian's Discipline
Make Me Soar
With Parker Williams: Dom of Ages

LEARNING TO LOVE
Michael & Sean
Evan & Daniel
Josh & Chris
Final Exam

Published by Dreamspinner Press
www.dreamspinnerpress.com

DEBT
K.C. Wells

Published by
DREAMSPINNER PRESS

5032 Capital Circle SW, Suite 2, PMB# 279, Tallahassee, FL 32305-7886 USA
www.dreamspinnerpress.com

This is a work of fiction. Names, characters, places, and incidents either are the product of author imagination or are used fictitiously, and any resemblance to actual persons, living or dead, business establishments, events, or locales is entirely coincidental.

Debt
© 2016 K.C. Wells.

Cover Art
© 2016 Ethan James Photography.
ethanjamesphotography.com
Cover Design
© 2016 Paul Richmond.
http://www.paulrichmondstudio.com
Cover content is for illustrative purposes only and any person depicted on the cover is a model.

All rights reserved. This book is licensed to the original purchaser only. Duplication or distribution via any means is illegal and a violation of international copyright law, subject to criminal prosecution and upon conviction, fines, and/or imprisonment. Any eBook format cannot be legally loaned or given to others. No part of this book may be reproduced or transmitted in any form or by any means, electronic or mechanical, including photocopying, recording, or by any information storage and retrieval system, without the written permission of the Publisher, except where permitted by law. To request permission and all other inquiries, contact Dreamspinner Press, 5032 Capital Circle SW, Suite 2, PMB# 279, Tallahassee, FL 32305-7886, USA, or www.dreamspinnerpress.com.

ISBN: 978-1-63477-285-3
Digital ISBN: 978-1-63477-286-0
Library of Congress Control Number: 2016901420
Published May 2016
v. 1.0

Printed in the United States of America
∞
This paper meets the requirements of
ANSI/NISO Z39.48-1992 (Permanence of Paper).

Acknowledgments

MY THANKS to my wonderful team of betas: Bev, Debra, Jason, Mardee, Michelle, and Helena.

And a very special thank-you to Andrew Q. Gordon for all his help and advice.

Chapter One

MITCH JENKINS threw down his pen with a groan. "You know what? They must think we're idiots." He put his head in his hands and closed his eyes as if that would wipe away all traces of Bronwen Dempsey's pathetic excuse for an essay. No such luck—it was still lying there when he peeked at his desk.

Angela Frampton raised her head from her grading and chuckled. "What have the dear little darlings done now?" She put down her pen and stretched. "Go on, tell me. I could use a laugh." She gestured toward her neat pile of assignments. "Anything not to have to look at yet another paper that proves my students don't listen to a word I say." Angela tilted her head to one side. "So go on, spill." She started packing away her pens.

"I assigned an essay on *Lord of the Flies* for my tenth grade class," Mitch told her as he leaned back in his chair, his laced fingers cradling his head. "So far, I count ten, maybe twelve students who've all used goddamn *CliffsNotes* in their 'research.'" He hooked his fingers in the air and snorted. "Yeah, right. The extent of their research was to repeat the notes verbatim or copy and paste whole paragraphs from the Internet. I bet they all thought they were being *so* clever, *so* original. Did they think I wouldn't notice? Oh, *course* not, I forgot, I'm just some dumb schmuck of an English teacher with a degree in English literature and obviously don't have enough brain cells to recognize what is basically the same essay repeated over and over again." He shook his head. "And these will be the same kids who'll go running home to mommy and daddy to complain I'm being unfair and harsh when I give them an F. Is it wrong of me to expect an essay to contain at least *one* original thought?" Mitch exhaled, pushing all of the tension out of him in one long breath. "Are we there yet?" It had been a long fucking week.

Angela got up from her chair and came over to him, placing her hands on his shoulders and kneading the tense muscles. She bent lower to speak quietly next to his ear. "You've got three more weeks, Mitch, then it's adios to all this for the summer. C'mon, I know it's been a rough couple months, but you're nearly there." She pushed her thumbs into the flesh on either side of his spine and kneaded hard.

Mitch groaned and leaned forward, giving her room. "Damn, you're good at that. You'd make a fabulous masseuse, do you know that?" He grunted when she dug in deeper, her agile fingers finding the knots of tension at the base of his neck and between his shoulder blades. He gave a low moan of pleasure; it felt that good. Clearly there was some recompense for staying behind to work when everyone else had left for the evening. The teachers' lounge was deserted, save for the two of them. Not that this was the first time he'd benefited from Angela's magical fingers. It was getting to be a regular Friday night habit.

Angela chuckled. "Can you *not* make those noises, Mitch? If anyone passes by in the hall, they'd be forgiven for thinking something awfully dirty is going on in here."

"Who cares?" he groused. "The students have gone, 'cause who would stick around school on a Friday after four o'clock?" He guffawed. "Oh yeah, I forgot—the poor teachers who have to grade their plagiarized crap." Mitch chuckled. "And if there's anyone out there perverted enough to listen with their ear pressed up to the door? Screw 'em. Let 'em think what they like."

"You're a wicked man," Angela said, laughing. "You'll ruin my reputation."

"Honey, your reputation is quite safe, trust me." It wasn't as if he made a big thing about his sexuality, but he didn't hide it. Besides, Angela was an absolute sweetheart. She and Mitch often chatted during their prep period or over coffee during their lunch break. "And one day, you're gonna make some lucky man very happy with those fingers." Angela snorted and Mitch snickered. "Okay, that sounded dirty even to me. I think we'd better call it a night."

"Why, Mr. Jenkins, Miss Frampton, what*ever* are you doing?" A theatrical gasp accompanied the words.

Right on time. "Hey, Aaron, you ready to leave?" Angela hastily withdrew her hands and straightened. Mitch grabbed hold and patted one hand, gazing up into her sweet face. "Thank you," he said sincerely. He kissed her fingertips. "These are wonderful."

Angela blushed from the neck of her blouse up to the roots of her auburn hair as she pulled free of him. "Oh hush. Have a good weekend, Mitch." She glanced over his head and gave a slight nod.

"Aaron." Once she'd picked up her purse, she fled the teachers' lounge, cheeks still flushed.

Aaron Weldon flopped into the chair facing Mitch. "I don't get it. What do *you* have that I don't?"

Mitch arched his eyebrows. "Excuse me?" He stretched, his spine popping.

Aaron flung out his hand, gesturing toward the closed door. "You get back rubs, giggles, '*have a good weekend, Mitch,*'" he mimicked, "whereas all *I* get is a cursory nod and my name." He let out an exaggerated sigh. "And what makes it worse? She knows we're both gay."

"God, you talk a load of crap," Mitch groused, rising from his chair to get his jacket. He was more than ready to leave.

Aaron gave a knowing smile. "I get it. You've got that whole *wounded by love* thing going for you. Women are suckers for a guy with a broken heart." No sooner had the words left his lips than he froze. "Oh. Yeah. Sorry, Mitch, I didn't—"

"Save it, okay?" Mitch said stiffly. He didn't want to think about Jerry. Two months had passed, but the pain was still fresh, still raw.

Aaron sighed. "I was meaning to talk to you on the way home. I wondered if you wanted to meet up tonight."

Mitch glanced at the pile of essays. He'd be spending most of Saturday grading them.

That made the decision a damn sight easier.

"Sure. What do you have in mind? And *don't* say meeting up with some guys you found on Grindr, 'cause if that's the case, I'm changing my mind." He shoved the papers into his bag.

Aaron pulled a face. "What have you got against Grindr?"

From the hall came the sound of a door closing.

"Not in here," Mitch said hurriedly. "You never know who's hanging around. We can talk on the train." Not that he wanted to.

Aaron nodded and rose, grabbing his backpack. "Let's get out of here, then."

As they headed down the quiet hallway toward the exit, one of the custodians, Bertha, greeted them with a cheery wave. "Have a good one, fellas."

Mitch grinned. "Same to you, Bertha. And thanks for those books you left on my desk this morning. Books are always welcome." They'd gone straight onto the shelf in his classroom where he kept paperbacks for the kids to borrow.

Bertha waved her hand dismissively. "Pfft. You were doin' me a favor. Now the eldest is off to college soon, he's clearin' out his room. He was gonna throw 'em out!" She shook her head. "Kids. Don't appreciate nothin'. I figured you'd have a use for 'em." Her smile lit up her face. "He still says you're one of the best teachers in the place. And he had some damn good teachers in Atlanta, so that is really sayin' somethin'."

Damn. Mitch was too long in the tooth to be blushing at a compliment, but his cheeks heated up regardless. "Your Tony was a sweet kid who loved learning. Kids like that are a joy to teach." He gave her one last smile before he and Aaron departed. "Enjoy deciding what you're going to do with that room once he's gone."

Bertha let out a whoop. "Honey, got that one *all* figured out. That's gonna be my new sewin' room. You know how long I've wanted me one of those?" She grinned. "Soon as Tony is out, my sewin' machine is *in*, baby."

Mitch could still hear her chuckling as he and Aaron descended the stone steps in front of the main building, hurrying to 77th Street to catch the subway. The Upper East Side was gearing up for rush hour, the traffic already swelling along with the noise. Mitch swung his jacket over his shoulder, enjoying the warmth of the late afternoon sun. Early June was a lovely time of year in New York City, and right then the temperature had to be in the high seventies. Perfect, as far as Mitch was concerned.

"I remember Tony Blasco," Aaron remarked. "Nice kid."

Mitch chuffed. "And gay as a three-dollar bill." He adjusted his backpack to a more comfortable position. "He took a lot of crap from the jocks when he was a sophomore and he joined the theater group."

"What—you think he's gay just because he was into the arts?" Aaron rolled his eyes. "Geez, talk about stereotyping a guy."

Mitch chuckled. "No, I think he's gay because I caught sight of him one weekend in Central Park his senior year. He was sitting on a bench with Sammy Williams, and they were doing their damnedest not to look like they were holding hands." The memory made him smile. "Young love, huh?"

"You think his mom knows he's gay?"

"Not for me to speculate," Mitch replied with a shrug. "All I can do is hope she's one of those parents who supports their children, whatever their sexual orientation. Lord knows, we have plenty of the other kind in this country." He pushed aside the familiar pulse of rage toward parents who could abandon their children simply because they were LGBT. He'd been damned lucky with his family. "Talk to me about your plans for this evening."

"There's a bar I'd like to take you to," Aaron said as they descended into the bowels of the city and through the turnstile that led onto the subway platform. "Well, it's sort of a club too."

Mitch groaned. "Please, not another strip joint. That last one was embarrassing."

"What was wrong with it?" Aaron's tone was indignant.

Mitch leaned in close and lowered his voice. "They were supposed to be strippers, right? Sorry, but I do *not* class playing around with the hem of your sleeveless shirt as stripping." He sighed. "Now Atlanta, *there's* a city that has good strip clubs. For one thing, you get to see the whole package, not like in this puritanical city."

Aaron coughed. "New York—puritanical? Hell, I've heard the Big Apple called a lotta things, but that is not one of them." He grinned. "NYC is the Gay Mecca."

Mitch arched his eyebrows. "Well, your Gay Mecca has some pretty strict ideas about sex."

Their train pulled into the station, and they quickly got on board. Aaron grabbed two empty seats near the door and flopped down into one of them. Mitch joined him, his backpack sitting on his lap.

He sighed heavily. "Go on, then—tell me about this club."

"It's on West 38th Street between Eighth and Ninth Avenue, and it's called the Black Lounge. It's more of a bar-*cum*-restaurant, but it has three floors. The second floor is quieter, with leather couches, soft music—you know, more conducive to talking. And then there's the third floor, which is where the dancing happens."

"A gay restaurant?" Mitch didn't think the Garment District had such a thing, although it wasn't often he ate far from his home turf of 4th and Perry. He knew the area; it was frequented by a young gay crowd, the perfect spot for a club.

Aaron shrugged. "To be honest, I don't eat much in the restaurant. I just take the stairs up to the second or third floor. Both have bars, and the music's not bad."

"Are we talking casual, swanky, what?"

"It's a swanky spot, for sure. Pretty classy." Aaron leveled a keen glance at Mitch. "So… you still wanna meet me there tonight?"

The mood he was in right then, Mitch would've agreed to anything. "Sure. I'll meet you outside. What time?"

"I was thinking maybe nine, ten o'clock."

Mitch could do that. He leaned his head against the window and closed his eyes. He hadn't been to a club for a while. Jerry's exit had been a real kick to the balls. He'd only started to venture out after he'd grown tired of jerking off. What he hadn't counted on were his own hang-ups getting in the way of a good time.

"You okay, Mitch?"

He popped open one eye and peered at Aaron. "Yeah. Why'd you ask?"

Aaron stared at him. "Why'd I ask? Really? You've been one badass moody bitch ever since… you know."

Shit. "That bad?"

Aaron snorted. "Why'd ya think I'm taking you out on the town tonight? I figured you really needed a fun night out. You know, music, hot guys…. You never know, you might get lucky."

Mitch could've told him *that* wasn't about to happen, but he didn't want to put a damper on things. He knew Aaron's heart was in the right place. He regarded his colleague with affection. "Thanks. I do appreciate it. And I'm sorry for having my head stuck up my ass the last couple of months. I guess being dumped really knocked the wind out of my sails."

"I haven't asked you about it 'cause I figured you didn't wanna talk about it."

"Well, get a few drinks in me tonight," Mitch confided, "and I may spill my guts." Not that he wanted to talk about it, but Aaron deserved that much.

When the train pulled into the station, he and Aaron parted company with the promise that he'd call if he changed his mind. Mitch didn't think it likely. A night of alcohol with the possibility of eye candy was definitely an improvement. He changed lines and headed across to

West 10th Street. He had time to grab a bite to eat and maybe even a nap before showering and taking the train up to 34th Street. It would be a lovely night to walk the remaining four blocks.

Aaron was right. Mitch needed a night out. Anything to get away from the constant nagging voice telling him it was *his* fault Jerry left.

THE BLACK Lounge was definitely upmarket. Mitch took one look around the crowded space and felt shabby. He'd never seen so many smartly dressed men in one place. The bar was a sea of Hugo Boss, Gucci, and Ferragamo. The background music was low and unobtrusive, and the bar top seemed to be one long line of cocktails and glasses of white wine. There were small tables set up with two or three chairs, and at least four couches that Mitch had spied so far. From above came the pulse of dance music.

"When you said classy, you weren't kidding," he said quietly, leaning closer to Aaron while they waited at the bar. "I keep looking over my shoulder for the bouncer to walk up to me and ask me to leave because I don't meet their dress code."

Aaron cackled, the sound just a shade too loud. Heads turned in their direction before conversations resumed. "Mitch, you look fine. Stop worrying."

Mitch glanced at his black shirt, the top two buttons open to reveal the black hair that covered his chest. He wore black jeans that had been sitting in his drawer for months, the tags still intact, and he'd polished his boots until they shone. No jewelry except his heavy watch, a silver thumb ring, and the single diamond stud in his earlobe.

Maybe a tie would help?

The bartender placed a beer in front of him, and he nervously swallowed half of it. "Feeling a little underdressed, to be honest."

Aaron snickered. "Will you quit stressing? I repeat: you look *fine*. Now finish that up so I can get you another. Maybe something classier, like a cocktail." He winked and sipped his Manhattan.

Mitch bit back his groan. "See? Even my choice of drink is all wrong for this place." He gazed at the tables and couches, taking in the men of all shapes and sizes. Lord, but there were some good-looking guys, not one of them badly dressed. He estimated one man's suit would cost as much as Mitch made in a month.

Aaron appeared completely relaxed, as though he spent every night in the bar.

Come to think of it....

"How often do you come here?" Mitch asked him.

Aaron's face flushed. "Oh, I've only been here a few times." He took a longer drink from his cocktail and peered into the distance, as if studying his environs. Mitch regarded him steadily, but Aaron was doing a good job of avoiding his gaze.

Okay, that's weird.

Mitch huffed and returned his attention to his beer while drinking in the scenery. His earlier estimation had been entirely correct—the guys in this bar were gorgeous. His gaze was drawn in particular to one tall hunk of good-looking sitting alone, sipping a cocktail. Now and again the guy would flick his gaze in Mitch's direction and smile. Mitch tried hard not to stare, but damn, Mr. Tall, Dark, and Sexy just drew the eye. When he shifted position, drawing Mitch's attention to his crotch—*fuck, how in hell did I miss that?*—it became apparent, even at a distance, that the man was hung.

The blatancy of his calculated action was enough to pour ice water over Mitch's groin.

Uh-uh, not going there.

"You got good taste," Aaron murmured, nudging Mitch's arm. "Why not stroll over and say hi?"

"Because that's not me," Mitch returned under his breath.

Aaron stared at him sardonically. "Wanna explain that one to me? 'Cause last time I looked, you've been single for two whole months and he is fucking *gorgeous*." He arched his eyebrows. "You telling me you haven't been laid in two months?"

Mitch did his best to breathe evenly. "Look, you're perfectly happy to go on Grindr or Scruff or whatever and hook up with random guys based on the way they look and how their profile reads, but not me, all right?" He knew all about Aaron's sex life. His colleague wasn't the shy, retiring type, and when he got lucky, Mitch always got to hear the gory details—whether he wanted to or not.

Aaron rolled his eyes. "Geez, Grindr again? Consenting adults, right?"

Mitch drained half his glass before turning to face Aaron. "I've used it too, okay? I had a couple of hookups about a month ago, but honestly, I'm just not sold on the whole one-night stand thing. I'm not happy about going to some guy's place, and as for them coming to mine? Forget it."

"Sounds like you got issues," Aaron remarked.

"You're damn right I have issues!"

That came out louder than Mitch had intended. His cheeks grew hot as he took in the glances in their direction, but Aaron said nothing.

Mitch took a deep, calming breath. "I like situations where I feel in control. Hookups, one-night stands, call 'em what you will—there are too many unknowns for my liking, especially nowadays."

"Like what?"

"Well, there's disease, for one. You don't know anything about the guy you're fucking, or who's fucking you. Plus there are some real crazies out there. Most of all, I guess I'm scared of that lack of control." He drained the rest of his beer and met Aaron's gaze. "Can't believe I'm telling you this, but… I've been thinking about using some site like RentMen.com." He'd done more than think about it, but Aaron didn't need to know that.

Aaron frowned. "Why them and not Grindr?"

"It seems legit, and it looks like all the guys are vetted."

Aaron stared at him in silence. After a moment he put down his cocktail glass and shifted closer on his barstool. "Okay, I know RentMen has a good reputation, but you've got it all wrong. *Anyone* can advertise on that site. You still don't know what you're getting. All the company does is provide the site." He tilted his head. "What if…?" Aaron grabbed his Manhattan and took a gulp, his face contorting as he swallowed.

For some inexplicable reason, Mitch had goosebumps. He watched Aaron without a word. Aaron studied his face intently, and Mitch wondered what the hell was going on.

When he couldn't take the silence anymore, he gestured wildly. "All this is driving me crazy. Spit it out, Aaron, whatever it is."

"Correct me if I'm wrong," Aaron began, enunciating slowly. "You wanna get laid, but you're not happy taking home some stranger you know nothing about. You're even less happy about going to his place."

"It just doesn't feel… safe," Mitch admitted. He knew it was a hang-up, but it was proving difficult to overcome. *At this rate I'll never get laid again.* The alternative was the slow and steady dating route, but *Lord*, there were times when all he really needed was a good, hot fuck.

"So what if I told you about a club I joined recently?" Aaron's gaze never wandered from Mitch's face.

The goosebumps were back, big-time.

"What kind of club?" Mitch knew he sounded cautious, but he couldn't help it.

Aaron leaned closer, his voice barely audible. "A secret club, which provides any type of guy you could imagine. Guys who are vetted. You get to spend time with them in a controlled, secure environment. Would that be of interest to you?"

Mitch smirked. "Christ, Aaron, sounds like you're describing a brothel."

Aaron's eyes widened. "Shh, not so loud." He glanced around them, biting his lip.

Fuck. "Oh my God, you *are*." Mitch gaped. "You're talking about a fucking *brothel*."

Aaron straightened. "I'm talking about a club where you can only get in if you're a member, or a member's guest. And they run background checks before they accept you as a member. They don't advertise, it's all word of mouth. Everything the client wants, they provide—and I do mean everything. You pay by the hour, and you get to see before you buy, if you catch my drift. The guys are taken care of, tested, checked out, you name it. When you become a member, you have to sign a contract stipulating that you do *not* disclose any details about the club to anyone."

"What, like you're now disclosing to me?" Mitch raised his eyebrows.

"You, I trust. And if I take you there, you'll have to sign the same contract, okay?"

Mitch breathed deeply. "You're serious, aren't you?"

Aaron nodded. "Why not come along, see what you think? And if someone catches your eye, he's yours for a couple of hours, on me." He held up his hands. "No pressure, Mitch. If you're not happy, then we leave. I don't mention it again." A faint smile twisted his lips. "But if you do spy someone who pushes all the right buttons…."

"Sounds like an awfully expensive gift, Aaron." Mitch knew what the guys on RentMen charged per hour for their time, and what Aaron was describing didn't come across as cheap. "Why would you do that for me?"

He snorted. "Look, we may get along, but I'm not about to shell out *that* kinda money for you to get laid. Think of it more like bonus points I've accrued. I don't have a clue what happened with Jerry, but it's obvious you've been through some shit. You need this." He sat back and drained his glass. "Well?"

Mitch thought fast. A look wouldn't hurt. He could get an impression of this club and make a decision based on his gut feeling. And of course, there was always the possibility that he could get laid. God knows, he'd had enough of fucking his fist.

"Okay, let's do it," he said quickly. "Where is this place?" He grabbed his jacket from the stool next to him and rose to his feet.

Aaron simply raised his gaze to the ceiling before looking Mitch in the eye.

It's upstairs?

Chapter Two

"You're kidding." Mitch wondered at the sheer nerve of whoever had created the club. It certainly wasn't the first place he'd think of when it came to locating a brothel. No wonder the owners wanted it to remain a secret.

Aaron shook his head. "So far no one on the street level has a clue of its existence, and that's how they'd like to keep it." He led them out of the bar and back to the stairs they'd used to reach it. On the third floor, the dance floor was packed with male bodies in varying states of undress, the least amount of clothing being a pair of skimpy shorts. Aaron worked his way around the room to the back of the club where a thick-necked gorilla of a man dressed entirely in black sat on a stool, ostensibly watching the cavorting on the dance floor. Behind him was a narrow hallway, its walls black.

His gaze flickered over Aaron and Mitch as they approached him. He nodded to Aaron. "Mr. Weldon." Dark eyes regarded Mitch, no trace of emotion, before returning to Aaron. "Got your ID?"

Aaron nodded. "This is my guest," Aaron said, his hand at Mitch's back. "I can vouch for him."

The man's stare was unnerving. "I'm glad about that, but I still need to see some ID before he goes anywhere," he observed dryly.

Mitch took the hint and handed over his driver's license. The bouncer examined it carefully before handing it back. "Des will fill out the paperwork through there." He gestured with his head. "You can go on through."

Mitch followed Aaron into the dark hallway. "'Oh, I've only been here a few times,'" he mimicked. "Yeah, right. When a bouncer knows you by name at a sex club? Hate to tell you, Aaron, but you are *so* busted."

Aaron muttered under his breath, something about this being the last time he'd do Mitch a favor, but he fell silent when they reached a door with yet another bouncer leaning against the wall. The heavy guard straightened at the sight of them and examined the card Aaron held up. He peered at Mitch.

"ID," he said brusquely. Mitch waited while the guard perused his driver's license. He reached up to take a clipboard and pen from a hook on the wall. "You need to sign this before I can let you in. You can collect your ID on the way out."

Mitch nodded. Attached to the clipboard was a nondisclosure agreement, outlining Mitch's acceptance of the rules. He read it through and signed the form. Clearly, security was of the utmost importance. He handed the clipboard back and waited while it was scrutinized.

"Okay, Mr. Jenkins. You understand the rules?"

"I'm not to disclose the existence of the club to anyone," Mitch confirmed.

The guard nodded. "That includes its location, and anything—or any*one*—you see while you're on the premises. Our members value their privacy, as you can imagine. No photographs, no recording. We reserve the right to examine your phone before you leave."

"Understood."

He gave Mitch a card with Mitch's name written on it. "This is for this evening. It states that you have been made aware of the rules and have signed the agreement. Once you get upstairs, someone will show you around the facilities. Should you wish to visit the club again, you'll need to take out a membership. The options will be presented to you at that time." The guard stared at Mitch, unblinking. "You understand that if you break this agreement, the club *will* take legal action against you."

He'd been thinking about that. "What exactly can the club do if I—"

"Don't go there," Aaron cut in. "Seriously. Don't be a smartass." The guard's eyes bulged and he clenched his jaw.

Mitch thanked him politely, and the guard rapped on the door, which swung open for them. He followed Aaron past another security guard into a long hallway, at the end of which was a staircase.

"I see what you mean about it being a secure environment," he muttered as they walked along the hallway. "It's probably easier getting into Fort Knox."

"But that's a good thing, right?" Aaron gave him a sideways glance. "These guys don't want just *anyone* wandering in off the street. Someone at the dance club gets to wondering about what's up here, there's not much likelihood of getting past three security guards."

He had a point.

"Aaron, think about it," he said under his breath. "They're a secret club, for Christ's sake. They couldn't sue me without drawing attention to themselves, which they do *not* want to do. So if I did break the rules, they couldn't do a thing."

Aaron stopped dead before they reached the stairs. "Look, I signed the same form you did, okay? It's just your average, basic intimidation technique, right? Just trust me on this. Do *not* mess with these guys." He fixed Mitch with a hard stare.

Mitch caved—for the moment. "Okay, okay," he said, attempting to mollify Aaron. "I'll behave, all right?"

"You'd better," Aaron muttered.

They climbed the stairs, at the top of which was a plain black door. Aaron knocked and waited.

The man who opened it was dressed smartly in a suit. He smiled at Aaron and stepped aside to let them enter. "Good evening, gentlemen."

Mitch took a moment to assimilate his surroundings. They were standing in a reception area, the only furniture being a low desk with a monitor and keyboard and three fat leather armchairs facing it. Piano music filtered through the air. The walls were plain, a deep red that matched the thick carpet and the highly painted door to the left of the desk. The overall impression was one of class.

Suit Guy took their cards and went over to the desk where he tapped on the keyboard, peering at the monitor. He raised his head to glance at Mitch. "Are you here to check us out?" he asked, that smile still in place.

Mitch opened his mouth to speak, but Aaron got in first. "I've brought him to take a look at the club, Seb," he said, licking his lips. "And if he'd like to spend some time here, it can go on my account, right?" He gazed levelly at Seb, who nodded. "I won't be staying this evening," Aaron continued, rubbing the back of his neck. "But I'll wait to see what my friend decides to do."

Mitch had never seen Aaron act so nervously, and he didn't like it. *What the fuck has he got to be nervous about?*

Seb regarded the monitor. "If you become a member, you'll have to undergo our health screening, of course. Before we go any further, do you have any health issues that we should know about right now?"

That was a new one. Still, Mitch could understand why; they were concerned for the health of their assets.

"I recently had my biannual checkup with my doctor," he told Seb. "Also, I get tested every six months and my last test was two months ago. I'm negative, no STIs." He arched his eyebrows. "If I'd known I was coming here, I could've brought you my documentation," he added, tongue in cheek.

"I understand," Seb replied smoothly. "We still need to see it, however. A formality, of course, but we have to cover ourselves, you understand. What can you leave with us as a guarantee of your return with the necessary documentation within two days at the most? A bank card? Your driver's license?" He gave Mitch a thin-lipped smile.

Fuck. He was being serious. "One of your staff already has my driver's license," Mitch said slowly. "Will that do?" *I suppose they're only covering their own asses, but geez....*

Seb beamed. "Excellent. Now, for this evening, if you choose to engage the services of one of our staff, without proof of your health status, these are the acts that are permissible." He handed over a sheet of paper. Mitch stared at the contents.

It was a very short list: *kissing; oral sex with condom; rimming with dental dam; anal sex with....*

"The club operates a strict safe-sex policy, but you'll also need to stick to these activities, until such time as we have your documentation."

"And when you have that, is there a different list?"

Seb nodded.

"And what's on that list?" Mitch wanted to know.

Seb's gaze met his. "Everything," he said simply.

Fuck.

Seb stepped out from behind the desk and walked up to the red door. He opened it and turned to them without dimming the wattage of that smile. "Welcome to the Black Lounge private club, Mr. Jenkins."

Mitch had no clue what to expect, so he took a breath and followed Aaron into the unknown.

The door closed behind them, and Mitch found himself in a spacious lounge furnished with low couches in red leather, all with deep seat cushions. Some of the couches were occupied, but he tried not to stare at the clients who were busy talking quietly, kissing and stroking their "companions" for the evening. The sight of one huge bear of a guy leaning back on a couch with a naked twink in his lap was particularly mesmerizing. The young man was stroking the bear's beard and bare, furry chest, and both men were smiling, seemingly very content.

Mitch leaned close to Aaron and lowered his voice. "Aaron, how are they going to know if I do something that's not on the list? I mean, how will they know if I don't use their supplied finger cots? Not that I'm thinking of *not* using them, you understand," he hastened to add.

Aaron gave him a dark look. "Oh, they'll know. There are cameras everywhere—*some* of them you'll even be able to spot."

It took a moment for Mitch to realize his friend wasn't kidding.

He glanced around the room, trying to avoid staring at the couches. There were no external windows, just long, heavy black drapes. Lamps sat on low tables, giving off a warm glow. Mitch found it unsettling that he couldn't see a single camera; they were either nonexistent or extremely well hidden. At one end of the lounge was another red door, ajar, and through it Mitch caught the unmistakable—though muted—sounds of fucking. But the other end of the room was dominated by a vast window that took up the entire wall except for a door to the side of it.

Aaron led Mitch to it and gestured with his arm. "Take your pick."

Mitch stared through the glass at another room, maybe twenty feet across and just as deep. It was full of men. Tall, short, lean, muscled, some naked, others scantily clothed, Caucasian, black, Asian—the club catered for all tastes. The room resembled a lavish studio apartment. A king-sized bed sat against one wall, and a couple of guys were rolling around under white sheets, glancing occasionally toward the window. Young men posed directly in front of it, giving provocative looks. Another sat in a big armchair, nude, his legs spread wide over the arms while he stroked his erect cock, his gaze focused on the glass.

For Mitch, it seemed like a room full of peacocks, preening and primping themselves, all trying to attract attention. *Peacocks in a pretty, comfortable cage.*

"They can't see us," Aaron whispered at Mitch's side.

Mitch snorted. "That doesn't seem to stop them from parading themselves."

Aaron chuckled. "I'd have thought that was part of the job, ya know, selling themselves to whomever is out here watching." He nudged Mitch. "They all look good, though, don't they?"

Mitch couldn't argue with that. There had to be about fifteen guys in the room, maybe more, and all of the ones he could see appeared healthy and happy. Of course, a smile could be pasted on, but no one seemed unwilling to be there.

So why doesn't one of them appeal to me?

"So?" Aaron nudged him again. "Which one lights your candle?" He grinned. "You've got to admit, there are some beautiful men in there." He nodded toward one young man standing nearest the window. He was stroking down over his chest and well-defined abs, to where a thick cock jutted out toward them. Just then the young man turned and bent over, reaching back to spread his cheeks and reveal a pink, glistening hole, clearly lubed. He wiggled his ass, his dick bobbing stiffly.

Aaron smothered a chuckle. "Wow. He's eager."

That wasn't the word in Mitch's mind. He preferred blatant, and it wasn't turning him on. In fact, none of them were.

"This is a mistake," he said quietly. "Thanks for bringing me here, but honestly, this isn't me. And there isn't one guy who does it for me." His gaze swept across the room, taking in the smiling, pouting faces and….

Mitch stopped, his pulse quickening. "Him." *How did I miss him?*

Aaron peered in the direction of Mitch's stare. "Which one?"

At the back of the room was a small table and a couple of armchairs facing each other. In one of them sat a young man with long, black hair tied in a single braid down his back. He was Japanese in appearance, with small, round glasses perched on his nose. Physically he was slight, not that tall as far as Mitch could tell. Unlike the others, he wore a pair of jeans and a white shirt.

What caught Mitch's attention was the fact that he was reading a book, his legs curled up under him, lost in his own world.

"Mitch?" Aaron pinched his arm.

"Hey!" Mitch grumbled, rubbing the spot near his elbow. "What was that for?"

"You were off in cloud cuckoo land." Aaron cocked his eyebrows. "Well? I repeat, which one?"

"The one with the book." There was something so delightfully incongruous about him that Mitch was intrigued.

"Really?"

Mitch dragged his gaze away to give Aaron a firm stare. "You said to take my pick, so I pick him." He couldn't account for the way his body reacted to the young man. His heart pounded and his mouth was dry.

"That's Nikko. He's new here."

Mitch turned toward the speaker. A dark-haired man wearing a black suit and matching shirt smiled at him. "My name is Randy. I'm here to give you any information you require." He gave a flick of his head toward the window. "Nikko only joined us recently. Would you like to meet him, and if so, for how long?"

His heart still racing, Mitch regarded the young man who was oblivious to his surroundings. "An hour?"

Beside him Aaron chuckled. "And that's my cue to leave." He patted Mitch on the arm. "Enjoy, with my blessing. You can tell me all about it on Monday."

"Thanks, Aaron." Mitch gave him a warm smile. "And as for Monday? Uh-uh." The smile became a grin. "I don't kiss and tell."

He snorted. "Spoilsport. And you have nothing to thank me for yet." Aaron grinned. "See ya." He walked toward the door and gave one last wave before disappearing through it.

Mitch returned his attention to Randy, who was regarding him with a hint of amusement. Mitch cleared his throat. "I'm sorry, I'm new to all this."

Randy's smile widened. "Then you and Nikko have something in common. Do you have your card?" Mitch held it up and Randy peered at it. "Okay, that's fine. If you'll come with me, please?"

He led Mitch through the door at the end of the lounge. They were in a long hallway with doors on either side. Randy escorted Mitch to door number seven and opened it. The room was small, but what it lacked in size, it made up for in furnishings. In the corner was a Chinese painted screen and a washbasin with a thick towel hanging from a rail beside it. Most of the space was taken up by a bed adorned with white sheets, a soft gray comforter, pillows, and cushions. A wide chair faced the bed, its cushions deep. There were no windows. At the head of the bed was a large mirror, and beside it, a small cabinet with two drawers.

"You'll find condoms and packets of lube in the cabinet," Randy said. "You're aware of the club's strict safe-sex policy."

Mitch nodded. He had no problem with that. He'd never had bareback sex in his life.

"There are also some toys, should you require them. If there's something particular you'd like, simply ask. We do cater for those clients who are into S&M, but they generally stipulate their needs ahead of time. Would that be of interest to you this evening?"

Mitch was sure his face was bright red. "Uh, not for me, thank you."

Randy gave a polite nod. "Then I shall go and bring Nikko to you." He exited the room.

Mitch gazed around him while he removed his jacket. He placed it on the chair and examined the prints on the wall. The room was definitely nothing like he'd expected; he'd had something much more austere in mind. A glance behind the screen revealed a toilet, tastefully hidden from view.

They really do think of everything.

Mitch scanned the walls and corners for any sign of a camera. Nothing. But from a safety aspect alone, he knew there had to be one in there somewhere.

Damn, they're good.

He came back to the bed and sat, bouncing on it to test its springiness.

"Are we to be using it as a trampoline?" a soft voice asked.

Mitch jerked his head toward the door just as it closed gently. Nikko stood there, his fingers laced together in front of him, dark brown eyes focused on Mitch, his braid not visible, his expression impassive.

Mitch coughed and rose to his feet. "Maybe not." He took a few steps toward Nikko, his hand extended, his belly tensed. Inwardly he cursed his uncertainty. It wasn't as if he was a stranger to meeting guys, but after two years of being in a relationship, he felt decidedly out of practice. And this was definitely a new experience.

Nikko took his hand almost shyly and shook it, his fingers cool to the touch. "I'm Nikko." The handshake over, he laced his fingers once more and stepped back, maintaining his distance from Mitch. His manner had Mitch retreating too.

"Is that your real name, or just one you use here?" Mitch wanted to know. When Nikko raised his eyebrows, Mitch felt the warm flush that rose up his chest and neck. "I'm sorry. This is my first time in a... in one of these places."

Nikko became still for a moment, tension evident in his posture. When he smiled, it didn't reach his eyes. "Then we have something in common. And to answer your question, Nikko is my real name. May I know yours?" Those eyes were captivating, a rich, deep brown framed with long, sooty black lashes, and set in a pale, unblemished face.

"I'm Mitch." It was on the tip of his tongue to say *Pleased to meet you*, but the words sounded wrong given the circumstances. *I don't suppose there are etiquette rules for greeting a hooker in a brothel.*

Not that Nikko resembled his preconceptions of what a hooker looked like. The young man was beautiful, maybe five foot five, six max. He felt tiny next to Mitch's five foot eleven. Those clasped fingers were slim, his hands delicate. Mitch was reminded of one of his mother's ethereal porcelain figurines in her china cabinet back home. They shared that same fragile quality.

"Are... are you feeling awkward too?" Nikko asked, biting his bottom lip. "You're my first... client." A flush crept across his cheeks and his ears turned red.

His words stirred something in Mitch's chest, an absurd desire to enfold Nikko in his arms, to protect him. The yearning took him by surprise. Maybe it was Nikko's slight build, his fragility, that engendered the inclination. Whatever it was, it sent a rush of warmth through Mitch's body.

He beckoned to Nikko. "Come here."

Slowly Nikko walked over to him, his gaze fixed on Mitch's face. He stopped a few feet in front of him and tilted his chin up, not quite meeting Mitch's gaze. The rapid rise and fall of Nikko's chest, the ragged breathing, betrayed the nerves he hid. Mitch stretched out his hand to cup Nikko's face, his large hand exaggerating the diminutive young man's size.

"How old are you?" Mitch asked quietly. Nikko had to be barely legal.

"I-I'm twenty-two," Nikko said in a low voice that cracked. "I know how I look, Mitch. I'm old enough to work here. This may be my first time with a client, but I'm not a virgin."

"I never thought for a second that a virgin *would* be working here," Mitch admitted. He tilted his head. "You can come closer, you know. I won't hurt you."

Nikko swallowed, blinking. "I… I'm sorry. It's just that you're not how I expected a client to be."

Mitch took a step closer. "How did you think I would be?" He kept his voice low and soothing. Nikko reminded him of a colt he'd spent time with on his uncle's farm as a boy. The young man gave an impression of being about to bolt at any second.

Nikko took a deep breath. "I didn't expect to be treated with so much… respect."

Now Mitch got it. "Come closer," he said, coaxingly. When Nikko hesitated, Mitch gave him a warm smile. "Nikko, I meant it. I will not hurt you. I don't have it in me to do that."

Nikko regarded him in silence. "I believe you." He inhaled slowly and took that last step to bring him to Mitch.

Mitch couldn't help himself. He bent his head lower and took Nikko's mouth in a gentle kiss. Nikko held himself still for a moment longer before putting his slim arms around Mitch's neck and responding, his lips parting.

When Mitch broke the kiss, Nikko looked up at him with shining eyes. "Thank you."

"For what?"

Nikko smiled, this time genuinely. "For being gentle." His breathing hitched. "You… you make this easier than I thought it would be, Mitch."

Mitch's first reaction was a surge of pleasure, until a thought nagged at him. He paused, his hands on Nikko's shoulders. "Are you here because you want to be?" Something about Nikko's choice of words tugged at his mind.

Nikko regarded him, face calm. "I chose to be here, Mitch. Have no doubt about that." There was no trace of deception in his voice or expression. He reached up with both hands and cupped Mitch's face. "Kiss me again?" His Adam's apple bobbed.

"Are you asking because you want to be kissed or because you feel you should ask?"

Nikko stared at him, lowering his hands, his eyes wide. "You are… perceptive."

Mitch shrugged. "I use my eyes, is all. If you'd rather we sit on the bed for a while, maybe chat, that's okay, I don't mind." He waited for Nikko to make the next move. The young man was skittish enough without Mitch making matters worse.

Nikko's breathing grew more even. "Then I should like you to kiss me, because"—he stroked Mitch's cheek, the touch light, and for the first time, he looked Mitch in the eye—"because I want you to."

Mitch smiled. "That's better." He caressed Nikko's cheek, brushing his fingertips over his cheekbones. "Because I want to kiss you."

Nikko closed his eyes, lips parted, waiting.

Fuck. Nikko was beautiful.

Chapter Three

MITCH WAS surprised to find his fingers trembling as he cupped Nikko's face. *For God's sake, get a hold of yourself.* He was acting like a teenager. What the fuck was there to be nervous about?

He almost snorted aloud at the thought. Like having sex with a hooker was an everyday occurrence....

Nikko opened his eyes. "Is it okay for me to tell you I'm nervous too?" His words were a whisper.

Mitch stilled his shaking hands and gazed at Nikko's upturned face. He smiled. "The sound of your breathing told me that much." He stared at Nikko's mouth, his lips pink, shining where he'd licked them apprehensively.

This was nothing like he'd anticipated. Scrap that last thought—*Nikko* was nothing like what he'd expected. Mitch was off-balance and he didn't like it. This was all new territory for him, and he was uncertain of what to do next.

"You made me feel good when you kissed me," Nikko said, biting his plump lower lip.

That was reason enough for Mitch to do it again, not that he needed an excuse. He loved kissing. He lowered his head and took Nikko's mouth, liking the way Nikko opened for him. He deepened the kiss, his cock stiffening in his jeans when Nikko pressed against him and moaned. Tremors rippled through Nikko's body, and Mitch slipped his arms around the young man, pulling him closer. Nikko looped his arms around Mitch's neck.

"Mitch," he whispered. "I… I feel you." He rocked his hips gently, forcing a groan from Mitch's lips when the hardness of his dick met the pliant warmth of Nikko's body. "There." His breathing quickened.

"You make me feel good, Nikko." It was probably the understatement of the year. Nikko was damn good at his job. "But I want to do more than kiss you." Fuck, his dick was a rock in his jeans.

Nikko's breath caught and his eyes widened. Mitch would have thought him scared if it weren't for the gentle push of Nikko's stiffening cock against his hip. Nikko didn't break eye contact, although his skin flushed against the white of his shirt. He turned his head slightly to one side, presenting his neck, and Mitch buried his face in the soft curve, kissing from under his ear down to the base of his throat. He traced over Nikko's Adam's apple with his tongue, and Nikko rolled his head back to give Mitch greater access.

"Oh." The word shivered out of Nikko, his eyes closing, arms tightening around Mitch's neck. Mitch supported him as he kissed the hollows of his collarbones, feeling the shudders that coursed through Nikko. He opened his eyes, lips parted, his breathing staccato. "Undress me?"

Fuck, yeah.

Mitch was glad Nikko was taking the lead. *That's because it's his job, dumbass. Just… go with the flow.*

Mitch began the task of unfastening buttons, tugging Nikko's shirt free of his jeans and slipping the soft cotton garment off his shoulders. Nikko's skin was pale and smooth, and Mitch couldn't resist. He pressed his lips to Nikko's shoulder in a soft kiss.

Nikko sighed. "Yes." He allowed Mitch to remove the shirt before peering up at him through those long lashes. "My turn." His hands shook as he fumbled with the buttons of Mitch's shirt, and Mitch reached up to cover Nikko's hands with his.

"No need to rush," he said quietly. "We have time." Although Mitch had a sneaking suspicion that the hour was going to fly by.

His words had the desired effect. Nikko relaxed and the tension in his body dissipated a little. He managed to undo three buttons and then smiled. "Wow. You have a lot of hair." He slipped his hand under the fabric to fondle Mitch's chest and tugged gently at the mat of hair that covered Mitch's pecs. "I like it," he admitted shyly.

Mitch unfastened the remaining buttons and shrugged off the shirt. Nikko applied both hands to the task of petting Mitch's chest, moving in slow circles. Mitch cupped Nikko's head and guided him closer until his lips were scant millimeters away from his nipple.

"Flick it with your tongue," he suggested, his own breathing growing more ragged. Inside his jeans, his cock was a solid rod of flesh.

It had been a long time since Mitch had been this aroused. Maybe it was the illicitness of the whole situation, a sense of the forbidden. He was about to do something illegal, after all. That thought alone had his heart pounding.

Nikko's eyes lit up, and he smiled before taking the tiny nub between his lips and sucking it, rolling his tongue over it. The sensation went straight to Mitch's dick, and he had to reach down to palm his aching shaft. He grasped it tightly through the fabric and squeezed.

Nikko pulled free and glanced down. "That's my job," he said in a low voice, and before Mitch could say a word, Nikko lowered himself gracefully to his knees and unfastened his waistband. The slow intake of breath when he tugged at the jeans and Mitch's cock sprang free was very gratifying, but the sight of Nikko's delicate hand wrapped around his girth raised a question in Mitch's mind.

He wasn't small by any means. But Nikko….

Nikko stared at the thick dick in his hand, before raising his head to meet Mitch's gaze. "I didn't expect… this." He bit his lip and sucked in a deep breath.

Mitch slipped his hands under Nikko's armpits and drew him up into a standing position. "Let's finish what we started, okay?" He undid the button on Nikko's jeans and slowly lowered them over his slim hips, leaving him in just his briefs. Nikko stepped free of the jeans. Mitch toed off his shoes, shoved his own jeans down to his ankles and kicked them off.

Naked, he knelt before Nikko, gazing up at him while he pulled off his black briefs, his fingers caressing the firm globes of Nikko's ass before leaving the underwear in a puddle of fabric around his ankles.

Nikko stepped out of them and stood beside the bed, his hands clasped together again, covering his genitals, gaze focused on Mitch. He was slim, his waist narrow, his body devoid of hair. In spite of Mitch's efforts to calm him, apprehension and anxiety rolled off him in waves.

Mitch rose to his feet. "Nikko, don't hide yourself from me. Let me see you, please?" The thought, *let me see what I'm buying here* rose unbidden in his mind, and his dick twitched.

Nikko hesitated for a moment and then lowered his hands, revealing a slim, pretty cock and a smooth sac. His pubes were scant and neat. He held his breath while Mitch gazed at him.

Mitch smiled. "Very nice." He supposed it was polite to compliment the guy he was about to fuck. Mitch pulled back the sheets and got into the bed. He held out his hand. "Come here."

Nikko climbed into the bed, swallowing. Mitch lay on his back and drew Nikko to lie at his side, his head on the pillow beside Mitch's. He covered them with the sheet.

For a moment he floundered. This wasn't like getting into bed with a lover, but at the same time, he didn't want it to be a clinical experience. The recent couple of hookups had been something new, a knee-jerk reaction to Jerry's leaving that had left him more convinced than ever that casual sex just wasn't for him. In the past if he'd taken a guy to bed, it was because it had meant something to both of them.

And yet here I am, in bed with a male prostitute, about to fuck him. How the hell did I let Aaron talk me into this?

This was *all* kinds of fucked-up.

Nikko gave a shy smile and trailed his fingers across Mitch's chest, his touch light. "I'm always fascinated by hairy men," he admitted. "Japanese men are pretty much smooth-skinned."

Mitch twisted his head to look at Nikko. "Yeah, but it's nice." He caressed Nikko's chest, brushing his thumb over his nipple. Nikko shuddered and Mitch grinned. "Oh, you like that, huh?" He pushed Nikko flat to the bed and leaned over him to where Nikko's nipples stood proud. The way Nikko arched his back told Mitch plenty. He sucked on the taut nub, listening to Nikko's breath stuttering out of him. Mitch flicked it with his tongue while tweaking the other. Nikko's soft sighs grew more numerous, and he grabbed hold of Mitch's shoulders and hung on. Mitch freed the now tender nipple and kissed his way up Nikko's chest to the base of his neck. Nikko pushed his head back into the pillow, a low moan escaping his lips as Mitch licked a line up to his jaw.

Mitch couldn't resist the call of that beautiful mouth any longer.

He held Nikko's face in one hand while he kissed him, slowly and thoroughly, slipping his tongue between parted lips to explore. Nikko moaned into his mouth, hips pushing up off the mattress. What Nikko lacked in expertise, he made up for in enthusiasm, his low noises of pleasure giving Mitch the impression that he was loving every minute of it. Mitch lost himself in the sensuality of the moment and responded to Nikko's eagerness with a degree of passion that surprised him.

Until reality smacked him hard upside the head.

If he didn't look like he was enjoying it, he'd be a crap hooker, right?

Mitch had almost forgotten where he was and exactly who he was with.

Mitch wanted to slow things down, take his time, but his body was crying out with need. *Get with the program.*

He rolled them until Nikko was on top, chest pressed against his. Nikko put his weight on his forearms and kissed Mitch, tongue pushing deep, feeding gasps and sighs into Mitch's mouth. He pulled Nikko down and kissed him, hard, tilting his hips to grind against Nikko's now rigid dick. Nikko groaned, the sound unguarded and spontaneous, his body writhing, pushing down on Mitch's shaft.

"You ready?" Mitch asked. Nikko stretched out his hand to the drawer beside the bed. "I've got this," Mitch told him, and yanked it open. He pulled out a packet of lube, a couple of condoms and some finger cots. After dropping them onto the cabinet, he flipped Nikko until he lay beneath him. Mitch didn't let up kissing him, rolling his hips, letting their dicks rub against each other. Nikko's breathing was in sync with each slide of hot, stiff flesh, and as Mitch picked up speed, Nikko's soft moans kept pace with him, until Mitch couldn't wait a moment longer.

He tore open a foil and unfurled the condom down Nikko's long, slim dick. Their gazes met and Mitch grimaced. "You have no idea how much I'd rather be tasting your cock than latex, but rules are rules." He shifted until he was between Nikko's legs, Nikko spreading for him, knees bent, feet flat to the mattress.

Nikko bit his lip. "Rules are important." The words came out as a gasp. He didn't take his eyes off Mitch, his belly quivering when Mitch grasped his cock around the base and slowly took the head into his mouth. The latex didn't mute his heat, and Mitch sucked hard, enjoying how Nikko's hips jerked up from the bed, how he clutched at the sheet beneath him, fingers clawing at the fabric.

Fuck, he's so responsive. Mitch took him deeper, working his shaft, determined to elicit more noises from the young man. Nikko cried out, hips bucking. "Oh, Mitch, that's…." Shudders coursed through him.

Mitch rolled Nikko's balls through his fingers, squeezing lightly, before rubbing over his perineum, massaging his prostate from the outside. Nikko's dick swelled in his mouth, and Mitch groaned around his length, feeling heat within the condom. He pulled free, and Nikko lay there shivering, pulsing come into the latex, his breath escaping in short bursts. He stared at Mitch, eyes wide and sparkling, the condom clinging to his cock.

"S-sorry." Nikko's voice shook. "I couldn't hold it back." His chest heaved.

"Nothing to be sorry about." Mitch chuckled. "At your age, I could come three times in one night. I doubt you're any different." He left the bed and grabbed the towel from the rail. When he returned, he stripped Nikko's dick of its latex barrier and wiped him clean. The temptation to clean the pretty cock with his tongue was huge, but he knew better than to break the rules. Who knew what eyes were watching them that very second?

Mitch put aside the towel and knelt up on the bed, his cock so hard it hurt. He reached across to the cabinet for the supplies, Nikko watching him with those dark eyes. Mitch smiled at him as he slipped on a couple of finger cots and opened the packet of lube. He lay down beside Nikko and maneuvered him until his head rested on Mitch's arm. Mitch lifted Nikko's leg.

"Catch hold," he told him.

Nikko did as instructed, and Mitch slowly stroked over his balls, moving lower, lower, until his fingers reached their prize. Nikko's breathing caught when Mitch rubbed the pad of his finger over his hole, feeling the muscle tighten. He cursed silently. Okay, he'd stick to the rules but *damn*, the thought of rimming Nikko until he came all over the bed was fucking delicious. Using a dental dam made sense, but what he really wanted was to taste him there.

Mitch grabbed the opened packet of lube and slicked up his fingers, before carefully placing the remainder back on top of the cabinet. Nikko clutched his thigh, and Mitch stroked over his hole, slowly sinking one finger into him up to the first knuckle. Fuck, the heat inside him….

"God, but you're tight."

Nikko closed his eyes and let out a sweet whimper. "It's… been a while." He lay still, his body cuddled up to Mitch's side, his fingers digging into the meat of his thigh, right hand gently stroking his already hardening shaft. *Geez, the joys of being that age….*

Mitch leaned over, his finger still just inside Nikko's channel, and kissed him, sliding his tongue slowly between Nikko's lips. Nikko responded, letting out a soft moan, and Mitch waited until Nikko began to move, pushing down on his finger, clearly wanting more. Mitch pressed deeper, until his finger was buried in Nikko's tight heat. He stilled, focusing on the kiss, the noises Nikko made, the smell of clean hair, clean skin, the feel of his warm body next to Mitch's.

Yeah, this was *nothing* like he'd expected.

When he couldn't wait a moment longer, Mitch slowly added a second finger. Nikko stiffened and then relaxed, moaning into the kiss. He rolled his hips, taking Mitch deeper. By the time Nikko was pushing down hard, Mitch was leaking precome in a steady stream. He pulled free of Nikko's body and reached for the condom.

"Can I...?" Nikko asked, hand already outstretched.

Mitch nodded, and Nikko knelt up beside him to unroll the latex over his granite dick. He picked up the remaining lube from the cabinet and wiped slick fingers over Mitch's cock before reaching behind him to swipe his hand through his own crease. Nikko straddled Mitch once more, bending over him to kiss him, his braid falling over one shoulder. He leaned back and steadied Mitch's dick, moving into position so that its head gently kissed his hole.

Mitch didn't want to breathe. He wanted to lie there in the stillness and focus on the sensations as Nikko slowly lowered himself onto his dick, controlling his descent inch by inch, until Mitch's cock was sheathed in exquisite tightness. One look at Nikko's face told Mitch the young man was feeling every one of those eight inches.

It's not the length he has to deal with, more like the width. Jerry had always told him it was like being fucked by a Coke can. Mitch was content to let Nikko do the driving—it was his ass, after all—but hell, he wanted to *move....*

Nikko let out a long sigh. "That feels... good." He leaned forward to kiss Mitch on the lips, and Mitch moved with him, keeping his shaft buried to the hilt. Nikko broke the kiss and sat upright, his gaze focused on Mitch's face. He rolled his hips, his lower body undulating, dick rising skyward again. Mitch placed his hands on Nikko's waist and helped to lift him up and down, slowly at first while Nikko adjusted to Mitch's girth. Nikko's tight channel gripped him, clinging to his cock as he tilted his hips and pushed up into glorious heat.

Then Nikko's movements gathered speed.

"Mitch, so... so good," Nikko gasped, bracing his arms, hands flat to Mitch's chest while he rocked on top of him, his cock bouncing, leaving spots of precome on Mitch's belly.

He wasn't moving fast enough for Mitch's liking.

Mitch squeezed out the last drops of lube and ran his fingers over his shaft. He grabbed Nikko's hips and held on tight while he thrust up, dick sliding into his channel, going deeper than ever, until Nikko was moaning constantly. Nikko grasped his own length and tugged, mouth open.

Mitch wanted to groan out loud when his balls tingled and drew up tight against his body. *Too soon.* He closed his eyes to shut out the sight of Nikko, breathless, a sheen of perspiration on his chest and abs, dick sliding through his fist. Mitch thought about grading papers. Teaching. Wrinkled old grandmothers. *Anything* but the prospect of coming *any fucking second now....*

Yeah, like that's gonna work....

He thrust deep and shot his load into the condom, his body jolted by his orgasm, overtaken by the enormous pleasure of coming inside Nikko while he rode Mitch's dick. Nikko groaned, and Mitch felt it reverberate through him, felt the ripples along his cock as Nikko came, spunk jetting out in thin trails over Mitch's belly. Nikko arched his back and shuddered, his body trembling. Mitch pulled him down into a hot, drawn-out kiss, leaving both of them breathless.

Nikko dropped his head to Mitch's shoulder, his chest damp against Mitch's, the stickiness of his come lying between them. Mitch kept his arms around Nikko until they were breathing in sync, the aftershocks fading away. Warmth seeped through Mitch's body, and he surrendered to the afterglow.

Nikko lifted his head to gaze at Mitch. "Thank you."

Mitch arched his eyebrows. "You're thanking me?" Damn it. Nikko messed with his head.

"For my first time here, I couldn't have asked for a more attentive client." Nikko lowered his gaze. "As I said before, you made things so much easier than I had anticipated." He fell silent.

Mitch was at a loss. What was he supposed to do until their hour was up? This was a first for him too. He rolled Nikko onto his side and put his arm around him. Now that the sex was over, an awkwardness seemed to have descended. He could probably get it up again in about twenty minutes, if he worked at it. At forty-five years old, the recuperative powers he'd once enjoyed had long since fucked off.

Nikko snuggled up to him, his head on Mitch's arm, appearing far more relaxed than Mitch. "Do you think you will come back to the club?" he asked Mitch, almost shyly.

In other words, am I gonna be a regular? Nikko's words were yet another reminder of what he was, and the realization was like a flush of cold water over Mitch's skin. *This was just a job to him. The first fuck of what will probably be a damn good career on his back.* For some reason Mitch was filled with a sense of disappointment.

"I don't know," he said truthfully. "I wouldn't have come here tonight, but for a friend insisting." He peered at Nikko. "Mind if I ask you something personal?"

Nikko became still. "Go ahead."

"Why are you working here, Nikko? Surely someone with your looks could find a job modeling, working on a reception desk somewhere…. What made you choose to do this? I mean, it's not exactly one of the career choices they tell you about in high school, right?"

There was no mistaking Nikko's reaction—he froze. The silence that ensued had all the hairs standing up on Mitch's arms and the nape of his neck.

"I work here. That is all you need to know." Nikko's words were as stiff as his body posture, his breathing rapid and harsh. The message could not have been clearer.

Fuck. Mitch had put his foot right in it. The last thing he'd wanted was to upset the young man. Hooker or not, he'd given Mitch a lot of pleasure.

"I'm sorry, I had no right to ask," he said quietly. "It's your body, your choices." He waited in the silence, willing Nikko to loosen up. After a moment, the rigidity in his body eased and Nikko breathed more evenly. To Mitch's surprise, Nikko pulled free of his embrace and sat up.

"I know you've paid for an hour," he began, his voice low, "but I'd like you to go now."

Well, fuck.

Mitch sat up in bed, reaching out to put his hand around Nikko's toned upper arm. "I'm sorry I upset you," he said quickly. "Please, can't we just lie here and talk?"

Nikko's face and neck flushed, and his expression tightened. He pulled free of Mitch's grasp. "You'd be within your rights to complain to the club management. If that's the course of action you decide upon, I will accept any… reprimand they feel is appropriate." He got off the bed and began to dress himself hurriedly, his every movement making it obvious he was trying to control himself.

I'm just making this worse.

Mitch clambered off the bed and pulled on his jeans. "I'm sorry," he repeated, buttoning up his shirt. "I never meant to upset you. I'll go, okay? But just so you know, I won't say a word about why. They can think it's my decision, okay? I figure telling them the truth would only cause you problems, and I'd hate that." His chest tightened and his stomach roiled. *Me and my big mouth.* He couldn't look at Nikko while he dressed. When he was ready, he tried to get past Nikko, but the young man grabbed hold of his arm.

"Please do not judge the club based on my actions. I'm sure if you were to return, you would find someone else to please you." He released Mitch and bowed his head. "Thank you for making my first time so… enjoyable." He swallowed and then rapped on the door.

Within seconds Randy opened it, frowning. "Is everything okay?"

Before Nikko could say a word, Mitch stepped forward. "Everything was fine," he said smoothly, "but I've just realized I need to go home urgently." He smiled, doing his damnedest to appear relaxed and confident. "Sorry to mess you about like this, but I'd clean forgotten I had a late-night visitor due to arrive at my place anytime now."

Randy's face cleared. "I see. Well, if you'd like to come with me, I'll take you through to reception." He glanced at Nikko. "You can go now."

Nikko dipped his chin toward his chest and stepped past Randy into the hallway. For one brief moment, he turned his head and caught Mitch's gaze. Nikko bit his lip and walked out of sight.

Mitch followed Randy back into Seb's office, his mind in a mess. It had been a very pleasant experience, up until the point where he'd ruined it. He didn't blame Nikko—the guy clearly had his reasons for selling his body, and they had nothing to do with Mitch. He'd had no right to ask the question in the first place. The only reason he was keeping quiet about Nikko's demand that he leave was due to his own feelings of guilt.

"Mr. Jenkins?"

Mitch was dragged back into the moment. Seb was addressing him. "Sorry, did you say something?"

From his seat behind the desk, Seb gave him a polite smile. "I asked if you'd remembered you had to bring—"

"My documentation? Yes, yes. I'll bring it by tomorrow." Mitch just wanted to get out of there.

Seb handed over a sealed envelope. "I hope you enjoyed your evening with us. You'll find details of membership fees and hourly rates in here. These are, of course, for your eyes only and not for public consumption." His eyes glittered. "We look forward to having you join our elite club." He rose to his feet, extending a hand, and Mitch shook it. "We already have your driver's license as collateral until such time as we receive your medical information."

They really do take this shit seriously.

"I won't forget," Mitch assured him.

Seb's smile widened. "Excellent. And now I'll bid you good-bye." He walked across to the door and opened it. "Until we meet again, Mr. Jenkins."

Mitch scurried past him, his heart pounding. He wanted to get out of there.

He hurried along the hallway, barely hearing the security guard's words as he passed him. He just wanted to go home and take a shower.

Mitch had never felt so fucking dirty in his life.

Chapter Four

MITCH DRANK his coffee and stared at the still-sealed envelope on his tiny kitchen table. He knew he had to open it sometime, but that would make the previous night all the more real. He told himself the only difference between the club and a hookup was the fact that money exchanged hands. And even *that* was inaccurate; last night had been on Aaron, in more ways than one.

It didn't make him feel any better, though.

There was still the matter of his medical test results….

He drained the mug and ran hot water into it before placing it next to the sink. The sun had risen about an hour before, and its light spilled into the kitchen, reflecting off the cream walls. Mitch liked his apartment well enough, but he missed the large expanses of sky that he'd enjoyed growing up in York, Maine. His present view of apartment buildings and treetops was sadly lacking in comparison.

It was my choice to work here, so I can't really complain.

His parents would have been delighted all those years ago if he'd chosen to remain in his native state, but the lure of New York and the freedom it offered had been too great to ignore. Sure, Ogunquit on the coast to the north of York was a great little town with its own gay beach, but it had nothing on the Big Apple. Mitch had been in his early twenties when he'd made the move, the ink barely dry on his teaching credentials. Of course, that had meant more testing in New York before he could teach there. Twenty years on and he was in his fourth appointment. Park View High School wasn't as big as his previous schools, with fewer than six hundred students, but the small, screened school in Manhattan was exactly what he'd needed after teaching in the South Bronx school district for six years. He'd figured his last teaching position would have counted against him, but apparently Park View's principal, Dominic Galletta, had seen something else apart from the years of working in what was arguably the worst school in NYC. After five years at Park View, Mitch finally felt settled. He liked the teaching staff, and on the whole, the students were hard-working and ambitious.

Except for that twelfth grade English class, the lazy bunch. There was the odd diamond shining out among the dross even there, so he couldn't complain.

The envelope was still sitting on his table.

With a sigh Mitch grabbed it and tore it open. It contained a copy of his nondisclosure agreement—like he was gonna forget that—a list of rules, contact information, and the financial details, not that he was interested. He had no intention of becoming a member. All the same, he couldn't help peeking at the annual fee, and when he saw it he wasn't sure he believed it. *$5,000? Is that all?* Then he kept reading. On top of that, there was still an hourly rate to be paid. He supposed the annual fee was for the privilege of being a member. He wondered how often Aaron used their services.

Even if Mitch wasn't going to be a member, he still had to return to the club.

He glanced at the kitchen clock. Since when was he awake at six thirty on a Saturday morning? He knew the answer to that one—a huge guilt trip. Ever since he'd walked out of the Black Lounge and called up an Uber car, he couldn't stop thinking about it. He'd had sex with a prostitute! The recollections had him tossing and turning all night.

Was I that *horny? I mean, really?* His face tingled. Before Jerry, he'd had three or four relationships, none lasting more than a year, and the splits had always been amicable. But between guys, Mitch had never resorted to one-night stands. He made do with his hand and the occasional toy. And it had only been *two freaking months* since Jerry had left him, for Christ's sake. It wasn't as if he'd been sex-starved during their two years together either. Sex had been frequent and, as far as Mitch had been concerned, satisfactory. It wasn't until Jerry had hit him with that final nail in the coffin remark that he'd learned what his lover had really thought.

Mitch shuddered. He had better things to do with his time than think about Jerry. The bile still threatened to rise in his throat whenever the bastard popped into his head. Besides, if he were really honest with himself, he knew his decision to stay in the club was all about Nikko. And a lot of the shame and guilt that plagued him was how the whole fuckfest had ended.

Not gonna go there. It was bad enough that he had to return to the place.

Mitch checked the contact info. Apparently, there was a buzzer at street level that would bring a member of staff, 24-7. He huffed aloud. *Not at this time of the morning, surely.* He glimpsed his backpack on a stool by the door, those assignments waiting for him to grade. At least the task would bring respite from the stuff going on inside his head. *And what about the rest of the weekend, huh?*

What he needed was a distraction, something to keep his mind occupied, such as….

Mitch smiled to himself. What the situation called for was a few good games of chess.

He grabbed his phone from the table and scrolled through. As a kid, Gareth was always wide-awake with the dawn. There was a reason Mitch and the rest of his family had nicknamed him Tigger. It was a habit he'd apparently grown out of, but these days, having three dogs all whining to be let out would be a very effective alarm clock. Mitch hit Call and poured himself another cup of coffee while he waited for Gareth to answer. He'd need it if he was going to grade those assignments.

"Oh my God. They've announced the end of the world. That can be the only reason for you calling me at this hour on the weekend." His brother chuckled. "Wassup, Mitch? Hangover? Or have you just had a late one and you're only getting in now?"

"I *can* hang up, you know."

Gareth laughed, a rich sound that boomed out of his phone and made his heart that little bit lighter. It had been way too long since they'd met up for one of their Sunday brunches and chess marathons.

"Hey, you made it this far. What can I do for you?"

"I wondered if you wanted to meet up tomorrow for brunch and chess."

The moment of silence made Mitch's heart sink. Damn. His big brother clearly had other plans.

"Sorry, Mitch. I'm driving to see the folks this weekend." A pause. "You could come with me, you know. We haven't done that in a while."

Mitch didn't miss the wistful edge to Gareth's voice. *Yeah, sure, make me feel even* more *guilty, why dontcha?* What made it worse was that he knew Gareth was right. He hadn't been home for one of Mom's mega Sunday get-togethers in at least three months. Mitch usually managed to get up there once a month. He and Gareth would meet up around noon on Saturday and share the driving for the five-hour-plus trip. On Sunday they'd stay long past the sensible time for departing, only because Mom wouldn't let them leave. It was nearly always midnight by the time Gareth dropped him back at his apartment before continuing across the river for another hour of driving to reach Mount Kisco. It meant retracing their journey for Gareth, but he wasn't put out in the slightest—that was just the kind of man he was. Mitch was damn lucky when it came to family.

Home. Mitch closed his eyes as the longing overwhelmed him. Maybe getting out of the city was a good idea, even only for a day or so. He knew it wouldn't be a picnic. His folks hadn't seen him since Jerry's… departure, and there were sure to be questions. But still, a chance to spend some time in his former home….

Fuck it. He'd spend a few hours grading, go into the city to the club, and then meet up with Gareth. He could grab some snacks and beverages for the trip, the least he could do, and they could hit the road. The thought of hearing his mom's voice when she found out he was coming was the clincher. *She'll be ecstatic. When she stops whacking me on the behind for staying away so long.*

"Okay, where did you go?" Gareth's amused tone broke through. "Mitch, you still there?"

"Okay," Mitch said with an air of finality.

"Okay?" Silence. "What—you mean you're coming too?" The note of genuine joy in his brother's voice had Mitch welling up. "Aww, that's great. I'll let you tell Mom." He snickered. "So, am I picking you up at the apartment?"

"No, I've got something I have to do in the city first. How about I get the train as far as North White Plains and you meet me there? It'll save you coming into the city, and that way we can just carry on. I'll bring snacks." Mitch couldn't resist. "Only this time, for the love of Mike, *please* bring some decent music?" He was teasing—he loved Gareth's predilection for seventies rock—but damn it, poking Gareth was *fun*. Mitch took his role of annoying little brother very seriously, although there were only five years between them.

"Just for that," Gareth said slowly, "I will be bringing my new collection of hits of the seventies. A *five CD* collection, I might add."

Mitch snorted. "There can't have been that many good songs from back then. I call bullshit."

Gareth laughed. "I'll aim to be at the train station for one o'clock. Think you can make that?"

"Sure." It took just over half an hour to get there, unless he caught the local train and then it was nearly an hour. Mitch had a few hours of work, a trip up to West 38th Street, and back to Grand Central for the Metro North train. "Any preferences for snacks or beverages?"

"Yeah—some of those new Oreos would be nice. And some diet soda."

Mitch snickered. "Let me guess—the calories in the Oreos are canceled out by the diet shit."

More chuckling from Gareth's end. "You know me too well. Don't bring too much. We can stop for a bite on the way as usual. See you at the station." He hung up.

Mitch was still smiling and shaking his head when he grabbed the backpack and went into his living room to start work. The call to Mom could wait until later.

IN DAYLIGHT, the restaurant looked pretty much the same—an expanse of glass at street level set in a frame of polished black marble slabs, a black canopy protecting the main door from the elements, and several floors above that, windows of obscured glass, with AC units protruding from them. Black carpet stretched out beneath the canopy. Through the windows Mitch could see the tables already starting to fill with the early lunch crowd.

The smaller door to the bar and club was off to the left, plain black glass bearing the words Black Lounge Bar in red. He spotted the buzzer for the club, located above what looked like an intercom, set into the black metallic doorframe. He pressed it firmly and waited.

"Mr. Jenkins?" The tinny voice made him jump, the response had been that fast.

What the fuck? Now *that* was scary. Mitch glanced upward and spied the security camera pointing at him. He leaned closer to the intercom. "Yes. I-I've brought the documentation." He stepped back and held up the brown envelope.

"Someone will be down right away." The voice died with a click.

Mitch lowered his hand and glanced around. For some reason, something about this felt... wrong. It wasn't that he now knew the building housed a brothel, albeit a top-end one. It wasn't the clandestine way of contacting the club. Whatever was bugging him remained frustratingly out of reach, something he couldn't put his finger on.

The club door opened, and Mitch recognized one of the security guards from the night before, dressed in a black suit. "Good morning, Mr. Jenkins. We've been expecting you. If you'd follow me, please."

"Uh, is that necessary?" Mitch really didn't want to go back up to the club. He held out the envelope. "This is all you want, right?"

The guard frowned. "I was under instructions to take copies."

Mitch breathed a sigh of relief. "That's fine. These *are* copies, so keep 'em, okay?" He figured if he went upstairs, someone would try to sweet-talk him into becoming a member, and he wanted to avoid that at all costs.

The guard studied him for a moment. "One second, please." He took out a phone and made a call, stepping away from Mitch while he talked quietly. The whole time Mitch's belly was turning somersaults. After a brief conversation, the guard disconnected and faced Mitch. "That will be fine." He held out his hand for the envelope, and Mitch handed it over, restraining himself from heaving yet another sigh of relief. The guard gave him a tight smile and reached into his jacket pocket. "Here's your driver's license. Have a good day, sir." He gave it to Mitch, reentered the club, and closed the door behind him with a metallic click.

Mitch huffed out his breath. Done. Another step closer to forgetting it had ever happened.

Except he knew he was lying to himself. After Jerry's cruel jibe, Mitch had been determined to step out of his comfort zone, do something he'd never done before, hence the idea—the *fantasy*—of using an escort site. He'd wanted it, all right, but now he was paying for it.

Guess I'm going to stay a serial monogamist. Maybe Jerry was right after all.

Damn but that was a depressing thought.

"Hey!" Gareth's cheerful greeting boomed out across the quiet parking lot of the train station. He walked across to Mitch, grinning widely. "Good to see you."

Gareth embraced him in a brief but extremely firm hug. Mitch patted Gareth on the back. "You too."

Gareth released him and stepped back. "So? Did Mom have a meltdown when you told her you were coming?" His eyes sparkled.

"For all of five seconds, and then she launched into her tirade. Apparently, I'm gonna get my ass kicked when she sees me."

"Good."

Mitch arched his eyebrows. "Geez. Really feeling the love here."

Gareth shrugged. "Sorry. I call it as I see it. You've stayed away from home far too long." He peered intently at Mitch. "We could've supported you, ya know, when he left. That's what families do, right?"

They reached Gareth's tired-looking but fully functional Jeep. Mitch sighed as he climbed into the passenger seat and dropped the backpack and plastic bag of goodies at his feet. "Look, I… I didn't want to see anyone, okay? And I certainly didn't want Mom lecturing me on how it didn't matter, there'd be another guy along, yadda, yadda, yadda…." His folks had welcomed every guy Mitch had ever brought home with open arms. He knew they just wanted him to be happy. "Maybe I'm tired of being the black sheep of the family."

Gareth paused in midaction, about to switch on the engine. He stared at Mitch, his eyes wide. "Huh? You're kidding, right? Christ, you're Mom's blue-eyed boy! You followed in her footsteps and became a teacher. I swear, her heart nearly bursts with pride when she talks about you." He shook his head. "For a supposedly intelligent man, you come out with some shit sometimes." The engine roared into life, and they pulled out of the parking lot, Gareth's phone sitting on the dashboard in its plastic rest, displaying their location.

Mitch was having none of it. "You think about it. Deirdre is happily married to her childhood sweetheart, and they have three adorable kids, one of whom in turn has made Mom and Dad great-grandparents. Monica and Shaun have two kids who'll both be in college come September. Both girls live near enough for Mom to visit them, or vice versa." Deirdre and Eric were in Saco, and Monica and her husband Shaun lived in Wells.

"According to your theory, I should be the black sheep," Gareth said as they joined 15 north. "At least you've *had* relationships. I'm just a big ol' confirmed bachelor."

"Who happens to be one of the most accomplished architects in the business," Mitch butted in. "You design some amazing houses. Of course they're proud of you. And it doesn't matter if you're a bachelor. You're happy." He gave his brother a sideways glance. "Aren't you?"

Gareth sighed. "Yeah, I can't deny that. I love my life. I have my house, the forest at my back door, my dogs, peace and quiet...." He fell silent, his gaze fixed on the freeway ahead.

Mitch couldn't say what really bothered him—that he'd been ashamed when Jerry had left. Another failed relationship, only this one had lasted longer than the others. The thought of seeing *that look* on his parents' faces yet again....

"Mitch, for what it's worth, I'm sorry about Jerry, okay?"

Fuck. Mitch really didn't need this, even if it came from his adored big brother. "I don't—"

"Yeah, yeah, you don't wanna talk about it. I get that," Gareth interrupted, "but knowing how Mom and the rest of the family are going to monopolize you the second you get through that front door, this might be the only chance I get, so you're gonna listen, okay?"

Mitch sagged into the seat. "Okay." There was little point in arguing. They had a long journey ahead of them.

Gareth gave a satisfied nod. "Good. So, like I was saying.... Jerry was okay."

"Only okay?" Mitch couldn't help but smile.

Another shrug. "Sorry. I liked him well enough, but if I'm being truthful...."

When Gareth paused, Mitch jumped right in. "Oh, please, be my guest. Say what's on your mind. It's not like you to hold back."

"I thought you could do better."

Silence.

Mitch stared out of the windshield at the steady stream of cars in front of them. He was at a loss for words.

"Mitch, you need someone who looks at you like you hung the moon. Someone who clearly loves being with you. Someone who makes you laugh, makes you smile. Someone who looks like he can't wait to have some alone time, just the two of you." Gareth turned his head for a moment to regard Mitch. "And that wasn't Jerry. It was none of the guys you've had over the years. But I believe he's out there, bro." He let go of the steering wheel and gestured to the windshield. "Somewhere out there, someone is waiting for you. I feel it. And when you meet him?" He grinned. "Fourth of July, Mitch. Freakin' Fourth of July."

Mitch's chest heaved at the thought. *Please, God, yeah.*

"Now let's change the subject. It's catch-up time. Tell me what's going on in the life of Mitch Jenkins, teacher extraordinaire. And then tell me you brought Oreos in that bag."

Mitch thought the little edge of a whine in Gareth's voice was cute.

Chapter Five

GARETH PULLED onto the driveway and switched off the engine. He glanced through Mitch's window and grinned. "Uh-oh. Your welcoming committee is here."

Mitch looked across at the front porch. Mom was at the door, smiling broadly. "Yeah, like that smile's gonna last once she gets me indoors. I can hear it now." He raised his voice up a notch or two and folded his arms across his chest. "'*Where have you* been, *Mitchell Seymour Jenkins? You are supposed to come see your mother* occasionally.'"

Gareth guffawed. "God, that was uncanny. I could've been sitting next to her." Mitch whacked him hard on the upper arm. "Hey, no hitting the driver. Especially as I did all the driving." He frowned, his face etched with concern. "Didn't you get any sleep last night?"

Mitch sighed. "I'm sorry. I… I had stuff on my mind, so yeah, sleep was a rare commodity." He bent down and picked up his backpack. "Time to face the music."

Gareth stopped him with a large but gentle hand to his arm. "It'll be fine," he stressed softly. "Just remember they love you."

It was a good thought.

Mitch climbed out of the Jeep and walked past the three vehicles in the driveway. It seemed like the whole family was there. *Talk about baptism by fire.* By the time he climbed the steps and reached Mom, her arms were already wide.

"Come here, you."

Mitch smiled and enveloped her in a tight hug. Her head just reached his shoulder. "Are you shrinking, Mom?"

She huffed. "You're not too old to slap, you know." She turned her face up to his, her blue eyes shining. "Hey there, sweetheart." Her voice was soft, as was the hand that caressed his cheek.

Mitch gazed at her. "You could give Susan Sarandon a run for her money in the looks department. Just saying."

Mom giggled. "Flatterer. Now get inside. I've got Deirdre's homemade lemonade waiting for you boys."

Gareth was behind him. "Make mine a spiked one and I'll be interested."

Mom released Mitch and speared Gareth with a hard stare. "And you can wait. Your dad's making his special punch for later."

Both of them groaned. Dad's punch had a kick like a mule. Mitch had vivid memories of many mornings after a night of "special" punch, aching head, suede tongue….

He stepped into the cool interior and sniffed the air. God, that smell…. It was a mixture of lavender furniture polish, flowers, and books—a scent that hadn't changed since he was a kid. It enveloped him, sinking into his skin and pervading his senses.

It was the smell of home.

"Hey, stranger." Monica came out of the living room, smiling. "About time you decided to grace us with your presence." She hugged him, her face buried in his neck. "You have been missed," she whispered.

"Aw, Mon," he remonstrated, but she didn't release him. Mitch sighed and went with the flow. "Missed you too, sis."

Sometimes it was good to be the nice big brother too.

Monica let him go, and Mitch kissed her cheek before walking through and into the living room. He smiled at the sight of the Steinway grand piano, the warm maple gleaming in the sunlight filtering through the lace curtains that frothed at the windows. Mitch couldn't resist. He lifted the lid and ran his fingers over the keys, loving the mellow tone of the piano. Another part of his childhood.

His mom appeared at his side. "I bet you haven't played since you were last here."

He chuckled. "You'd win that bet." He lowered the lid. "Do you still have your sticky-fingered pupils?"

"Unfortunately, yes." His dad stood in the doorway that led into the dining room. "I've told her it's time to call it a day. She'll be seventy next birthday. That's far too old to be dealing with some of the entitled little brats that expect her to drop everything and arrange their lessons to fit in around their social calendar. You know, only last week—"

"Malcolm." There was a warning note in Mom's voice. Mitch bit his lip when his dad snapped his mouth shut. Malcolm Jenkins was ex-Navy, but there was no doubt who ruled the roost—and who had him wrapped around her tiny little finger.

His dad came over to give Mitch a hug. "Good to see you, Mitch." His voice was gruff. "Are you hungry yet? We're having pizza. I was waiting until you two arrived before putting in the order."

"Malcolm, they've just gotten through the door," Mom exclaimed, exasperated. "Let them sit for a while. Besides, it's only just turned six o'clock." She peered at him over the rim of her glasses. "And if you're that hungry, there's cold turkey in the refrigerator."

His dad opened his mouth as if to retort, which made Mom stare even harder.

"Yes, dear," he said meekly.

Monica walked over to the couch and flopped down onto it, chuckling. "Nice to see some things don't change, isn't it, Mitch?"

From behind him came the sound of someone clearing their throat. Mitch turned and smiled to see one of his brothers-in-law, Shaun. Mitch extended his hand and the two men shook, before Shaun joined his wife on the couch.

"Did you bring the kids?" Mitch asked. He liked the company of his nephew and niece. They were always a laugh, both intelligent, easygoing people.

Shaun shook his head. "Cal is at home planning a camping trip with his buddies to Acadia National Park. It's their last vacation before they all head off to college. One of them has an RV, and they're going hiking, biking, canoeing, you name it." He shook his head. "Five guys camping. When I was his age, I was—"

"Already dating me," Monica butted in, "and no, I would *not* have let you disappear off for weeks on end with your buddies. And the only reason Cal wants to go is because he doesn't have a girlfriend."

Shaun returned his attention to Mitch. "Lisa has gone on vacation with her college girlfriends. They've flown down to Florida for a couple of weeks." He patted Monica's knee. "All the chicks leaving the nest."

She shook her head. "Don't. You'll only get me started again." Monica got up abruptly and exited the room. Mitch and Gareth stared after her. Shaun hesitated for a few seconds before following her.

Mom sighed. "She'll be all right. She's just not looking forward to losing her baby." She reached up and stroked Gareth's cheek. "It's one of those things all parents have to go through. Sooner or later, everyone leaves."

Dad cackled. "Yes, and then we got the house all to ourselves again. No more kids leaving their stuff everywhere, no more mess, blessed peace and quiet...."

"Oh hush." His mom gave his dad a fond glance. "You'd have those days again in a heartbeat, don't think I don't know that. Besides, *I* was the one dealing with all the mess while *you* were off gallivanting for the Navy."

Dad spluttered. "Gallivanting? Well, I...."

"Isn't it great to be back?" Deirdre appeared at Mitch's side from the hallway.

He turned and hugged her. "Be it ever so humble," he whispered. She was right, of course.

It was great to be back.

MITCH SAT in the swing, his feet still touching the ground, a bottle of beer in his hand. The night was warm, a gentle breeze carrying the sweet fragrance of hydrangea. All around him in the fading light was the evidence of his mom's passion—her garden. The neatly cut lawn was bordered by well-stocked flower beds and trees of differing heights and ages. The swing was suspended from a bough of one of the oldest trees in the garden—a magnificent, mature red oak. Higher up, the remains of Gareth's tree house were still visible, although the elements had taken their toll. All of his siblings had played in it at one time or another. Deirdre, two years older than Mitch, had sometimes complained when he followed her to the hideaway, but more often than not, she'd let him climb the ladder and sit there while she arranged a tea party for her dolls and soft toys. Mitch had to take part, pouring lemonade into tiny cups and serving tiny squares of a PBJ. It was only years later that he figured out she'd done it on purpose to punish him for being her irritating little brother.

He closed his eyes and let the heavenly aroma of the gardens fill his senses. Summer was a wonderful time to be in Maine, away from the noise, dirt, and fumes of the city. Some weekends he'd go into Central Park and sit on the grass, reading a book and trying to blot out the noise of the traffic. But it was times like this, sitting in his parents' garden, that brought home to him just how much he missed Maine. He intended to get up early Sunday morning, take his old bike and cycle to Cape

Neddick, one of his favorite places as a child. He used to stare at the Nubble Lighthouse and imagine living there, surrounded by the constant noise of the sea and the cries of gulls.

"So you came all the way from New York to hide out in my backyard?"

Mitch turned to regard his mom. "But it's a beautiful backyard," he said with a smile.

She walked across the lawn and came to stand behind him, her hands on the ropes. "I remember when I used to push you on this. You'd have spent hours at a time on this swing if I'd let you."

He chuckled. "Yeah, I remember that. Gareth used to whine and bitch that it was his turn all the time, but I figured he'd already had years of playing on it before I came along."

His mom came around to stand in front of him, arching her thin eyebrows. "Yes, but some of those years, he'd had to fight off Deirdre too." She shook her head, tut-tutting. "Poor Gareth. Being the oldest child is never easy." She narrowed her eyes. "And you…."

Mitch laughed, knowing what was coming next. "Yeah, yeah, I was a brat, I know." Everything had changed when Mitch hit sixteen years old. It was to his older brother that he'd turned to share what had been on his mind for almost six months. Gareth had come home from college for the summer, bursting with news. He'd decided what he wanted out of life—to become an architect. He was so excited, so hopeful for the future. And when Mitch grabbed him and took him to the tree house, out of sight and hearing of the rest of the family, Gareth had been in a great mood, so he'd acquiesced. He could have had no idea of what his little brother was about to confess—that he thought he was gay.

That was the day Mitch realized how much he loved Gareth.

"Honey, why did you stay away so long?"

Damn. He really thought he'd gotten away with it. No one had said a word about it through dinner, but there'd been a lot of pizza, punch, and laughter, and little time for interrogation. Mitch knew that was mean of him—no one was about to quiz him mercilessly—but he also knew what his family was like.

Mitch took hold of his mom's hands. "I'm sorry." He spoke softly, his words audible above the buzz of the cicadas. "I was… it's not that… I…."

"Mitch." Mom pulled a hand free and lifted his chin to look him in the eye. "I thought you and I could talk about anything."

He sighed. "I was ashamed, Mom."

She stared at him. "Honey, forgive me if I've got this all wrong, but it was Jerry who left you, right?" He nodded, and Mom shook her head. "Then what in the world do *you* have to be ashamed about? He's the asshole in this equation."

Mitch was awfully glad he wasn't drinking beer right then—his mom might have ended up wearing some of it. He gaped at her, openmouthed.

Mom giggled. "Didn't know I had it in me, huh?"

That made him laugh. "Love you, lady."

She stroked his cheek. "Love you right back. So tell me. Why were you ashamed?"

He took a moment to find the words. "Mom, you know what I really want? What you and Dad have. What Deirdre and Eric have. What Monica and Shaun have. I want to find someone who completes me." He smiled at her. "Someone who loves me."

"Oh, sweetheart." Mom stepped closer and leaned over to hold him, wrapping her arms around him and squeezing tight. "Do you think I don't know that? I *saw* you, every time you brought someone home. I saw the hope in you. And no matter who walked through that door with you, I made them feel at home, because you know what? One of these days it could be my future son-in-law." She kissed his cheek. "But you think Jerry leaving you makes you a failure, is that it?"

He nodded once more. "I thought I'd found him, Mom, I really did. But at the end, he was honest with me—brutally honest—and it made me look at myself."

"And you didn't like what you saw?"

"No, Mom. I think… I think I need to make some changes in my life. Because my way hasn't worked so far."

She stared at him. "Mitch, promise me you won't do anything rash."

His heart pounded. *Too late for that, Mom.*

He laughed and rose to his feet, gazing at her fondly. "This is me talking. Mr. Sober-sides, right? Since when have I ever done anything rash?" *How about last night, when you fucked a hooker?* He gave himself an angry mental shake. Thinking about Nikko was not a good idea.

His bluff appeared to have worked. Mom smiled. "Okay, okay, I'll stop worrying."

That did make him smile. He snorted. "Yeah, that'll be the day." He put his arm around her shoulders. "How about we go to the kitchen and see if we can't find some of your homemade ice cream in the freezer?"

"Hah. Like I wouldn't have made some with you horde of locusts about to descend." She grinned. "There's peach and honey, and I also made maple and pecan."

Mitch let out a whoop. "Well, come on, then. Before that horde of locusts finds your ice-cream stash."

She peered at the bottle in his hand. "I see you avoided the punch." That grin didn't alter. "I always said you had brains."

Laughing together, his arm still around her, they walked back to the house.

Mitch couldn't complain. It had been less painful than he'd expected. A whole lot less.

"Any more slaw, Mom?" Deirdre asked, putting down the bowl of potato chips and glancing toward the table with its piles of neatly sliced burger buns and hot dog rolls, and containers of relish and ketchup.

"In the refrigerator. But you'll have to go get it." Mom grinned. "I'm supervising your father." Deirdre chuckled and set off toward the house.

His dad brandished the tongs. "Heavens, woman, do I *look* like I need supervising?"

There was a brief moment's silence before everyone assembled around the gas grill burst out laughing. Monica snorted and spluttered, spraying Coke all over her blouse.

She looked down at her stained clothing in disgust. "Great, now I have to go change into something else." She scowled at her dad. "Way to go, Dad." She put down her glass and marched back to the house.

Eric was still laughing. "Oh, come on, Malcolm, you have to admit, you haven't exactly got a good track record when it comes to barbecues."

Dad huffed. "I'll have you know, I always do the grilling in this house."

"Yeah, and you always burn it," Deirdre called out, coming along the path with a container of slaw. "I'm with Mom on this one—you need watching."

"Nonsense. Anyone can grill. Why, I—"

"Watch the sausages!" Mom shrieked, digging him in the ribs with her elbow. Dad gave the grill his full attention, and Mom caught Mitch's gaze. He bit his lip, trying hard to stop the laughter that was right there, dying to escape.

"Hey, Mitch, did you see what I bought last month on Amazon?" Dad gestured with the tongs to the opened aluminum case beside the grill, his chest puffed out.

"Yeah, I did." Mitch was still struggling. "But Dad? An eighteen-piece stainless steel barbecue utensil set? In its own case? Don't you think that's a bit… excessive?"

Dad stared. "But look what it comes with! Spatula, knife, barbecue fork, tongs, eight corn holders…."

Mitch held up his hands. "Oh, it's wonderful, don't get me wrong. I was just thinking… how often does Mom let you near—I mean, how often do you grill?"

His dad narrowed his gaze. "Well, if you're going to be like that about it…."

"It's a beautiful set, Malcolm," Shaun interjected quickly, his lips twitching. Eric murmured in agreement. Mitch mouthed *ass-kissers* at them, and both men grinned.

"Steaks!" Mom yelled.

With a groan Dad turned back to flip the steaks. "See?" he said, pointing toward them. "Not burnt."

His mom grinned. "That was the point in yelling. I didn't want them to get that far." She peered at her husband. "And they put you in charge of an entire boat?"

He glared. "A naval destroyer is hardly a boat."

By that point the laughter had started up again.

Sunday was a perfect day for a barbecue. Little or no wind, temperature in the high seventies, and not a cloud in the sky. And judging by the aromas in the neighborhood, they weren't the only ones taking advantage of the day. Garden chairs had been set up on the patio, and on the small table were glasses, bottles of soda and water in a bucket filled with ice, and a jug full of Dad's punch poured over yet more ice.

Mitch gazed at his family. They were a wonderful group of people, generous and loving, but not without their mischievous side at times. It was at events like this that he counted himself lucky.

"So, no new man yet, Mitch?" Deirdre asked, an innocent expression on her face, as Monica rejoined them.

Fuck. Maybe not so lucky after all.

"Give him a chance," Monica said quickly. "It's only been, what, two months?"

"Leave your brother alone," Mom said firmly. She gave him a warm, sympathetic glance.

Like Deirdre was going to pay heed to *that*.

"Want to know what I think?" Deirdre said, waving her chicken leg in the air.

"No, but I'm pretty sure that won't stop you from telling us anyway," Mitch said dryly. His heartbeat quickened.

"Where did you find that chicken?" Mom squinted at Deirdre. "That's for later."

Mitch could've kissed her. He knew she was trying to deflect Deirdre, but there was little chance of that happening. He knew his sister. If Gareth was Tigger, she was a terrier.

"I think you need to stop looking for Mr. Right, and try finding Mr. Right Now," Deirdre said with an evil grin, ignoring their mother completely.

What the fuck?

"Well, it's not like you're getting any younger, is it?" she added with a shrug.

"Deirdre!" Mom gasped.

"Mom!" she mimicked, before meeting Mitch's hard stare. "I mean it. Stop looking for The One, and settle instead for someone who's, you know, fun to be with, sexy"—she winked at him—"not weird...."

"Excuse me?" Mitch put down the plate containing his food and glowered at his sister. "Since when did I *ever* bring home a guy who was weird?"

A moment of silence followed. Deirdre slowly put down her plate of chicken and faced him.

Oh fuck.

"Well now, let's see," she said, smiling sweetly and counting off on her fingers. "There was that guy who must've known the words to every show tune going, and who could—and did—burst into song at the drop of a hat, no matter in whose company he found himself."

"He was a musical theater student," Mitch protested, "and I was nineteen at the time." He didn't miss the snickers of the rest of his family.

Deirdre pursed her lips. "No excuse. Then there was the one who never stopped talking. I mean, *ever*."

"So Mike was a Chatty Cathy, so what?" If he were honest, even Mitch had found Mike's constant chatter an annoyance. They'd lasted two months before he'd called it a day.

"Did he talk in his sleep too?" Deirdre asked, that evil smile still in evidence.

"Deirdre!" This time it was his dad.

"And what about—oh, what was his name?—Andy!" she exclaimed in triumph, totally ignoring her dad's hard stares. "Did he *ever* stop eating? And where did he put it all? He was as thin as a rake."

Mitch groaned. "I stopped taking him out to dinner after the third or fourth time. He was costing me a fortune." He bit his lip. "Whenever we went out after that, it was always to one of those all-you-can-eat restaurants. Except the Chinese one barred us after a couple of visits." He smothered a chuckle. "I swear, he must've had a tapeworm."

By then, everyone was laughing, Mitch included.

When the laughter died away, Deirdre walked across to him and placed her hands on his upper arms. "Mitch, whatever happens, you need to remember one thing, all right?" She looked him in the eye. "We all love you. We will always love you, and we will always be here for you. And that goes double for when some bastard dumps you. Don't shut us out, okay?" She leaned forward and kissed his cheek.

Mitch held his sister close, his stubbled cheek against her smooth one. "Thanks, sis," he whispered.

"For what it's worth?" she whispered back. "I hope you find him. I really do."

Mitch tightened his grip. "Me too." Mr. Right Now was a nice idea, but it wasn't him.

"Dad!" Monica's hoarse yell had everyone turning, just as the sausages caught fire.

His dad stared in dismay at the blackening lumps of meat, while Eric reached for the fire extinguisher. Dad swallowed and reached into his back pocket for his wallet. "Pizza, anyone?"

Chapter Six

NIKKO KUROKAWA poured himself a glass of water and placed it on the tiny table before pulling open the huge refrigerator and peering inside. He couldn't complain at the food provided for them, that was certain. Anything he could have wanted was in there: fruit, yogurt, cheese, eggs, cold meat.... And if there was something else they wanted, they only had to ask. The Black Lounge took care of its... merchandise.

Merchandise. A shiver ran through him. It was still difficult to think of himself in those terms, even after two weeks. Only, he'd stopped thinking of his time in the club in terms of days. He was all about the hours. Nikko kept an exact tally of every hour he spent, sitting in that chair, reading, avoiding meeting anyone's gaze. He wasn't there to make friends.

He just wanted to do what he had to and get out of there.

The kitchen was set behind the scenes, away from the gaze of the club's patrons. No food or drink was allowed onto the "floor." Everything was to be consumed out of sight. Unlike Nikko, not all the men who worked in the club were there all the time. There were some who only worked weekends, when there was the highest demand. Others turned up for the evenings and only worked a couple of hours. Apart from Nikko, there were three other men who resided at the club 24-7 simply because that was their choice. They shared what could only be described as a dorm on the floor above the club.

Not that Nikko was allowed to share it with them. His accommodation was very different. For one thing, he doubted they would have put up with the cameras. Nikko was by nature a very private individual, which made his situation all the more ironic. There was nothing he could say to change it—complaining was not an option. It was simply a matter of doing what needed to be done, so that he and Ichy could walk out of there one day soon.

Their room was comfortable, clean and tidy, but there was no privacy, not even when taking a shower—the camera saw to that. No phones. They lived in a cage with no bars, but a cage nonetheless.

He helped himself to a plate of cold meat and salad, and sat at the table on one of the three chairs. When the club was at capacity, there could be more than twenty young men located in that mock-up of a studio apartment. Time spent in the kitchen area was done on a rotation basis. Nikko had chosen to eat before the boys started to arrive. He'd already made sure Ichy had eaten something. It was Friday evening, and if the previous two Fridays were anything to go by, business would be brisk.

Business. Merchandise. Just listen to yourself. Don't try to make it sound better than it is.

"Don't be too long, Nikko." Randy stuck his head around the corner. "Things are heating up out there."

Nikko bit back his sigh. "How long do I have?" It wasn't as if nobody was on the floor. The seven or eight guys out there should have been plenty to service whomever required them.

Randy tilted his head to one side. "Twenty minutes tops, okay?" His glance wasn't entirely unsympathetic.

Nikko nodded. "Thanks, Randy." He dove into his food without delay as Randy disappeared from view.

"Hey, slow down there." The voice bubbled with an undercurrent of amusement. "You don't wanna barf when you're with a john, right?"

Nikko glanced at the speaker. All he knew of the tousled blond-haired, blue-eyed young man was his name, Jesse, and that he appeared to love his occupation. Jesse worked a few nights during the week and had been around both weekends so far. Nikko estimated him to be in his early twenties. Jesse was slim with a body that showed evidence of gym activity, but what had struck Nikko from the first was Jesse's face. The young man was always smiling.

Jesse had a point.

Nikko nodded. "Good thinking," he said with a polite smile and went back to his food.

Jesse didn't take the hint. He launched himself into the chair next to Nikko's and pulled up his legs, his feet balanced on the edge of the plastic seat. Jesse hugged his knees. "You don't talk much, do you?"

Nikko lowered his fork. "Not while I'm eating, no."

Jesse smiled. "I'm interrupting you, aren't I? Sorry. I'll leave you alone. Besides, we can talk later." He winked. "That is, if I'm not otherwise occupied." With a chuckle he lurched from his chair, poured himself a glass of water, and gulped it down before exiting the kitchen.

Nikko went back to eating. He had no intention of chatting with Jesse. He wasn't there to make friends.

He had a job to do.

Nikko finished his meal, washed the plate and fork, and put them away. He knew he was putting off the moment when he'd walk back onto the floor. Not that he'd been in demand all day. He'd curled up in what was now his chair, book in hand, and tried to blend into the background. It was a subterfuge that hadn't always paid off, but he couldn't complain. So far there had only been three guys who'd requested him. The last two had been okay, nothing outlandish, immediately forgettable, in fact. Certainly nothing like Mitch. It seemed Nikko's first encounter with a john was going to be the yardstick by which he measured everyone else who followed. Mitch had been…. Nikko closed his eyes and tried to sum up the tall man with the abundant chest hair and the warm brown eyes.

Kind. Gentle. Thoughtful. And unfortunately, inquisitive.

With an internal sigh, Nikko walked into the bathroom to brush his teeth. He glanced at his reflection, checking his appearance. Everything in order. He went back to the kitchen, picked up his book from the table where he'd left it, and walked onto the floor.

Jesse was already in full swing. Nikko had to admire his boundless energy. He was always right there at the glass, strutting his stuff and doing his best to attract attention. He usually managed it too, displaying his already lubed hole to anyone who was watching was apparently a crowd pleaser.

That glass. Nikko hated it with a passion. It reflected the room, reminding him exactly where he was—like he needed a reminder. But what was worse was that he couldn't see who was out there. It was like a lottery, every time Randy opened the door and summoned one of them. The second time Randy had called him, Nikko had walked over to him, heart pounding, hoping maybe Mitch had come back for a return visit. When he'd spied the middle-aged man in a suit that barely covered his middle-aged spread, Nikko's heart sank. Not that he disliked the look of the guy. He just wasn't Mitch.

I really need to stop thinking about him. It wasn't the first time that thought had crossed his mind in the—he did a quick count-up in his head—one hundred fifty hours he'd spent on the floor. One hundred fifty hours closer to his goal—freedom.

Nikko curled up in his armchair and opened his book.

"Randy likes you, you know."

Nikko stuck his thumb in the page and closed the book, before lifting his chin to regard Jesse. "What makes you say that?" It appeared Jesse wasn't about to be put off.

Jesse crouched down next to him. "The way he looks at you. I'm not suggesting he has the hots for you, but I do think he has a soft spot for you. I mean, you get *smiles*, for God's sake." Jesse rose to his feet and dragged over a chair to face Nikko's. He glanced around and grabbed a towel from a neat pile on a rack. Jesse spread it over the seat cushion and sat down carefully. "Don't wanna get lube everywhere, do I?" he said brightly.

Yeah, Nikko couldn't help but like Jesse.

"Nikko, can I ask a question? Kinda personal?"

Nikko blinked, surprised that Jesse even knew his name. "Sure," he said cautiously.

"What are you doing here? Because it seems to me, at least, that you don't belong in a place like this." Jesse's expression was kind. "I mean, I know why *I'm* here—why most of us are here—to make a few bucks. But you? You sit back here; you don't draw attention to yourself. If anything, you seem to avoid it." He regarded Nikko intently. "*You* are an enigma."

"How long have you worked here?" Nikko wanted to know. Anything rather than answer Jesse's question.

"A couple, maybe three weeks. One of the guys in my class at college suggested it."

"College?" Nikko schooled his features. He couldn't imagine Jesse as a student.

Jesse arched his eyebrows. "This isn't what I want to do in life, Nikko. I study, I have loans. This helps to pay them off." He smiled. "I'm doing my master's right now, so I can only work a few nights a week and most of the weekend, but it all helps." He peered intently at Nikko. "But every time I'm here, so are you. So what's your story?"

Nikko stiffened. "I'd rather not talk about it." He fell silent, praying Jesse took the hint but didn't take offense. He liked the young man, but one conversation wasn't about to make them best buddies.

Jesse blinked. "Oh. Okay. I didn't mean to pry. You don't have to tell me a thing."

The door next to the glass opened and Randy appeared. His gaze went straight to Nikko and he beckoned. Nikko got up and placed his book on the seat.

Here we go again. He sent up a silent prayer. *Please, make him gentle? Like Mitch?* As an afterthought, he added, *how about just cutting to the chase and making him Mitch?*

It was a pleasant thought.

"Oh shit," Jesse whispered.

Nikko froze and turned to face him. "What?"

Jesse's expression was grave. "Randy isn't smiling."

MITCH STRETCHED, his spine popping. His workload was increasing the closer they got to the last day of the semester. End-of-term papers to grade, textbooks to collect and check, grades to assign, a classroom to clear.... One week left, and he was more than ready for a vacation. Not that he'd planned anything, but there was always his grandparents' house in Maine if nothing else materialized. His parents kept it as a vacation rental property, but if no one had booked it, he often spent a week or two there. It was literally a short walk along a path from the house to the rocky shoreline, a peaceful, beautiful place that Mitch had fond recollections of from childhood.

"We okay to talk now?"

Mitch sighed. "Hey. How was your day?"

Aaron pulled out the chair facing him and sat. The teachers' lounge was empty, not surprising as it was already close to six o'clock. It wouldn't be long before the custodians were shooing them both out of there with brooms. Everyone was eager to start their weekend—everyone except Aaron, it seemed.

Aaron leaned back in his chair. "Haven't seen much of you this week." His manner was cautious.

"Oh?" Mitch feigned surprise. He'd done his level best to keep out of Aaron's way for the last two weeks, ever since that first day back after their trip to the Black Lounge. All Aaron had done was to ask if Mitch had enjoyed himself, but it was enough. Mitch had replied tersely that he didn't want to talk about it, and Aaron had backed right off. "I've been busy with the end-of-year assessments." That was partially true. Every time he caught a glimpse of Aaron, in the hallway or the lounge, even crossing the school yard during the lunch break, it had brought that whole episode back. Not that it had ever been that far from Mitch's thoughts.

He couldn't stop thinking about Nikko.

What surprised him was the nature of his thoughts. Mitch wasn't thinking about the sex. What bothered him was something more complex. He kept recalling Nikko's manner, his quiet way of speaking, the way he held himself, his gentleness. Mitch couldn't for the life of him imagine what Nikko was doing working in a brothel, and yet Nikko had insisted he was there of his own volition.

Something wasn't right. Between what Nikko said and how Nikko behaved, something just didn't… mesh.

"Seeing as we're alone, can I ask you something?"

Mitch stifled a sigh. There was no way he was going to discuss that night. *Christ, can't he take a hint?* Some things were private. "You can ask," he said with a shrug.

"Have you given any thought to becoming a member of the club?" Aaron's face was flushed, his tongue flicking out to lick his lips.

"To be honest? No." That at least was the truth.

Aaron's face fell. "Oh. I thought maybe you'd changed your mind after…." He shut up.

Mitch stared at him. "Why should it matter to you if I become a member or not?" He couldn't resist a little poke. "You're not on commission, are you, Aaron? You bought shares in the club? Is that it?"

Aaron's eyes widened. "Fuck, no! Shit, why would you even think a thing like that?" He blinked rapidly, rubbing at his neck where his shirt collar rubbed up against it.

Mitch held up his hands. "Easy there. Boy, you sure are touchy tonight. Maybe you need to get out of here." He glanced at the clock on the wall. "He—heck, maybe we both should." He scowled. *Six o'clock on a Friday night and I'm having to watch my goddamn language.* Like there was anyone around who gave a fuck if he said hell. The incongruity of his last thought struck him as funny. He piled up his papers and left them neat, before rising to pick up his jacket and backpack. "C'mon, let's get out of here. We've earned our keep for this week."

"Yeah, sure," Aaron muttered, copying his actions.

Mitch gazed at him, perplexed. Aaron's behavior was odd, even for him. "You okay?"

"What?" Aaron blinked. "Oh, sure. Yeah. I'm fine. Absolutely fine." He followed Mitch to the door.

Mitch chuckled. "I think I got the message with 'sure,' but thanks for the clarification." When Aaron didn't respond, Mitch gave up. His colleague clearly had something on his mind, and Mitch wasn't one to pry.

They left the building and walked briskly to the station, the roar of traffic a constant drone in the background. Mitch was on autopilot, his head elsewhere. It hadn't taken much to bring Nikko to the forefront of his mind. He could still see him, standing there in the doorway, hands clasped in front of him, those dark eyes focused on Mitch.

Why are you there? What is it you're not saying? The more Mitch thought about it, the more convinced he became. There was something there that required answers. By the time he and Aaron squeezed onto the train packed full of commuters, the smell of sweat heavy in the air, Mitch had made up his mind. He wasn't going to take out a membership to the club, but that didn't mean he couldn't go back there and see if they'd let him have more time with Nikko.

This time, however, he'd be paying for it.

"I'M SORRY, Mr. Jenkins, but that will not be possible. We don't operate like that." Seb's tone was patient but firm. He sat across the desk from Mitch, arms folded across his chest.

Mitch could be patient too. "You guys have an hourly rate, right? Why not let me pay for an hour with one of your boys, as a sort of incentive?"

Seb gave a thin smile, a perfect replica of the one he'd given Mitch two weeks previously. "A 'try before you buy' deal? I believe that's what you were given the last time you were here." He tapped the application form that lay on the desk between them with a long, thin finger. "If you wish to use the services of the club, I'm afraid that can only be in one capacity—as a member." He leaned back in his chair, his expression saying what his mouth did not: *that sensation pressing against your middle is the barrel we have you over, Mr. Jenkins.*

What made it infinitely worse was that the smug bastard was right.

Mitch stared at him, but Seb stared serenely back. *Talk about an immovable object.*

He had two choices. He could walk out of there and put Nikko from his mind—it was only Nikko that had brought him back there, after all—or he could shell out $5,000 that might be used for much more practical purposes, like feeding, clothing, and housing him. The latter sounded crazy, ridiculous, sheer lunacy. Finding out more about Nikko was not worth paying that price.

Was it?

Then why was he reaching for Seb's pen?

His heart thumping wildly, Mitch read the form. It was another version of the one he'd signed last time. His fingers shaking, he signed on the dotted line.

Seb slid another sheet across to him. "Some details are required for our files. Just for demographic purposes, you understand."

Mitch scanned the sheet. They wanted to know personal details such as his age, address, phone number, place of work, job title.... *Geez, they don't want much, do they?* He raised his head to meet Seb's cool gaze. "I suppose you'd like payment now. Credit card okay?"

Seb nodded. "I'm assuming your credit limit is good."

"Excuse me?"

Seb merely arched his eyebrows. "Mr. Jenkins. You are a high-school English teacher. And although you may be wonderful at your job, it is hardly a career someone takes on if they are looking for a *highly paid* job, is it? I am simply verifying that your credit limit is adequate for our purposes."

That was when Mitch decided he didn't like Seb.

He reached into his wallet, withdrew his credit card, and handed it over before returning to his task of form-filling. Seb pulled open a drawer and took out a card payment machine.

When the transaction had gone through successfully, Seb handed back the card and pointed to the webcam secured to the monitor. "Look at the camera, please."

Mitch did as instructed, still smarting from Seb's comments about his financial situation.

"Thank you. That's everything." Seb gave him a thick plastic card. "This is your membership card, to be shown on request. Please ensure you have it with you each time you visit the club. Payment is to be either by credit card or we can set up autopay from your checking account."

Mitch wasn't too happy about that idea. "Think I'll stick with the credit card." It wasn't like he planned on making that many visits. "So you still need to take a payment for tonight?"

"Payment is due before leaving," Seb told him, "and as you are now a member, your first visit is our welcome gift."

Mitch was tempted to retort, *after just taking me for five grand? I should fucking think so.* Fortunately, Valerie Jenkins had raised all her kids to be polite, so he just nodded and smiled as he pocketed his wallet.

Seb rose from his chair, came around the desk, and walked over to the door that led into the club. "Enjoy."

Mitch gave another polite nod and entered the club.

The couches were empty this time, but a couple of guys were standing in front of the glass, staring in at the… *hookers? Rent boys?* Mitch thought both of those terms ugly, and neither of them fit in with his memory of Nikko. After two weeks of thinking about him, Mitch was starting to wonder if he was recalling Nikko through rose-colored glasses. It would be interesting to see if the reality matched up to his fantasy.

He walked up to the glass, his gaze drawn to where Nikko had been sitting, but the chair was empty. *Damn.* To go through all that rigmarole with Seb and then find Nikko was already in someone else's bed was just irritating.

"Good evening."

Mitch turned to see the security guard—Randy?—from before. "Hi." He went back to scanning the room in front of him, in case Nikko was somewhere else in there.

"Looking for something—or someone—in particular?" Randy asked him quietly.

Mitch got the feeling Randy knew exactly who he was looking for. "Yeah, but I don't see him. Nikko." When Randy didn't reply, Mitch regarded him. "Is that a problem?"

Randy's expression tightened. "Nikko is… unavailable."

Fuck. He is *with someone else.* The thought made Mitch's stomach churn, though he had no idea why that should be. He'd gone to this much trouble, he wasn't gonna leave until he'd seen Nikko. Not so much because he was that desperate to fuck him. Mitch just wanted to see him to make sure he was okay. The vague disquieting feeling that something was wrong hadn't left him.

"How long will he be?" Mitch had plenty of time.

Randy's expression softened. "He won't be available tonight."

That churning sensation in his stomach intensified. "When *will* he be available, then?"

Randy sighed. "Perhaps you should come back toward the end of the week?"

Fuck. Mitch was getting a bad feeling about this.

"Is there someone else you'd like to see while you're here?" Randy gestured to the window.

Mitch didn't even bother looking. "No, thank you." He just wanted to get out of there. It was bad enough that he'd returned in the first place.

Without another word he left the room, walked past a surprised-looking Seb, and out the door. His heart was racing, his breathing rapid.

I just wanna go home.

It wasn't until he reached the street level that something about his encounter with Seb finally filtered through his consciousness.

I hadn't filled in the form, yet he knew I was a high-school teacher. He even knew my subject. The only person who could have given Seb that information was Aaron.

So why the fuck is Aaron talking about me to Seb?

Chapter Seven

"OKAY, QUIET down."

As usual, the majority of students followed Mitch's instructions. There were still those who kept on chatting excitedly. He couldn't blame them; he still remembered how it felt to finally be there, the last day of the year before summer vacation.

The noise level rose, and he glared at them. "What did I just say?"

"But Mr. Jenkins, it's the last day!" Emma Talbot bleated.

"No, really?" he said, feigning shock. A wave of laughter rippled through the room. He was excited too but for a whole different set of reasons. Right then the last place he wanted to be was in a classroom.

He wanted to be in front of a TV screen.

When the laughter had died down, he began handing out the summer vacation assignment sheets to a chorus of groans. "Yeah, yeah, I'm mean. I know," he said with an evil grin, glancing at the clock. It was eleven o'clock, and he had ten minutes until the bell. *Geez, c'mon, surely there must be news by now?* Reluctantly he returned his attention to his tenth grade class. "Make sure you read the entire sheet before you begin. And yes, class points will be deducted if you return in September and you haven't completed it." More groans rose up. Mitch shook his head. "Do I mean what I say?"

"Yes, Mr. Jenkins," they responded in a doleful chorus.

"Are you going to do your assignments?"

"Yes, Mr. Jenkins."

He opened his mouth but snapped it shut when a few muted cheers and shouts were heard from the street below. More voices joined them, too indistinct for Mitch to make out the words, but the sound was joyful.

Oh my God. He didn't dare breathe for fear it would somehow alter the outcome. Well, what he fervently prayed was the outcome.

The door to the hallway opened, and the principal entered, his face flushed.

As one, the students rose to their feet and addressed him. "Good morning, Principal Galletta."

He smiled at them. "Good morning, students. Please, be seated." When this had been achieved, he turned to Mitch. "A moment of your time, Mr. Jenkins?"

Puzzled, Mitch nodded and followed him into the hallway. Once on the other side of the door, Dominic Galletta broke into a huge beaming smile. "The news just broke on CNN. SCOTUS ruled in favor."

Mitch stared at him, his heart pounding.

Dominic nodded. "It was close, Mitch. Five votes to four. I wanted to let you know. I figured you'd have been on tenterhooks all morning." He extended his hand. "Congratulations. This is an historic day."

Dominic's words finally sank in. Mitch beamed as he gripped Dominic's hand and shook it vigorously. "You bet it is." From behind the door came the swell of lively chatter. "I'd better get back in there. And... thank you for telling me."

"To be honest, I wanted to see the look on your face," Dominic admitted. He released Mitch's hand and left him standing by the door, still grinning like an idiot.

Mitch walked back into his classroom, and the noise level died down a little.

"Okay, put away your assignments, please. I don't want anyone running to me the first day back, claiming they left it on the desk." This raised chuckles among them. He glanced at the clock. "Stand please. It's time for lunch period." As the words left his lips, the bell sounded. "Class dismissed."

He fought the urge to duck as the kids surged past, chatting and laughing. Mitch hurried into the teachers' lounge and dug out his phone, which was on silent. He grinned when he saw the two missed calls. Mom had called first at 11:05, then a few minutes later. He was about to call her back when the phone vibrated in his hand.

"Oh my God, Mitch." From the sound of it, Mom was crying. "Have you heard?" Mitch could hear his dad talking animatedly in the background and, beyond that, the sound of the TV.

The overwhelming joy in her voice was enough to make him tear up. "Yeah, just now."

"Honey, I'm just so happy for you. I think it's wonderful." Noisy sniffs. "Did you ever think this day would come?"

"I hoped, Mom." He was shaking. Teachers were coming into the lounge, most of them smiling when they caught sight of him. Angela gave him two thumbs up, her face one big grin. When Aaron entered, making a beeline for Mitch, he knew he had to get off his phone. "Mom, I have to go. I'll call you tonight, okay? And thanks for calling."

"Like I'd let *this* pass without speaking to you," she said with a loud sniffle. "Go teach. I love you."

"Love you, Mitch," his dad called out.

"I love you both." Mitch disconnected and wiped his eyes. He was immediately surrounded by five or six colleagues, patting him on the back or grasping his hand. Mitch accepted their congratulations with a wide smile, murmuring his thanks. Aaron was not so restrained. After doing his share of accepting hugs and handshakes, he seized Mitch in an enthusiastic hug, damn near squeezing every bit of air out of his lungs.

"Fuck, Mitch, can you believe this?" Aaron looked as overwhelmed as Mitch felt. He gave a shaky laugh. "It's not like I'm gonna go out and get married, like, *tomorrow* or anything, but *fuck*...." He released Mitch and stepped back, shaking his head. "I never thought I'd see the day."

Mitch glanced around the room. Not everyone seemed as welcoming of the news as those who'd approached him. A couple of teachers watched the proceedings with tight expressions. He indicated them with a slight flick of his head in their direction.

"Neither did they, probably. Although that might be due in part to your choice of expletive just now. No swearing policy, Mr. Weldon, remember?" Mitch couldn't hold back his grin. Right then he couldn't have cared less about a couple of people who looked like they were sucking on lemons. Dominic was correct—this day was momentous.

"I hear some bigwigs in Washington just made an announcement."

Mitch jerked his head across to where NYPD officer Donna Michaels stood a few feet away, in full uniform and beaming at him. "Hey!" He walked over, hand outstretched. "I didn't know you'd be in today."

Donna ignored his hand and pulled him into a tight hug. "Great news, Mitch," she whispered. "I'm so happy for you." She let him go and gave Aaron a polite nod. "Mr. Weldon. Good to see you again."

He returned her nod and glanced at Mitch. "I'm gonna go grab some lunch from the cafeteria. You want anything?"

Mitch shook his head. "I'm good, thanks."

Aaron gave another brisk nod and strode away, without giving Donna a second look.

Mitch frowned. "Who's put a burr up his ass?"

"Oh, never mind him. You got time for a chat?"

Mitch grinned. "You can have me until 11:55, when my next class begins. That good enough?"

She smiled. "Yeah, that's great." They walked over to an empty table, and Donna pulled out a chair. "You got any coffee going around here?"

Mitch gasped in mock horror. "Honey, this is a teachers' lounge. Around here we hook ourselves up to it and take it intravenously." He left her laughing while he crossed the lounge to the little kitchen that contained a microwave, refrigerator, coffee machine, electric kettle, and a couple of cabinets. Armed with two full mugs of coffee, Mitch returned to their table and sat facing Donna. "So, what brings you here today?" Donna was the school's liaison with the NYPD and was regularly seen in the hallways of the school.

She cocked one sculpted eyebrow. "Sweetie, what is today? Apart from being a wonderful day for anyone in the LGBT community, of course," she added.

It took one look at the D.A.R.E. badge on her lapel to provide him with the answer. "Ah. You're here to talk to the kids."

She nodded. "The principal asked if I'd come along and talk to the kids. It's my standard end-of-year address before they all disappear off on vacation. Just reinforcing the message, as usual."

Mitch knew all about Donna's work as part of the Drug Abuse Resistance Education program. Most of the kids in school would have taken part in some form or other since they were in eighth grade. With the senior students, it was more a case of helping them to recognize and cope with feelings of anger without causing harm to themselves or others—and without resorting to the use of alcohol or drugs. Donna's role was one of the things Dominic had made part of the curriculum once he'd convinced the school board of its necessity. There were too many temptations out there and far too many people ready to place them in the students' paths.

"Trouble is, kids this age think they can handle anything," Mitch said with a sigh. Then it struck him. "I think you're speaking to one of my classes this afternoon."

She smiled. "Good. I'll expect lots of nodding and appropriate, supportive comments then." Donna sipped her coffee. "So how's life treating you? I haven't heard from you lately. I was starting to worry."

Mitch had met Donna four years previously when she became the liaison officer. Not long after their first meeting, they'd run into each other in the city one evening and had remained friends ever since. They would meet up in a bar every so often for a drink or three, and their chief topic of conversation was usually Donna's brother, Frank, who was the same age as Mitch, and gay. Donna wanted him to settle down with a partner, but it seemed Frank had other ideas. Tales of his exploits had kept Mitch laughing through quite a few nights out with Donna, especially when she joked about introducing the two of them.

Mitch's heart sank. He hadn't been in touch with her for the last four months, and that meant....

"How's Jerry?"

Damn it. "We broke up, two months ago."

Donna's jaw dropped. She lowered her voice. "Oh hell. I had no idea. No wonder you haven't called me." She laid her hand on his arm. "How you doing?"

He snorted. "How'd you think? Would you mind if we didn't talk about this?"

She withdrew her hand. "Sure. Look, I'm sorry, for what it's worth. I really thought after this long that you'd found your Mr. Right."

Her words brought back to him the family lunch three weeks previously. "Yeah, well, I've been advised to stop looking for him. Apparently, I need to think about something more... short-term."

She bit her lip. "There's always Frank, you know. He's still single."

Mitch did his best to keep a straight face. "Yeah, what a shocker."

They stared at each other before simultaneously erupting into laughter. Donna relaxed in her chair and took another drink of coffee. "You gonna celebrate after work? I imagine there'll be a party down on Christopher Street that'll last long into the night." She grinned. "I might take a look myself when I'm off duty."

Mitch laughed. "That'll be more than a party. You won't be able to move down there tonight, trust me." It was a tempting thought, but he had other ideas about what to do with his Friday evening, and they revolved around finding out why the hell Nikko had been unavailable. If Randy had told him Nikko had left their employ, that would have been the end of it. Mitch would probably have canceled his membership there and then, and Nikko would have slipped from his memory.

The one word "unavailable" conjured up all kinds of images in Mitch's mind, and he didn't like any of them.

"Hey, you weren't serious, were you?"

Mitch was back in the moment. "About what?"

"Looking for something short-term." She tilted her head to one side. "I don't see you as a one-night-stand kinda guy. You're more the faithful, monogamous type." Her smile was warm. "That's what I like about you."

"And yet you try to hook me up with Frank?" Mitch said, smirking.

Donna snorted. "Yeah, right, like I'd let you anywhere near him." When Mitch raised his eyebrows, her face flushed. She leaned forward. "God, that came out all wrong. What I mean is, you'd probably be just what he needs, but there's always the possibility that he'd corrupt you." She shrugged. "C'mon, we both know he's a slu—" Her eyes twinkled. "Right?"

Mitch stared at her, fighting the laughter that bubbled inside him. "Okay, I promise. I'll stay away from your brother."

She patted his arm. "Patience is a virtue, or so I'm told. Somewhere out there is a guy who is perfect for you; I know it. You just haven't met him yet." She grinned. "I was gonna say, if I meet someone I think fits the bill, I'll be sure to send him your way. Only thing is, I don't think you'd wanna meet the kinda guys I run into on a regular basis. They tend to be—oh, what's that word again? Oh yeah—crooks." She waggled her eyebrows. "Hey, maybe you'll meet someone nice if you go down to Christopher Street tonight. Sure to be some hot men hanging out there."

"Okay, that's it. You need to keep the… *heck* out of my love life," Mitch said good-naturedly. "I was going to fetch my sandwich from the kitchen and wolf it down before my next class. I can grab you something if you haven't eaten."

Donna waved her hand. "Nah, I'm good. You go ahead and eat, though. I'll just keep you company." She gave him a mischievous smile. "I can relate some of my brother's latest exploits."

Mitch groaned. "Please—not while I'm eating." He got up from the table and went to fetch his lunch. His day was shaping up to be a good one.

Let's see how the day ends up.

He'd feel better when he saw Nikko was okay.

"Nikko, come with me, please."

Nikko put down his bottle of water and stared at Randy in dismay. "Now?" He'd only just been given the all clear by the club's doctor to go back onto the floor. Nikko didn't want to think about all the hours he'd missed out on that past week.

Randy nodded. "Mr. Richards wants to see you."

That got his heart pounding. Mr. Richards was one of the owners of the club. They'd spoken twice—once in the hospital when Ichy had been there and the second time when Nikko had visited the club in a bid to save Ichy's hide. On first meeting Mr. Richards hadn't seemed so bad. It wasn't until reality bit hard and Nikko learned the truth that he'd seen the club owner in a whole new light.

The man scared Nikko. Period.

He followed Randy through the door and was puzzled when he led him toward the playrooms. Nikko's heart hammered even harder when Randy paused at the door of the Red Room.

Why there, for God's sake? It was the last place Nikko wanted to see.

Randy opened the door and stepped to one side to let Nikko enter. He swallowed hard and crossed the threshold, barely hearing the soft *snick* behind him as the door closed.

Mr. Richards sat on a chair in the middle of the space. It was a larger room than the ones where Nikko usually met clients, but that was all to do with its... purpose. Nikko focused on the seated man, trying to ignore the large wooden cross against the red wall, the implements hanging next to it, the benches, the cage, the smell of leather….

The room terrified him more than the club owner.

"Come here." Mr. Richards beckoned with a finger.

Nikko walked slowly across the floor toward him, his pulse racing. Cool, dark eyes watched him. Nikko came to a halt in front of him, his hands by his sides. He wiped them on his jeans.

"I understand you've been cleared to return to the floor." Even his voice was cool.

Nikko nodded.

"Mr. M was very pleased, by the way." Mr. Richards smiled. "You did well."

Nikko didn't trust that smile, not for a second, but he wasn't about to let the moment pass, not when he'd been given an opening. "Can I ask… why would you let him do that to me? Obviously… if I'm unable to work for a week, that's revenue you miss out on. You're running a business, after all." It was the question that had plagued him all week, every time he'd recalled his hours spent in that room. Not that he wanted to think about it, because it just made him feel *ill*.

Mr. Richards leaned back, crossing his long legs at the ankles, hands laced in his lap. "Nikko, what you fail to understand is that certain of our clients come to this club to act out their fantasies, things they don't want others discovering. Perhaps things other men might use against them." He smiled. "We offer them whatever they desire, and for that they are willing to pay a premium." His gaze was unwavering. "What Mr. M paid us for two hours of your time more than made up for you not being on the floor last week. And as I mentioned, he was very pleased. So pleased, in fact, that I can see him using your services again."

The thought sent chills coursing through Nikko. *God, no. Please… no.*

Something else occurred to him, helping him to push down the rising panic. "Seeing as he paid more, I think those two hours should count more. Maybe… double?" There had to be *some* benefit for enduring the attentions of Mr. M.

Mr. Richards stared at him in silence for a moment. Finally he nodded. "Agreed. But should Mr. M require you in the future, make sure that you please him. Is that understood?"

Nikko swallowed but nodded. "Yes, Mr. Richards." It would almost be worth putting up with Mr. M again if it meant getting out of there sooner than they'd anticipated.

Almost.

Mr. Richards rose and pressed a button on the wall. "Randy will take you back now."

And that was that. Nikko had been dismissed.

He bowed his head once, turned, and went to the door. Randy opened it, and Nikko followed him along the hallway where some of the playrooms were already in use, judging from the sounds that emanated from them. He averted his gaze when he walked past the couches, where two men in suits sat on either side of a naked young man, both of them fondling his dick and balls while he closed his eyes and sighed with contentment.

When Nikko entered the "apartment," he found ten or twelve guys there, preening in front of the glass, Jesse among them. He grinned when he saw Nikko.

"Hey, you're back!"

Nikko couldn't help but smile at the genuine warmth in Jesse's smile. "Hi."

To his surprise Jesse walked over to him and regarded him closely. "Are you okay?" he asked quietly.

There was a lump in Nikko's throat. "Yes, I'm fine." He sat down in his usual chair, and Jesse sat facing him.

"When I didn't see you last weekend, I thought maybe you'd left us."

The thought flashed across his mind. *No, you didn't see me because the bastards who run this place had me in lockdown.* Not that he'd say it aloud, not when there were eyes and ears *everywhere*.

Jesse dropped his voice. "Until word got around that you were sort of out of action." He cocked his head. "What happened?"

Nikko had spent a week keeping everything bottled up, with only Ichy for company, and Ichy had panicked enough when he'd seen the results of Mr. M's… handiwork. It was about time Nikko told someone.

"Have you heard of Mr. M?"

Jesse paled. "Shit. The one who's into whips and chains and stuff like that?" When Nikko nodded, Jesse grimaced. "Some of the guys have told me about the Red Room, and a few of them have serviced him. Apparently he gets very… enthusiastic."

Nikko laughed bitterly. "That's one way of putting it." He could still recall the sting of that riding crop, the sound of the whip slicing through the air before it descended on his back and ass.

"Aren't there places he can go to do that?"

Nikko recalled what Mr. Richards had said. "Maybe not. Maybe he doesn't want anyone to know that he likes dressing up in leather, tying up boys, and…. " Nikko couldn't finish the sentence.

"What do you think he does for a living?" Jesse's eyes widened. "Maybe he's a priest. Or a social worker. Maybe he's a kindergarten teacher or a principal." He chuckled. "Yeah, that's it. Imagine if word got around." His expression sobered. "I'm sorry you had to go through that. If you're lucky, you might not get him again."

If what Mr. Richards had said was anything to go by, Nikko didn't hold out much hope.

The door opened and Randy entered. "Nikko."

Nikko's heart sank. *God, no.* His heartbeat sped up.

"Nikko," Jesse whispered, taking hold of his hand and squeezing it. "It's gonna be okay."

"Yeah?" Nikko couldn't keep the cynical edge from his voice. "And just how do you know that, hmm?" He knew it was wrong to take his fears out on Jesse, especially when the young man had been nothing but kind to him. But *damn it*, he was scared.

"Look at Randy's face," Jesse suggested, releasing his hand.

Nikko glanced in the security guard's direction. Randy was smiling. Just like that, something eased in Nikko's chest, and he found it less difficult to breathe. He gave Jesse a grateful look and walked toward Randy. Without a word, he followed him through the door and barely held back his sigh of relief when Randy didn't head for the Red Room.

"You're in here," Randy told him, opening the door to one of the playrooms.

Nikko entered, and his legs almost gave way under him when he saw who was sitting on the bed.

It was Mitch.

Chapter Eight

MITCH DIDN'T miss the look of relief that crossed Nikko's face. It was probably the mirror image of his own expression. "You have no idea how many times I've thought about you this past week." He did a quick scan of Nikko's body, looking for any sign the young man had been injured, but there was nothing visible. Nikko wore jeans and a black T-shirt that hugged his torso. "I'll be honest, I thought the worst."

Nikko stood there by the door, his gaze unwavering. "I don't understand."

"I was here last week."

Nikko's eyes widened. "You were?"

Mitch nodded. "I was told you were… unavailable."

"Oh." Nikko swallowed. Still he didn't move.

Mitch got tired of the chasm between them. He held out a hand. "Come here." Nikko walked over to him slowly, until he was standing in front of him. Mitch spread his legs and pulled Nikko to stand between them. He put his hands on Nikko's slim waist before moving them to stroke up and down his bare arms. "You really are okay." When Nikko gave him a quizzical look, Mitch smiled, not bothering to hide his relief. "The things that have been going through my head…."

"It's been three weeks since I saw you," Nikko said quietly. "I know I ended our time together abruptly, but… I'd thought to see you before this." His face fell. "I… I thought you liked me."

What Mitch was dying to know in that moment was exactly who was saying this—Nikko the hooker, or Nikko the young man? He stared into those dark eyes and spoke from the heart.

"Being totally honest, I didn't plan on coming back here."

Nikko's breathing caught, and he pressed closer. "I'm so glad you did." His voice was whisper-soft. He placed his hands lightly on Mitch's shoulders. "How long do we have?"

After all this time thinking about Nikko, then worrying about him, Mitch's emotions were a mess. He knew he couldn't allow himself to read more into Nikko's responses, but *damn* it, he wanted to. "An hour, at least." What with paying for his membership the previous Friday, it was proving to be an expensive week.

Nikko's smile was gentle. "Then we shouldn't waste any of your time and money."

Mitch's heart sank. *Looks like it's Nikko the hooker, after all.* When Nikko grasped the hem of his T-shirt to lift it over his head, Mitch stopped him. "Let me." Nikko nodded and raised his arms into the air, while Mitch eased the garment up and off him. He dropped it to the floor and stared at the expanse of creamy, smooth skin before him. Unable to resist, Mitch leaned forward and flicked one of Nikko's nipples with his tongue, and a sigh shuddered out of him. Mitch put his arms around Nikko and drew him closer still, pressing his face against Nikko's chest, while he stroked over—

What the fucking hell....

Mitch froze, his fingers tracing the skin on Nikko's back. "Turn around," he commanded.

Nikko stiffened. "Mitch...." His breathing quickened.

He grabbed hold of Nikko's arms and spun him around. Where there had been unblemished, soft skin three weeks previously, there was a pattern of welts covering Nikko's shoulders and upper back. Mitch stared at them in horror and then froze when another thought crept into his mind. He reached around to Nikko's front, unfastened the button at his waist, slid down the zip and roughly pulled Nikko's jeans down to reveal his ass. He swallowed at the sight of yet more welts and ran his fingers lightly over them, feeling the ridges in the flesh.

He couldn't breathe. His hands fell to his lap.

Slowly Nikko turned to look at him. "Mitch?" He pulled up his jeans and zipped them.

Blood pounded in his ears. His pulse raced. His throat dried up and his vision clouded. Mitch rose unsteadily to his feet, hands shaking.

Nikko grabbed hold of his arms. "Mitch… you're scaring me."

"Let go of me," he ground out. "Let me out of here."

Nikko's eyes widened. "To do what, exactly?" He tightened his grip on Mitch's arms. "Mitch?"

"Someone did that to you." His voice cracked at the thought of someone taking a whip or whatever the fuck it was to Nikko. It didn't matter in that moment what Nikko did for a living—no one deserved to be so brutally treated. All he could think of was that it had to have been worse than he was seeing now to put the young man out of action.

Jerry's face was suddenly there in his mind, those… things on the bed between them. That whole conversation. Mitch's stomach roiled as the memory took hold of him.

It took a moment or two to realize Nikko was calling his name.

Mitch's vision cleared, and he stared at him.

Nikko let out his breath in unmistakable relief. "Okay, now you need to listen. You're a member of this club, right?" Mitch nodded, his throat still tight. Nikko's gaze was focused on his face. "So you know how it works, right? Anything goes, Mitch. *Anything*. And if I wasn't happy about what was done to me, I would've walked, okay? But I didn't. I'm still here." He lifted his chin. "I know I said it last time, but I'll say it again. I'm here of my own volition, Mitch." Nikko stood very still, his gaze unwavering. "And if we're being honest… I'm here to do a job. Okay, sometimes my job has elements that aren't… pretty, but it's still my job. Nothing was done to me against my will." Those eyes were almost mesmerizing. "You have to trust me on this."

Something clicked in Mitch's head. "And if I were to barge out of here, shooting my mouth off, it would look bad. Your boss might think you'd been complaining, and that would cause trouble for you."

Nikko nodded slowly. "Exactly." He cupped Mitch's face tenderly. "And because we're being honest—" He leaned closer and gave Mitch a chaste kiss on the lips. "—I meant what I said. I really am glad you came back." Another kiss, only this time Nikko let his lips linger, his soft fingers tracing the curve of Mitch's cheek.

Mitch was unsure how to react. The thought of someone hurting Nikko still burned in his brain, and he couldn't seem to shake it loose. And then there was the way Nikko was acting. Mitch found it increasingly difficult to remember that Nikko was paid to be attentive, especially when everything he did or said made him seem more like a lover and less like a….

Whore.

Mitch closed his eyes. The word felt… wrong. Ugly.

"You said you were thinking about me," Nikko said, his hand gentle against Mitch's face. "Well, I was thinking about you too." His dark brown eyes held a hint of sorrow. "I didn't like how it ended between us, because up until that point, you made me feel really good."

"Yeah?" Mitch stilled. The way Nikko's gaze never faltered, the calmness in his voice and stance... everything about him spoke to Mitch of sincerity.

Nikko nodded. "You told me I made you feel good too." He moved closer, until Mitch could feel Nikko's body heat. "Let me do that again?" He placed his hands on Mitch's shoulders and rubbed. "You're tense. I can help."

In spite of his internal confusion, Mitch couldn't hold back his smile at the line. "Oh? How might you do that?"

"I was thinking of a shoulder rub, unless you have something else in mind." Nikko grinned. Before Mitch could retort, Nikko stepped back. "Take off your shirt, please."

This was definitely not what Mitch had expected. The memory of those welts was still there at the forefront of his mind.

"Do I have to tell you again?" There was a hint of amusement in Nikko's voice, and hearing it went some way to calming Mitch.

Maybe he's okay with it. I don't know what his sexual preferences are, do I? What if he likes it rough? Maybe I'm overreacting.

He unbuttoned his light cotton shirt and shrugged out of it. Nikko took it from him and placed it neatly on the chair. He crouched down beside the bed and pulled out a drawer. When he stood, Mitch was surprised to see a bottle of massage oil in Nikko's hands.

"Lie face down on the bed," Nikko instructed. "Place your head on your folded arms."

Mitch was smiling again. "You're a bossy little thing, aren't you?" Chuckling, he complied and stretched out on the gray comforter, turning his head to one side to watch Nikko.

Nikko put down the bottle, unfastened his jeans, and shoved them down to his ankles, revealing his soft dick. He stepped out of them and climbed onto the bed, sitting astride Mitch's ass. He reached for the massage oil and poured a quantity across Mitch's shoulders. Once he'd set aside the bottle, Nikko began to rub.

Mitch hadn't known what to expect, and to feel Nikko's slow, even strokes across his upper back with the palms of his hands was a pleasant surprise. Not only that—it felt damn good. The movements were unhurried, like they had all the time in the world. When Nikko used his thumbs to push down into the fleshy part of his shoulders, Mitch let out a groan.

Nikko stopped. "Am I hurting you?"

"God, no. It feels fantastic." Mitch closed his eyes and let the sensations overwhelm him as Nikko moved slowly down his back, working the muscles.

"Good. Just relax and enjoy it." He reached Mitch's hips, and placing his hand flat, he pushed down with his body weight and performed a rocking motion that felt amazing.

"Where did you learn to do this?"

"My first boyfriend. He was training to be a masseur, and he used to practice on me." Nikko rubbed in slow circles, one hand on either side of his spine. "You're stiff here, but then you're supposed to be. The two columns of muscle in your lower back are made to be tight. If they weren't, you'd fall over. But a gentle rub can ease them if they cause you pain. I think you spend a lot of time standing up."

Mitch smiled to himself. He had to remind himself Nikko didn't know what he did for a living. Everyone always assumed teachers spent their days sitting at a desk. The truth was quite the opposite, and the number of times Mitch had gone home at the end of a long day with an aching back were too numerous to mention.

"You're right; I do." A feeling of languid contentment spread throughout Mitch's body. For the first time in a long while, he felt totally relaxed, almost melting into the mattress. What surprised him was a lack of arousal. He lay there and enjoyed the back rub, the feeling of Nikko's weight on him as he gave Mitch what felt like an expert massage. "You could make a fortune as a masseur," he said with a groan when Nikko dug deep, his fingers working a knot in Mitch's shoulder muscle.

Nikko chuckled. "That would be a waste of my degree."

And being a hooker isn't? It was on the tip of Mitch's tongue to ask more questions, but the memory of their last encounter was still vivid in his mind. He kept silent, his eyes closed, content to let Nikko's hands work their magic. When Nikko rubbed him briskly, he knew the pleasurable experience was at an end. His heart sank when he realized Nikko would expect to be fucked. After all, why else would anyone visit a brothel?

It wasn't what Mitch wanted.

After the abrupt way their last meeting had ended, Mitch had no wish to cause Nikko offense, but sex was the last thing on his mind. Then he recalled Nikko's words: *anything goes*. Mitch had another phrase in mind: *the customer is always right*.

Damn it, he was the customer, and right then this customer craved something very different. Mitch wanted warmth, conversation… intimacy.

Nikko shifted off him to stand next to the bed, and Mitch rolled onto his side. His heart pounding, he looked Nikko in the eye. "Would you mind joining me here for a while? I'd like to hold you and maybe talk, if that's okay." He gestured with his head to the floor where Nikko's jeans lay in a heap. "You can put those back on."

NIKKO STARED at Mitch, unsure for a moment that he'd heard right. Mitch met his gaze, his expression neutral. "Sure," Nikko said, reaching for his jeans.

Since when does a guy pay for a hooker and not fuck him?

He couldn't figure Mitch out, but he was beginning to like that about him.

Nikko climbed back onto the bed, and Mitch rolled onto his back, arm outstretched, inviting Nikko to lie beside him. Nikko rested his head on Mitch's arm, his braid pulled around to lie over his shoulder. Mitch reached across and ran his fingers along its length.

"This is beautiful," he said quietly. "How long has it taken you to grow your hair this long?"

Nikko smiled. "All my life. Well, as soon as I was able to tell my mom I didn't want it cut." As always, the thought of her brought a brief stab of pain, and he fought hard to push it down deep. He could think about her later. This room was no place for grief or sorrow, only lust and desire.

Except right then? There was no lust. The whole situation had a surreal quality to it, not that he was complaining. To find himself lying in Mitch's arms felt… right, the perfect ending to his massage. Mitch appeared relaxed and happy.

"Some of my male students have long hair, but nothing like this."

"You're a teacher?" Somehow that fit. He could visualize Mitch in front of a class of kids.

Mitch nodded. "I teach English in a high school on the Upper East Side."

"Do you enjoy your job?"

He shrugged. "Most of the time. It's hard work and the kids can be a total pain in the ass, but now and again there are days that make up for all the crap." He smiled. "Like today."

Nikko loved the way Mitch's face lit up when he smiled. "What was so good about today?"

"Two reasons. School is now out for the summer, and today the Supreme Court pulled their heads out of their asses and made a momentous decision."

Nikko had to smile too. "I would love to have been in Washington. Can you imagine what the mood would have been like there?" His had been a quiet day, reading or watching the news on the TV. No, scrap that—it had been a lonely day, broken up by brief visits to see Ichy, who remained in seclusion. Nikko knew that was of his own doing. He wanted nothing to do with the men around him.

He wasn't going to be there all that long.

Mitch chuckled. "My mom called me—twice—when the news broke."

Nikko craned his neck to gaze at Mitch's face. "If you announced to your parents that you were going to be married, would they be happy for you?"

Mitch guffawed. "Happy? My mom would start planning the wedding that *second*. Then my dad would want to get involved, and before you know it, the pair of them would be coming up with the most outlandish ideas." He peered at Nikko. "What about your parents? How would they react?"

Nikko swallowed. "My parents are dead."

Mitch stilled instantly. "God, I'm so sorry. You're so young to have lost them." He stroked Nikko's cheek.

Nikko had been fourteen, Ichy eighteen. His brother seemed to cope with his grief better than Nikko did. "My grandmother brought me up, helped put me through college, but she's very… traditional. When I told her I was gay, it was sort of a… nonevent. It wasn't that she was unhappy about it—at least, not to my face—she just… accepted it without comment." He let out a heartfelt sigh. "I knew what was going through her mind, though."

"Yeah?" Mitch pulled Nikko closer, as if he sensed that Nikko needed some comfort.

Nikko put his arm around Mitch's waist, holding on to him like an anchor. "She was thinking about the future—you know, children, the continuation of the family line. I suppose all she saw was that there'd be no great-grandchildren from me."

"Do you have any brothers or sisters?" Mitch asked him, stroking his back slowly and gently.

Nikko sighed. "I have a brother, Ichiro." His throat tightened. "We sort of clung to each other when Mom and Dad died. Although Grandma was my legal guardian, it was really Ichy who raised me. He put off going to school so he could be there for me while I finished high school. As soon as I went off to college, he left home for New York to study."

"Is he here in New York now?"

Shit. It was good that Mitch was reaching out, trying to connect with him, but Ichy was the last thing Nikko wanted to discuss. "Can… can we not talk about this, please?"

Mitch rolled onto his side, pulling Nikko with him, and Nikko found his face buried in Mitch's wide, furry chest. He inhaled deeply, drawing the scent into his nostrils. It was a warm, comforting smell.

"I'm sorry," Mitch whispered. "Forgive me. It's clear I've upset you." He kissed Nikko's forehead and then cupped his chin to tilt his face upward. Mitch kissed him softly on the lips.

Nikko didn't want to feel. He shoved down hard on his emotions and lost himself in the tender kiss, molding himself to Mitch's firm body, his arms reaching around to hold Mitch in place. Mitch responded, kissing him deeply, hands sliding down Nikko's back to cup his ass and squeeze lightly. Nikko waited for the bubble to burst, for Mitch to reach inside his jeans to fondle his dick, for Mitch to fuck him.

It didn't happen.

They spent the rest of the time making out, Mitch apparently content to hold Nikko, to kiss him and caress him, occasionally letting his fingers trail lower to brush over Nikko's crotch before beginning his ascent once more. In the quiet of the room, Mitch told him stories about his teaching career, asking nothing of him except his attention, which Nikko gave willingly. There was a languid feel to those precious minutes that provided a balm for Nikko's soul. In that bubble of time, he forgot about Mr. M, the club, and his own private pain. He was lying in another man's arms where he felt safe and warm.

It didn't resemble the reality Nikko knew, and for that brief spell, he was glad of it.

NIKKO WALKED through the floor area and into the kitchen to pour himself a glass of water. Mitch had just left, and Nikko was in a daze.

Is every visit from Mitch going to be like this? Is he always gonna be nothing like anyone else?

Nikko hoped there'd be more. Mitch's gentle ways, soft words, and tender kisses provided an oasis where Nikko could escape and leave behind those parts of his life over which he had no control.

"You look happy."

Nikko looked across to where Jesse stood by the door, smiling. He shrugged. "I guess I am." The encounter with Mitch hadn't worn off yet, and Nikko felt good. "Mitch is a nice guy."

"Mitch? So it's Mitch?" Jesse arched his eyebrows. "I think we need to talk."

There was a fluttering in Nikko's stomach. "What about?"

Jesse sighed. "Look, I know you're a newbie at this—that's not meant as an insult, by the way, because I am too—but there are some things you have to do if you're gonna be any good at this. Number one on the list is stay objective."

"I am," Nikko remonstrated, but Jesse cut him short.

"I don't know how many johns *you* see a week, and personally it's none of my business, but I see quite a few. I don't know their names. I don't *ask* for their names. They arrive, they fuck me, we have a good time, they leave. End of." He glared at Nikko. "*That* is being objective."

"You know Mr. M's name."

Jesse snorted. "Yeah, like that's really his name. Do you know the names of the other guys who've fucked you?"

Nikko's chest grew tight. "No."

Jesse stared at him. "Oh, Nikko, this is not good." He came closer and put his hands on Nikko's upper arms, their faces level. "Don't get attached, babe. It starts with 'Mitch,' and before you know it, you're developing feelings for him. And that road only leads to one thing."

"And what's that?" Nikko stood straight, meeting Jesse's gaze.

"You getting hurt." Jesse sighed. "Always remember what he is, Nikko—a guy who's paid to fuck you. That's all you are to him, okay?" He squeezed Nikko's arms. "Be objective. It's easier in the long run. Enjoy it, but always make sure the client is pleased. And keep your emotions out of it." He released Nikko, gave him a flash of a smile and exited the kitchen.

Nikko stared after him, his heart sinking.

Oh God. I'm in trouble.

Chapter Nine

"CHECKMATE."

Mitch frowned. "Wait. What? How did that happen?" He stared at the board in consternation. "How did you sneak that move in there?"

Gareth sat back in his chair and smiled smugly. "Clearly you have forgotten that, when it comes to chess, you are playing with the master." He wiggled his fingers in the air. "See? The hands of the master."

Mitch snorted. "I must've also forgotten what a modest, shy, retiring person you are."

Gareth laughed out loud. "Seriously, what were you thinking? I thought when you castled that you were playing up to your usual high standard, but that last move with your queen was just dumb." He peered intently at Mitch. "Are you feeling ill? You almost always beat me."

Mitch began packing away the pieces into their wooden box. "You're complaining about winning? Geez, some people are never satisfied." Around them was the noise of traffic and chatter from the tables adjacent to theirs. The west side of Union Square Park was far less noisy than Washington Square Park had been in recent months. The construction had driven lots of players away. Mitch liked Union Square, and it was good to see some familiar faces at the tables. "You wanna go to Irving Farm for a coffee?"

Gareth's eyes sparkled. "Add a pastry or two to that and you're on."

Mitch chuckled. "I wasn't gonna mention that you've put on a little weight lately, but now I see why."

Gareth gave Mitch one of his looks. "What is it you gay guys say to each other? Oh yeah. Bitch." He snorted. "You're just being mean because you lost."

"Ah, but maybe I *let* you win," Mitch said with a grin as they began walking to the coffee shop. "Ever think of that scenario?"

"Nope." Gareth grinned back. "I am simply the superior player. Suck it up." He glanced across the street at the coffee shop and grabbed Mitch's arm. "Quick! I see one table left outside." Gareth dodged a taxi and made a dive for the little round table on street level, Mitch in his wake. He sank into one of the chairs with a satisfied smile. "It's usually full down in the basement, and it gets so noisy in there, you can't hear yourself think." He peered expectantly at Mitch. "Seeing as I won, these are on you. I'll have a chai latte and a piece of their delicious key lime pie for starters, and then I'll see how I feel after that." He patted his belly. "And less of the comments, if you please. I'm in damn good shape for my age."

Much as Mitch liked to poke his brother, he knew this was true. Gareth ran every day along the quiet paths through the forest that backed onto his property. He swam in his pool. And despite a fondness for pastries—which Mitch knew all about—he ate pretty healthily. Mitch just loved to tease. He figured the day he stopped doing that was the day to hand in his Annoying Little Brother card.

Mitch entered the coffee house and ordered their beverages and treats before joining Gareth at their table. Gareth was people watching, his forehead scrunched up.

"What are you thinking about?" Mitch asked him, sitting down across from him.

"You, if you must know." Gareth cocked his head to one side. "I was thinking about the last time we were home. You do know Deirdre wasn't serious, right? About you settling for Mr. Right Now?"

Mitch laughed. "What on earth made you think of that?" For one fleeting moment, the image of Nikko rose up in his mind.

Gareth's expression sobered. "I want you to be happy, okay? And I think in your case, that means you being in a long-term, satisfying relationship. Don't settle for second best. Yeah, I still believe the perfect guy is out there, just waiting for you, but I don't like the thought of you going through men like they're gonna run out any time soon." He smiled. "You weren't built for promiscuity, Mitch."

Mitch's first thought was one of déjà vu, his brother's words uncannily resembling Donna's. The love in Gareth's voice was so evident, Mitch's throat tightened and something pricked the corners of his eyes.

"Okay, where's our damn coffee?"

Gareth chuckled. "That's the only fly in the ointment about coming here. Sometimes they take a while to get the orders out"—he winked at Mitch—"but by God, it's worth it when they do." He relaxed into his chair. "So how will you be spending your summer vacation this year? Thinking of going anywhere nice?"

A vacation sounded like a wonderful idea—Mitch sorely needed to recharge his batteries before September—but there was no way he could afford it, not after paying for his club membership. He suppressed a sigh. That damn club. Every time it came to mind, he tried to push it out again. He justified his last visit to Nikko with the argument that if nothing had happened between them, he hadn't *really* paid for sex.

Yeah, right.

Gareth was staring at him.

Mitch cleared his throat. "I may stay in the cottage this summer." When Gareth arched his eyebrows, he shrugged. "So? I like staying there. It reminds me of being a kid." All true, but he wasn't about to share his finances with his big brother.

Gareth regarded him closely for a moment. "Everything okay with you, Mitch?"

He feigned innocence. "Yeah, sure, why wouldn't it be?" Their order arrived at that moment. *Phew—saved by the server.* Spending his Sundays with Gareth had one huge drawback—his brother knew him too well.

NIKKO SQUEEZED out the last drops of water from his hair and then scrubbed at his skin with the towel. The shower had served its purpose, taking with it the physical reminders of his last client and the invisible layer of shame he could feel clinging to him every time he emerged from one of the playrooms. He'd watched some of the others walk back onto the floor, heard them laughing and joking, sharing their exploits.

How can they do that? Does it weigh so lightly on them that they can just... shrug it off, like a jacket?

The days came and went, and with them the clients, an ever increasing number of them. He'd begun to notice a trend. Most of the men who paid for his services were big guys, men who had a penchant for rough sex.

Is it something about me? The way I look? Nikko knew he appeared younger than his years. Add to that his slight physique, and perhaps some men interpreted the combination as an invitation to manhandle him. There had already been one client who'd requested that he act out a role. It had taken Nikko less than a minute to realize exactly what the guy wanted.

Nikko was to play the part of an underage, virginal boy, taken against his will.

Just thinking about the scene sent shudders itching down his spine. Some logical part of his brain could see the club had a purpose in that respect. *At least he's in here, acting out his fantasy with me. He's not out there, raping some teenager.* Oh God, Nikko hoped not.

Nikko wrapped the towel around his hips and padded barefoot from the bathroom to the door that led upstairs. On the floor above was the small dorm-like room that contained six beds, of which three were in use, and a couple of closets and cabinets for clothes. His destination was one floor higher. He paused at the door to the "apartment" and glanced up at the camera that tracked his movement. The door clicked opened and Nikko entered. There was another click as it closed behind him.

The room had no windows and the door through which Nikko had entered was the only way in or out. What worried him was the lack of a fire escape. He knew there was one at the top of the stairs, so that was something. A small bathroom equipped with a toilet, washbasin, and tiny shower took up a corner of the room.

Ichy was lying on his bed, his Kindle beside him. The tray next to him contained a glass of water and a half-empty plate, the remains of a sandwich still in evidence. He opened his eyes and gazed in silence at Nikko, his expression solemn.

"Not hungry?" Nikko asked him as he removed the towel and walked across to the closet to retrieve a pair of jeans and a clean T-shirt. He'd forgone wearing underwear. There seemed little point.

Ichy said nothing, his gaze focused on Nikko.

"How are you feeling?" Nikko asked him as he stepped into his jeans.

He shrugged. "I'm okay."

"No more headaches or nausea?" Nikko persisted, his stomach churning at the memory of seeing Ichy in that hospital bed. He'd never been so scared in his whole life.

"Jesus, Nikko, will you just leave it alone?"

Nikko stiffened. "I… I'm—"

"Come here." Ichy sat up and held his arms wide. Nikko walked into them, and Ichy pressed his face against Nikko's belly, enveloping him in a hug. "I'm sorry. I shouldn't take it out on you." The words were muffled. Nikko gazed down at Ichy, stroking his hair, his throat tight. It was strange to have their roles reversed, but Nikko didn't care. He would do anything for his brother.

"Hey," he said softly. "It's going to be okay."

Ichy released him and sat back, staring up at him. "Really? You still feel that, after everything that's happened so far?" His dark eyes held so much pain. "This is all my fault."

"Hush." Nikko crouched in front of him. "I thought we'd gotten past the blaming."

Ichy's eyes widened. "But it is! When I think of what you're doing—" He swallowed. "You're my little brother. I'm supposed to be the one protecting *you*, remember? And yet you're the one who's down there, doing God knows what, just because of my stupid mistake." He blinked rapidly. "Can we call the home soon? She'll only worry if she doesn't hear from us."

It had been three weeks since they'd been allowed a phone call to their grandmother, and then only under supervision. Not that Nikko would have said a word to share their present location or circumstances. Mr. Richards knew exactly where she was, right down to her room number in the retirement home in Oregon. The thought sent a shudder rippling through him.

Ichy had a point, however.

"I'll ask if we can call her over the weekend, okay?" As for her worrying, Nikko was not so sure. The last few times he'd been to visit her, she hadn't known him. That knowledge clawed at his throat. He was losing his grandmother to Alzheimer's, slowly but surely.

Ichy nodded. "And I am feeling all right, honestly. Better than before."

"Has the doc been up to check on you?"

Ichy nodded again. "I suppose I should be grateful they took me to the hospital." He shivered. "God, Nikko. When I think how this might have gone…."

Nikko stretched out his hand to press a finger against Ichy's lips. "Don't, all right? Just… don't."

The intercom on the wall buzzed into life, making them both jump.

Ichy sighed. "You have to go."

Nikko rose to his feet and pulled on the T-shirt. "I'll see you later, okay?" Ichy gave a single nod, and on impulse Nikko gave him another hug. "It's only for a few more months, right? Then we can go home and put it behind us." He released his brother. Deftly he braided his damp hair, securing it with a fabric-covered band, and made to walk away, but Ichy stopped him, grabbing hold of his arm.

"You really believe that, don't you?" Ichy's eyes were large with wonder.

Nikko flashed him a tight smile. "I have to." The alternatives didn't bear thinking about.

Ichy laughed softly. "I'm unsure whether I find your naïveté endearing or incredible." He let Nikko go. "Now go do your stuff. Make 'em happy." His Adam's apple bobbed. "I'll pray you don't get Mr. M again." Ichy's face darkened.

Nikko couldn't take any more. He walked over to the door and gazed up at the camera. Another metallic click and he was out of there, down two flights of stairs and into the kitchen. Three or four guys were in there, standing around and drinking bottled water. They gave him passing glances but resumed their conversations. That suited Nikko just fine. Generally he stayed out of their way and kept conversations to a bare minimum, not giving a rat's ass if this made him seem cold and standoffish.

He had more important things to worry about than the hurt feelings of rent boys. Like keeping on the right side of Mr. Richards and his partners, and ensuring he and Ichy walked away from this mess. Speaking of which, it was time to go to work.

Nikko paused at the threshold that led to the couched area. Once past that point, he'd be on show again, unseen eyes watching him.

Maybe Mitch will come back.

It was a pleasant thought, but Nikko had to face facts. He couldn't live in hope of walking into a playroom and seeing the tall teacher with the soulful brown eyes. Not when each day was bringing men who were nothing like Mitch.

"You don't talk much, do ya, honey?"

Nikko glanced at the speaker, a tall drink of water with black spiky hair and the bluest eyes he'd ever seen. He was maybe in his late twenties. Blue Eyes was leaning against the table, bottle of water in his hand.

Nikko gave him a polite smile. "I've never been much of a talker."

Blue Eyes cocked his head. "You're new to all of this, ain'tcha?" He snickered. "You'll soon get used to it."

Nikko didn't want to get used to it.

"I'm only going to be here a few months," he said, still smiling.

"Well, honey, you must be something else in the sack, if you're earning enough to make a living *and* pay to stay in the boss's 'hospitality suite.'" He crooked his fingers in the air. "How he can charge so much for so little is beyond me. It's just the one room, right? Man, that place is locked up like a fortress too. Trent stayed in there once, said it was not a lot of space for $2000 a month."

Wait... what?

Nikko gaped at him. Mr. Richards had said nothing about charging them rent.

Blue Eyes chatted away, oblivious. "I mean, I know the food they provide for us is top notch, but then again it ain't free, right? The boss takes a cut from what we earn to pay for it."

Cold spread throughout Nikko's body. *Ichy's right. I am so naïve.* He hadn't given their room and board a second thought, but now it occurred to him that Mr. Richards wasn't the sort of man to do something out of the kindness of his heart. *If he has a heart.*

It wasn't as if Nikko was actually earning anything, which could only mean one thing.

Room and board was being added to his debt.

"Hey. Pretty boy. You okay?"

Nikko gave himself a shake and nodded. "Yeah, I'm fine. Just zoned out for a moment there." He walked out onto the floor and headed straight for "his" chair. He curled up in it, tucking his feet under him, absently toying with his braid, his mind in confusion.

What else haven't we been told? Are there any more surprises in store?

Nikko was starting to get a bad feeling about this.

"Hey, Nikko, you're up." Randy stood in the doorway.

There was no time to think.

He got out of his chair and walked to Randy in a daze. As he followed the guard along the hallway to the playrooms, noting with relief that the Red Room wasn't their destination, Nikko did his best to collect his thoughts. It wouldn't do to have a john complain about his "performance." He hoped and prayed it would just be some horny guy who wanted to fuck him and then go back to his wife and kids. Someone who wasn't expecting feats of sexual gymnastics or role-playing shit.

That last thought brought him up sharply—it sounded far too much like something the others would say. But at its heart lay a simple truth. He just wanted to switch off his brain and lose himself in the act, to not have to *think*.

Randy pushed open the door, and Nikko stepped past him into the room. He took one look at the bed and sent up a silent prayer of gratitude.

Apparently there was a God, because Mitch was waiting for him.

Chapter Ten

Either Mitch was imagining it, or Nikko looked pleased to see him. "Hey." When the door closed behind him, Mitch caught a whiff of soap or shampoo, something fresh and pleasant.

Nikko smiled. "Is it the weekend already?"

He laughed. "I'm on vacation, remember? I can visit the club whenever I like." He fought the urge to pull Nikko into his arms and kiss him, telling himself that was not how to greet a hooker. But that was the problem. Whenever Mitch was around Nikko, it proved more and more difficult to remember that he was paying for sex with the young man. All he saw was someone he was attracted to, a genuinely nice guy. Okay, so the sex that first time had been good, but it was more than just sex that had brought him back.

It was Nikko himself.

Nikko hovered by the door, his hands clasped in front of him.

To hell with whatever passes for etiquette in brothels. Mitch stood and held out a hand. "Come here."

Nikko walked across the floor and took Mitch's hand, squeezing it lightly. "I'm not complaining, you understand. It's always a good feeling when I walk into a room and it's you."

Mitch regarded him for a moment, taking in the faint lines across Nikko's forehead, a tightness in his expression that spoke of anxiety. "Is everything okay?"

"Everything's fine." Nikko sounded relaxed, but there was definite tension around his eyes. And not just there. There was something about the way he held himself….

Mitch wasn't buying it. What came out of Nikko's mouth did not match his body language. All he wanted to do right then was to hold Nikko again. He gestured to the bed. "Can we…?" It was going to sound weird to ask if they could cuddle up like the last time, but he'd loved the feeling of closeness. Then he remembered the maxim. *I'm the customer, right?* Mitch smiled. "Come and lie down with me for a while."

He didn't imagine the way Nikko's breathing changed or the way that tension eased up. Nikko nodded. "I'd like that."

Mitch lay down and held out his arm in invitation. Nikko stretched out beside him, his head resting on Mitch's chest, his arm across Mitch's waist. He listened to Nikko's breathing, slow and even, and found himself breathing in time with him.

Mitch curled his arm around the young man. "I was thinking about you this weekend, after my visit Friday."

"Hmm?" Nikko felt warm against Mitch's body.

"I'm sorry I reacted badly when I saw... your back." Nikko stiffened in his arms and Mitch groaned. "See, this is what I was afraid of. There I was, about to go bite someone's head off, and I didn't stop to think that maybe you... liked it."

Nikko froze. "What?"

Mitch tilted Nikko's chin upward. Those dark eyes were huge. Mitch swallowed. "You were so calm about it, so adamant that nothing happened unless you wanted it to. So it got me thinking... maybe you like rough sex. Maybe...." He swallowed again and looked Nikko in the eye. "It's okay, by the way. I mean, I just didn't want you to be disappointed." His stomach churned. He had no idea why it had been important to bring the matter up, but it had been on his mind. He got that what *he* wanted was the important thing, but part of him wanted Nikko to be satisfied too.

Why he felt that way, Mitch had no clue.

Nikko's jaw dropped. "No!" He sat up and stared at Mitch. "Why would I be disappointed? I love how you are with me, the way you treat me." He cocked his head. "Why on earth would I be disappointed with a man who is gentle, who treats me with respect?" His face was flushed.

Shit. Mitch really didn't need to hear that. If that was truly how Nikko felt, then Mitch was all the more concerned about the treatment he'd received at the hands of some whip-happy bastard. More than that, it meant Nikko had lied to him about not having a problem with it. And it was much too close for comfort to the whole Jerry mess.

Mitch opened his arms wide. "Come back here, please, Nikko." He waited until Nikko was in his arms again, his breathing uneven. "I guess I feel this way because someone...." He inhaled slowly and deeply, pushing out his own tension with each exhalation. "I need to share something with you."

Nikko said nothing but snuggled closer.

Reassured, Mitch continued. "My last relationship was with a guy called Jerry. We were together two years and things were good. At least, I thought they were, until the night he turned around and told me"—he closed his eyes, still hearing Jerry's voice in his head—"he told me I was boring in bed."

Nikko raised his head. "Wait a minute. Why would he have stayed two years if the sex was boring? Maybe he was trying to hurt you. Ever think of that?"

Mitch let out a sigh. "There was more to it than that. He… he'd wanted to 'spice things up,' as he put it. For him, that meant wanting me to… to hurt him, to choke him during sex. And then he brought out a few new toys." He shivered, seeing that riding crop lying there on their bed, the cane and whip next to it. "He wanted me to use them on him, but I couldn't do it. Just… couldn't."

Mitch stroked Nikko's cheek. "For me, sex was only part of our relationship. I think what hurt me the most was that it was clearly more important for Jerry. It brought home to me how different we really were. He accused me of not loving him enough to want to cater to his needs. Said I wasn't prepared to take risks. That I was boring." He sighed. "It made me look hard at myself. I've had a string of unsuccessful relationships. Maybe this was why. In the end I got angry. I thought, 'fuck it. I'll prove him wrong.' I decided to step out of my comfort zone and do something new."

Nikko's gaze was fixed on him. "What did you do?"

"I started looking at online sites, like RentMen.com. I created all these fantasies in my head, about hooking up with some stranger and just… letting go." He huffed. "Yeah, right. I couldn't do it. I just couldn't take that step." He smiled. "My brother calls me a serial monogamist, and maybe he's right."

Nikko smiled too. "That sounds funny, coming from you. Considering where we are right now."

Mitch snorted. "This is all the fault of my coworker. He caught me at a weak moment."

"And has reality lived up to the fantasy?" Nikko watched him, his hand slowly stroking Mitch's chest.

Mitch smiled. "It's better. I had no clue what to expect when I walked through those doors, but I do know one thing. I never expected to find someone like you." He paused for a moment, his heart pounding. *Fuck it. I've told him this much.* "I'll be honest, at first I was ashamed. I never thought I'd do this. But when I'm here with you?" He took a deep breath and took a further step out of his comfort zone. "There's no shame here. When I'm with you, it feels… right. I can be myself. So when I got to thinking about what Jerry had said, I—"

Nikko surprised the hell out of him by stopping his words with a finger to Mitch's lips. "Now you listen to me. You're a gentle, tender, sensual man. That's perfect in my book. Don't you change because of what Jerry said. Because he got it wrong, okay?" He leaned over and kissed Mitch on the mouth, his lips warm and soft.

Mitch closed his eyes and drank Nikko in—the smell of him, clean and warm, the feel of his mouth, the way his body felt against Mitch's. When the kiss came to an end, he slowly opened his eyes and gazed at the young man in his arms.

"You know what? I could get used to this."

"Used to what?" Nikko murmured, looking at him through long black lashes.

"Visiting here more often."

A slow, sweet smile spread across Nikko's face. "Like I said, I'm not complaining."

Something in that smile touched Mitch in his heart. He pushed Nikko onto his back and rolled leisurely to lie on top of him, his arms bracketing Nikko's head. Nikko gazed up at him, the remnants of his smile still in evidence, his lips parted in invitation. Mitch kissed him, tongue stroking languidly in and out, tasting him, savoring him, Nikko's body warm beneath his. Nikko reached up and looped his arms around Mitch's neck, fully invested in the kiss, a soft moan escaping now and again. Mitch rocked on top of him, liking how Nikko was starting to move too, a gentle undulation as he pushed up with his hips to meet Mitch. Nikko appeared more than happy to continue making out, their kisses long and deep.

It was slow and sexy as hell.

Without breaking the kiss, Mitch rubbed Nikko's belly, the cotton T-shirt sliding over his skin. Nikko nodded, running his fingers through

Mitch's short hair at his nape, sending shivers shooting down his spine when he caressed Mitch's neck.

"That's one surefire way to get me hot and bothered," Mitch murmured into Nikko's mouth. "You just found my major sweet spot." It drove him crazy when a guy touched his nape.

Damn it if Nikko didn't carry right on, his fingers tracing over the skin while their kisses intensified, the heat between them building. Mitch shuddered at Nikko's delicate touch. He slid his hand under the T-shirt and caressed Nikko's taut belly, earning a low moan from him that grew louder when he moved higher to brush his fingertips across Nikko's nipples. The sounds Nikko was making went straight to Mitch's dick, and he ground against Nikko, letting him feel the results.

Nikko's eyes widened and his breathing sped up. "Oh, you're so hard." He rocked up off the bed, and Mitch could plainly feel the heat of him through his jeans. He moved his hand lower until it covered Nikko's crotch, and Nikko pushed up into his touch. "Please, Mitch."

It took every ounce of Mitch's willpower not to pop open Nikko's jeans and slip his hand around that pretty cock he knew awaited him, already stiff beneath the fabric. He didn't want to rush this. Instead, he rubbed over the bulge, loving how Nikko rolled his hips, eager noises escaping his mouth. Mitch murmured against Nikko's soft lips. "You're pretty hard yourself." Nikko said nothing but let out a sweet whimper when Mitch brushed his fingers roughly over the head of his dick and then squeezed the firm length. "Oh, you like that," Mitch said, surprised by the breathless quality of his own voice. Nikko's responsiveness aroused him to the point where he was aching. He propped himself up on his hands and ground his cock against Nikko's, undulating against him, picking up speed.

Nikko's breathing grew more erratic, and he met Mitch's thrusts, his pupils huge and black. "Mitch? Do we get to ditch the latex?" He gave a half smile. "Want to feel my mouth on you?"

Fuck. Nikko's words brought the situation home to Mitch in a rush of heat that spread through him in seconds. That initial list of Seb's was a thing of the past. No more blow jobs with a condom. No more finger cots. And the last thought was what sent the blood surging into his shaft.

He'd finally get to eat Nikko's ass.

Mitch moved swiftly to kneel between Nikko's already spreading legs and fumbled with the button on his jeans. Nikko lifted his hips from the bed as Mitch tugged at the offending garment before dropping it to the floor. Nikko's slender but hard, uncut cock rose up in greeting, bobbing before him in a delicious invitation. Mitch ignored it and leaned over to remove Nikko's T-shirt, pulling it up and off in one quick movement, Nikko sitting up to help him, arms raised above his head. Mitch didn't give a damn about his own clothing—he was focused on Nikko. He stared at the slim dick, wet-tipped, and licked his lips. With a grin he bent over, inhaling that clean, fresh scent once more, but underlying it was the same musky aroma he remembered from his first time with the young man. He met Nikko's gaze.

Nikko's face was flushed, his mouth open. "I… I thought it was supposed to be my mouth on you."

Mitch's grin widened. "All in good time. Right now I want to find out how you taste." He held Nikko's cock steady around the base while he lapped at the head, smiling to himself to hear the desperate note in Nikko's whimpers and moans. With his other hand he stroked and caressed Nikko's belly and chest, keeping his touch sensual and lingering, keeping them connected.

Nikko seemed unable to lie still. He pushed up into Mitch's mouth, his movements lacking their usual grace, his hand on Mitch's head, exerting just enough pressure to keep him at his task. Mitch didn't mind in the slightest. He wanted Nikko to lose it, to let himself go in a tide of ecstasy. Besides, there was plenty of time for Nikko to come at least twice before Mitch was done with him.

"Please, don't stop," Nikko moaned, his hips speeding up as he gave small thrusts into Mitch's mouth.

Mitch had no intention of stopping. He had a goal—to make Nikko come, hopefully down Mitch's throat. And there was still that gorgeous ass awaiting his tongue….

NIKKO WAS in heaven. None—not a single one—of his johns ever sucked him off. It was always Nikko on his knees, head moving frantically, or between their thighs, bobbing up and down while they thrust deep into his mouth, him gagging around a thick dick. It didn't seem to matter to most of them that he couldn't deep-throat them. They appeared to like it when Nikko coughed and spluttered, his mouth full of hard cock. So for him to be lying on the bed while Mitch gave him what was undoubtedly the best blow job of Nikko's life was sheer bliss. Mitch's hands were gentle, stroking over his chest and belly, before moving lower to roll Nikko's balls between his fingers while he licked a line down Nikko's dick to give them a tongue bath. Nikko grabbed at the sheet beneath him, clutching it tightly to anchor himself to the bed as he pushed up into Mitch's hot mouth. When Mitch hummed in approval, Nikko thrust faster, letting go of the bed and taking hold of Mitch's head so he could get deeper. Mitch swallowed around his length and Nikko let out a harsh groan of pleasure at the sensation of a tight throat around the head of his cock.

"Feels... amazing." Not that amazing conveyed half of what he was feeling. Mitch pulled off and dragged his tongue the whole length of Nikko's dick, slow and deliberate, before heading back down to suck gently on his balls, one at a time, until Nikko was gasping, desperate for more. Mitch focused his gaze on Nikko as he went down on him, and all it took was one look at those brown eyes, hooded with desire, for Nikko to realize this was not going to be like the last time.

Mitch was going to fuck him, and God, Nikko wanted him to.

Nikko groaned when Mitch slowly freed his cock, but then the sound died in his throat when Mitch slipped both hands under Nikko's ass, lifting him higher and spreading his cheeks as he lapped over Nikko's hole. He couldn't breathe, couldn't do anything except lie there and submit to the most sensual experience he'd ever had. Mitch was worshipping his ass. It was the only way to describe it. The slow licks, sucking kisses, the tantalizing way he circled Nikko's hole with his tongue, the feel of those large, capable hands on Nikko's ass, splaying him, making him vulnerable....

"Fuck, you taste good," Mitch muttered against his hole, before sinking both index fingers into Nikko and stretching his hole. Nikko cried out at the blissful sensation of Mitch's tongue in his ass, pushing insistently into him again and again. Mitch's chuckle tickled him. "God, you really like that."

He had no argument from Nikko, who grabbed hold of his knees and held on while Mitch sent him soaring higher and higher—and then everything stopped when Mitch pulled free and crawled up Nikko's body, planting soft kisses along the way, tracing the line of Nikko's hip bone with his tongue before briefly dipping into his navel. He gasped when Mitch took his nipple between his teeth and gently bit on it. When

Mitch's lips met his in a deep, heated kiss, Nikko was grateful for the respite. He wanted to savor every minute with Mitch.

"My turn," Mitch uttered breathlessly and crouched at his head, that thick, heavy cock right where Nikko wanted it. He laid his hand on Mitch's firm thigh and wrapped the other around the base of Mitch's dick while he took him as deep as he could.

"Fuck, yeah, just like that," Mitch moaned, cupping Nikko's head and pulling him onto his cock, urging him to take more, to go faster. Nikko sucked him eagerly, running his tongue under the ridge of that flared head, his lips stretched as he tried to take in as much of Mitch's wide dick as he could. "That's so good, Nikko," Mitch praised him. "So very, very good." He knelt above Nikko, hips rocking, still holding Nikko steady, soft moans still stuttering from his lips. He pulled his cock free and smiled at Nikko. "I want that ass again."

Nikko's hole clenched at the thought. Mitch swung around until his thick dick was once again nudging Nikko's lips. Nikko held him steady and sucked him deep, but he let out a loud groan when Mitch bent over him, his weight on his elbows, and spread his legs wide once again. Mitch's mouth was at his hole, his hand cradling Nikko's ass while he probed him with his tongue, his fingers stretching him again. Nikko pushed his head back into the pillows and cried out, eyes closed, lost in the overwhelming pleasure of Mitch tongue-fucking him. His body trembled, his balls ached, and he didn't want it to end. When Mitch slowly pressed two fingers inside him, Nikko moaned loudly and grabbed hold of Mitch's furry butt, licking up his crease.

"That's it, lick my ass," Mitch urged, before diving back to resume his task of driving Nikko out of his mind with an agile tongue. Nikko rimmed him eagerly, the sensations Mitch was creating sending him higher still, until he knew he was about to come. He grasped his cock tightly in an effort to stave off the imminent orgasm, squeezing the firm shaft.

Mitch halted and thrust two fingers deep into his ass, brushing over his prostate while he sucked hard on the head of Nikko's dick.

It was more than Nikko was capable of withstanding. Without a word of warning, he pulsed come into Mitch's mouth, body shaking, breathing erratic, all his attention focused on the feel of that hot, wet mouth on his cock. Mitch moaned in appreciation and took every last drop until Nikko lay spent, chest heaving, tiny shocks jolting through him.

When Mitch sat up and yanked open the drawer to remove a condom and lube, Nikko wanted to howl with joy.

"You ready for me?" Mitch's gaze was fixed on him, his slick hand wiping over his rigid dick. Nikko's tight throat choked out whatever words he'd intended to say while Mitch rolled Nikko's ass up off the bed once again and licked at his hole. "Got to get you nice and wet for my cock."

"Yes." The croak was all Nikko would manage. He caught his legs behind the knees and held himself still for that first push of Mitch's dick into him. When Mitch entered him, unhurriedly and carefully, Nikko expelled a sigh. "So ready for you."

Mitch slowly filled him, hooked his arms under Nikko's knees and kissed him, long and slow, while he moved gently in and out of him. Nikko placed his hands on Mitch's shoulders and threw his whole being into that kiss, into the sensuality of the moment. They remained like that, lips locked in leisurely kisses while Mitch stroked his cock in and out of Nikko's ass like he belonged there.

It was freaking perfect.

Mitch straightened and lifted Nikko's legs to rest his ankles against Mitch's shoulders. He kissed the soles of Nikko's feet, making Nikko catch his breath at the intimacy of the gesture. But it wasn't long before Mitch was back to kissing him, his tongue sliding between Nikko's lips while his cock slid home in thrust after slow, deliberate thrust. Nikko cupped the back of Mitch's neck while they kissed, not wanting to lose the sensuality of it all.

"This feels so... nice," Mitch said with a smile, filling his ass with one long push of that hard dick. He bent lower, their lips brushing against each other's. "You like that?"

Before he could stop himself, Nikko blurted out the truth. "I love it," he replied breathlessly.

Mitch's face lit up and he kissed Nikko hard. "Fuck, yeah," he murmured into Nikko's open mouth. "Me too." He stroked Mitch's neck, loving the shivers that rippled through him as he bent to suck Nikko's nipple, his tongue playing with the taut nub. Nikko groaned and rubbed Mitch's shoulders, a slow caress that kept them connected, Mitch never ceasing in those long, deep thrusts, like they had all the time in the world.

Mitch cradled Nikko's head in his hands and kissed him, beginning to move a little faster, his thrusts more shallow. Nikko sensed the growing need in him, the way Mitch's eyes were focused on him, their breathing in synch. "Look at you." There was a touch of awe in Mitch's voice. "You're so beautiful." He eased his cock from Nikko's body and lay down on the bed, shifting Nikko until they lay spooned together, Mitch behind him.

"Oh, God, yes," Nikko groaned when Mitch pushed back inside him, his dick still hard. Nikko lifted his leg into the air and let out moans of sheer bliss when Mitch began to fuck him, his arm across Nikko's waist, holding him close. "Mitch, so good." He didn't have the words—Mitch's lovemaking was scrambling his brain.

Mitch grabbed onto Nikko's thigh and fucked up into him, cock sliding with ease, the friction delicious. Now and again he'd slow everything down and they'd kiss, Nikko gasping into Mitch's mouth when Mitch picked up the pace and fucked him again. Mitch reached lower and grasped Nikko's already stiff dick, stroking him, fondling his balls, until Nikko was more than ready to come again.

"Onto your knees," Mitch whispered, helping him to move. Nikko placed his elbows on the bed and let out a harsh moan when he felt hot breath over his hole. "Your hole is perfect."

Nikko tilted his hips, offering Mitch his ass and then dropped his chest to the mattress when Mitch fucked him again, alternating between tongue and fingers. The pressure of a hard cock entering him in one long thrust of hot flesh, and once again Mitch was fucking him, fingers digging into his hips.

A joyful laugh rang out. "Fuck, Nikko, you feel amazing." Mitch punched his dick into Nikko's body, and Nikko stretched out his hands to grab onto the pillows. Mitch curved his body over Nikko's, his arms wrapped tight around him, and kissed between his shoulder blades and down his back. Mitch pulled Nikko upright until he was almost sitting in Mitch's lap.

Nikko reached back to curve his arm around Mitch's head, leaning into him. "Won't be long now." His balls were already starting to tingle, the heat growing inside him.

Mitch held on to him and pumped his hips, the movement speeding up along with his breathing. Mitch pushed Nikko back onto all fours, rested his chin on Nikko's back and fucked him hard, their flesh slapping together each time Mitch pistoned into him. "Oh, fuck, Nikko...."

Nikko braced himself, elbows locked, and pushed back to meet Mitch's urgent thrusts. He looked along the line of his body to where his cock pointed straight toward him, hard as steel. Mitch's arm was still tight around him, anchoring them together.

"Want to watch your face when you come," Mitch said hoarsely. "On your back, baby."

The unexpected endearment made Nikko catch his breath, but he stamped hard on the emotion it kindled in his chest. *It's just a word. He probably always uses it when he's fucking someone.* Only Mitch hadn't used it their first time together. He rolled onto his back and drew his knees up to his chest. Mitch positioned the head of his dick at Nikko's hole and slid into him until he was balls-deep. Mitch hooked his arms under Nikko's legs once again.

Nikko didn't hesitate. He grabbed onto Mitch's nape and tugged him down into a kiss, all teeth and tongues, while Mitch thrust into him, hips slamming, his breathing staccato, low moans building into groans of ecstasy as he neared his climax. Nikko slipped a hand between their damp bodies and worked his cock, wanting them to hit that plateau together.

"Fuck. So close." Mitch's gaze was locked on him, and Nikko nodded, hand moving faster. Mitch's eyes widened and he fed gasps into Nikko's open mouth, his body stiffening as Nikko felt heat inside him. Nikko squeezed his muscles tight around Mitch's dick, forcing a loud cry from Mitch's lips. Then Nikko was coming, hot come spilling over his hand onto his belly, still feeling the throb of Mitch's cock in his ass.

Mitch slid his arms under Nikko's shoulders and held on to him through his orgasm, their bodies gently moving together as the waves of pleasure ebbed. Nikko clung to him, unwilling to let go. He knew why he was feeling so emotional. Yet again, Mitch had made him feel like he'd been a part of the act, not simply the recipient of another guy's dick. Mitch had made him feel like his enjoyment mattered, that it wasn't all about Mitch getting off. Nikko couldn't let the moment go without saying something.

"God, that was so good."

Mitch smiled, his eyes alight. "You felt amazing." He brought his mouth to Nikko's and kissed him, slowly, languidly, his hips in motion, a gentle wave that left Nikko aware of Mitch's cock still buried inside him. Nikko closed his eyes to shut out everything that might have intruded on his little bubble of happiness—the club, Mr. Richards, Mr. M, even Ichy, although that last thought made his face burn hot with shame. He wanted to forget about everything except the strong, wonderful man who held him like he was something to be treasured.

That didn't mean he could shut out everything, however. Jesse's warning still rang inside his head, making his stomach churn—it was already way too late to be thinking about being objective. Nikko knew it made sense not to become attached, but fuck, that boat had sailed.

Nikko was falling for Mitch.

Chapter Eleven

"Mom really thought you were going to make this month's Sunday family fest," Gareth said as they packed away the chessboard. Mitch had been of two minds as to whether to meet up for their chess game. The temperature had been stuck in the eighties for the last week, typical of mid-July, and the humidity was unbearable. Not the weather for sitting outdoors playing chess.

Mitch's mind had been anywhere but on the games. Trying to concentrate on his moves had been next to impossible, and it had been a foregone conclusion that Gareth was going to win.

"Yeah, I know." Mitch ignored the knots in his stomach as they walked across the street toward the coffee house. He hadn't given the family meal a second's thought. When Saturday had arrived, all he'd been thinking about was going back to the Black Lounge. But the club—scrap that, *Nikko*—had been on his mind a lot lately.

He was a mess.

That had been the deciding factor when it came to the chess game. Mitch needed to talk to his big brother, although he was dreading the moment when he'd have to put his cards on the table. He'd been imagining Gareth's questions, because there'd be no getting away from them. Worse, he'd been imagining the look on his brother's face.

What's he gonna think of me?

Mitch wasn't sure he wanted to know the answer to that one.

They entered the coffee house, and Mitch headed for an empty table in the corner. It wasn't perfect—a public place was totally the wrong location for what he had in mind—but it would have to do in the time available. He sat with his back to the red brick wall and watched Gareth at the counter, ordering their coffees and pastries. It always surprised him that Gareth was alone. His brother was a good-looking man. Mitch was sure there had to be women interested in him, but Gareth had never spoken of being in a relationship, or even going on a date. It had crossed Mitch's mind on more than one occasion that maybe Gareth was gay but in denial, but he'd always pushed the thought aside. If that had been the case, Gareth would have said something.

"So, you want to tell me what was on your mind this afternoon?" Gareth pulled out the chair facing him and sat, folding his arms across his wide chest. "This is getting to be a habit, me beating the pants off you. Not that I'm complaining, you understand. It's kinda nice to be on a winning streak." He grinned, but after a moment his expression grew more serious. He unfolded his arms and leaned forward, elbows on the table. "What's wrong, Mitch?" His voice was gentle.

Mitch stared at him, his heart pounding. He'd woken up that morning with so many thoughts buzzing in his head. Talking to Gareth always helped. His brother had a lot of common sense, and Mitch had lost count of the number of times he'd gotten good, sound advice. He'd considered long and hard how to broach the subject all that morning, but now that the moment had arrived, he couldn't get the words out.

"Mitch?"

"Something's happened," he blurted out.

Gareth's expression didn't change. "Go on."

"This is difficult, okay? Just bear with me."

"Hey." There was that gentleness again. "Whatever it is, take your time, all right?" Gareth clammed up when the barista called out their order, and crossed the floor to collect the tray with its danishes and tall cups of coffee. After placing Mitch's order in front of him, Gareth took a sip of his dark roast and regarded him with warm eyes. "Okay. Start at the beginning."

Mitch took a mouthful of coffee, relishing the smoky flavor. "Just over a month ago, a coworker took me out for a drink one Friday night. We went to a bar on 38th, kinda swanky place. Anyhow, we got to talking, and he invited me to take a look at this secret club he belonged to."

Gareth raised his eyebrows. "Secret club? Why do I not like the sound of that?"

"Probably because you have good instincts, and in this case, you'd be right. It was a brothel."

Gareth stared at him. "Seriously? Did you go with him?" Mitch nodded, his chest tightening. "You… okay, there's no delicate way to say this, so I'll come right out with it. Did you pay for sex?"

"Not that night, no." The muscles in Mitch's belly were tight too.

Gareth sagged into his chair. "Your words imply there have been other nights. Am I reading the situation correctly?" When Mitch nodded once more, Gareth shook his head. "Whoa. What did I say about not taking Deirdre seriously?"

Mitch huffed. "By then it was too late. I'd already met him."

"Him," Gareth said heavily. "Oh God, there's a *him*. Okay, back to that in a second. How many times have you visited this club?"

Mitch paused for a moment. "In the last two weeks, I've been back maybe five, six times. Before that, maybe three times since the beginning of June."

Gareth's jaw dropped. "Fuck." He gaped at Mitch. "Right, I've got to ask something here. Why keep going back? Is the sex that good? Is it something you couldn't find anyplace else, like maybe somewhere that wasn't fucking *illegal*?"

"It's not just the sex," Mitch said in a quiet voice.

"And now we're back to him. Tell me about this guy who is proving impossible to resist."

Mitch took in Gareth's expression. There was no judgment in his brother's eyes, thank God. It was enough to make him continue. He related how Nikko had caught his eye, but skipped the part about the amazing sex—some things were *not* to be shared. He told Gareth about the welts on Nikko's back and ass, and how things just didn't add up.

"You're worried about him."

Mitch nodded. "That's why I keep going back." Okay, so it wasn't the only reason, but Gareth didn't need to know that. "I know he told me he's there because he wants to be, but every time I go there and I'm told he's unavailable, it scares me. And the next time I see him, I'm checking that he's okay." He took a long drink of coffee, ignoring his pastry. "He's such a beautiful person, Gareth. And I don't just mean how he looks, either. He's a good man."

Gareth frowned. "How can you know that? And based on what?"

"I trust my gut," Mitch replied simply. "Okay, we might not have talked that much"—he glared when Gareth smothered a chuckle—"but I didn't need to have in-depth conversations with him to get the feeling he's hiding something. And that worries me."

Gareth locked gazes with him. "Mitch? Are you falling in love with him?"

It crossed Mitch's mind to say love didn't happen that fast, but that felt just plain wrong. He smiled. "I think I am. Well, either I'm on the way to falling in love or I'm already there." Mitch expelled a heavy sigh. "I'm just so confused. I didn't expect this to happen. I mean, who falls in love with a prostitute?"

"What, like *Pretty Woman?*"

Mitch gritted his teeth. "This is not *Pretty* fucking *Woman*."

Gareth studied him for a moment. "Leaving aside whether you're in love or not, let's talk money for a second here. This must be costing you a fortune."

Trust Gareth to be all about the practicalities. "I've… dipped into my savings." Gareth didn't need to know that his savings were all but depleted. And he wasn't about to share how he'd maxed out his credit card too. Yet another thing to give him a few sleepless nights.

Gareth said nothing but tore pieces off his pastry and ate in silence. Mitch was just starting to get uncomfortable when Gareth leaned forward and looked him in the eye. "Okay, I'm gonna be honest here. You're worrying me. Top of the list is you going to a brothel and paying for sex. Bro, you don't need me to tell you this is dangerous shit and you're in it up to your neck. What if the club gets raided? I don't want to see you getting arrested or losing your job. Because you can be damn sure your fancy school will take a very dim view of one of its teachers getting caught up in *that*."

Mitch's heart sank. The last thing he'd wanted was to worry Gareth. Never mind that everything he was saying was correct.

"And then there's Nikko. From what you've told me, I'd say you're right to worry about him." He gazed at Mitch, his eyes full of love. "I'd say stay away, but I know that's not gonna happen. So all I will say is this. If you need anything—money, an ear to bend, whatever—come to me, okay? A problem shared, and all that crap, right?" He gave Mitch a half smile. "Love you, you idiot." He tilted his head to one side. "So, did telling me help, or make matters worse?"

"Both?"

Gareth smiled. "Just remember I'm here for you, okay?" He sat back. "You're gonna go back there soon, aren't you?"

Mitch nodded. "Thank God I get paid tomorrow." Things had gotten more than a little tight, and he'd been trying not to panic. Staying away wasn't an option, however. He'd just have to work out how many visits he could feasibly afford until the next paycheck.

Geez, I sound like an addict.

It was a sobering thought, but Nikko was an addiction Mitch wasn't willing to give up.

Not yet. Not until it got so he couldn't afford it. And if it got that far, he'd have to consider his options.

Fuck. I've got it bad.

NIKKO WASHED his glass, dried it, and put it away in the cabinet. It had been a quiet day so far, and he couldn't help wondering if he'd see Mitch. It seemed like every couple of days the sexy, gentle teacher would be waiting for him, that great smile just for him. The last couple of weeks had been wonderful.

"Wow. You look happy."

Nikko glanced at Jesse who was helping himself to some salad from the refrigerator. "Do I?"

Jesse laughed. "Don't play the innocent with me. You're happy, so don't deny it." He grinned. "It's a good look on you. To be honest, I was getting worried."

"About what?" Nikko checked the clock. He didn't want Randy chasing him, reminding him of the time.

"I watch you," Jesse said with a shrug. "And that's not me being all creepy, okay? I told you before, you don't look like you should be here, so I kinda look out for you. But I see you when you come back from a john. Most of the time you look like you've just been through torture. And I have to ask myself, why would someone who doesn't seem to enjoy sex work in a place like this? Plus there's the whole top floor scenario going on."

"Excuse me?" Nikko stiffened. He had no clue how much or how little Jesse knew about the club's other "business" interests, and the last thing he wanted was for someone to think he was divulging their secrets.

"Word gets around," Jesse said with a smile. "You're staying in that room on the top floor, the one with the camera above the door?" He held up his hands. "I'm not gonna pry, okay? I just wanted to say if you ever need to talk, grab me. I'm here more often now it's vacation time." The smile widened into a grin. "Gotta pay off those loans, right?" He regarded Nikko carefully. "I'm just glad to see you with a smile on your face. But you gotta know, I'm dying to know what put it there."

"That would be Mitch." Nikko was tired of secrets. Mitch was the one thing he could be open about.

Jesse stared at him. "Still with Mitch, huh? Did you not listen to me? Did we not have this conversation already?" His jaw set. "What is my cardinal rule?"

Nikko swallowed. "Sorry. He's the one thing that keeps me going. Most of the guys treat me like a piece of meat, manhandling me—and worse—but he's the only one who treats me well. He's gentle. He cares—"

"Well, shit." Jesse's face fell. "You went and did it, didn't you? You fell for him."

"Nikko." Randy poked his head around the corner. "You're wanted."

Saved by the security guard. Nikko gave Jesse an apologetic smile. "Sorry. This will have to wait."

Jesse shook his head. "This conversation is not finished, just postponed. You got that?"

"Nikko." Randy was more insistent.

"Later," Nikko promised Jesse. He went to follow Randy, but the guard stopped him.

"You need to strip off now. The client expects you naked." Randy's face was grave.

Okay, that was unusual. "Sure." Maybe he was going to be on one of the couches. Nikko got out of his clothes and folded them, leaving them on a chair. Randy waited and then led him through to the door. The area with the couches was unoccupied. As Randy led him along the hallway, Nikko's heart grew heavy when they approached the door of the Red Room.

Oh hell, no.

Randy stopped outside the door and met Nikko's gaze. "Ready?" Nikko knew Randy well enough to read his expression. What he saw was sympathy, and that could mean only one thing.

Mr. M was back.

Nikko entered the room to find the tall, heavyset man standing in the center, dressed as before in leather chaps and harness, his bare cock already hard and curving upward, the light reflecting off his shaved head. He grinned when he saw Nikko, and then nodded to Randy behind him. "Okay, I've got this."

The door closed softly behind him, and Nikko was alone with Mr. M.

"Well, Nikko, we meet again," he began, still grinning. "This is going to be a little different from last time."

Nikko couldn't speak. His throat seized up and breathing became difficult.

Mr. M's eyes glittered. "You are mine for twenty-four hours, boy."

Fuck, no. Nikko didn't think that was even possible. "Oh?" It was all he could manage. He watched in dismay as Mr. M strode over to the cage that stood against the wall. It was about three feet high and four feet across, its floor covered in a padded, vinyl-covered cushion. He unlocked the cage door and gestured to the interior with a flick of his head.

"Get in there."

Shit. Shit. Nikko tried not to succumb to the panic that clawed at his chest. He moved slowly in an effort to put off the inevitable.

"On your knees, boy. Crawl into it," Mr. M growled.

Shaking, Nikko got down on all fours and crawled his way across the floor, legs trembling. He climbed into the cage, which was just tall enough for him to sit upright. Mr. M closed the door and locked it with the padlock. When he straightened, he stared hard at Nikko.

"Now, you are gonna sit there until I come back. Not sure when that's gonna be, but hey, it'll give you plenty of time to think about what's coming, right?" He walked over to the large wooden X standing against the wall and patted it before regarding Nikko once more. "You and I are gonna have some fun, boy." His grin widened, and the sight of it sent shivers surging along Nikko's spine. "All kinds of fun."

And with that he turned and strolled out of the room like he was taking a walk in the park. The door opened and closed, and Nikko was alone in the Red Room, locked in a cage, with only a very active imagination for company. No clocks in the room. His heart pounded and there was an invisible iron band around his chest, forcing him to take shallow breaths. He closed his eyes to shut out the sight of that hateful space, as if that would stop the fear that rose up in his throat.

Yeah. Like that was going to work.

NIKKO SAT on the floor in the corner, arms wrapped around his knees, head bowed. He stank of piss, his hair damp with it, and the air was heavy with the smell of sex and come. Speaking of which, he could still feel Mr. M's come on his back and belly, the skin tight where it had dried. He ached all over, he was exhausted, and his hole was fucking sore. He knew there would be bruises from where large hands had gripped his hips and dug into his thighs. He yearned for sleep.

Mr. M had left the room, but he was still in Nikko's head. He couldn't shut out the humiliation he'd been forced to endure. It had to be over, not that he had any idea of how long he'd been in the Red Room. There had been moments when he'd fallen asleep on the floor, only to be awoken by a rough hand yanking on his braid, and then sleep had no longer been an option. There had been no crop or whip, thank God, just hours of rough hands, rough handling, and even rougher sex. At one point he'd thought Mr. M was going to sleep on the bed, but the man seemed to possess endless supplies of energy. Judging by his dilated pupils and the sheen of sweat that covered him, Nikko hazarded a guess that some of that energy was drug-induced.

Well, that'd be right. And no guesses as to who would have supplied him.

After a while, the hours seemed to roll into one another, until the whole experience was one painful blur, memories of being taken again and again, an endless stream of verbal abuse and being tossed around like a limp rag doll.

Nikko listened for some sign that Mr. M had finally gone. All he wanted right then was a hot shower to scrub off the layers of shame and degradation, and ease his aching body, followed by hours of the sweet oblivion of sleep. More than anything, he didn't want to *think*.

The door opened and Nikko froze. *Please, God, no more.* Slowly he raised his head and heaved a sigh of relief at the sight of Mr. Richards. The guy might be scary as shit, but he was still an improvement over Mr. M. The club owner walked up to him and came to a stop, forcing Nikko to crane his neck to look up at him.

"In case you were wondering, the twenty-four hours is up."

His words brought a lightness Nikko hadn't thought possible in his exhausted state. He gave a short nod, too tired to do much more, and waited for the instruction to leave.

It didn't come.

"You and I are going to have a little chat." The steel in Mr. Richards's voice belied the innocence of his words.

Nikko's arms and the back of his neck erupted into a carpet of goosebumps.

Mr. Richards dragged a chair across and placed it in front of Nikko. He sat, hands clasped in his lap, his long legs stretched out, his shiny black shoes almost touching Nikko's bare feet. His dark eyes focused on Nikko, no trace of a smile.

"I know what you've been doing."

Nikko's heartbeat sped up, and his hands grew clammy. "What… what do you mean?"

Mr. Richards arched his eyebrows. "Did you think I hadn't noticed? I see everything, Nikko." He smiled thinly. "You sit at the back, hoping to blend into the furniture, almost as if you're trying not to attract attention. That *is* what you were doing, right?"

Holy fuck. Nikko swallowed hard.

"My question has to be, why?" Mr. Richard's voice was cool. "You're here for one purpose, and that is to pay off what your brother owes me."

"And that's what I'm doing." Nikko found his voice at last. "Every hour I sit in that room is one hour closer to when we can leave here, the debt paid off."

Mr. Richards laughed, and the sound of it sent a shudder coursing through him. "Oh dear. We appear to have our lines crossed. Your debt does not diminish with every hour you spend sitting in that chair with your book *and* those times when you are with a client." He leaned forward, his voice soft with a menacing edge. "Your debt only decreases when you spend time with the clients. Except we also have to take into consideration your room and board. You work a few hours on your back, but with every day, the debt grows just that little bit more."

Ice filled Nikko's veins as his fears were realized. "Why didn't you say all this at the start?" he whispered.

Mr. Richards raised his eyebrows again. "Oh, didn't I mention that? How remiss of me." His smile was predatory. "Mind you, your time with Mr. M paid back a large chunk. I suggested it, by the way."

"Why?" Nikko asked, his voice hoarse.

Mr. Richards shrugged. "I knew he'd go for it. More importantly, I wanted to show you that you are *mine*, Nikko. Your looks attract a certain kind of clientele, but you'll only be of use to me for a few years."

That one word was like a knife in his gut. "Years?"

The club owner widened his eyes in mock surprise. "Why, how long did you think you'd be here?"

Nikko didn't want to answer. He had a sinking feeling he knew what the response would be.

"Well?"

He forced himself to take a deep breath. "I'd thought we'd be out of here by Christmas at the latest. That *was* what you said, wasn't it?" He winced at the sound of loud, sardonic laughter that followed his words.

"Oh, that's priceless. I can't deny I may have given you that impression, but that was before I saw the reaction of our clients." White teeth gleamed in a wide smile. "My dear little Nikko, you are going to be with me for much longer than that. I know a good thing when I see one." His eyes shone. "Mr. M is very pleased with you. And there are a great many men like him, with similar… tastes." He laughed again. "But that's good, isn't it? Because now you know how busy you need to be." He rose to his feet and advanced upon Nikko. Mr. Richards bent down and grabbed Nikko's braid, pulling it down forcefully so that Nikko had no choice but to look at him. "Are you regretting your noble gesture, Mr. Kurokawa?" he hissed. "How fortuitous for me that you were in that hospital room when I came to visit your brother. I hadn't bargained on you stepping into the breach, so to speak. Maybe it was for the best. If Ichiro had gone back to work for me, I doubt he'd be alive at this point." That cruel smile. "Lucky for him. Even luckier for me."

Nikko shivered as Mr. Richards released him and straightened. He couldn't move. The bleakness of his situation seeped into his bones until he felt numb.

"So things are going to change around here. No more sitting with a book. No more trying not to be noticed. You need to work that cute little ass, Nikko. If I look in on you, I want to see you actively trying to attract clients. You've seen the others, seen how they do it. Well, now it's your turn." He cleared his throat. "Now I suggest you go and take a shower before another client arrives. The stench is making me gag." Mr. Richards turned and walked away without another word. The door opened and closed.

Nikko stared at it, still frozen to the spot. *Years. He intends on keeping me here for years.* He couldn't even comprehend it. Then it hit him.

Ichy. I have to talk to Ichy. With a supreme effort he attempted to hoist himself up off the floor, wincing at the aches pervading his body, but his legs gave way and he retreated farther into the corner. He knew he couldn't stay there. He had to talk to his brother.

Ichy will know what to do.

Even as the thought crossed his mind, he was filled with a sense of dread.

Maybe this was beyond his big brother. And if that were true?

They were both fucked.

Chapter Twelve

Randy entered the Red Room, saw Nikko and came over to kneel in front of him. "Are you okay?"

Nikko choked back tears at the concern he heard in Randy's voice. "Yeah," he lied. Randy was a nice guy, but he still worked for the club, after all. Nikko didn't want it to get back to Richards that he'd lost it. "I just need to get out of here and see my brother." He glanced at his own body and grimaced. That God-awful smell. "I just don't want anyone to see me like this."

Randy shook his head. "I've already made sure it's clear out there. I kinda figured you wouldn't appreciate spectators after…."

God. That nearly did for him. Nikko's emotions were way too close to the surface. "Thank you," he replied sincerely.

Randy waved his hand. "Pfft. It's my job."

That was probably true, but Nikko had the feeling Randy was a really nice guy, maybe someone who could have been a friend in a life beyond the club. He struggled to get to his feet, wincing.

"Hey." Randy's voice was soft. He slipped his arms around Nikko and picked him up like he was no heavier than a bag of groceries. "Come on, hold on to me."

"Randy, no," Nikko protested. "I can do this." Besides, he was acutely aware of his present… state.

Randy ignored him and rose to his feet, Nikko cradled in his arms. "And I'm not taking you through the apartment room. Those guys don't need to see you like this. We'll go the back way to the stairs. You can shower in your room, okay?"

Too choked up to say a word, Nikko nodded against Randy's chest.

Nikko held on as the big guard exited the room and walked slowly along the hallway, pausing at the desk where Randy usually sat, a monitor facing away from the couch area. Randy stopped at the desk and put Nikko down to press a button under his desk. A door to the left clicked open. "Okay, this takes you to the stairs." He went to pick Nikko up, but Nikko held out his hands.

"It's fine, Randy. I can make it on my own." Gratitude for the guard's actions threatened to overwhelm him. He stretched up on his toes and kissed Randy's cheek on instinct. "Thank you."

Randy's face flushed. He leveled a keen glance in his direction. "Are you sure you'll be okay?"

Nikko choked down hard on his emotions. Everything was so raw, so close to the surface. Too close.

No one got to see him lose it, not even Randy.

"I just need to take a shower." Not that hot water was going to take away the memory. Nothing short of a mental enema would do that. And he had to get away from Randy. He had the feeling it would only take a few kind words from the sweet-natured guard to have him dissolving into a pool of tears. Besides, Nikko had to see Ichy. He forced a smile. "Thank you."

Randy waved his hand. "Just go see your brother and get yourself cleaned up. You'll feel a whole lot better then." He held open the door and Nikko stepped through it.

Slowly, carefully, he climbed the stairs to their room and waited for the click. When he entered, Ichy sat up instantly, concern etched on his face. "Where have you been? I was so worried." He sniffed and grimaced. "Oh my God, what happened to you?"

Nikko ignored the question. "I just had an illuminating conversation with Mr. Richards." He was so tired he felt like his legs could give way at any second, but he had to get this out.

Ichy's face fell. "Oh shit. Now what?"

"It seems I got it all wrong about how long we're going to be here." He took a deep breath. "Looks like Mr. Richards has no intention of letting me go anytime soon." That part still had him shaking.

Ichy groaned. "You're just figuring this out? Really? God, I knew you were naïve, but…." He met Nikko's gaze. "Why do you think I'm here? Why do you think he sent his goons to the hospital when I got discharged? To bring me here so we could be together? Out of the kindness of his heart? Hell, Nikko, I'm *collateral*. That fucker Richards knows as long as he has me under lock and key, you're going nowhere." He sighed. "I really fucked up both our lives, didn't I?"

Nikko couldn't speak. He felt as if one small tap would shatter him into a million fragments. He didn't trust himself to talk, because he didn't want all the dark shit bubbling inside him to spew out over his brother. Ichy had been through enough, but the mood Nikko was in, he was afraid he'd say something he'd later regret.

"I have to go take a shower," he said abruptly. He had to find a way to scrape off some of this horrendous day, and right then he couldn't be around Ichy. He hoped there'd be some respite from clients, because the last thing he needed was to have to deal with a john, not after what he'd just gone through in the last twenty-four hours. Shower and sleep. That was it.

Nikko grabbed a towel and staggered into the small bathroom. Dropping his towel to the floor, he opened the door to the tiny cubicle, climbed in, turned on the jets full force and leaned against the tiles, arms braced, the water hitting his head and back, almost pummeling his skin. He bowed his head and closed his eyes, welcoming the opportunity to drop the mask, but he couldn't let go. Everything was still too bright, too sharp. The water sluiced away every trace of Mr. M, but inside Nikko's head a loop was playing. It was a collision of images and words, rough fucking, Mr. Richard's barely concealed cruel delight, and the thread woven through it all—the futility of Nikko's situation.

Can't do this. I have to hold on, just a little longer. All he wanted to do was collapse onto his bed and sleep, at least for a few hours, to put some distance between himself and recent events.

Nikko picked up the soap and scrubbed at his skin with enough vigor that he was soon red and tender. He pulled the band from his hair and washed it through twice, until all he could smell was soap and shampoo. When he was happy he'd gotten rid of the physical evidence of the encounter, he turned off the water and dried off, beyond tired. He didn't have the energy to braid his hair, so he left it hanging loose. By the time he wearily emerged from the bathroom, Nikko was ready to drop. He acknowledged Ichy with a wave, flopped onto the bed, and pulled the pillow against him, already sinking into the dark, soft arms of a deep sleep.

Until the buzzer sounded.

What the fuck?

Nikko opened his eyes and groaned. "They have got to be kidding!"

"Tell them to go to hell," Ichy growled. "You need to sleep, even I can see that."

Weary to his bones, Nikko sat up, rubbing his eyes. "Yeah, like that'll work. You know I can't say that, right?" He rose unsteadily to his feet, fumbled through his clothing for a pair of sweats, pulled them on, and headed for the door. He felt as brittle as old glass, as fragile as a cobweb.

"It wouldn't surprise me to learn Richards is behind this. I'm telling you, the guy is a bastard. He just wants to show you who's boss." Ichy's expression was unhappy. "Please, Nikko, tell them you need to sleep. You're worrying me here."

"I'll be okay," Nikko replied, lying through his teeth. He couldn't let Ichy see how close to the breaking point he really was. One glance up at the camera and the door clicked open. Nikko half walked, half stumbled down the stairs and through the 'apartment.' Jesse saw him and opened his mouth to speak, but Nikko waved his hand. "I'm wanted," he murmured. The door opened and Randy was there, his green eyes troubled.

Nikko kept a tight hold on his emotions. "Let's do this." He couldn't paste on a smile to save his life, but he schooled his features enough to reassure the guard. He followed Randy through the open area toward the playrooms, pushing down the desire to sigh heavily with relief when he saw their destination was not the Red Room. That knowledge kindled a hope in him.

Maybe it's Mitch.

In that moment, the desire to see him welled up from someplace deep inside Nikko, catching in his throat and making breathing a chore. Mitch always held him. Comforted him. The only thing Mitch didn't do was feel the same way about Nikko that he felt about Mitch.

Mitch wasn't in love with him.

"Randy, a moment?"

Randy came to a halt and Nikko stiffened at the sound of Mr. Richards's voice. He didn't want to face the man but knew that would attract attention. Nikko took a deep breath and turned around.

Randy frowned. "Sir? Is there a problem?"

Mr. Richards gave Nikko a cursory glance and regarded Randy. "You're taking Nikko to his next client?"

"Yes, sir."

Mr. Richards nodded. "Good. I just wanted to say that as far as Mr. Mitch Jenkins is concerned, Nikko is unavailable. Is that understood?"

Nikko froze at the mention of Mitch. *What the fuck?*

Randy became very still, not responding right away.

"Is there a problem?" Mr. Richards's voice was cool.

Randy straightened. "No, sir," he replied decisively. "I've got it."

"Good." Mr. Richards's gaze flicked in Nikko's direction and then he smiled. The sight of it sent a shiver through Nikko. "Please don't let me keep you. Nikko has a client awaiting him, after all." Without another word he strode away.

Nikko stared after him, his heart sinking. *That bastard.* The club owner had taken Nikko's one lifeline, the man who made this fucked-up situation just one bit more bearable, and severed the tie. For a moment it crossed Nikko's mind that Richards knew how he felt about Mitch. *But how can he? And even if he did, why do that?* Unless....

The moment the thought crossed Nikko's mind, he dismissed it as too fantastical, but it wouldn't be pushed aside. And the more he thought about it, the more it made sense.

What if he's doing this because he knows it will break me? What if he just wants to show me that I really am under his thumb? That there's no way out?

Cold spread from his core, sliding down his spine and radiating outward until he felt numb from it.

"Nikko? *Nikko!*"

With a shock he realized Randy was calling him. The guard had stopped outside room three and was pointing at the door. Nikko walked up to him in a daze, his mind in a muddle. Randy placed his hand on Nikko's back, his eyes focused on him. "I'm sorry," he whispered. "I know you're tired, but—"

"Just open the door," Nikko told him. He didn't mean to sound so brusque, but acting like everything was okay was wearing pretty thin, especially after this last blow. Nikko wasn't sure how much more he could take.

Randy didn't seem to take offense. If anything, his expression was sympathetic. He pushed open the door and stepped to one side to allow Nikko to enter.

When Nikko saw the room's occupant, he was flooded with a sense of relief. He recognized the client and knew it wouldn't be so bad—the guy was strictly the suck 'n' fuck type, vanilla to the bone, with a wedding ring. Nikko inhaled deeply and began to strip, knowing the drill.

He dropped to his knees and blew the guy, functioning on autopilot, his mind focused on a simple mantra—*watch the teeth, watch the teeth*—

while he choked on his client's thick, short dick. When he ended up on all fours, being plowed into from behind with an accompaniment of loud grunts, Nikko ignored the pain and simply retreated into himself. In his head he replayed his times with Mitch, recalling each caress, each slow thrust, the feel of Mitch's body curved around his, the smell of him, the *taste* of him…. He let the memories have their way with him, pushing out low moans that had nothing to do with the balding man fucking him and *everything* to do with the man who held his heart. He let go and fantasized about a life outside of the club, where he and Mitch could be together, in a pain-free world where Mitch loved him.

It was such a beautiful dream, and when he came, it was with tears trickling down his face.

If the client's rapture was anything to go by, it had been a convincing performance.

MITCH STARED at Randy. "Again? When will he become available?" He knew he came across as a whining asshole, but he couldn't help it. Every time he turned up to the club and heard those words, shivers ran down his back and his heart pounded. All he could see in his head was some fucker taking a whip or something similar to Nikko, and the thought was pure torture.

How can anyone hurt him?

He wanted to march into Seb's office, bring his fist down onto that wide desk and demand to see Nikko, demand that no son of a bitch be allowed to hurt him anymore.

Yeah, like I'd really do that. Mitch might not have liked it, but this was Nikko's living, and he wouldn't do anything that could jeopardize the young man's way of life.

Randy stared back at him. "I don't know. Maybe you should come back another time."

"Uh-uh." Mitch folded his arms across his chest. "I'll stay. I don't care how long it takes, I'm not leaving here until I've seen Nikko." He clenched his jaw.

Randy regarded him in silence, until Mitch was convinced he was about to be escorted from the club for being a nuisance. But there was something in Randy's expression that piqued his interest.

"Come with me." Randy beckoned for Mitch to follow him, and led him to a room at the far end of the hallway. He pushed open the door. "Wait in here and I'll see what I can do."

Randy's low tone and manner almost had Mitch believing he was doing something illicit, but that didn't make sense. Still, he wasn't about to say no, not if it meant he got to see Nikko. He thanked him and entered the room. A quick look around showed him it was the same as any other room he'd seen thus far. He sat on the bed and leaned back against the pillows.

He could wait.

NIKKO GROANED at the sight of Randy when he appeared in the bathroom. "Please, don't tell me you're here to take me to another client." What did Richards want—blood? Nikko didn't think his ass could take another pounding, not unless the club wanted him out of action for a while. There was no *way* anyone was fucking him again that night. He shook his head angrily while he dried himself off. "I can't, Randy. I'm plain exhausted. I can barely stand, and I fucking *hurt*." It was on the tip of his tongue to tell the guard that Richards had won, that Nikko couldn't take it anymore. Instead, he couched his plea in different terms. "What kind of advert for the club am I right now, anyway? Surely it would be better to let me rest, give my body a chance to heal?" It was the closest he'd get to telling Randy just how bad he was feeling.

"Listen to me." Randy stepped closer. "Just see this last client, and I promise, I'll take you up to your room myself, okay? I'll let you sleep for a minimum of eight hours because I know you need to, no matter what anyone says." His eyes were earnest. "Just one more, all right?"

Nikko was too exhausted to argue, his emotions too close to the surface yet again. "Fine. Take me to him," he exclaimed bitterly. *So much for Randy liking me.* He was as bad as the rest of them.

Randy nodded. "Come with me."

Nikko followed him through the "apartment" and out into the couched area. When they headed along the hallway that led to the Red Room, the blood froze in Nikko's veins. "Aw, shit, no," he moaned.

Randy surprised him by whirling around to face him, gesturing for him to hush. He stopped at a door and beckoned Nikko closer. "This is gonna get me into so much trouble, but you know what? Fuck it. Some things are worth it." His jaw was set.

Before Nikko could question him further, Randy opened the door and pushed him inside, closing it behind him.

"Hey, you."

At the sound of Mitch's voice, it was all Nikko could do not to break down then and there. "Hey." He pulled himself upright and walked over to where Mitch was sitting on the bed with a warm smile just for him. Nikko felt like he was in a dream. Hadn't Richards said…? He wondered if he was losing his grip on reality.

"Nikko?" Mitch's brow furrowed. "What's wrong, baby?" His voice was as gentle as a caress. He stood and held his arms wide.

Oh, fuck. Nikko couldn't hold it in a second longer. He stepped into the safe circle of Mitch's arms, pressed his face to Mitch's wide chest, and broke.

It began slowly, with sobs that hitched out of him, and swelled into a crescendo of grief. He kept his face hidden from the camera he knew was behind the mirror. They didn't get to see him lose it.

Mitch reacted instantly. He scooped Nikko up into his arms and carried him to the bed, cradling him protectively against his body. Gently, *so* gently, he laid Nikko down and stretched out next to him, curling up around him, his arm across Nikko's chest, holding him close. "I've got you," he whispered. "It's okay, just let it out. I've got you."

Nikko took Mitch at his word and let it all roll out of him in a never-ending wave of pent-up emotion. Grief, rage at his own impotence, desperation, and sorrow bubbled up out of him and burst forth in hot tears and harsh sobs. He wept, his body trembling in Mitch's arms, his tears soaking into the pillow.

Mitch didn't make any attempt to quiet him. He simply held Nikko tightly and let him cry it all out until, little by little, the pain inside him abated and he could breathe more easily. He hiccupped, sucking in gulps of air, shudders racking his body. Nikko rolled over and wrapped his arms around Mitch, a warm, solid anchor to cling to while the last vestiges of his emotional outburst ebbed away, leaving him limp and mentally exhausted.

"That's it," Mitch told him, stroking his hair that fell unfettered down his back. "Feel better?"

Nikko nodded against his chest, inhaling Mitch's warm, earthy scent, drawing it deep into him. "I'm sorry," he murmured.

"For what?" The gentle stroking soothed him. "You obviously needed to get that out of your system." He pressed his lips to Nikko's hair and kissed it. "We can just lie here and snuggle, if you like." Another soft kiss. "Unless… you want to talk?"

The thought of sharing his load, after keeping it locked up tight within him for the last month or so, was a tempting one. "Maybe."

Mitch lifted Nikko's chin with his hand. "Look, I'm not about to judge you, okay? If it helps to talk, then I'll just lie here and listen. I'm a good listener." His deep brown eyes held nothing but warmth and concern. Mitch caressed his cheek and then kissed him, a chaste brushing of lips.

Nikko sighed into the kiss. Yet again, Mitch was exactly the balm his soul needed.

Maybe telling him will bring me some relief too.

God knew, he needed some of that.

"It's a long story," he said after a moment, shifting in Mitch's arms to get more comfortable.

"I have time. Take as long as you need." The confidence in Mitch's voice was a comfort. "Start at the beginning." He held Nikko against him, stroking up and down his back.

"That would be with a phone call in early June from my brother, Ichiro—Ichy." Nikko closed his eyes and took succor from Mitch's comforting presence, letting it seep into him. "I'd just gotten home from college—home is in Oregon, by the way—when I got the call to say he was in the hospital. I got on the first plane to New York."

It seemed like a lifetime ago.

Chapter Thirteen

Early June

NIKKO WENT up to the door where the nurse had directed him and pushed it open. There were two beds, one of which was occupied. Ichy lay beneath white sheets, his skin pale, his breathing uneven. An IV dripped into the tube that went to the crook of Ichy's arm. Nikko's gaze flickered to the monitor where he saw Ichy's heart rate and other vital signs. Okay, he knew shit about such things, but to his mind it looked like Ichy was doing okay. He took a breath at that point. Ever since the hospital had called him, he'd been balanced on a knife-edge. He'd gotten a little sleep during the flight from Portland to NYC, but he still felt like he was running on fumes.

"Nikko?" Ichy had turned his head in Nikko's direction, his eyes wide, his voice hoarse. "What are you doing here?"

Nikko walked over to his brother's bed and took his hand, squeezing it tight. "Well, when someone calls from a hospital to say my brother has been admitted, what do you think I'm going to do?" He smiled, although inside he was still wound up tight. He had so many questions, but Ichy didn't look up to answering them. "I got here as soon as I could." Only twenty-four hours had elapsed since the call, but it had seemed like the trip had taken forever.

When Ichy closed his eyes and tears leaked from beneath his lashes, Nikko's heart started hammering. "Hey." He dropped his backpack to the floor and sat on the edge of the bed, still holding Ichy's hand. "It's okay. I'm here now."

Ichy's eyes flew open. "I didn't want you to know about this!"

"Well, I do," Nikko responded practically, "so how about you tell me what's going on? And start by telling me what's wrong with you."

Ichy turned his head away. "That was the part I didn't want you to know about." Nikko was barely able to catch his whispered words.

It was so unlike his brother that Nikko was seized by stone-cold panic.

"Ichy, please, talk to me." He stroked Ichy's forehead and found it warm and damp with perspiration. Nikko looked around and saw a jug of water and a box of tissues. He grabbed a handful and sprinkled them with water, before dabbing Ichy's brow. "You can tell me anything, you know that." Ichy had been Nikko's rock while he'd been growing up, especially after their parents had died in a pileup on the freeway.

Ichy rolled onto his side to face him, his face more pallid than before. "They're treating me for a drug overdose," he whispered and then closed his eyes.

Nikko was unable to move. The notion that Ichy would take drugs was beyond him. Ichy wasn't like that. Ichy was….

Up on a pedestal.

Ichy's breathing grew shallower, and Nikko gazed in alarm at the monitor where his heartbeat was looking erratic. He let go of Ichy's hand and dove for the door, desperately scanning the hallway. "Nurse!"

A nurse poked her head around the corner and came running. She glanced at the monitor and left the room instantly, returning with medication. Once she'd injected a colorless liquid into the IV line, she checked Ichy's vital signs. Nikko was relieved when, after a few moments, Ichy's breathing became more even and his heartbeat dropped back down to near normal.

"Thank you." Nikko found himself breathing in sync with Ichy.

The nurse acknowledged his words with a quick smile and left the room.

Nikko retook his position on the bed and placed Ichy's cool hand in his.

"You still want to talk to me?" Ichy opened his eyes and met Nikko's gaze.

"Only if you're prepared to give me some answers." Nikko didn't look away. "What happened?"

Ichy took several deep breaths. "I'm not a drug addict, okay?" When Nikko nodded, Ichy relaxed a fraction. "I… maybe I smoked a little pot with one of my college friends, once or twice, but that was it. Anyway, I was with this friend, and he asked me to do him a favor. He wanted me to pick up a package for him, because he had a term paper to finish, and I was done with mine. He gave me the address, and I went to collect it."

Nikko gaped at him. "Did you at least ask him what was in the package?" When Ichy shook his head, Nikko's jaw dropped. "And you call *me* naïve?" A single tear slid down Ichy's cheek, and Nikko cursed himself silently. "When was this?" He pulled another tissue from the box and wiped Ichy's face.

"A-about six months ago."

Roughly about the time that Nikko had stopped receiving regular calls and texts.

"Go on." Nikko kept his voice steady and calm. Ichy didn't need to be more upset than he already was.

"I picked it up, no problem. The guy seemed nice and I didn't get a bad feeling or anything. But when I got closer to the campus, I… I was jumped by three or four guys, all bigger than me."

That wasn't difficult. Ichy was only an inch taller than Nikko, and just as slight.

Ichy shivered. "I think they were watching for me. Well, maybe not me, more like the package."

"Did they take it?"

Ichy nodded. "And they beat the shit out of me."

Nikko frowned. "Wait a minute. How would they know about the package? Surely they'd be watching your friend."

"Yeah, I wondered about that. I think he blabbed to someone he shouldn't have, and set me up to save his own scrawny neck. Anyway, when I got back to the dorm and told him what had happened, he seemed horrified. He got on his phone right away, and within half an hour, a black SUV pulled up outside the dorm, three men got out, and I got whisked away in it to someplace in the city." His breathing hitched. "This was the point I found out I'd just been robbed of a substantial amount of cocaine—and they wanted their money back."

Nikko stared at him, aghast. "Fuck, Ichy. How much money are we talking here?"

"That's just it, I don't know! Judging by the size of the package, it must have been a fuckload." A sob escaped Ichy. "I was so afraid. I had no idea what was going to happen to me. I mean, these were big, bruising guys, and scary as fuck. And that was *without* the guns they were all packing. Then their boss arrived, and man, this dude was like *ice*. He spoke really calmly, didn't even raise his voice once, but *fuck*, just listening to him, I wanted to shit myself." He gulped in air. "So, he told me he had a… proposition for me. They wanted their money, so I was gonna work for them."

Nikko's skin was cold. "Doing what?"

Ichy locked gazes with him, shaking. "Being their… delivery boy."

"Delivering drugs?" Nikko whispered. When Ichy nodded, his hand so cold in Nikko's, he wanted to reach around the tubes and wires and just hold his brother close. "Oh, my God, Ichy."

"What choice did I have? Especially when that cold bastard, Richards, tells me I have two options. Either I work for them, or—" He choked out a sob. "—or they get the money from someone else."

"Like who?" Nikko gaped at him incredulously.

"Grandma."

Nikko swore his heart skipped a beat. "Grandma doesn't have that kind of money. And how the hell did they know about her in the first place?"

Ichy's laugh was bitter. "Oh, bro, these guys knew *everything* about me. I swear they even knew where I shopped for toilet paper. But when he mentioned Grandma, that was when I got really frightened. She might not have that kinda money, but that wasn't why he talked about her. That was a warning, Nikko, clear as anything."

Now Nikko understood. "So you started working for them?"

Ichy nodded. "At first it was easy. They had me running all over the city, then the state. I thought this wasn't so bad. Okay, some days I had to skip classes because there was a schedule to keep to. Then it got heavier. I was being driven to the airport and put on a plane. They sent me all over the place. South America. Antigua. You name it, I got the stamp on my passport."

Nikko widened his eyes. "But, surely if you got caught carrying drugs…."

"I wasn't exactly carrying them." Ichy's face flushed. "Well, I suppose I was, only… internally."

His meaning registered and Nikko gasped. "Oh. My. God. Have you done this often?"

Ichy nodded glumly. "Never had a problem, until I got off a flight from Antigua, came back here and when they went to… remove the drugs, they discovered one of the condoms was leaking. So they got everything out of there, shoved me in a taxi, and sent me to the nearest hospital. When they did their tests here, it just looked like I was ODing."

"That's fucking serious!" Nikko was appalled. "You could have died!"

Ichy's hand tightened on his. "Keep your voice down!" he hissed. "I'm okay, all right? They gave me this stuff that absorbs the cocaine, as far as I can make out. They say I can be discharged tomorrow." His eyes focused on Nikko, large and wide. "Honest, Nikko, I'm okay. I'm just not feeling so good right now, but I'm not gonna die."

"I'm delighted to hear it." A dry voice from behind Nikko made him jump. He saw Ichy pale and turned to see the speaker. A tall, dark man in a dark gray suit stood inside the doorway, his gaze fixed on Ichy. Dark eyes too, almost black. "I came to see how you were doing, Mr. Kurokawa." Those cool eyes flickered as he glanced at Nikko. "This must be your brother Nikko." The man stretched his lips in a thin smile.

Nikko had no doubt who he was looking at. "Mr. Richards?" The guy had a faint British accent.

Mr. Richards gave a polite nod. "I see Ichiro has been speaking about me." His eyes flashed and Nikko felt Ichy's hand tremble in his. "We can talk about this another time. When you are discharged, I look forward to seeing you back at the club, Ichy. We have lots of work for you to do."

Nikko almost bounced up off the bed. "He can't. Just look at him. He needs to rest."

"Nikko, please," Ichy begged in a low voice.

He glared at Ichy. "You are in no state to work. You should be resting."

"Unfortunately, there is the not-so-small matter of a debt," Mr. Richards interjected. "To which has now been added the quantity that was lost during transit. Ichy has no choice." He walked over to Nikko and handed him a stiff white card. "Should you ever need to contact me," he said, that thin smile still in evidence. Then he gave Ichy a final nod. "I will see you at the club." He exited the room.

Nikko examined the card. "This is where you work from? The Black Lounge?"

Ichy nodded. "And now throw that thing in the trash, because you have absolutely no use for it."

"How much do you still owe him?"

Ichy groaned. "I don't know. I'm too scared to ask, because if it's some horrendous amount, I don't *wanna* know." He gulped. "And if I don't pay it back? I'm a dead man."

Nikko shivered. "So he was serious, then?"

Ichy became very still. "About what?"

"You needing to go back to work for him."

Ichy struggled to lift himself into a sitting position. "I know that look. Whatever you're thinking, forget it."

"What?" Nikko kept his face straight. "I don't know what you mean."

Ichy shook his head. "This is *my* mess, bro. I will be the one to fix things. And there is no *way* I am letting you get mixed up in any of this shit. I've already fucked up my life by being stupid and naïve—I'm not about to let you do the same. So you are gonna march right back to that airport, get on a plane, and fly back to Oregon." He coughed and his face flushed once more.

"Lie down," Nikko urged him. "You need to rest, remember?" He didn't like the strained look on Ichy's face. "I'll stay here until you fall asleep." He helped Ichy lie down and stroked his hand, hoping the action was soothing. Within a few minutes, Ichy's forehead smoothed out and he fell asleep. Nikko doubted his brother's physical condition was as cut and dried as he seemed to think. He gazed at Ichy's face, his thoughts in a whirl. Okay, so he'd been dumb to agree to collect the package, but what had resulted was hardly his fault. Nikko knew Ichy had acted to protect their grandmother. An elderly woman suffering from Alzheimer's, she'd gone into a retirement home where she was receiving the best care. She'd put both her grandsons through college and had provided for them. The last thing Nikko wanted was for her to be on the receiving end of threats.

And now Nikko had to figure out what to do next. There was no way he'd let Ichy shoulder the burden alone. There had to be something he could do to help his brother pay off his debt. He stared at the white card on the bed where he'd placed it, an idea forming.

Maybe Mr. Richards needed staff for the Black Lounge. Nikko was adamant that Ichy would not be delivering drugs any longer, but maybe the two of them could work in the club. He had three months until he started his master's degree. If it came to the worst, he'd see about deferring entry until Ichy was better. Maybe by Christmas the debt would be cleared.

Except I have no clue just how big that debt is. Will seven months be enough?

Just thinking about it made him feel nauseous.

The idea of leaving Ichy to pay off the debt—however much it turned out to be—on his own was unthinkable. This was a matter of honor. This was what families did when someone was in trouble. And right then Ichy needed him.

It was time to go talk with Mr. Richards.

Nikko waited until he was sure Ichy was sound asleep, and then he eased off the bed and left the room clutching his backpack. Outside the hospital, he hailed a taxi and gave the address on the card to the driver. As the cab sped through the busy streets, Nikko ignored the sights and sounds of New York City. He and Ichy had planned to spend time together that summer. Ichy had been looking forward to showing him around the city once their studies were over. Nikko couldn't think about that. All that consumed him was the idea of helping his brother out of a tight spot.

Tight? That had to be the understatement of the year.

The taxi pulled up in front of a classy looking restaurant. After paying the driver, Nikko got out and gazed up at the building. This had to be wrong. No one looking at the elegant frontage would have believed drug dealing took place behind the swanky facade. Then he reconsidered. Maybe that was the whole point.

A tall man dressed in black opened the glass door for him and offered to show him to a table. Nikko showed him the card and was directed to a staircase. On the second floor was a gay bar, but he knew from the doorman that he needed to head up one more floor to the dance club. When he got there, he was lost for a moment. There was no sign of Ichy's boss. The dance floor was packed with gyrating bodies, the music loud, pulsing through his feet.

"Can I help you?"

Nikko turned to find a burly security guard standing behind him. A glance at his own clothing told him why he'd attracted attention. In his jeans and T-shirt, with a backpack and his jacket over his shoulder, he certainly didn't look like the guys who were already dancing.

He held out the card. "I need to see Mr. Richards." When the guard raised his eyebrows, Nikko pushed on. "My name is Nikko Kurokawa. I met him a while ago, when he gave me this."

The guard spoke into a walkie-talkie, the words indistinct. After a moment he gave a nod. "Follow me." He led Nikko to the back of the club where another guard sat on a stool in front of a door. Nikko's guide gestured to him with a flick of his head. "To see the boss."

Nikko was shown into a long hallway, up a flight of stairs, until he found himself in an office, its walls painted red. Two men were there in deep discussion, and one of them was Mr. Richards. He didn't seem surprised to see Nikko.

"Mr. Kurokawa. What can I do for you?" He nodded to the other man. "Can you see that we're not disturbed?" The man nodded and left the room. Mr. Richards gestured to a chair across from a wide desk and then sat facing him.

"I want to help pay off Ichy's debt," Nikko blurted out as he sat in the chair. He didn't see any point in wasting time, and as a businessman, Mr. Richards would appreciate him coming to the point.

Mr. Richards arched his eyebrows. "Indeed. Are you fully aware of the terms involved?"

Nikko swallowed. "Ichy wasn't sure how much he still owed you. He didn't mention an amount." He waited with bated breath to hear the final amount.

"I engaged your brother to work for me until I was satisfied the debt had been paid. However, that was before the unfortunate incident following his last delivery. The debt has now increased." He fixed Nikko with a piecing gaze. "Are you prepared to carry on his delivery duties?"

Nikko shook his head. "Sorry, but I won't deliver drugs for you." He wouldn't be moved on that point. "Couldn't I work for you in the club?" Even as he said it, the reality of the situation sank in. *Working tables and tending bar—is that going to be enough to pay the man back?*

He was in the dark here, and it scared the shit out of him.

Mr. Richards observed him in silence for a moment. "I admire you, Nikko, for wanting to help your brother out like this, so here's what I'll do. Whatever he owes me at this point, I'll halve it. How does that sound?"

To Nikko's way of thinking, it sounded too good to be true. Mr. Richards didn't strike him as a kindly soul. "Better," he said cautiously. "But I still don't know how much we're talking about."

"Nor do you need to," Mr. Richards said, his eyes glinting. "All *you* need to know is it will take a great many hours working for me to pay it back."

"Working in the club or the bar? That's got to be a hell of a lot of hours." Forget about being free of debt by Christmas—this way, Nikko doubted he'd be done by *next* Christmas.

Mr. Richards smiled, and for some reason it sent a shiver down Nikko's spine. "Ah, but I have something very different in mind, a much more lucrative position where you would be able to pay off the debt in less time." He rose to his feet. "Come with me."

Nikko followed him through a door into a large open area with several couches placed around it. A hallway led off to the left, from which came the obvious, although muted, sounds of sex. Nikko stared. *Oh my God.* To the right was a huge window. Nikko walked over to it and froze. Behind the glass were several young men in various states of undress, some of them posing in front of it.

He turned to Mr. Richards. "What… what is this place?" Not that he didn't have a damned good idea already—the sound effects had seen to that.

"This is a very exclusive club." Mr. Richards gestured to the young men. "You would join them." He looked Nikko up and down, his eyes glittering. "I can think of several clients who would be *very* interested in making your acquaintance."

That was one way of putting it. Nikko was under no illusions about the club or what he would be expected to do. *But could I do it?* That part he wasn't so sure about. He didn't have a lot of sexual experience, and the thought of selling his body sent icy waves pulsing through him. *He hasn't even asked me if I'm gay.* Then he realized it wouldn't matter to the guys who would pay to fuck him.

That one thought made him shudder.

"How much do you love your brother, Nikko?"

Shit. *Talk about hitting me where it hurts.*

"Let me put it another way. I have an apartment here on the top floor, where you could both stay. Ichy would have a place to recuperate. You'd be together." Mr. Richards folded his arms across his chest. "And with your looks, that fragile quality about you, I'm certain you'd be able to pay off what Ichy owes me in a matter of months."

That brought Nikko down to earth. He was due to start his master's in September. There was no way he'd be able to do that if he did what Mr. Richards was suggesting.

Only it's not a suggestion, is it?

"I… I'm not sure I can do this."

Mr. Richards narrowed his eyes. "Let me put this in terms you will understand, Mr. Kurokawa. You have refused to deliver my drugs. Working in my club is the only way I will be able to recuperate my money. Therefore you have no choice in the matter."

Nikko's heart sank as reality bit hard. He swallowed. "When… when would you want me to start?"

Mr. Richards smiled. "Tomorrow seems ideal."

"Can I go back to the hospital and see Ichy?" Nikko knew the shit would really hit the fan when Ichy learned about this, but it wasn't like they had a choice here. He couldn't let Ichy carry this on his own. Maybe when he was feeling better, he could work in the club, help pay it off even quicker.

"No need." Mr. Richards got out his phone. "He's due to be discharged tomorrow. I'll have someone go to the hospital and bring him here. Are you staying anywhere?"

Nikko shook his head. "I went to the hospital straight from the airport."

"Excellent." Mr. Richards tapped his phone. "You can stay here tonight, and Ichy will join you tomorrow. You'll be very secure here." His white teeth gleamed. "I can guarantee that." He stared at Nikko. "So, do you agree?"

Nikko's heart pounded. "Why are you even asking? It's not like I have a choice, right?" He swallowed hard. "A matter of months, you said."

Mr. Richards said nothing, the same cool expression fixed on his face.

Nikko ignored the uneasy rolling in his gut. "Okay, I'll do it."

"Excellent." There was that thin smile again. "A verbal agreement. That will do." A security guard, tall and muscled, appeared from another doorway. "Randy will take you up to where you'll be staying, and then he'll show you our facilities. Don't worry about meals—we will take care of you while you're with us." He nodded to Randy. "This is Nikko. Take him to the suite." He gave Nikko one final chilling smile. "I think you'll fit in very nicely." With that he turned and left the room.

Nikko followed Randy, his heart pounding.

Why do I get the feeling I just made a big mistake?

Chapter Fourteen

Mitch was not a violent man. Sure, he had his moments when his anger seemed to bubble right below the surface, but he never acted on it. Right then? He wanted to kill that fucker Richards.

Nikko was quiet in his arms, all his energy clearly spent. Mitch held him close, his mind turning over and over everything Nikko had told him. At least he had all the answers to his questions—he just didn't like what he'd discovered. He couldn't help feeling anger toward Ichy, though he knew it hadn't been totally his fault. Wrong place, wrong time. He wasn't surprised at how Nikko had stepped in to help his brother. From what Mitch already knew of Nikko, the young man had a warm heart.

And right then, that warmhearted young man was in a mess.

Mitch couldn't stand back while Nikko was going through hell.

"What's to stop me walking out of here with you, right now?" His heart beat faster. "That's what we need to do—walk out that door, out of the club, and away from this place."

Nikko lifted his chin and regarded him with wide eyes. "You're kidding, right? Mitch, you're not thinking straight. For one thing, you really think they'll let you do that? How many security checks do you have to go through to get in here? And you think they'll just let you walk out with me?"

Mitch's stomach churned. He hated that Nikko was right.

"Let's not forget the next important point—Ichy. You imagine I'm going to leave him behind? And what would happen to him if I did?"

Mitch cursed himself for being a selfish bastard. He hadn't thought about Ichy.

"And the last point?" Nikko locked gazes with him. "They know all about my family. They know about Grandma. Richards as much as threatened her. I can't protect her if they go after her." He swallowed. "I love that you want to help me, but to be honest? I don't see a way out, I really don't."

Mitch pressed his lips to Nikko's head and kissed him. "Okay, okay." Nikko trembled against him. "You're right, I wasn't thinking clearly. It was just a knee-jerk reaction."

"I know," Nikko murmured into his chest. "But being hotheaded is not the answer. What kills me is I don't think there *is* an answer."

Mitch tightened his arms around Nikko. "Now you listen to me. I am going to get you out of here. I don't know how yet, but I'll think of something." He meant it with every fiber of his being. He couldn't bear the thought of Nikko being held in the club a moment longer. He had to do something.

Nikko's sigh was heavy. "There's nothing you can do." His words were laced with weariness. "I appreciate the thought, but—"

"You've got to think positive, sweetheart." Mitch kissed him again, this time on the forehead. "I promise, I'm not gonna rest until I come up with an idea." He lifted Nikko's chin and looked him in the eye. "I cannot let you go on with this. There *has* to be a way to get you out of here."

"Mitch. Richards is not going to let me go." His voice was patient, but underlying it was a tone that spoke of futility. It tore at Mitch's heart to hear Nikko so despondent, so devoid of all hope.

"Please, baby, don't give up yet." He held Nikko close, feeling his heart beating against Mitch's. "Just one thing. If you don't see me as much, it's because... well... I don't want you to think I'm avoiding you. It's just that I have a few... financial issues at the moment."

Nikko sat up abruptly, staring at him. "Because of me, right? Because you've been here so often." He pushed Mitch off him and climbed down from the bed. "God, I've been so stupid. I was so pleased to see you every time you turned up here, it never once crossed my mind that this must be costing you a fortune." He shook his head angrily. "I've been so selfish."

"Selfish?" Mitch sat up and grabbed him, pulling him back into his arms. "You are the least selfish man I have ever met. Look at what you've done for Ichy. Is that selfish? Hell, no." He focused on Nikko's sweet face. "You are a beautiful human being, Nikko Kurokawa, and I'm privileged to know you." He kissed him softly on the lips and held him, eyes closed, dismayed to feel tremors through Nikko's body. "Just hold on, Nikko, okay? Let me see what I can do." He'd find *something*, God help him, because the alternatives just didn't bear thinking about.

"Would you mind if we didn't...?" Nikko's voice tailed off.

Mitch opened his eyes and stared at him. "You think that's even crossed my mind? You're exhausted; I saw that as soon as you came through the door. I wasn't sure I'd get to see you, but Randy let me stay." He peered at Nikko's pale face. "Are they going to make you carry on working today? Because you look like you're about to fall down, baby."

Nikko gave him a faint smile, his first since he'd stepped through the door. "I like that, you know."

"What?" Mitch stroked his hair.

"You calling me baby."

Warmth surged through him. "Then I'll go right on using it." He paused. "We could lie on the bed and cuddle, but to be honest, I'd be happier if you went and got some sleep."

Nikko nodded. "Thanks, Mitch. Maybe next time, whenever that is."

Mitch silently cursed his financial situation. "I'll get back to you as soon as I can, and maybe then I'll have some news." He stood up and hugged Nikko. "Now you go to bed."

Nikko smiled. "Randy promised to make sure I got some sleep." Mitch led him toward the door, not surprised when it opened before they reached it. Randy stood in the doorway.

Mitch gave him a nod and turned to Nikko, cupping his face. "I'll be back, okay?" Not giving a damn about the security guard, Mitch kissed Nikko on the mouth, keeping it chaste but taking his time, reassured when Nikko put his arms around Mitch and returned the kiss. When they parted, Mitch gave Randy a hard stare. "You gonna make sure this young man gets to his bed?"

Randy smiled. "You can count on it." He glanced at Nikko. "Let's go."

Mitch watched Nikko walk away from him, turning once to give him a weary smile. Mitch wasn't fooled for a minute. Nikko didn't hold out any hope of him finding a solution.

Fuck it. If there's a way, I'll find it.

Mitch left the club, thankful he didn't run into Mr. Richards. By that point he felt sure he'd recognize the man if he saw him, and the way he was feeling, he'd probably end up getting arrested. Once outside in the warm July night air, he stood for a moment and took a few deep breaths. *What do I do now?*

It took only a couple of seconds to have him reaching for his phone. He had a few questions for someone. Mitch scrolled through his contacts and pressed Call, walking away from the restaurant as he waited for it to connect.

"Hey! I was beginning to think I wasn't gonna hear from you until September." Aaron spoke loudly over the noise of voices and music in the background. He was clearly out for the night.

"You got a minute?"

There was a pause and then everything got a little quieter. "Okay, I'm in the restroom. You okay?"

"Not really, no." Mitch drew in a lungful of air and went for the jugular. "Aaron, did you know the Black Lounge is part of a drug racket?"

The silence that followed was almost deafening.

"Shit. You did." Mitch clenched his fist.

Silence.

A thought began to fester in Mitch's brain. "Aaron, are you taking drugs?"

There was only the slightest hesitation before Aaron lurched into speech. "I never take them during a school week," he protested hurriedly. "Just the weekend. And it's not like I do drugs all the time, just now and then."

Fuck. Mitch fought hard to push down on his rage. It was men like Aaron who indirectly had put Nikko in such an abysmal situation. "You bastard. You let me go to that club, knowing what goes on there?"

"M-Mitch?" Aaron's voice shook.

"Why, Aaron? Why did you really take me there that night? And tell me the goddamn truth!"

Aaron sighed. "I owe them money. They said if I brought in new members, they'd reduce the amount."

The more Mitch heard about the club, the less he liked it. Then a thought occurred to him. "You told them all about me, didn't you?"

"Huh?"

"The night I went to become a member, that guy, Seb, he knew I taught English before I wrote down a word. He could only have gotten that from you. So you must have mentioned me."

"Yeah." Aaron sounded uncomfortable. "Seb... asked lots of questions, about my friends, my coworkers. He must've taken notes, I guess."

"You *guess*? Do you know what these people do with information like that? They fucking *threaten* people, you son of a bitch!"

"Fuck, Mitch, I'm... I'm sorry. I didn't know, all right?"

He could hear the teary edge to Aaron's voice, but right then, he really didn't give a fuck. "I don't want to hear it, okay?"

"How... how did you find out? About the drugs, I mean. 'Cause I can't see *you* taking drugs."

"Funny. Until just now, I'd have said the same thing about you," Mitch said in a clipped tone. "And it doesn't matter how I know." His rage was still boiling, even if some tiny, logical part of his brain told him that if it hadn't been for Aaron, Mitch would never have met Nikko. But the idea of Aaron doing drugs made him see his coworker in a whole new light. And he didn't like what he saw. He was glad he wasn't face-to-face with Aaron. Mitch's clenched fist was itching to connect with Aaron's jaw.

"We okay, Mitch?" He heard the cautious note in Aaron's voice.

Mitch was in no mood to make Aaron feel better, not after what he'd just learned. He gave a derisive laugh. "Good night, Aaron." He disconnected before Aaron could say another word. Right then Mitch didn't trust himself.

He stood on the street corner, oblivious to the crowds of people out enjoying their Friday night. All he could think about was Nikko and the money he owed those bastards at the club. There had to be something Mitch could do.

When the idea came to him, he dismissed it, but he couldn't shake it loose. Then he decided to go with it, because he was desperate enough to try anything.

Mitch hit speed dial and waited, hoping Gareth was home. When Gareth answered, his voice mellow and low, Mitch heaved a sigh of relief. "Hey, you got a minute?"

"For you? I'll be generous. You can have five." Gareth chuckled. "I'm kidding. It's Friday night, my plans for a museum in Decatur have just been approved, and I'm kicking back with a glass of wine. What can I do for you?"

"I know nothing's planned for Sunday, but do you think you could drive me up to Maine tomorrow? I… I need to see Mom and Dad about something." During the pause that followed, he surged on. "I can give you gas money." He just couldn't afford the bus fare or a plane ticket.

"You can stop right there," Gareth said gruffly. "It's okay. I know things are tight right now." He paused. "Has something happened?"

Mitch wanted to let it all spill out of him, right there and then, but he didn't dare. "I can't really talk about it now."

"Well, call Mom first, make sure they're home before we make any plans." Gareth snorted. "What am I saying? Like she wouldn't change plans if she knew her baby was coming to see her."

In spite of his worries, Mitch had to laugh. "I think I'm a little old to be her baby."

"Yeah, right. Call her, then call me when you know."

"So you're okay about this?"

Gareth chuckled once more. "Of course I am, you idiot. Now get off this phone so you can call Mom and make her day." He hung up.

Mitch took a moment before calling home to collect himself. He didn't intend to worry his parents, just let them think it was an impromptu visit. The reason for it could wait until he got there. The last thing he wanted was them worrying all night, so he'd keep the tone light and cheerful.

That's if I can actually do *light and cheerful right now.*

If he pulled this off, he'd deserve an Oscar.

GARETH PULLED up at the curb and stared at the two cars in the driveway. "Did you ask Mom to invite Deirdre and Monica?"

Mitch shook his head unhappily. "I didn't ask because I didn't want them to hear what's coming." *Shit.* His stomach roiled.

"It'll be fine," Gareth said, his voice soothing. "They love you, remember? And I'm assuming this is something to do with Nikko, since you hardly said a word to me all the way here. I figured you didn't want to repeat yourself."

"Yeah, but I hadn't counted on telling my sisters about it." It was bad enough that he was going to tell Mom and Dad.

"Are you two coming in the house or what?" Dad was standing on the front porch, looking vaguely amused.

"Bite the bullet, bro." Gareth patted Mitch's knee. "I'm here for you."

Mitch expelled a long breath and then inhaled slowly. "Thanks. Think I'm gonna need all the help I can get."

They got out of the car and made their way past the parked vehicles to the porch. Dad smiled at Mitch. "She was cursing your hide when you didn't turn up a few weeks ago. Not that you'd know it *now*, of course. *Now* she's all sweetness and light, and 'are they here yet?'"

"The fatted calf all trussed up and in the oven?" Gareth asked with a grin.

"Not helping," Mitch muttered under his breath, but his dad guffawed.

"Get in the house. Deirdre is making cocktails. She and Monica have come on their own, so it'll be quieter than the usual family clambakes."

Well, that was better than Mitch had anticipated. They entered the cool interior and he heard the tinkling sounds of a piano immediately. Mom was playing a Beethoven concerto. He stood still in the bright hallway and soaked it up as always—the smells, the sounds, the sight of Mom sitting at the gleaming Steinway, moving gently in harmony with the music. She glanced up and smiled widely, and a wave of love so intense crashed over him that Mitch was left shaken in its wake.

Mom was on her feet in an instant. "Mitch, are you okay?" She reached up to caress his cheek, her touch light, her eyes troubled. "You looked so odd for a moment there."

He gave her a warm hug. "I'm fine," he lied. "It's just good to be home." He held on to her for a minute, her head barely up to his shoulder. When he was himself again, he released her and glanced at his sisters. "Hey. Didn't think I'd be seeing you here." Mom patted his arm and disappeared in the direction of the kitchen.

Deirdre grinned as she poured out a cocktail. "You think Mom was going to let you come up here and not see all of us? Yeah, right." She walked over to him and handed him the glass. "I made you a Manhattan. You like those, don't you?"

Mitch ignored the glass and kissed her on the cheek. "It's good to see you too." He took the drink and sipped it. "Wow. I'm impressed. It's perfect. Just the right amount of cherry juice."

Deirdre buffed her fingernails on her blouse. "I remembered how you liked them that Christmas when we had an evening experimenting." Her eyes twinkled.

Mitch snorted. "That's one way of putting it. All I can recollect about that Christmas is the hangover from hell."

Monica came up to him and kissed his cheek. "Glad you made it." She gave him a whack to the arm, fortunately not the one holding the cocktail glass.

"Ow! What was that for?" Mitch demanded, glaring.

"That's for being late. Sunday family lunch was two weeks ago." Monica glared right back at him.

"Leave your brother alone," Mom admonished, coming back into the living room with plates of nibbles. "He's here now, and that's the main thing. Now sit down, all of you, and let's enjoy some cocktails." She peered at Deirdre who was pouring out another Manhattan. "I take it you're staying the night?" she said dryly.

Deirdre rolled her eyes. "Yes, Mom. I'm not going to drive tonight." She flashed Mitch a grin.

"Where's my cocktail?" Dad was behind him. "Did anyone think to make their poor old dad a cocktail?"

Deirdre sighed and handed him the glass. "Here, have this one. Anything for a quiet life." Her gaze met Mitch's and she winked.

Mitch laughed. He knew the mood would change once he started talking, but right then he was happy to be back with his family. He sat on the big couch under the window and took a long sip of his Manhattan. He figured the alcohol might have a calming effect on his insides.

Gareth sat next to him, Monica at the far end. Mom and Dad were in their armchairs by the fireplace, and Deirdre was on the smaller couch facing Mitch. Dad gazed at his family and let out a contented sigh. "I do love it when we're all together. I'm just sorry Shaun and Eric couldn't be with us."

"It was a last minute thing, Dad," Monica said. "You'll see them in August." She peered at Mitch. "Actually, there was something I wanted to ask you, but it can wait." She held up her glass. "To family."

Her words echoed around the living room as everyone copied her action. Mitch was grateful for the warmth that spread through his belly. In spite of the hot summer evening, his skin felt cold as he anticipated the conversation to come.

"So, anyone met your eye yet, Mitch?" Deirdre asked innocently. "Did you follow my advice?"

His dad groaned. "For God's sake, Mitch hasn't even been in the house half an hour and already you're on about his love life. If he'd found someone, he'd tell us. Right?" He looked to Mitch for confirmation.

Gareth leaned closer. "I do believe that was your cue," he said quietly.

Mitch leaned forward. "I… I need to talk to you all." He took a drink; his mouth had dried up. His heartbeat sped up and breathing became a chore. He'd intended to wait until later, but Gareth was correct—the timing seemed perfect.

Mom straightened. "Something *is* wrong. I knew it." She stared at him, the lines across her forehead more pronounced than ever. "What is it?" His dad put down his glass and studied him.

Mitch cursed himself for making them worry. They didn't need this, for God's sake. They'd been through all the worrying that accompanied being parents. "You know what? I… nothing." He drained his glass, wincing as the whiskey burned the back of his throat. He held out the empty glass to Deirdre. "Can I get another of these, please?"

"Sure." She frowned. "You okay, Mitch?" Deirdre got up and walked over to the bar in the corner where Dad kept all the liquor.

"Mitch." Gareth's hand was at his lower back. "It'll be okay. Just tell them."

Mitch hung his head. "You have no idea what I'm about to say, so how can you know that?" He glanced at his brother. "You don't know the whole story." His chest tightened.

"Fair enough, but I know our family. Leap of faith, bro."

"Mitch?"

He raised his head and gazed at his dad.

"Start at the beginning, son. That's usually the best way." Dad's smile was sympathetic.

Deirdre came over to him and handed him another glass. "And here's some lubrication for your throat," she whispered.

Mitch took it gratefully and nodded. He could do this.

For the next fifteen or twenty minutes, he talked. He told them everything, leaving out the details they had no business knowing. He was conscious of how quiet the house was. No one asked a question, no one commented. They simply listened, and with each passing minute, Mitch grew more and more nervous. His palms were clammy and yet he felt so hot, though that might have had something to do with the two

Manhattans he'd downed. When he got to where he'd left the club the previous night, he sagged into the couch and awaited the interrogation.

He didn't have to wait long.

"I can't believe this of you." Monica's expression was grim. "How can you sit there and tell us all so calmly that you went to a *brothel*?"

Mitch stared at her. "You think I'm calm?" He struggled to breathe evenly. "And it's not like I knew where he was taking me. I didn't know."

"Then you should have turned and run out of that… place when you realized!" Her eyes were wild. "How could you have stayed there? Worse, how could you have paid to have sex with a prostitute?" She shook her head. "I have always looked up to you, admired you, but this…."

Bile rose in Mitch's throat, and he swallowed it back down with a grimace. He hadn't expected total acceptance, but *fuck*, this hurt. "I couldn't leave once I'd seen Nikko. There was just something about him."

"I really don't get where you're coming from, you know that?" Monica glared at him. "What you did makes no sense. You risked everything, and for what? For some *criminal*?"

"Whoa, hold on there." Gareth stared across the room at his sister. "I think you're being a bit harsh here. I was just as shocked as you when I heard about this."

Monica's mouth fell open. "How long have you known about this?"

Gareth set his jaw. "A few weeks, but that doesn't change a thing. Weren't you listening? Nikko's not doing this out of choice, is he?"

"You know, I can't help agreeing with Monica a little," Dad interjected.

Mitch's heart sank, and he put his head in his hands.

"Wait a minute, let me finish. I'm more concerned about the practical implications. What if you'd gotten arrested? What if you lost your job? Mitch, you're playing with your future here."

"Dad, I said exactly the same thing," Gareth said quietly.

Mitch couldn't look at any of them. *They're so disappointed in me.* The silence that ensued cut into him, leaving him feeling raw.

A smothered sob broke the silence. Mitch raised his head to find Deirdre staring at him with wet eyes. "That poor boy. Mitch, that just about broke my heart." She shook her head. "That's just… wrong." Deirdre wiped her eyes on the paper napkin from her plate and stared defensively at the others. "Well, Gareth is right. It's not like Nikko chose to do… that, is it? He's in real trouble."

Mitch gave her a grateful glance. It was good to know someone else in his family had his back.

"You love him, don't you?"

Mitch jerked his head up to gaze at his mom.

She smiled. "I'm not going to say it's too soon or anything like that. You're old enough to know your own mind by now." She tilted her head. "But you do, don't you?"

He'd just bared his soul; the least he could do was take one more step. "Yeah, I do," he admitted. "Not that I've told Nikko. That can wait until he's out of there."

"Why are you here, Mitch?" His dad's voice was thoughtful and quiet.

"Sir?"

"I don't think you came all this way to get all this off your chest. You came here for a reason. I'm just curious as to what that reason might be."

Mitch took a deep breath. "I can't sit by and do nothing, Dad. I have to get him out of there."

"I can understand that," Dad said slowly, "but I have an inkling you have something specific in mind."

He nodded. "I… I want to pay off his debt. Not that I have any idea how much that is, but I know it's more money than I have right now. So I…." He couldn't continue. The previous night it had seemed logical. In the light of day, sitting in his parents' living room, it felt like the worst idea in the history of bad ideas.

"Did you want to ask us for money, son?"

Mitch stared at his dad, his heart hammering. "Y-yes, sir."

Dad smiled. "Did you think I'd be shocked? After what I've just heard? Hell, you're in love. People in love have the craziest ideas. I should know. I remember how I was when I first met your mother." He sat forward and fixed his gaze on Mitch. "I understand that you need to get him away from that club and these people, but you're looking at this situation from the wrong angle, Mitch. Suppose you do get him out of there. Suppose by some miracle this Mr. Richards agrees to let go of his little cash cow. What about the others? There may well be young men working in that club by choice, but what about those who aren't?" He shook his head. "Getting Nikko out of there isn't the answer. You need to get that cesspit closed down, and the only way to do that, son, is by going through the proper authorities. You have to take this to the police." He sat back and took a sip of his Manhattan.

Mitch regarded him in silence for a moment. "You're right, of course. I can't think why I—"

His dad laughed. "Oh, *I* sure can. You love Nikko, and you're worried about him. This was the first thing to come into your head, right?" Mitch nodded, and Dad smiled. "See, I get that. You're just not thinking straight right now."

"Uh, Dad? He's gay. He doesn't think straight, *ever*," Deirdre said with a chuckle. Mom giggled and Gareth stifled a snort.

"I can't believe you'd put us all in danger like this," Monica muttered.

"What the hell?" Gareth gaped at her. "What are you talking about?" Deirdre murmured something similar.

Monica set her jaw. "Were none of you listening? These people are dangerous. If they can find out about Nikko's grandmother, they can find out about our family too. It'd be easy. If Mitch goes to the police and they find out, what's to stop them taking their revenge on us?"

Deirdre's jaw dropped. "Okay, you've been reading way too many thrillers."

"Now wait a minute." Monica bristled. "I'm entitled to my opinion, same as you. I don't like what's happened to Nikko any more than you do, but I'm being realistic. It's not like we even know him and—"

"Monica, sweetheart? You need to hush now."

Monica snapped her mouth shut and looked at her mom.

Mom smiled. "The whole idea of Mitch going to the police and getting that boy out of there is so one day you *will* know him. How foolish do you think you'll feel, recalling this conversation, the first time you meet your future brother-in-law?"

Mitch gasped and Mom turned to regard him, her eyes wide. "Well, I'm right, aren't I? Isn't that what you want?"

Mitch was dumbfounded.

Dad laughed. "This is why I love you, Valerie Jenkins. You always say exactly what is on your mind." He met Mitch's gaze. "First thing Monday morning, go to the police. Tell them everything you know."

"What—including the fact that he paid a prostitute for sex?" Gareth sat up. "What if they arrest him? He'd be admitting it; he wouldn't have a leg to stand on."

"Maybe that's for Mitch to decide," Mom said quietly. "It depends how important Nikko is to him."

Mitch hadn't considered that scenario. "Important enough." He didn't want to think about the repercussions, not then anyway.

Monica scoffed. "Yeah, good luck with that. I've heard about the NYPD. They're one of the worst in the US."

"I think you've said enough for one night," Mom said firmly. Monica opened her mouth to retort but apparently thought better of it. She sat back, her face flushed.

Mitch sighed. "Monica has a point, but I have a friend who's a cop. I was planning on telling her and see what she advises." He glared at Monica. "And I resent the remark about the NYPD."

"Me too," Gareth added. "It's just unfortunate that the ones doing their job badly always get more press than the ones doing everything right."

Dad cleared his throat. "Whatever you decide, you'll keep us informed?"

He smiled at his Dad. "Yes, sir, I promise."

"I don't know about anyone else, but I'm starving." Gareth patted his belly. "What's for dinner?"

Mitch wanted to hug him for that. He gave Gareth a half smile and relaxed a little as the talk turned to what Mom had prepared for dinner. It wasn't long before the conversation was a whole lot calmer. He let the comments and laughter flow over and around him. His thoughts were of Nikko.

I'll get you out of there.

He'd given his promise.

Chapter Fifteen

MITCH STUFFED his toiletries into his backpack and had one last look around the bedroom to make sure he hadn't missed anything. Gareth was ready to drive back to the city and as usual they'd left it as late as possible. At least there was no school tomorrow. The weeks were flying by; it would be September before he could blink.

"Hey." Monica stood in the doorway. "You got a minute?" She bit her lip. "That's if you're still speaking to me."

Mitch stiffened. "I'd have thought it was more the other way around." Monica had been quiet throughout the previous night's dinner and all through Sunday. They hadn't talked much, which was unusual. Mitch was sickened to think the whole Nikko business had come between them. She was entitled to her opinion. The only thing was, Monica was never one for keeping her opinions to herself.

Her face fell. "Look, I'm sorry, okay? I shouldn't have flown off the handle like that. I was lying awake all night, thinking about it."

God, he was *so* tempted to say *Good*. The hurt she'd inflicted was still there, although muted. But it wasn't him. "Since when have I ever held grudges?" Besides, he needed all the goodwill he could lay his hands on.

"We-ell, there *was* that time when you were eight and I—"

"Mon."

She smiled. "Just kidding." Her expression grew more serious. "But I meant it when I said I'd been thinking about it. I know it must be a scary thought, telling the police about… what you were doing. But couldn't you do a deal? You know, give them all the information you have on the place in return for immunity from prosecution? They do that all the time on *Law & Order*."

Mitch had to smile at that. "Thanks, Mon. I'm sure Donna will have some ideas."

"Your cop friend?" He nodded. "Well, that's good." She bit her lip, stepped into the room, and pushed the door shut behind her.

That got his attention straight away. "Everything okay?"

She did a seesawing motion with her hand. "You going to be here in August?"

"Probably." Right then he couldn't see past Monday. He gazed at his sister with interest. She shifted from one foot to the other, seemingly unable to keep still. "Monica, what is it?"

Monica sat down on the bed, staring at the rug. "I was hoping you could find time to have a talk with Cal."

Mitch stared. "Why, what's wrong? Is he okay?" It wouldn't be long before his nephew would be leaving for college.

Slowly she raised her head to look at him directly. "Remember I said last month that he hasn't got a girlfriend?"

He frowned. "Uh, yeah." Then the penny dropped. "Hoo boy. Are you telling me what I think you're telling me?"

Monica gave a weak laugh. "I guess some things do run in families." She swallowed. "I don't know what to say to him."

He gave her another hard stare. "What is there to say? If he brings a boy home, you treat him exactly as you'd treat a girlfriend. You sit them down, feed them, ask how they met, you know, regular shit like that." He cocked his head. "You don't have a problem with Cal being gay, do you?" He didn't think it likely. He'd have noticed something while they were growing up.

"No, not at all," she returned swiftly. "It's just... well, what if he has questions?"

Mitch smiled. "I think if he has questions, he'll go to someone more knowledgeable than his mom."

She nodded enthusiastically. "Exactly what I was thinking. Like, maybe, his gay uncle."

He sighed. "I was thinking more of someone nearer his own age. There'll most likely be a group he can join at college." One look at her anxious expression was enough to make him continue. "But sure, I'll talk with Cal. If he wants that," he stressed.

Monica beamed. "Thanks, Mitch. I'm really grateful."

"Save your gratitude. Just make sure that boy knows you love him no matter what, you got that?"

"I got it." She rose to her feet. "Oh, and Gareth says will you hurry the bleep up." She grinned. "I'm paraphrasing, of course."

He laughed. "Then we'd better go find Mr. Impatient, hadn't we?" He grabbed his backpack and followed her from the room. The rest of the family was in the kitchen, saying their good-byes to Gareth.

His brother gave him a hard stare. "You do want to get back to New York tonight, right?"

"Oh hush." Mitch hugged his mom. "Thank you, as always."

She smiled up at him. "I'll expect to see you next month, only come prepared to stay longer than a night, all right? We'll probably have a house full, but we can always find room for you. There's the cottage if things get too crowded around here."

He kissed the top of her head. "I promise, I'll be here." Mitch extended a hand to his dad but was pulled into a gruff hug.

"Keep us in the loop, son," Dad said into his ear. "And don't forget what you have to do tomorrow."

Like he could forget. "Sure. I'll call my friend first thing in the morning." The prospect of telling Donna what had been going on filled him with trepidation. It got a little easier each time he told the tale, but this was different.

How do I tell my cop friend that I've been breaking the law?

He didn't want to think about the way she might look at him.

"Are we ready yet?" Gareth said with a sigh. "We need to go. According to my phone, traffic is heavy. There's still roadwork on 95 and 495."

Mitch hugged his sisters and followed Gareth to the car. He stood for a moment on the street, breathing in the sweet air and the peace.

"You'll be back soon enough."

He smiled. "Yeah, I know. I'm just enjoying it while I can." After seeing part of its seedy underbelly, the luster of New York was wearing pretty thin.

"Here's a nice thought for you," Gareth said as he unlocked the car and they climbed in. "Imagine bringing Nikko here."

The idea made him stop dead. "Wow," he said softly.

Now there was a goal.

DONNA STARED at her empty coffee cup. "Wow. I'm not sure what to react to first—the 'Guess what, Donna, I've been to a brothel' part, or the 'I'm in love with a hooker' part, or maybe it's the 'I need your help' part." She huffed. "You want to help me out a little here, Mitch?"

Shit. "I couldn't tell you," Mitch said quietly. "It's not the sort of thing you share with a friend who happens to be a cop. And I never intended to go looking for it."

"But you sure as hell found it." She raised her chin and stared at him. "When you knew what sort of a place Aaron had taken you to, why didn't you leave, there and then?"

"Great. First Gareth, then Monica, now you. I was going to," Mitch protested, "but then I saw Nikko, and—"

"Yeah, yeah, I got that part." She sighed. "Okay. You ready?"

Mitch frowned. "Ready?"

She nodded and rose to her feet, dropping some bills on the table. "Yup. You're coming with me to my precinct. That's what you want to do, right?" He nodded, swallowing. Donna smiled. "Well, then, let's get a move on. I'm not letting you go there on your own." She chuckled. "You have no idea, do you? Do you know how long you'd sit there, just waiting for someone to come speak to you? And besides, some of the detectives are real sons of bitches." She laughed when Mitch gaped at her. "I can say that, honey, I get to work with them. But there are a few good ones. I'll get you to talk to Andy Farrio. He's a damn good detective."

"Thanks, Donna. I owe you." The churning in his belly eased up a little.

"I'll stay with you while you give them a statement." She cocked her head. "You sure you want to put your hand up to paying Nikko for his services? Because if they decide to press charges, I—"

Mitch rose swiftly and placed a finger to her lips. "It's okay, I have thought about this, but I'd rather not think about it right now. Let's just see what happens, all right?"

He pulled back his hand and she nodded. "You're nervous. Understandable under the circumstances. Now, I know this is my day off, but do you want me walking in there wearing my uniform?" She patted his arm. "Would that make you feel less nervous?"

Mitch snorted. "You know what? I think I can manage without that."

They left the coffeehouse and took the F line to Lexington Avenue and 63rd Street. Mitch knew Donna worked out of the 19th precinct. When they came up out of the subway and walked up to 67th Street, his heart was pounding. He was scared to death of the repercussions, but the thought of doing nothing was plain selfish.

Nikko needed him.

When they arrived at the precinct, Mitch stared up at the redbrick and tan four-story block building and swallowed. Donna patted him on the back.

"I'm right here with you, remember? It'll be okay."

He nodded, and they walked under the arch into the precinct. The reception area was comprised of a large space with a long chest-high counter across one side. People sat on benches facing the desk. There were two or three officers on duty, chatting with each other. One of them caught sight of Donna and grinned.

"You can't keep away, huh?"

Donna smiled. "Yeah, that's me, Frank, a slave to my job. Can you do me a favor? Call up to Vice and see if Detective Farrio is available?"

He nodded. "Sure. Wanna take a seat while I find out?"

She smiled and guided Mitch to an empty bench. When they were seated, Mitch regarded her keenly. "Vice?"

Donna shrugged. "Yeah, Andy works Vice. You got a problem with that? I figured he'd be a good one to talk to."

"You're right, I suppose."

She smiled. "Just as long as you don't expect them to go in tomorrow, all guns blazing. It doesn't work like that."

Mitch snickered. "Yeah, I did know that. But at least if I tell them, I'll know I've done something to help him."

Donna gazed at him, her eyes wide. "Wow. You really do love this guy, don't you?"

Before Mitch could answer, a voice called out from the stairs. "Hey, Donna! Don't you ever take a day off?"

"Bite me," she replied with a sweet smile. "Andy, this is Mitch Jenkins, a good friend of mine. You need to hear what he has to tell you."

Andy Farrio was tall with short, black hair, pale blue eyes, and a very firm handshake. He gave Donna a speculative glance and turned his attention to Mitch. "Pleased to meet you. Come with me and we'll find a place to talk."

"Okay, sure." Mitch and Donna followed the detective up the stairs until they reached the third floor. Andy led them into a small room with a single window covered in wire mesh, a table, and three or four chairs around it. A writing pad and pen lay on the table. Andy gestured to one side and they sat. Mitch's pulse was racing and his chest was constricted. When he felt Donna's hand on his leg, just resting there, he took a couple of deep breaths. She smiled encouragingly at him.

Andy shoved the pad and pen across the table toward Mitch. "Can you write down your full name, address, and contact details, please?" He handed him the pen.

"Sure." Mitch did as instructed. When he'd finished, he put down the pen.

"Okay—Mitch, yeah?—tell me why you're here." Andy relaxed in his chair, his gaze focused on Mitch.

Slowly, with a lot of hesitation at first, Mitch told him everything he knew about Nikko, Ichy, the club, Richards, anything he felt was relevant. When he mentioned the brothel, Andy opened up the writing pad and began taking notes, nodding now and again. Sometimes he'd stop to ask a question or two, his expression neutral. When Mitch paused, his throat dry, Andy cocked his head.

"You need some water?"

Mitch nodded gratefully. "That would be good, yeah." Andy left the room and Mitch turned to Donna. "How am I doing?" He felt hot and nervous in the small interview room.

"You're doing great," she reassured him. "And there's not much more to tell, right?"

He nodded again, straightening when Andy reentered the room with two glasses of water. He placed them on the table and grinned at Donna. "I figured with this heat, you'd need one too."

She smiled and took a drink. The pink on Donna's cheeks distracted Mitch for a moment, and he resolved to question her later. He took a long swig of water, which cooled him down a little.

"So, is that everything?" Andy asked, taking up his pen once more.

"I think so."

"What about this coworker who took you to the club? You haven't mentioned his name."

Mitch hesitated. He'd fully intended on sharing that information, but he wasn't sure of his motivation. He wasn't a vindictive man, even if Aaron had royally pissed him off. "Do you need to know that?"

"Not now," Andy told him. "But there may come a point later if we do something with this information." He leaned back. "Okay, well, if that's all, thank you for coming forward."

Mitch stared in surprise. "That's… that's it?"

"For the moment, yes. If we investigate this further, we may want to interview you again."

"If?" Mitch clenched his fists unseen under the table. "I've just told you that there's a brothel where they're not only holding a couple of men against their will, but they're also running drugs, and you say *if* you investigate?"

"Mitch, honey, you need to calm down." Donna's voice was firm.

Andy nodded, not taking his eyes off Mitch's face. Those blue eyes were cool. "Maybe you should listen to Donna, Mitch, because that's good advice. I get that you're a little… overwrought right now, but you really don't want to piss me off, okay?" He enunciated every word clearly.

"But…." Mitch inhaled deeply, the sharp intake of air making him dizzy. He took a few seconds to collect himself before regarding Andy in dismay. "I… I wanted to go back to Nikko and tell him something was being done about this."

Andy frowned. "Go back…. Mitch, I'm telling you in the strongest possible terms *not* to go back to that club. You got that? You *stay away*."

"Yes, sir." Mitch did his best to meet Andy's gaze.

"I mean it," Andy said, more forcefully. "Right now I only have your statement that you've visited the club. If you go back and the police raid the place while you're there, that's it. That's evidence. And besides that, you have nothing to tell Nikko." He leaned forward. "Am I making myself clear?"

"Perfectly." Mitch maintained eye contact.

Andy studied him for a moment and then gave a nod. "Okay. Well, if that's everything…."

"It is," Donna said, rising to her feet and pulling Mitch up with her. "Thanks, Andy."

"Thanks for coming in, Mitch." Andy extended his hand and Mitch shook it. "I'll show you guys out." He picked up his notes from the table and walked with them to the top of the stairs. "You know where you're going from here, right?" he said with a wink to Donna.

"Oh, I might." She grinned at him and took hold of Mitch's arm to lead him down the stairs. Mitch went with her in a daze.

Donna glanced at him as they reached the first floor. "You okay, Mitch?"

He shrugged. "I guess I didn't expect to be walking out of here. I thought they'd arrest me."

Donna regarded him closely for a moment. Then she led him by the arm into a small room off the reception area. Once inside she closed the door behind them and indicated a chair. Mitch sat, perplexed. Donna sighed. "Sorry, but we couldn't talk out there. Anyone might have been listening." She gazed at him, rubbing the back of her neck with her hand. "Okay, this is only my opinion, so don't quote me on it, all right?" He nodded and she continued. "Yes, solicitation is a crime, but typically, we don't charge customers unless they solicit an undercover agent. You came here of your own free will, so it's unlikely they'd charge you."

"But why?" Mitch raked his fingers across his scalp. "Not that I'm complaining, you understand. I just… don't get it."

She lowered her voice. "In order to charge someone with a crime, we'd need a confession *and* corroboration, however slight, to prove it. So if they went ahead and closed the place down, unless there are records with your name on them, or unless Nikko admits you paid him for sex, we wouldn't have the second element."

"But…." Mitch let out a heavy sigh. "There would be evidence. I'm a member of the club. They have all my details."

Donna stared at him for a moment before speaking. "I did not hear that, okay? And I think you should just wait and see what happens. If something does go down, I can't see them wanting you as a witness, but like I said, that's just my opinion. All you've done so far is give them information that you learned from Nikko." She patted his knee. "So stop panicking. You've done everything you could."

It didn't feel like he'd done nearly enough.

"Andy was right about one thing, though." She speared him with an intense gaze. "Don't go back there. You got me?"

"Sure," he responded quickly. "Can we go now?" He tried to stand, but she caught hold of his arm.

"Mitch." There was a warning note to her voice. "Promise me."

Shit. "I… I can't do that, Donna, and don't ask me to." He couldn't look her in the eye.

After a moment she sighed. "What am I going to do with you?"

"You could try taking me to lunch." He hadn't felt like eating that morning; he'd been too nervous.

She snorted. "Subtle. Okay, how about brunch? There's Alice's Tea Cup on 64th." She rose to her feet, pulling him with her.

"Sounds good. And while we're eating you can tell me how long you've had the hots for Andy Farrio." He smirked.

Donna gaped. "Shit, how did you...?" She schooled her features instantly. "Okay, you know what? I'm gonna plead the fifth." She strode out of the precinct, waving to the officer behind the desk. Mitch had to jog to keep up with her.

Maybe a little brunch and talking with a friend seemed trite compared to what Nikko was going through, but Mitch needed some respite. Besides, he knew in his heart Donna was right. He'd done everything he could. All he could do now was keep Nikko's spirits up and help him not to lose hope.

Because there had to be some hope on the horizon.

Chapter Sixteen

NIKKO EXITED the downstairs bathroom and went into the kitchen area, a towel wrapped around his hips. He stopped dead at the sight of Ichy making a sandwich. "Hey, I don't often see you down here." He walked over to the sink to get a glass of water.

Ichy sliced the sandwich in two and placed it on a plate. "Yeah, well, there's a reason for that." His face flushed. "I… I just don't like to see you walk through that door." He pointed out toward the floor.

Nikko sat at the table and stared at his brother. "Why?"

Ichy rubbed at his neck below the neckband of his T-shirt. "Look, when you walk through the door of our room, I can pretend, okay? You could have been playing cards with someone, or watching TV, or any number of activities. But when I see you come through *that* door—" His Adam's apple bobbed. "—I know that someone just fucked you and that was my fault."

Nikko's heart sank. "Ichy… it was my choice to come here, all right?"

"But you wouldn't have had to *make* that choice in the first place if I hadn't fucked up!" Ichy wailed.

Nikko was out of his chair in a heartbeat. He threw his arms around Ichy and held him tightly. "Listen to me," he whispered. "You need to stop beating yourself up about this. What's done is done. We need to focus on getting through this and getting out of here." Ichy didn't need to know about the feelings of hopelessness and resignation that filled him.

Ichy wasn't the only one who could pretend.

His brother sagged in his arms, and Nikko was dismayed to feel hot tears on his cheek. "I'm sorry. It's just so difficult to think like that, when all I feel is that he's never gonna let us go."

Nikko closed his eyes, as if that would shut out the thought. No such luck.

"Nikko?"

Damn it. Randy.

He sighed. "Ichy? I have to go."

Ichy stiffened and pulled away, wiping his eyes. "Sure. I'm going upstairs to eat my sandwich. Not that I feel hungry anymore." He picked up the plate and walked away without a backward glance.

With a heavy heart, Nikko turned to face Randy. "Ready. Sorry about that."

Randy's smile was sympathetic. "S'okay." He led the way out into the couch area, Nikko behind him.

Nikko suppressed the usual sigh of relief when they didn't go toward the Red Room. He saw far too much of that room as it was. Randy paused at the door to playroom five and regarded him, his expression neutral. "When you're ready to leave, don't be surprised if I don't turn up right away like I usually do, okay?" Nikko frowned and opened his mouth to ask what was up, but Randy put a finger to his lips. "I've got to be careful."

Before Nikko could ask what he meant, Randy opened the door and let him into the room.

"Hey there, beautiful."

A feeling of lightness suffused Nikko's body, and he lurched eagerly into Mitch's waiting arms. Mitch held him so close he felt the beat of his heart. Nikko buried his face in Mitch's chest and inhaled the familiar scent of soap and the musky aroma that was pure Mitch.

Mitch kissed the top of his head. "It's okay, I'm here. I've got you."

Nikko raised his chin to meet Mitch's warm gaze. "I didn't think I'd see you so soon."

Mitch laughed softly. "I only stayed away a week. I don't think I could've gone longer than that without seeing you." He stroked Nikko's cheek. "How are you?"

Nikko couldn't repress the shiver that coursed through him. "I've become very... popular." He wasn't imagining how Mitch's body stiffened at his words. He stared into those deep brown eyes. "Are you all right?"

"I'm fine," Mitch said with a slight nod. "I... I missed you."

His words sent Nikko's heart soaring. "I've missed you too."

"But I can't stay long," Mitch added. "Not this time."

Nikko swallowed down his disappointment. "Can we... would you just hold me?" He was so tired of being used by guys who only saw him as a hole to be filled, a body to be manhandled. Right then all he wanted was a little intimacy. Mitch wasn't there to cuddle, he knew that, but it didn't mean they couldn't start off with a little snuggling.

To his surprise, Mitch smiled. "That sounds perfect." He released him and took his hand to lead him to the bed. Mitch stretched out and held his arms wide. Nikko joined him and cuddled up against that firm, warm body, his head on Mitch's chest. They lay like that for a while, Mitch gently stroking up and down his back, saying nothing. Nikko rubbed Mitch's belly and chest in slow circles, enjoying the feel of solid flesh beneath his fingertips.

It *was* perfect.

"Okay, I need to tell you something."

Nikko paused. "Okay," he said slowly.

"I went to the police. I told them everything."

He gulped. "Seriously?" He fell silent for a minute. "What did they say?"

Mitch's sigh expanded his chest. "Thank you for dropping by? I guess it's up to them now." He tightened his arm around Nikko. "But at least I've done something. Don't give up hope, baby."

Nikko shifted to lie on top of Mitch, cradling Mitch's head in his hands. "Thank you for doing that much." He moved closer and kissed Mitch's lips, keeping the kiss chaste. Then he pulled back and smiled.

Mitch smiled too. "Oh, I think we can do better than that." He cupped Nikko's face in those large, strong hands and brought him close once more. They kissed, a series of sweet, lingering kisses, and Mitch pressed his lips to Nikko's cheeks, forehead, nose, and chin before returning to his mouth. There was no pressure to do anything else, and Nikko was glad of it. Making out with Mitch was exactly what he'd needed. The club faded into the background and Nikko felt safe. They could have been two lovers idling away a rainy afternoon, lost in their own little world, where nothing and no one could reach them. He could forget about Richards, Mr. M….

When Mitch stirred, the bubble burst.

"I need to go."

Nikko sat up. "Sure." At least they'd had this little oasis. He just wasn't sure when they'd have it again.

Mitch's eyes seemed sad. "I don't want to go, but…."

Nikko tilted his head. "But?"

There was a moment's hesitation before Mitch spoke. "Randy sort of gave me the impression that I shouldn't be here. Nothing concrete I could put my finger on, but yeah, that's how it felt."

Nikko recalled Randy's words. In that second he remembered Richards's instruction. *Hell. How could I have forgotten?* "Maybe he knows something you don't, but it's better to be safe, right?" He didn't want to put Mitch in any danger, and Richards had danger written all over him.

Mitch nodded and sat upright. He caressed Nikko's cheek. "One last kiss?"

Nikko had no qualms about that. He smiled and leaned forward, closing his eyes as their lips met, Mitch's tongue sliding between his lips for the first time, slow and sensual. Nikko pushed a sigh into Mitch's mouth and surrendered to the kiss. When Mitch broke away from him and climbed off the bed, Nikko wanted to hold on to him in spite of his worries, but he knew better.

They walked to the door and Nikko waited for the click of the lock that would signify an end to their idyllic but way too short interlude.

"I don't know when I'll be back," Mitch murmured, stroking down the length of Nikko's braid, still caressing his face.

Nikko wasn't stupid. It no longer felt like Mitch was a client. This was something else. He wasn't about to question it, for fear of saying the wrong thing. And the timing was all wrong. Neither of them knew what was around the corner. "Be safe," he whispered. He couldn't bear the idea of Mitch getting hurt because of him.

Mitch kissed his head. "I'll do my best."

The door opened and Randy was there, waiting for them. He gave a nod in Mitch's direction and turned to Nikko. "Everything okay here?"

Nikko managed a smile. "Everything's fine," he lied.

"If you'll wait here, I'll see Mr. Jenkins out."

Nikko nodded and watched Mitch walk away, turning once before he disappeared out of sight. That last glance had made Nikko want to run after him. There had been an unexpected look of longing on Mitch's face that tore at his heart.

When Randy returned to him, Nikko followed him back to the others without a sound. The apartment was filling, everyone gearing up for a busy Friday night. Music was playing in the background, something with a rapid beat that had a few guys bouncing on the balls of their feet, clearly eager for a night's work. Jesse was already there, wearing a skimpy pair of shorts that fit him like a second skin. He smiled when he saw Nikko, but his face changed after a second or two.

"Hey, are you okay?"

Nikko stopped on his way to the kitchen. "Yeah, I'm fine. Why'd you ask?"

Jesse crossed the room and placed his hand on Nikko's shoulder. "Because you look like someone just told you your cat had died. What happened?"

He couldn't share his heartache, not when Jesse was always warning him about not being objective enough. "I'm just tired," he said with a wave of his hand.

Jesse snorted. "Like I'm surprised. Every time I looked up this week, you were walking out that door. You seem to be flavor of the week."

"Then I wish someone would change the menu," Nikko growled. When Jesse stared at him, mouth open, Nikko sighed. "I'm sorry. I didn't mean to take it out on you. I just...."

"It's okay," Jesse assured him. "We all get a bit tetchy now and again." He studied Nikko intently. "If there was something wrong, I hope you'd talk to me about it. I mean, I know we're not exactly bosom buddies, but you're one of the few people in here I really like talking to. And you're a nice guy, Nikko."

Jesse was a sweetheart.

"Let's just say life's kinda kicking my ass at the moment, and leave it at that."

Jesse nodded. "Gotcha."

"Jesse!"

At the sound of Randy's call, Jesse grinned. "Ooh, someone wants me. Gotta go." He leaned forward and surprised the hell out of Nikko by kissing his cheek. "Stay strong, babe." His genuine smile warmed Nikko. Jesse sashayed across the floor toward Randy, hips swinging. "Ready for my public." He looked over his shoulder and winked at Nikko before disappearing through the door.

In spite of his anxiety, Nikko had to smile.

Maybe I should take a leaf out of Jesse's book and try and enjoy it.

Then he dismissed the idea. Like he could enjoy Mr. M's less than tender treatment.

NIKKO DRIED off and got dressed quickly. Saturday was shaping up to be another busy night—he'd already seen three clients. At least there'd been time for a shower between each one. There was no way Nikko was budging from his personal regime. That five minutes of hot water and soap was important, not only to get clean, but as a means of wiping away the stains on his soul. What both worried and relieved him was how detached he was becoming. Sex had been something he'd always enjoyed with the couple of boyfriends he'd had. The fact that he could now switch off internally and yet give the impression he was enjoying getting fucked made sex seem almost cold. And while that was probably a good thing, faced with the number of clients he was now seeing, it also made him anxious.

What happens if I do get out of here? Will it always feel that way?

God, he hoped not.

Nikko walked back into the apartment to find about twenty guys working that night. Jesse was there, just walking through the door with his usual well-fucked grin.

"That's a little more paid off the loans," he said, heading toward the bathroom.

An alarm rent the air, loud and piercing.

Nikko froze. "What in God's name is that?" Judging from the expressions on the faces of some of the guys who'd worked there awhile, they didn't have a clue either. The effect of the alarm was electric. The men surged toward the door, clamoring to know what was going on, voices raised in agitation.

Randy burst through it. "Okay, you all need to follow me." The sight of a semiautomatic pistol in his hand sent ice racing down Nikko's spine. "Come on, guys, move it!"

"What's going on, Randy?" Jordan yelled. Everyone began pushing at that point, heading for the door, but as Randy reached it, one of the guys, Baz, dashed through.

"Something's going on. There's a hell of a commotion coming from downstairs," Baz said, his face ashen. The rest of the men started talking loudly, asking questions. He gesticulated with his hands. "I heard loud voices, doors breaking. I tell ya, something's going down." He shoved the door closed and put his back to it.

"Hey, we gotta get outta here!"

"Fucking move out of the way, Baz!"

Randy appeared a damn sight calmer. "Okay, everyone quiet down. Baz, get away from the door."

His walkie-talkie burst into life. "Randy, you copy me? Negative on the fire escape. Cops were waiting."

"Copy that." He raised his voice and addressed the men surrounding him. "Check the bathrooms, the kitchen, all the back rooms. Get everyone in here, fast." A couple of men nodded and ran toward the kitchen and bathroom.

"Cops? Did he say cops?" Jordan stared at Randy, wide-eyed. "Fuck, I can't get arrested again."

One of the security guards flung the door open, brandishing a gun. "You got everyone, Randy?" His eyes were huge.

"Doing it now," Randy barked back at him. The guard nodded and disappeared from view, shutting the door after him.

The sound of gunfire from the floor below shattered the now quiet room.

"Fuck!" Baz backed away from the door, the others copying him.

Nikko gulped. "Oh my God." His heart hammered. Ichy was upstairs.

"What the fuck?" Jesse was at his side, clutching his arm, panic evident in his voice. "Randy, what's going on?"

"Police raid," Randy said shortly. His walkie-talkie spewed out a burst of static and garbled words. "Repeat," he yelled into it. "I didn't get that last message." Another spurt of static. "Fucking piece of shit!" Randy growled and then took a deep breath. "Okay, everyone? We need to stay calm."

"Who the fuck is firing?" someone cried out. "Are we gonna get shot?"

"Fuck," Jesse wailed. "I can't get arrested. My family'll have a fit if they find out about this." The others edged closer to each other, some whimpering with fright.

"I have to get to Ichy," Nikko said to Jesse. "I have to get upstairs."

Jesse gaped at him. "Are you nuts? The police are probably coming in that way."

"Up, down, it don't make no difference," Jordan spat out. "The cops are gonna get us, 'cause we're sitting ducks." Some of the others grumbled that he was correct.

More gunfire sounded, closer this time. Loud voices infiltrated the room, growing louder with each second. "Put down your weapons! Now!"

"This is fucking scary shit, Randy," Baz said, his voice quavering. There was agitated agreement around him.

"Randy, get us out of here, man!"

"Look, you're all unarmed, they're not gonna hurt you," Randy reasoned. "And they'll be coming through that door. Just do whatever they say and you'll be fine, okay? Just don't panic." He holstered his pistol.

"Listen to Randy." This came from Steve. "This is not the first raid I've experienced, all right? They're gonna detain us and question us. We just gotta stay calm."

"Calm? You're kidding, right? I just about shit myself."

"Don't the police shoot first, ask questions later?"

"Who's gonna know, man? They can do what the fuck they want."

"Will you all just *quiet the fuck down*!" Randy yelled. Nikko shivered and hugged Jesse tight. When the noise only died down a little, Randy raised his voice. "That's *enough*!" Around them the men fell silent. "Okay, that's better. Now—"

The door flew open, and Nikko staggered back in a blind panic as at least ten men in black riot gear spilled into the room, POLICE emblazoned across their protective vests. All of them carried rifles. In seconds they had surrounded the group, weapons pointing at them.

"Everyone on your knees, hands laced behind your heads. Do it *now*, people!" The officer pointed his rifle in their direction. "NOW!"

Nikko was about to piss himself, he was so frightened. He dropped to his knees, the pain of hitting the floor sending a shockwave through his thighs. He laced numb fingers at the back of his head, body trembling. Everyone else complied in silence. Fear prickled his skin.

"You!" The lead officer swung his rifle and aimed it at Randy. "Why are you still on your feet? You got a weapon?"

Randy nodded and glanced down at his holster. The officer stepped forward and took it roughly, handing it to another officer. "Okay, on your knees, hands behind your head." Randy did as instructed without hesitation. "Evans, don't forget the top floor," the lead officer called out toward the main area of the club.

"Got it" came the answering call.

"Marks, Talbot, Dennison, you're up," he said with a nod to the other officers. At once they stepped forward and began securing the men's arms behind their backs, plastic ties around their wrists. The other officers stood with their rifles trained on the men.

"Where you taking us?" Jordan demanded.

"You're all under arrest. You'll be questioned later. That's all you need to know."

As each man was secured, an officer hauled him to his feet and led him out of the room.

Nikko's heart was pounding so hard, he thought it would burst. When it was his turn, he staggered to his feet and stumbled out of the room, Jesse not far behind him. Everywhere he looked there were officers, some with FBI on the back of their jackets, and all of them shoving him to keep moving. Randy's computer was being unplugged and a couple of officers were in the hallway, checking all the playrooms. Nikko caught cries from some of the clients and saw a few guys being led out, their hands tied behind their backs.

"Rooms emptied, sir."

"Upstairs is secured, sir. Had to break into a room to find this guy."

Nikko twisted his head to see Ichy being brought through the door by an officer. His brother was pale and shaking, but he gave Nikko a nod.

"You need to move," the officer at his side said, nudging him hard in the ribs with the butt of his rifle.

Nikko winced. He nodded and walked through the outer office to the door beyond, except it was hanging off its hinges. None of the security guards were in sight. An officer was wrapping the cable around the office computer. Once he was in the hallway, he could hear the loud murmur of voices from below. He and the others were hurried along the hall. The dance club patrons were seated on the floor, with three officers guarding them. He didn't have time to notice much as he was ushered down the stairs to the street, where six white NYPD vans and several patrol cars sat in front of the restaurant. The area around them was deserted, but about forty feet to either side, barriers had been erected, behind which were crowds of people, some holding up phones. Officers stood around talking among themselves, some on walkie-talkies. One of them pointed down the street to a white NBC van that had pulled up beyond the barricade, a FOX van not far behind them.

"Someone's called the media. Get these guys out of here before the vultures descend!"

Nikko was led to the back of one of the vans and pushed inside. There were already four guys seated, including Steven and Baz, all looking nervous and twitchy. Nikko was shoved onto an empty seat and strapped in. Jesse was the last one in and the doors slammed shut.

Through the windshield, Nikko watched Randy being led away. Ichy emerged from the restaurant, still pale, and was taken to another van.

The van pulled away from the curb and moved out slowly into the street where officers removed the barricades to let them through. Nikko watched as the crowds were pushed back.

"Fuck, this is really bad, Nikko," Jesse whispered.

Nikko forced himself to take a couple of calming breaths. At least Ichy was safe. A thought crossed his mind and laughter bubbled up out of him.

Jesse stared at him. "Have you lost it? What the fuck is funny about any of this?"

Nikko got himself under control. "Mitch told me he'd gone to the police, but that was yesterday. Either they already had this operation planned, or Mitch is a mighty persuasive guy."

Jesse's jaw dropped. "He did *what*?" He narrowed his gaze. "You mean this is all going down because of Mitch?"

"Unlikely," Steve said from across the van. "My guess is the club has to have been on their radar for a while."

Jesse nudged Nikko with his shoulder. "My mom and dad are gonna be super pissed when they find out," he said gloomily. "A police record will really fuck up my chances of finding a decent job too."

"And I haven't been thinking the same thing?" Nikko retorted. If this got back to Grandma, the shock would probably kill her. Then it occurred to him.

He was free of the club. Out of Richards's clutches. Free to be with Mitch.

If he wants me.

That thought precipitated a slew of logic that left him depressed as hell.

What kind of future could we possibly have together? He'll be teaching in New York and I'll have my master's. And what sort of relationship would we have, beginning like this? We'd always remember how we met.

Whichever way he looked at it, they were never going to work out.

Nikko shut his eyes to force back the tears that threatened to spill.

Chapter Seventeen

MITCH LAY on the couch, Beethoven playing quietly in the background. It was supposed to help him think clearly, but shit, that wasn't happening. He knew he was playing with fire, but he wanted to see Nikko. Which was crazy.

It's only been twenty-four hours since I saw him. Am I that addicted? Stupid question.

His phone trilled, shattering the reflective mood. Mitch glanced over at the screen and scowled. Aaron. "Go away," he groused. He ignored the phone's shrill call and went back to his thoughts. Eventually Aaron gave up.

He was trying to pinpoint the moment when Nikko had found his way into Mitch's heart, but it wasn't easy. All he knew was that when he was with Nikko, it felt right. Never mind the sex—though that was so damned good—there was more to their relationship than the physical. And if he ever got Nikko out of that fucking brothel, Mitch wanted to see where things led.

That was if Nikko felt the same way.

His phone trilled again. Aaron.

Mitch snorted. He had no desire whatsoever to speak with his coworker. It was going to be enough of a strain when September arrived and he had to see him in school. He knew too much about Aaron to be comfortable around him anymore.

Can't think about school. Not now.

When his phone burst into life for the third time, Mitch had had enough. He grabbed it and accepted the call. "What the fuck do you want?" he growled.

There was a moment of quiet. "You really need to watch the channel 7 news right now."

Something in Aaron's voice had the hairs standing on Mitch's arms. He sat up and hit the TV remote, flipping through the channels to find it. His breath stuttered out of him when he saw the restaurant in the background amid a scene of armed police officers and detention vans.

"What the hell?" He put his phone to his ear. "When was this?"

"An hour ago, apparently. Someone caught it on their phone and uploaded it to YouTube, which was where I saw it first," Aaron explained. "The report doesn't say where they've taken everyone." He sighed. "Shit, Mitch, I was gonna go there tonight."

Mitch didn't give a rat's ass about Aaron, but he was grateful for the information. "Thanks for telling me," he said gruffly.

"That's okay, I figured you'd want to know. Bye." Aaron disconnected before Mitch could utter another word.

Mitch's mind went into overdrive. He hadn't expected things to move so fast. The one thought that consumed him was finding Nikko.

He checked the time on his phone before scrolling through to find Donna's number, drumming his fingers on the arm of the couch while he waited for her to pick up.

"I thought it wouldn't be long" was her first comment. "I saw the news."

"What do you know?" Pleasantries could wait.

"Well, I was in the process of getting more information when you called," she grumbled. "Gimme a few minutes and I'll call you back, okay?"

"Got it." Mitch disconnected the call and sagged into the couch.

What must Nikko be going through right now? The thought was tempered with relief that he was finally free of Richards. Mitch stared at his phone, willing it to ring. *C'mon, Donna, what's taking so long?* A more practical thought was that it was already past nine o'clock. It wasn't as if he could do anything once he knew where Nikko was.

When the phone rang, he grabbed it. "Okay, talk to me."

"He's been taken to a precinct where they'll question him. Once that's done, he'll be free to go."

"He's not under arrest?" That was one load off Mitch's mind.

"Nope. So if you get your ass down there, you can collect him when they release him. You got a pen?"

NIKKO GLANCED at the clock on the wall. An hour had passed since he'd arrived at the Midtown South Precinct, and a lot had already happened. He'd been placed in a room with the others, although there was no sign of Richards or any of the guards. Names and other personal details had been logged, and clothing had been provided for some of the guys who'd been wearing very little upon detention. At that point, they'd all been escorted to the cells. No one was cuffed, and yet he'd seen other people being escorted through the hallway in cuffs.

Then there were the uniformed officers who kept checking on him constantly with offers of food and drink, or to see if he needed anything. Everyone was so nice to him and the others, and nothing like Nikko had expected. Then he'd listened as the cells around him began to empty, when officers arrived to take away his fellow detainees. They didn't return.

When it was Nikko's turn, he got up from his bed, his heart beating fast. A uniformed officer led him through the hallway to a brightly lit interview room that contained little in the way of furniture, just a table and four chairs. There was no obvious recording equipment that he could see, but then he spied a microphone suspended from the ceiling. It didn't take long to spot the camera after that.

"Nikko, have a seat." The detective seated in one of the chairs gestured to the other side of the table. Nikko took the chair facing him and sat, his heartbeat still racing. The detective smiled at him. "I'm Detective Jamison, and we're just waiting for Detective Michaels, who is part of the arrest team. First things first. How are you?"

"I… I'm fine," Nikko lied. The whole experience had left him decidedly off-balance.

"Do you need anything? Some water, for example?"

Again with the offers? Nikko really didn't get it. He shook his head. "I'm fine, thank you."

Detective Jamison relaxed in his chair, still wearing a smile. "Okay. We'd like to talk to you, if you don't mind."

Now we're getting down to it. There was no way Nikko was about to incriminate himself. "I'm… not so sure that's in my best interests," he said after a moment's hesitation. "And shouldn't I have a lawyer present?" That much he knew from watching TV.

Detective Jamison straightened. "Firstly, you are not under arrest. Secondly, you are free to leave any time you like." He paused and regarded Nikko intently.

Nikko stared. "But… I thought I was under arrest. That officer at the club, he said…." His head hurt.

Detective Jamison nodded. "I know. That's why I'm stating this now." He leaned forward, his arms on the table. "Seriously, you can leave if you like, but we really do need to hear your side of things. And if you do decide to answer some questions, you're free to stop answering at any time and leave."

The way Nikko was feeling, he was ready to walk immediately.

"*But*"—the detective regarded him closely—"I'm hoping you'll decide to help us, Nikko. We already have a very good idea about what happened to you and your brother, but we don't know everything. Your version of events is of vital importance to our investigation if we're going to prosecute the people who put you through all that misery." His eyes were grave. "We don't want them walking away from this. I'm sure you don't want that either."

Aw, crap.

Nikko was still deciding how to respond when the door to the interview room opened. He took one look at the new arrival and stared at him in confusion. "I… I don't…." Then it sank in. "You have got to be kidding me!"

"Hi, Nikko." Randy pulled out the chair and sat facing him. He was dressed in jeans and a shirt, his detective's badge clipped to his breast pocket. His hair was tied back and he wore glasses. "Are you okay?" Those familiar eyes held sympathy.

Nikko ignored the question. "All that time in the club, you were undercover?" Randy nodded. Nikko forced himself to breathe. "Then why the hell didn't you act sooner? You knew what was going on. What on earth were you waiting for?" The one thought that dominated his head was that if the raid had taken place earlier, then maybe he wouldn't have gone through that hell with Mr. M. Maybe Ichy would have been spared his hospital visit.

Randy sighed. "It took a year at the club to get to the point where I was trusted. You're only seeing the last few months. I think my perspective is a little different from yours." He straightened. "But right now, that's not important. Are you going to help us?"

"What about Ichy?" Nikko demanded.

"Ichy's case is not like yours," Randy said patiently, "and his circumstances are very different. There's not much I can tell you—well, that I'm *allowed* to tell you—but I'll share what I can. But we still need to know if we can proceed. Because I know for a fact that there's someone waiting to see you once we're done." He stared levelly at Nikko.

That was enough to lift Nikko's spirits. *Mitch is here.* It could only be him.

"Ask your questions."

MITCH STARED at his laced fingers, his legs stretched out in front of him, and tried to remain calm. He'd been halfway to the Midtown South Precinct when he'd received a text from a Detective Michaels, informing him that Nikko was going to be released and that Mitch could collect him. The news had him speeding up, his heart soaring. Once he'd arrived at the precinct, however, it was a case of waiting for the red tape to be dealt with. It couldn't be that much longer.

"Mitch?"

He jerked his head up at the sound of that familiar voice. Nikko was standing in front of him, wearing jeans and a T-shirt. He was pale and there was a dazed look about him.

Mitch shot to his feet and threw his arms around the young man, pulling him close. Nikko didn't react at first, but after a moment he slowly moved his arms to encircle Mitch.

"Are you okay?" Mitch asked him. When Nikko's stomach gave out a loud rumble, Mitch chuckled. "I guess I know what the first order of business is. I need to get some food into you. One street down, there's the Skylight Diner, and it's open. What do you say?" He released Nikko and took a step back.

"Sure." Nikko gave a shrug. "It's not like I've got anyplace else to be right now." His words weren't uttered with bitterness but with an air of such resignation that Mitch was concerned.

He cocked his head. "What about Ichy?"

Nikko swallowed. "I'll tell you everything I know at the diner, okay?"

"Okay. Let's go. You all done here?" When Nikko nodded, Mitch put his hand to Nikko's back and rested it there as they exited the precinct. They walked along in silence to Ninth Avenue and then on to West 34th Street. Nikko's silence wasn't surprising. It had obviously been a long day.

When they got to the diner, Nikko glanced at the sign above the door and attempted a smile. "'Best diner in Manhattan,' eh? You trying to impress me, Mitch?"

Mitch returned his smile. "Wait until you've tried their Meatball Parmigiana Hero—then you can decide if you're impressed." When Nikko's belly growled again, Mitch chuckled. "Yeah, I agree, it sounds good. So let's go in and eat, all right?" He pushed open the door for Nikko and when they were inside, he pointed to an empty booth. "That'll do."

Nikko slid onto the gray vinyl-covered seat, and Mitch handed him the menu. Nikko gave it a quick glance and placed it back in its holder. "I'll go with your suggestion, with a glass of water, please."

"The Meatball Hero? Great." Mitch gave the choices a cursory glance. He'd eaten there often enough to know what he liked. "I'll go order, and when I get back, we can talk."

"Don't... don't the servers come to your table?"

Mitch grinned. "You forget, I've eaten here plenty of times. Trust me, with the speed some of these guys move at? This way is much faster."

Without giving Nikko a chance to say a word, he walked over to the counter and ordered their food and beverages. When he rejoined Nikko, he leaned back against the padded booth and regarded the young man. Nikko appeared exhausted. Maybe food would help.

"So, what happened? I saw on a news report that the club got raided." Mitch kept his voice low and even.

Nikko ran his finger along the edge of the table, but Mitch caught the shiver that rippled through him. "I was frightened, Mitch." Nikko wasn't looking at him, but was studying the Formica with apparent interest. "When that alarm went off... and then the gunfire...."

Fuck. Mitch's heart gave a stutter. It took a considerable effort to sound calm. "Was that the police or Richards's heavies?"

Nikko rolled his shoulders in a graceful shrug. "Not a clue. I just know I've never been so scared in my life. And when they surrounded us, all those rifles pointing at us...." He swallowed hard.

"But they treated you all right?" Mitch tensed, wary of the response.

Nikko jerked up his head. "They were so kind. I mean, they went out of their way to be nice. And then when one of the arresting officers walked into that interview room"—he shook his head—"you wouldn't believe me if I told you—and to be honest, I'm not sure I should."

"Hey, wait a minute." Mitch stared at him. "You can't do that. That's just mean, throwing out something to get me all curious and then backtracking."

Nikko studied him. "All I'm going to say is, he was undercover and you met him. Several times." He maintained eye contact.

Mitch frowned, until it hit him a couple of seconds later. He widened his eyes. "No, really?" he said heavily. "Well, that explains a lot." He wasn't about to say Randy's name aloud—if that was his name—because Nikko had a point. If Randy had been working undercover, the fewer people who knew about it the better. "And you definitely weren't under arrest?"

"Definitely. I told them everything I knew, which wasn't a lot, but they already knew why I was there." His bottom lip quivered.

"Nikko?" Mitch realized there was one topic left. "Where's your brother?"

There was a moment of silence. Nikko stared at him, eyes sparkling as tears welled in them, catching on his lower lashes like dewdrops. "I don't know," he whispered. He wiped his eyes with the back of his hand.

All talk ceased when the server appeared with their food and drinks. Mitch thanked him. Nikko gazed at his sandwich and fries as though he were looking straight through them to a spot under the table. He took a long drink of water, gulping it down. When he'd drained half the glass, he lifted his chin to gaze at Mitch. "All I know is he's cooperating with the police."

"So you think he's going to testify against Richards? It would make sense. He knew about the drug dealing, the deliveries. Do you think he's gone into a witness protection program?"

Nikko's Adam's apple bobbed twice. "I think so. I couldn't ask Ra—the police—if that was the case, but I did ask what would happen *hypothetically* if someone did."

Mitch nodded, his heart going out to the young man. If this was the case, heaven knew when Nikko would see his brother again. "What was the alternative?" he asked softly. "Did they say?"

Nikko gave a single nod. "If they arrest him, he'd go to jail, and they'd have to keep him apart for his safety until the trial. If they don't charge him, they'd have to let him go, and he'd take his chances that the bad guys didn't get to him. Because if they find him, he's dead. Or they could offer him witness protection. If he accepts, then he goes someplace to start a new life, and I may never see him again." Fresh dew sparkled on his lashes.

Mitch reached across the table and grasped Nikko's hand. "And the trial? How long before that might happen?"

"Anytime from six months to a year," Nikko informed him.

Mitch tried to look at the positives. "How long did the police have someone undercover at the club?"

"A year, apparently."

He nodded. "Then it stands to reason, Ichy can't be the only iron in their fire, not after all that time. Their whole case won't rest solely on his evidence. So maybe he's just lying low until the trial. Maybe he's afraid that if he contacts you, or vice versa, it'll get to the ears of the wrong people." He squeezed Nikko's hand. "Have courage, baby."

Nikko's eyes took on a soft glow, and for the first time since he'd left him last in the club, Mitch saw a genuine smile.

"Now eat, before your food gets cold," he admonished.

Nikko nodded and shook ketchup over his fries.

Mitch's phone vibrated in his pocket. He took it out and had to smile when he saw the text from his mom.

Saw the news. Was that Nikko's place? Is everything okay? Bless her.

It buzzed once more. This time it was from Gareth.

Call me when you get this. Is Nikko safe?

Mitch was still smiling when he raised his head to look at Nikko, who was watching him. "Anything bad?"

Mitch shook his head. "Texts from my family, wondering if you're okay."

Nikko's mouth dropped. "You... you told your family about me?"

"Of course." Then he realized his choice of words was telling. "Nikko, listen—"

A car backfired in the street outside, followed by the wail of several police sirens. Nikko gave a jolt and then shuddered. "Shit. This fucking city. The sooner I can go home, the better." Then he snorted. "Not that Oregon's much different."

He's bound to be nervous, after everything he's been through. A desire to protect him surged through Mitch, leaving him shaken. Nikko had suffered enough. What he needed right then was time and space to heal.

When the idea came to him in a sudden lucid burst, Mitch caught his breath.

"Are you okay?" Nikko was staring at him.

Mitch ignored the question and tightened his hold on Nikko's hand. "What happens when you get home?"

Nikko shrugged, a mask of misery slipping into place. "I visit Grandma. Get on with my life until September when I start my master's."

"Do you trust me?" Mitch demanded. He locked gazes with Nikko to watch his reaction.

"I...." Nikko flushed. He swallowed. "Yes," he whispered. Those dark eyes were almost black.

Mitch released his hand and scrolled through his contacts. Nikko watched him, his forehead creased, an air of puzzlement about him.

"Mom? I got your text."

"Mitch, oh, thank God. I was starting to panic. Is Nikko all right? When I saw the news, I was sick with worry."

"Mom, Nikko's fine. He's sitting opposite me as I speak."

"Malcolm! Nikko's okay!" he heard her shout.

"Mom, listen, I've had an idea." Mitch took a deep breath. "How would you feel about a couple of visitors?"

Nikko's eyes grew large, framed by long lashes.

"Visitors? Oh... you mean you and Nikko?" He didn't miss the note of joy in her voice. "When? And for how long?"

"Well, if I can arrange a car rental, tomorrow. And as for how long...." He met Nikko's gaze. "Let's say a few weeks to begin with." As long as it took for the peace of his home state to begin the task of healing Nikko.

"You're serious?"

"Yes, Mom." He smiled at Nikko. "I'm bringing Nikko home."

Chapter Eighteen

Nikko glanced around Mitch's bedroom in the dim light from the window. It was definitely a masculine room, done in shades of beige and brown. Even the comforter was a rich chocolate color. The furniture was all wood, solid and sturdy-looking. And the bed…. Nikko snuggled under the soft sheets, relishing the way the mattress supported him in comfort.

Sleep was a really good idea. Well, it would have been, except for the fact that he couldn't shut down his brain. He'd fallen into bed exhausted, convinced the next time he opened his eyes it would be Sunday morning.

Some hope. There he was, a couple of hours later and still awake.

So many thoughts were running through his head. Every now and then he'd find himself back in the club, on his knees, rifles trained on him, his body shaking uncontrollably. One thing he'd learned—it was possible to smell fear. It had pervaded the air, seeping from the pores of every man who'd knelt in that room, a stale smell that made Nikko's heart race. It didn't seem to matter how many times he told himself the danger had passed, that he was safe—he was still yanked back into that nightmare.

Can't keep doing this. In a few hours, I'll be getting up and traveling to Maine with Mitch.

And that was another thing. Why in hell had he agreed to this? When Mitch had finished his call to his mom and asked if he hadn't been too presumptive, Nikko had assured him it was fine.

Except it wasn't fine, not if Nikko's present circumstances were anything to go by. Because contrary to everything Nikko had expected, he was in Mitch's bed and Mitch was asleep on the couch. The mixed signals were driving Nikko crazy.

All those visits to the club—did he feel sorry for me? Is that as far as it went? The soft words, the caresses, the reassurances. I thought he wanted me, but if he did, surely he'd be in this bed with me. Sex was the last thing on Nikko's mind, but damn it, he needed Mitch's arms around him.

If this was how things were going to be between them, Maine was looking like a really bad idea.

It'd just be postponing the inevitable. Because at some point I'm going to have to leave. Two years at San Francisco State University awaited him, studying for his Master of Music degree. He'd be less than ninety minutes by air from Portland, and then Beaverton, where Grandma resided, was only seven miles away. Or if finances got tight, a bus ride away.

And in the meantime Mitch would be in New York.

So why am I deluding myself? Why not just call a halt to this whole charade right now, get out of here, and get on with my life? He'd have to contact the police, of course. The few belongings he'd brought with him were probably in an evidence lockup. Another thing to consider—he had no clothing with him, except the jeans, T-shirt, and sneakers he'd been wearing when they'd taken him from the club.

This is such a fucked-up situation. What the hell was I thinking, saying yes to him?

It didn't matter that he loved Mitch. This was no fairy-tale romance, with a Happily Ever After.

This was reality—and it sucked.

"Can't you sleep?"

Nikko's heart gave a jolt. He could just about make out Mitch's shadowy figure in the doorway. "No. You either?"

A sigh crept out of the darkness. "You were tossing and turning. The bed isn't exactly silent."

Shit. Nikko hadn't even noticed. "Go back to sleep," he told Mitch wearily. "I'm sorry I woke you up."

A rueful chuckle. "S'okay. The couch is a little on the lumpy side. I wasn't sleeping that well to begin with."

That did it.

"Mitch, can I ask you something?"

A moment's hesitation. "Okay."

"Why aren't you in this bed with me?" The words fell from his lips, sounding blunt to his ears, but he couldn't keep quiet. He wanted answers.

"Because...." Mitch's voice faltered for a second and then came back, firmer. "I thought you needed some space."

Damn it. Mitch was being a gentleman. *But is that really all?*

"I've been thinking about this Maine trip," Nikko began, his heart beating faster, "and I'm sorry, but I think I'd be making a big mistake if I went with you."

Stunned silence. "But… why?" Nikko could hear the bewilderment in Mitch's voice.

"Oh, come on, think about it. What are your parents going to think? You said they know about me, right? Does that mean they know about the club? What I did there?"

Moments ticked by, his scalp prickling while he waited for Mitch's reply. He was glad the darkness covered them both. He didn't want to see Mitch's face right then.

"Yes," Mitch said at last. "They know everything."

Nikko's heart sank. "And you think I can face them, knowing that?" He was feeling insecure enough without adding the shame that would fill him when he saw their faces, knowing they saw him as a prostitute. A flood of emotion, raw and sharp, burst through him, leaving him trembling in its wake. "Mitch, why did you bring me here? Why is it so important to you that I meet them?" His heart pounded. "Why did you keep coming back to visit me?"

There was a moment of silence, broken by a soft sigh. "Because I love you, that's why."

A wave of dizziness washed over him. A fluttery feeling spread through his belly. His skin tingled. "You… love me?" He had to see Mitch's face, had to see it written there.

Nikko reached for the bedside lamp and sent it flying.

"Hey, don't go destroying my bedroom, okay?" Mitch's form grew more solid as he approached. Some noise next to him and then the room was bathed in a warm light. Nikko blinked and gazed up at the man standing beside the bed, dressed in a pair of shorts. Mitch blinked too, scraping a hand through his hair. "Look, I didn't mean to tell you like that. I—"

Nikko shoved back the sheets and kneeled on the bed in front of Mitch, his hand across Mitch's mouth. "I love you too," he blurted out. He bit his lip and studied Mitch's face, withdrawing his hand.

Mitch's eyes widened and his cheeks glowed. He parted his lips as if to speak, but nothing came out. Then he grinned—a silly, huge grin that sent warmth flooding through Nikko's body and made him all shivery inside. "You love me," he echoed softly.

Mitch's strong arms encircled Nikko, pulling him closer until he could feel Mitch's heart beating against his. Mitch brought their mouths together in a kiss that sent jolts of electricity tingling through him, skittering down his spine, dancing along his arms, until he swore he could feel them in his fingers and toes. When the sensations died away, what remained was a slow, steady pulse of pleasure, like thick, rich cream flowing through his veins, slowing everything down to a crawl.

Mitch broke the kiss and cupped Nikko's chin. "I love you, Nikko Kurokawa." His voice was firm.

Nikko wanted to laugh, giggle, shout—*anything* to let out the exuberant joy that filled him. Instead he wrapped his arms around Mitch and held him, content to feel him in his arms, vital, warm....

And in love with me.

If it was a dream, Nikko didn't want to wake up.

"Although this is wonderful," Mitch murmured into his hair, "we have a long ride ahead of us. That is, if you still want to go."

Nikko nodded against Mitch's furry chest. He knew the awkwardness and insecurity at meeting Mitch's parents was not going to go away, but now Nikko had something else to cling to—the knowledge that Mitch loved him. Whether it would be enough to repel the shame of facing them, Nikko didn't know.

But it was a start.

"Don't go back to the couch," Nikko said suddenly. "Stay with me. I... I really don't want to be alone tonight."

Mitch's lips were on his once more, soft and warm, and Nikko breathed him in, relishing the strength that surrounded him. He felt, rather than saw, Mitch's smile.

"I finally get what I always wanted—a night with you in my arms." He chuckled. "Well, a few hours at any rate." One last kiss and Mitch turned out the light. "Let's get some sleep."

Nikko shifted across the mattress as it dipped beneath Mitch's weight. He waited until Mitch had lain down, and then he snuggled up against Mitch's side, his head resting on Mitch's chest.

Mitch held him in his arms. "Sleep, baby."

Nikko lay there in the darkness, listening as Mitch's breathing grew more regular, the sound of it and the rise and fall of Mitch's chest almost hypnotic, pulling him deeper and deeper into sleep....

"Wake up, sleepyhead."

Mitch's voice filtered through the cozy layers that cocooned Nikko, prizing him from sleep's tender but firm grip. Nikko opened his eyes and rubbed them. "Where are we?" All he could see was trees, interrupted now and again by quaint houses.

"We've just driven through York," Mitch informed him, "and now we're on Woodbridge Road. Not far to my parents' house."

That was enough to set off the butterflies in Nikko's belly.

As if he could read Nikko's mind, Mitch laid his hand on Nikko's thigh. "You have nothing to worry about, baby. They will love you."

It wasn't that Nikko doubted Mitch's words, it was just that he preferred to judge things as he saw them. "I'm sorry I slept most of the way."

Mitch laughed. "That's what I usually do when my brother drives us up here. And besides, you didn't get much sleep last night—"

"Well, neither did you," Nikko interjected.

"Maybe, but you were physically and mentally exhausted. I guarantee you'll sleep tonight, even if I have to wear you out to do it." He grinned.

The car turned left onto a leafy road with long driveways leading to large houses. Nikko swallowed. "These homes look pretty impressive."

Mitch chuckled. "That'll please my mom. She was always telling my dad the house wasn't big enough when we were growing up."

Nikko wound down the window and sniffed the air. "Can I smell the ocean?"

"Probably. We're not that far from it. There's a great cliff walk nearby, where my grandparents' house is. I used to stay with them when I was little. I'd walk to the end of their road, and there was this path that led to the edge of the cliff. I used to look down at the waves crashing onto the rocks below."

Nikko heard the love in Mitch's voice. "It must have been a beautiful place to grow up," he said quietly.

"It was. It still is. I don't come back here often enough." Mitch turned off the road and then turned right onto the first driveway. "This is it."

Nikko stared at the house, its boards painted pale blue with white trim. A porch ran across the front of the house, with two sets of steps leading up to it. Gardens surrounded it, and it was obvious how much care and attention had been lavished on both. "Mitch, it's lovely." A small figure appeared at the front door, and Nikko's heart gave a lurch. "Is that your mom?"

Mitch switched off the engine. "Yes, that's her." He took hold of Nikko's hand and squeezed it. "Please, try not to worry. It'll be fine, I promise." He got out of the car, and by the time Nikko had opened his door, Mitch was waiting for him. He gave Nikko a tight hug and kissed his cheek. "Remember what's important, right?" When Nikko raised his chin to look into Mitch's eyes, Mitch smiled. "I love you."

Nikko melted. Just… melted. "I love you too," he whispered. Mitch gazed at him with an expression that warmed him from head to toe.

Just then a sound drifted across the front yard—Mitch's mom gave a cough.

"I think that's our cue," Mitch said with a grin. Nikko waited while Mitch fetched a suitcase from the trunk, and sighed with pleasure when Mitch held out his hand. Nikko grasped it tightly, and together they walked up the driveway to where his mom awaited them.

Her lined face broke into a wide smile. "Nikko, I'm so pleased to meet you. I'm Valerie, Mitch's mom." She opened her arms in greeting, and in a daze, Nikko walked into them. There was a wonderful aroma that clung to her, a mixture of baking and the faintest hint of jasmine. It reminded him of the perfume Grandma used to wear.

"I'm pleased to be here." He smiled politely, and Mitch gave his hand a reassuring squeeze.

"Come on in." She led him into the house to a square living room with two couches, and two armchairs on either side of a fireplace. Nikko noticed the wall of bookshelves, not a space left on any of them. But what caught his eye was what lay beyond the french doors in a smaller room with a polished wooden floor.

It was a grand piano. A *Steinway*, no less.

Nikko walked slowly over to it and stroked the glowing maple wood.

"Do you play?" Valerie asked him.

In answer, Nikko sat on the piano stool and lifted the lid. The gleaming black and white keys were a temptation he couldn't withstand. Nikko closed his eyes, took a deep breath, opened them, and started to play. The melody began, deceptively simplistic chords such as any first year piano student might have played. He shut out the world and let the music build within him, welling up inside and pouring out of him through his fingers. A few minutes into the piece, the melody changed, becoming more complex. He exulted in the harmonies spun by his hands like the silken strands of a web, growing and swelling into a crescendo that filled the air and resounded throughout the room, spilling out the french doors and the open windows. The music returned to the initial simple harmony, and then Nikko let it carry him away, his heart soaring as his fingers moved quickly over the keys, the piece growing more fiendish and fiery as it neared its end. The last few notes, simple and slow, wove their way into the stillness of the room. When it was done, Nikko bowed his head and expelled his breath in one long push of air.

It had been far too long since he'd played.

"Val, what are you—"

Nikko halted at the sound of an unknown voice and turned to see the speaker. It was clear who Mitch resembled. His dad was the same height and build, his hair gray, but those brown eyes were so like Mitch's. Nikko gave him a hesitant smile.

Valerie ignored her husband and sat next to Nikko, her eyes shining. "Nikko, that was… amazing."

He flushed. "Thank you."

Mitch came into his line of sight, his mouth open. "You never told me you could play."

Nikko bit back a smile. "You never asked," he said with a shrug.

"That sounded very good," Mitch's dad said. "Well done."

Valerie swiveled around to glare at him. "'Very good'? Do you know what he just played?" When both Mitch and his dad shook their heads, she tut-tutted. "*That* was Chopin's Ballade No. 2 in F Major. Do you know how difficult that piece is to play? And Nikko just gave a performance that was worthy of a concert hall." She turned to face him, and this time her cheeks were wet. "That was truly beautiful. How long have you been playing?"

Nikko laughed. "Since I could reach the keys?"

"Perhaps I should introduce myself properly." Mitch's dad stepped forward, his hand outstretched. "I'm Malcolm. Welcome to our home, Nikko."

Nikko rose and shook the proffered hand. "Thank you for having me. You have a beautiful home, sir."

"Thank you—but it's still Malcolm."

Valerie patted his shoulder. "Why don't I show you to your room? I've put you in Mitch's old room." She glanced at Mitch. "And you're in Deirdre's old room."

Nikko tried not to smirk at the look of disappointment on Mitch's face. Not that he was about to suggest alternative arrangements. It was one thing to share Mitch's bed in his apartment, it was quite another under his parents' roof.

Valerie looked around. "Where's your bag?"

Shit. "I… I don't have one. The… police still have my backpack. Mitch has brought some of his T-shirts for me." He bit back a smile.

Valerie clearly got the joke. "Oh my. You'll be swimming in them. And I'm afraid I don't have any of the boys' clothes from when they were… smaller. Everything got sent to Goodwill." Her face lit up. "That's what we'll do tomorrow. You and I will go shopping. We'll get enough things to last you for your stay." She paused and gave him a stern glance. "And Nikko? *I* am buying the clothes."

Nikko was horrified. "Oh, you mustn't."

"Whyever not?" She seemed genuinely puzzled. "You need them, don't you?"

"Well, yes, but—"

"And you don't really intend to wear Mitch's T-shirts, do you?"

"No, I mean, I get your point, but—"

"And didn't you just finish saying that the police have all your belongings?"

"Yes, but—"

"Well, that's settled, then." She beamed.

Malcolm cackled. "Better give up now, son. It's a good deal easier in the long run." He winked. "Believe me. I speak from experience." Even Mitch was laughing quietly.

"Yes, sir—I mean, Malcolm," Nikko said with a sigh. It was obvious he didn't stand a cat-in-hell's chance of winning this particular argument. However, he aimed a look in Mitch's direction that promised retribution.

Mitch had the good grace to look scared—even if it was an act.

BY NINE o'clock, Nikko was already yawning. Mitch watched as he'd doze off at the far end of the couch, wake up with a start, and try to look alert, only for his eyelids to grow heavier by the second. Mom had noticed too.

Mitch shifted across the seat cushions and rubbed Nikko's thigh. "Hey, you," he said softly.

Nikko opened weary eyes to stare at him. "Wassup?"

Mitch chuckled. "You need to go to bed, sweetheart. Your ass is dragging." Dad smothered a chuckle and Mom mouthed *aww*.

Nikko nodded, still half-asleep. He rose unsteadily to his feet and turned to face Mitch's parents. "Good night."

"G'night, son. We can talk more tomorrow when you've had some rest." Dad smiled.

"Good night, Nikko. If you need anything, please let us know." Mom glanced at Mitch. "Or tell Mitch, of course."

"Thank you. You've both been so kind."

"Pfft." Mom waved her hand. "You just get a good night's sleep. You'll feel miles better in the morning."

Mitch guided Nikko from the room, but when he saw him stumble on the first set of stairs, that was it. Mitch scooped Nikko up into his arms and proceeded to carry him up the rest of the way.

Nikko glared at him. "You are *not* carrying me. I'm quite capable of walking."

Mitch laughed softly. "Well, it looks like I am carrying you, so there. My folks can't see, and you can't stop me, so suck it up." He cradled Nikko against him and climbed the second set of stairs to the room at the top of the house that had been his until he'd left home for college. When he reached the door, he carefully deposited Nikko. Mitch gazed at him, his heart swelling at the sight of those heavy-lidded eyes. Nikko was plainly exhausted. Mitch kissed his cheek. "Good night, baby."

Nikko stared at him. "That's it?"

Mitch laughed and pulled Nikko into his arms. He brushed his lips over Nikko's before deepening the kiss, loving the way Nikko wound his arms around him, his hands gently stroking Mitch's back. Mitch let the kiss continue until Nikko sagged against him. "If you're falling asleep midkiss, then you really are tired," he told Nikko with a smile. "Sleep well." He didn't want to leave it there, of course. He wanted to be in Nikko's room, in Nikko's bed, but he knew the young man really did need some space. "I'll see you in the morning." He pushed open Nikko's door and watched him walk over to the bed.

The last thing he saw as the door slowly closed was Nikko's sweet face, focused on him.

Mitch wondered how long it would take before his resolve broke. Because he didn't think it would be long. Spending those few hours the previous night with Nikko curled up in his arms had been heaven.

And now that Mitch had sampled heaven, he wanted more.

Chapter Nineteen

NIKKO SLIPPED on the robe that Valerie had left for him and quietly opened his bedroom door. The house was silent, not that he was surprised—the sun had barely risen. He'd awoken and watched the sky change color, loving how the sunlight tinged the treetops and made them glow warmly. Then it was time to go in search of coffee.

He crept downstairs to the kitchen and found a pot of coffee already brewed, but no one was in sight. It was a large, family kitchen, with a black granite-topped breakfast bar and a small, round table and chairs in front of the window. Nikko found himself a clean mug and poured some of the aromatic brew before walking barefoot out through the back door and onto the wooden deck. Malcolm was already sitting there in a garden chair, mug in hand, staring at the sky. He turned his head as Nikko approached hesitantly, and smiled.

"Good morning. Looks like I'm not the only one who's an early riser." He glanced at Nikko's hands. "I hope you like it strong. I always brew myself a pot of coffee the Navy way—strong enough to stand a spoon upright in it, with a pinch of salt." He grinned. "Valerie is always telling me it's a good thing I can't see what it's doing to my insides." Malcolm gestured to the chair next to his. "Come and sit down."

Nikko took the empty chair and sat. His first sip of coffee made him gasp. "Wow. You weren't kidding." He took another mouthful and smiled. "But you get used to it pretty quick."

Malcolm laughed. "Good lad." He gazed at the garden beyond the edge of the decking and the paved patio. "That is Valerie's domain. She designed it, dug it all out and laid out the beds as she wanted them, and chose all the shrubs and plants. I stayed out the way." He laughed. "You saw our front yard, right?"

Nikko nodded. Apart from the more formal flower beds closest to the house, the rest of the yard was a huge expanse of grass.

"Well, Val takes care of the beds, but the grass? That's *my* domain. Which is why I have a mower that I can ride around in." Malcolm winked. "Anything for an easy life."

After seeing them together the previous night, Nikko already liked how the couple interacted. Theirs was clearly a relationship of many years, where they knew each other's foibles and tastes, strengths and weaknesses. Watching them had given him a brief pang. He imagined his parents might have been like Mitch's parents, if they'd lived.

"You're not one of those people who talks for the sake of talking, simply to fill the air, are you?"

Nikko glanced up at Malcolm. "No, sir—I mean, Malcolm—not really. But generally mornings are when I like to be quiet, to sit and appreciate what's around me."

Malcolm gave him a warm smile. "You and I are going to get along just fine, Nikko." With that he resumed his coffee drinking, at peace in his yard.

Nikko drank from his mug, relaxing into his chair. Maybe this visit was going to be better than he'd anticipated.

MITCH DRIED off from his shower and pulled on his shorts and a T-shirt. He debated going up to Nikko's room to greet him good morning, but decided to let him sleep in.

Sleep's probably the best thing for him right now.

A night of uninterrupted sleep would have been good for him too, but unfortunately, his brain had decided otherwise. It had been the early hours of the morning when he'd finally fallen asleep. So much had been going through his mind, most of it to do with Nikko.

It had been wonderful to hear how Nikko felt about him, but that had only created more internal turmoil, raised more questions. Mitch figured they had time to talk while they were staying with his parents, but always at the back of his mind was the prospect of going back to New York, back to school—but without Nikko.

Mitch went down the staircase and into the kitchen. Mom was slicing bread, and on the counter, there were eggs, bacon, sausage, and the fixings for hash browns. He grinned. There was nothing like his mom's breakfast.

"Good morning." Mom stopped slicing to accept his kiss to her cheek. "You hungry?"

Mitch patted his belly. "For your breakfast? Always." He grabbed a mug and poured himself some coffee. "I should wake up Nikko."

Mom chuckled. "Would that be the same Nikko who is sitting out on the deck with your father?"

"What?" Mitch wandered over to the window and peered out. The two men appeared deep in conversation.

"They were talking out there when I came downstairs. Heaven knows how long they've been chewing the fat." She smiled. "But it seems Nikko likes your Dad's early morning coffee."

"You're kidding."

"Uh-uh. The pot was empty when I got here." Mom glanced at him. "Are you okay? You look a little peaky."

Mitch pulled out a stool and sat at the breakfast bar. "I just didn't sleep much."

Mom put down the bread knife, and after pouring herself a mug of coffee, she joined him. "Okay, the breakfast can wait. What's going on?"

Mitch stared into his coffee. "I love him," he began.

"As your nephew Cal is always saying—well, *duh*," Mom said with a grin.

He shook his head. "But I'm only now realizing how little I know about him. Like the fact that he's a goddamn piano prodigy. I didn't even know his degree was in music, or that he's going to do his master's in San Francisco." All of this had only come out after Nikko's magnificent performance.

Mom's smile was sympathetic. "Honey, how many times did you visit him in that club?" When he stared at her, lips parted, she sighed. "Just forget I'm your mother for a moment and answer the question."

"Ten, maybe twelve times." He knew his face was flushed.

Mom nodded. "Right. Now, I may be an old lady, but even I'm pretty sure you didn't go to see him to talk about his education. Did you actually talk all that much?" Her eyes were bright with amusement.

"Mom!"

She laughed. "Why is it all my children react the same way when I say something they don't expect?"

"Yeah, but it's not like we… I mean, we didn't…." His cheeks were hot. "Mom, sometimes, we just… cuddled, okay? And that was all!"

"Oh my." Mom bit her lip. "I'm sorry." She patted Mitch's hand. "What you need to understand is that you can talk to me about anything. The point I'm trying to make—without embarrassing you beyond endurance—is that during those visits, you two connected. You fell in love. Something in you saw something in Nikko, and vice versa. So what if you don't know a whole lot about him? You can change that by using the time you have now."

Mitch sipped his coffee. She had a point.

Mom glanced across the kitchen at her wall calendar. "Put it another way. Today is Monday. On Saturday the clan will invade. A whole lot of people under this roof, Mitch. So use this week to get to know Nikko while it's just the two of you. Spend time together—but don't crowd him."

"What do you mean?"

She sighed. "Sweetheart, that young man has been through a lot. And that's not based on what you've already told us, that's based on observing him. He needs time to come to terms with whatever is going on inside his head. So, take him for walks, go to the beach—but don't overwhelm him. He just needs some time and space to breathe."

Mitch nodded. It sounded like good advice. He got up and gazed through the window. Nikko was sitting quietly, his dad's head bobbing as he talked and Nikko listened.

"Maybe I should leave them be."

From behind him, Mom chuckled. "You think they'll stay out there when your father smells the bacon cooking? Hah!"

Mitch smiled to himself. Spending time with Nikko, maybe taking him along the coast to see more of Maine, going to the beach and walking along the shoreline….

This is just what I need too. Some time away from New York.

His chest tightened at the thought of September, but he pushed aside his anxiety.

Time enough to think about school when Nikko's left for San Francisco. I'm going to make every hour we spend together count.

"Now, is there anywhere else you'd like to go?" Valerie paused at the car, keys in her hand.

Nikko wanted to groan aloud, but his grandma would've pitched a fit at such bad manners. "I think we've got enough," he said, looking down at the five or six shopping bags, containing shorts, beach shorts, T-shirts, a couple of button-down shirts, a pair of brightly colored flip-flops, underwear—he still hadn't recovered from that part of the shopping trip—and even a cap.

"Are you sure?" Valerie frowned. "Mind you, it's been a long time since I took a young man shopping. I just want to make sure we've thought of everything."

"Well, if we haven't, Kittery is less than fifteen minutes' drive from your house." The last thing he'd expected to see was an outlet mall. He had to admit, they had everything anyone could possibly need in one place, but he loathed shopping for clothes. His mom used to tell stories of how she had to drag him kicking and screaming when it was time to buy him new shoes. The memory was both pleasant and painful.

"Where did you go just then?" Valerie lowered her voice and placed her hand on his forearm.

He smiled. "I was just remembering something about my mom."

Valerie unlocked the trunk, and he dropped the bags inside. She closed it and gave him a speculative glance. "How about we don't go straight home?"

The glint in her eye made his belly all fluttery again. "Uh, what did you have in mind?"

She raised her thin eyebrows. "Oh, nothing much. I just thought you and I could go for coffee and a snack in a place I know. We could sit outside at one of their tables that looks out over the ocean. Nothing fancy, maybe a grilled cheese sandwich and some fries?" She smiled. "What do you say?"

"Won't Malcolm and Mitch be expecting us back?"

Valerie laughed. "Those two are big enough to fend for themselves. I'd like to spend some time with you."

What is it with this family? Mitch, Valerie, Malcolm—they all had this quality to them, something that made it difficult to resist them. Nikko smiled to himself. *Maybe it's because they're genuine, good people.* Whatever it was, it was a very likable trait.

"Okay," he said at last. "That sounds great."

Valerie beamed at him, and the sight of that huge smile made Nikko feel warm inside. "Then it's off we go to the Lobster Cove restaurant."

Twenty minutes later they were seated at a table beneath a dark blue parasol, perusing the menu. Nikko looked out at the ocean and drew the fresh, salty air deep into his lungs. The breeze off the ocean was pleasant, and right at that moment, New York and all its misery seemed so very far away.

Valerie closed her menu with a sigh. "I already know what I'm having, so I don't know why I even bothered looking."

"The grilled cheese?"

She nodded. "With a Moxie." When Nikko tilted his head to one side, she laughed. "Sweetheart, you're in New England, the home of Moxie. It's a soft drink, not too sweet, with a flavor all its own. I know some who think it's bitter, but I like it." Her eyes gleamed. "You can have a taste of mine. Now, what are you going to have?"

Nikko peered at the menu, nothing really leaping out at him—until he saw…. "I'll have the mac and cheese." That had always been his go-to comfort food when he was a kid. "And a Coke, please."

By good timing, their server appeared to take their order. The drinks arrived not long after, and Nikko sipped his Coke through a straw, his face turned toward the ocean.

"Mitch said your parents died when you were only a teenager, and that your grandmother raised you." Valerie's tone was kind.

Nikko nodded. "Grandma and Ichy, my brother." He swallowed. "I wish I knew where he was."

Valerie reached across the table and wrapped thin, cool fingers around his. "Nikko, I'm sure wherever he is, he's safe, and that's what's important." She met his gaze. "Do the police want you to be a witness too?"

He shook his head. "They have my statement. I knew nothing about the drugs, and they'll have plenty of evidence about the… prostitution, seeing as they had an undercover detective there for a while. I can't see them needing me." He dropped his gaze and stared at the table. "It's just a case of waiting until they come to trial. Once they've been put away, maybe I'll get my brother back." The tears were there, threatening to spill out, but Nikko kept a tight rein on his emotions.

Valerie said nothing, but she tightened her grip on his hand and sipped her Moxie. After a few minutes of comfortable silence, she stroked the back of his hand. "Does your grandmother know you're here?"

Nikko shook his head once more. "At the club we were allowed to call the retirement home once every couple of weeks, but only with a guard sitting in on the call the whole time. I got to speak to her once, and she was awfully confused that day—I don't know if Mitch told you, she has Alzheimer's—but the last time the nurse came on and said Grandma was having a bad day, and that she'd pass on our love when it was a good time." His throat seized up and he took a drink of Coke.

"When we get home, I want you to call your grandmother," Valerie said, her voice quavering. "You make sure she knows you're okay."

"Yes, thank you," Nikko said gratefully.

Just then, their order arrived. Valerie thanked their server and smiled at Nikko. "Enjoy your lunch, and then we'll go see what our men have been up to."

Our men. It had a good sound to it. Nikko pictured Mitch, that handsome face, with a five-o'clock shadow because he hadn't bothered shaving for a day or two. Those deep brown eyes that could make Nikko weak at the knees when they focused on him.

My man.

Nikko liked the sound of that too.

LUNCH WAS over. It hadn't been much, just sandwiches and milk, Dad huffing because Mom had sent him a text to say she and Nikko were going to have lunch out. For one brief moment, Mitch's stomach had turned over, hoping Nikko wasn't being subjected to a barrage of questions. Then he considered his mom's words that morning and decided against it.

He and Dad were sitting in the living room, Dad in one of the armchairs and Mitch stretched out on the couch.

"I like Nikko, like him a lot," Dad said in a matter-of-fact tone. "He's interesting. More than that, the boy has integrity." He peered at Mitch over his glasses. "You sure he's only twenty-two? He seems very mature."

"Maybe because he's been through stuff that someone his age has no business going through," Mitch said softly, his hands laced behind his head. He had no idea what Mr. M looked like, or where he was, but right then Mitch prayed he was in a lot of pain.

Dad's face fell. "Maybe you're right." He paused and looked over at Mitch. "I wasn't sure what to expect, you know."

"What do you mean?" Mitch sat upright.

"Well, after everything you'd told us about him, and the way Monica went on...." Dad took off his glasses and cleaned them absently with his handkerchief. "But when I saw him, I was surprised by how… fragile he looked." He put his glasses back on, his eyes troubled. "Mind you, I'm not sure what I expected a…." He paused.

"A hooker? Prostitute? Whore?" Mitch sighed. "From the moment I met him, none of those words seemed to fit. It wasn't until I found out the truth that I realized why, of course. That wasn't him. That was *never* him." He closed his eyes. "I can still see him, sitting there in that chair, his feet curled under him, his nose in a book, while all around these guys were parading like peacocks. There was something about him, right from the start."

"When you know, you know," Dad murmured quietly. Mitch jerked his head up and stared at him. Dad laughed. "How many times did we tell you kids about how your mother and I met? Didn't you listen? Or was it a case of, 'Oh, it's just the old man going blah blah blah'?"

Mitch flushed guiltily.

Dad cackled. "Gotcha. My point is, I knew your mother was the one for me the moment I laid eyes on her. Well, my heart knew, at any rate. It took my head a little longer to work it out." He locked eyes with Mitch. "And you knew too, when you saw Nikko. Okay, so the way you two got together isn't exactly conventional, but who gives a damn about convention? When it comes to love, there *are* no rules."

Mitch's heart swelled with love for his Dad. "Yeah," he said, the word barely a whisper.

Dad cleared his throat. "I'm glad you're here, but I'm assuming at some point you'll be heading back to New York. You must have work to do to get ready for September."

Mitch's stomach churned. "I don't want to think about that right now." He wasn't about to tell his dad that he was dreading going back. Mitch knew it was the same every summer. He got to spend a few weeks in Maine and would recall how much he loved his home state. Then he'd get back to NYC, have a week of feeling homesick, and then life would get back on track.

Until the next visit.

"Could it be you're finally tired of the Big Apple?" Dad asked, his eyes twinkling. "I can understand why you wanted to live there—apart from Ogunquit, there are few places around here where you could feel free to be yourself—but maybe it's time to think about moving on. Or should I say, moving back." He tilted his head. "You're older, your tastes have changed, maybe your expectations too. There's nothing wrong in that. But don't let fear hold you back. I know it can be a damn scary thing to step out of your comfort zone, but you wouldn't be on your own." He smiled. "Not now."

God, Mitch wanted to believe that with every cell, molecule, and atom of him. "I don't know that for sure," he said slowly. "Nikko has plans too, and I don't figure in them."

Dad raised his eyebrows. "Are those plans set in stone? Nikko's perspective might have changed too, you know. It's not just you in this relationship." He smiled. "I've always liked that quote from Carl Jung. 'The meeting of two personalities is like the contact of two chemical substances: if there is any reaction, both are transformed.'" Dad peered over his glasses again. "Seems particularly apt to me."

Mitch remained silent, digesting his dad's words. *Can I allow myself the luxury of planning a future with Nikko?* Dad had set something in motion, deep inside Mitch.

Maybe I have some thinking to do.

Chapter Twenty

Mitch sat on the swing, the air full of music drifting from the house, a stunningly beautiful flow of melodies. Nikko had been playing since breakfast. In fact, apart from meals, Nikko had been playing most of the time for the last three days. Mitch had always been an average player, in spite of his mom's desire to have a concert pianist in the family. None of his siblings had realized her dream, either, so he guessed she was in heaven right then. He'd stood and watched Nikko as he played, marveling at the expression of intense concentration on his face.

It had taken him until this moment to work out what was really going on.

Nikko wasn't talking about whatever was plaguing his thoughts—he was letting it all out via his fingers. And if the choice of pieces was anything to go by, there was a lot of emotion bubbling away inside him. By the time dinner arrived, he looked worn out, but as each evening passed, Mitch detected an easing of tension in him, as though he'd come through a struggle and had won.

"He's amazing."

Mitch smiled at his mom as she walked through the yard to join him, two mugs in her hands. She handed one to him and sat on the stone bench near him. Mitch took a sip of coffee and nodded. "Yes, he is."

She sighed. "What blows me away is the pieces he's been playing. Chopin's Scherzo No. 2, Rachmaninoff's Prelude, Liszt's piano sonata…. These demand real skill."

"They're very emotional, the way he plays them," Mitch said quietly. "Almost as if he's fighting some battle internally, and using the music to vent."

Her gaze met his. "That's interesting. That was my thought too." She paused to drink but soon brought her attention back to Mitch. "Have you two talked?"

Mitch shrugged. "Yes, but not about important things. Nothing that tells me what's going on in his head." He was trying not to panic, but it felt like they were taking a backward step. And then there was the whole not sleeping together situation....

"I take it there's been no 'migration' in the night?"

He jerked his head up and stared at her. "Ever consider this might be something I don't want to discuss?" It had been bad enough at the start of the week. Mitch did *not* want to talk about his sex life with his mom.

"Sure, I considered it—then I thought, what the hell, some things need to be talked about." She raised her eyebrows. "You think I didn't know when Shaun used to sneak up from the basement to Monica's room when he stayed here for the weekend? Or that Deirdre never slept in her own bed once, from the first time she brought Eric to meet us? Pfft."

Mitch gaped. "Do they *know* you knew?"

Mom chuckled. "Are you crazy? This is good ammunition. I was saving it for when they got their own kids, if they ever tried the 'you can't sleep together' routine. I figured that would shut them up quickly."

Mitch laughed. "You are an evil woman."

She beamed. "It comes with being a mom. But back to you and Nikko. I didn't put you two in the same room because I was mindful of the circumstances. I thought maybe Nikko needed some space." She tilted her head to one side. "But I'd imagined you'd be going to his room by now. You surprise me."

He sighed. "I've been trying to give him space too. I didn't want to push him. I guess I was waiting for him to make the first move when he was ready."

The piano lapsed into silence. Mom glanced toward the house. "That boy needs to get out. Why don't you pack a picnic lunch and take him for a drive along the coast? Let him feel the wind in his hair, the sand in his toes."

"I took the rental back, remember?"

She stared at him. "So take my car. I'm not going anywhere today. And besides, I have a student arriving after lunch and I'll need my piano." She winked.

"Ah, now I see the real reason you want us out of the house," he said with a grin. He had to admit, the idea was alluring. Mitch nodded. "Okay, I'll suggest it to him."

"Don't suggest—insist," Mom said firmly. "You need this, both of you." She rose to her feet. "And now I'll go and see what delicious morsels I have in the refrigerator to sweeten the deal." She gazed at him fondly. "Love you, sweetheart. I just want you to be happy."

He got up and gave her a tight hug. "I love you too." He looked over at the house.

If I can make Nikko happy, then I'll be happy.

MITCH SWITCHED off the car engine. "Okay, this is it. We're here."

Nikko peered through the windshield. "Where is here, exactly?" He unfastened his seatbelt and got out of the car. The fresh, salty, warm air hit him instantly after the relative coolness of the AC. Mitch had parked along the road, a line of cars in front of him. To the left were huge, beautiful properties, but to the right were rocks, over which Nikko could just about see the ocean.

"Well, we drove through Kennebunkport, and this is Goose Rocks Beach." Mitch was at the trunk, taking out the cooler and a couple of beach towels. Nikko took the towels and grabbed his cap. Mitch pointed a little distance along the road. "There's a path right there that cuts through to the beach." They walked to where the rocks and shrubs were bisected by soft-looking sand. Nikko didn't hesitate. He removed his flip-flops and stepped onto warmth. He and Mitch strolled onto the beach that was already filling up. Mitch turned left and headed toward the far end of the beach where it curved. They found a spot close to the rocks and spread out their towels.

Nikko looked out at the waves rolling in, crashing onto the shore. "Can we go in?"

"To paddle or swim?"

He smiled. "I just want to get my feet wet." He stripped off his T-shirt, Mitch copying him, and dropped it onto the towel. One thought flitted through his mind. *Thank God there are no scars.* The welts left by Mr. M were all gone.

Mitch held out his hand and Nikko took it, the two of them walking over the hot sand to where the cool water frothed around their ankles. They strolled hand in hand along the shoreline, their pace unhurried, Nikko content to feel the heat of the sun on his body.

"Did you come here as a child?"

Mitch smiled. "My first memories of being on a beach are of here. Mom and Dad would pack up the car, strap us in, and head up to

Kennebunkport. You can imagine taking all the paraphernalia that comes with four kids—and two dogs—was some undertaking."

"Who is the oldest?"

"Gareth. He's fifty. Then there's Deirdre, she's forty-seven. Then me, then Monica who's forty-one."

"Wow." Nikko couldn't imagine growing up in such a large family. "I bet you were all a handful."

"We had our moments," Mitch admitted. He squeezed Nikko's hand. "You think you would have liked having a sister or two?"

Nikko considered the question. "Maybe. Sometimes it was hard, just being the two of us, when my parents died. Ichy was stronger than me. He coped better."

"Baby, how old were you and Ichy when they died?"

"I was fourteen and Ichy was eighteen."

Mitch nodded. "Then of course he coped better—he had to, for your sake."

Nikko fell silent, listening to the waves crashing around them.

"How are you doing? Really?"

He tensed, but he knew the conversation had been coming. Mitch had been so patient with him, but Nikko hadn't felt like talking.

Maybe it's time.

"I've been thinking a lot about the last two months," he said slowly. "I wasn't prepared for how much that whole episode affected me. I mean, when I knew what working for Richards would involve, a part of me was thinking, 'it's only sex.'" He swallowed hard. "Only it wasn't, of course." Mitch's hand tightened around his, and Nikko gave him a grateful glance. "And now that it's over, I'm finding it really difficult to shrug it off."

"Nikko, no one expects you to just shrug it off," Mitch said earnestly. "Okay, so I know you haven't told me everything that happened in that place, but even I know it has to have taken its toll on you."

"Yeah, but I'm trying to forget it and move on, and it's not happening as fast as I'd like it to." Nikko took a deep breath. "I have to be honest here. My head isn't in the right place to be starting my master's. I... I need more time." He halted and gazed at Mitch. "I've been considering deferring my entry until January. Maybe by then I'll have gotten my act together."

Mitch faced him and grasped his hands. "Listen to me. You do what you feel is right, okay? And your life will move on when *you're* ready for it to move on." He locked gazes with Nikko. "But you're the only one that can make that decision. No one gets to decide these things for you *ever again*."

Nikko closed his eyes, inhaling deeply. "Thank you." He opened his eyes and stared into Mitch's. "And thank you for putting up with me this week."

Mitch smiled and moved closer. He released Nikko's hand and cupped his cheek. "I wouldn't call it putting up with you. I just gave you the space you needed. I wasn't going to rush you." He brought their mouths together, and Nikko sighed into the kiss, looping his arms around Mitch's neck. Mitch put his arms around him and held him, the moment sweet and absolutely perfect.

Nikko was the first to break the kiss. "How about we go back to our towels and eat something? I'm starving." As if to corroborate his words, his stomach chose that moment to growl.

"Sounds like you need it," Mitch said with a chuckle. He took Nikko's hand. "Come on, let's go see what delights my mom packed for us."

They walked back up the beach, their hands clasped. For the first time since they'd arrived in Maine, Nikko felt at peace. He was enough of a realist to know it wouldn't last—his worries weren't about to disappear overnight—but the way Mitch supported him gave Nikko hope.

There was only one thing that continued to niggle away at him. Four nights under the same roof, and Mitch hadn't come once to Nikko's bedroom. Nikko was a mess. On the one hand he was grateful for the time to get his head around all the emotions that were warring inside him, but on the other, he wanted more of what they'd shared in New York—namely, Mitch in his bed. It was only Mitch's declaration that he loved him that kept Nikko going. But hearing him confess to not wanting to rush things lightened Nikko's heart. He smiled to himself. Mitch really was a gentleman.

So if anyone's going to make the first move, it has to be me.

MITCH STARED at the bedroom ceiling, the white paint now a pale blue in the light of the moon that filled the room. *Nikko is up there. Just one floor separating us.* All he had to do was get out of bed, creep up the narrow staircase and....

He sighed. If he got to spend the night with Nikko curled up in his arms again, it would be because Nikko wanted it. Once the rest of the family arrived on Saturday, things wouldn't be the same. Five bedrooms and thirteen adults made for some interesting logistics, and the chances of sneaking unnoticed up to Nikko's room would be practically zero. The last thing Mitch wanted was to make Nikko feel more awkward.

The bedroom door opened and closed.

Mitch rolled over to find Nikko standing there, a robe clutched around him, the moonlight catching in those dark eyes. "Hey." Mitch just about caught the whisper.

He sat up in bed, the sheet falling around his hips. "Is everything all right?" His pulse quickened.

Nikko gave a hesitant nod. "Can... can I join you?"

Mitch wanted to fist pump the air. He maintained a calm exterior and nodded, pulling back the sheet. Part of him liked that idea too—his dick twitched to life.

Nikko hadn't missed it. He hurriedly raised his chin to focus on Mitch's face. "Is this okay? I mean, would your parents object if they found out?"

Mitch covered his face with his hand. "Oh my God. You wouldn't even ask that if you'd heard the conversation I had with my mom this morning. And trust me, I am never, *ever* going to recount that talk."

Nikko smiled, the hesitation vanishing. "Okay, then." He undid the tie around his waist and shucked off the robe, letting it fall to the floor. His skin glowed pale in the moonlight that glinted off his hair. Mitch caught his breath at the sight—Nikko's nude, slight form, smooth skin, taut belly, and below that, his long, slim cock that already showed signs of growing harder.

"You are so beautiful." Mitch couldn't keep the words inside a moment longer. "Nikko, please... would you loosen your hair?"

Nikko's eyes widened just a fraction, and then he nodded. Swiftly he removed the hair tie and his fingers worked the long hair free of its braid. He shook his head and long, black hair fell down his back in a heavy silk curtain. "Like that?" he asked shyly.

Mitch nodded. "I love it when you wear it loose."

Nikko climbed into bed and lay down, staring up at him, his eyes large. "Come here," he beckoned, his arms reaching toward Mitch, his hair pulled around to fall over his shoulder.

Mitch wasn't about to refuse such a wonderful invitation.

He stretched out next to Nikko, lying on his side and gazing at him as if it were a dream and any second now he was going to wake up. "Couldn't you sleep?" He twisted the silken strands of Nikko's hair around his fingers, loving the feel of it.

Nikko smiled and reached down to slowly pump his stiffening dick. "What makes you think I'm here to sleep?"

It was enough to have all Mitch's blood heading south. He leaned over and kissed Nikko, loving how Nikko returned the kiss eagerly, hands cupping the back of Mitch's head to pull him in tighter, lips parting with a sigh. The soft sounds Nikko fed into his mouth were pure heaven. Mitch slid his hand over smooth skin, pausing to tweak Nikko's nipple. Nikko gave a low moan of pleasure and the sound went straight to Mitch's cock.

"That feels so good," Nikko said with a sigh. "Again."

Mitch went one better. He leaned across and took the tiny nub between his lips and sucked it, drawing the blood into it and making it stiff. When he tugged at it with his teeth, Nikko's groan grew louder. For one brief moment Mitch thought about his parents, their room a few feet away. Then all such thoughts fled when Nikko wrapped his hand around Mitch's dick and stroked him. When his thumb slid across the tip of Mitch's cock, it was Mitch's turn to groan, and he fell back against the pillows.

Nikko chuckled. "Oh, you like that?" He moved his hand down Mitch's shaft and squeezed his balls gently. "How about that?" One finger traced the skin between his balls and his hole, teasingly slowly. "Or how about this?"

Mitch spread for him. "More." This was a Nikko he'd never seen, and he was loving every second of it.

"You want more?" Nikko withdrew his hands, and Mitch wanted to growl at him to put them *right back*. Nikko sat up and stared at him. "Roll over onto your belly."

Okay, this was new.

Unable to repress the shudder that coursed through his body, Mitch did as he was instructed, grunting in surprise when Nikko moved swiftly to grab his thighs and spread his legs wide. The shudder grew more pronounced as the bed dipped and warm breath ghosted over his ass. Firm fingers pulled his cheeks apart, and Mitch trembled to feel that breath on his hole. "Fuck."

"I'm coming to that part." A rough chuckle was followed by a hot, wet tongue licking him from balls to hole.

Mitch's attention was torn between the wonderful sensations Nikko's tongue was inflicting and the idea that Nikko's words had engendered in his brain.

Who is going to be doing the fucking here? Mitch had a sneaking suspicion it wasn't going to be him. *Ho-ly fuck.*

"Up on your hands and knees," Nikko ordered. Mitch didn't hesitate, and he moaned when his cheeks were spread once more as Nikko buried his face in his crease. Mitch shivered when Nikko licked over his hole, pushing the tip of his tongue inside and humming. Mitch lowered his chest to the mattress, his weight on his forearms, and groaned. Nikko's only response was to push deeper until he was fucking Mitch with his tongue.

When Nikko broke off from his sensual onslaught, Mitch growled, "Don't stop!"

"Condom?" Nikko inquired breathlessly. "Because if you don't have one, I'm just going to have to fuck you with my fingers and tongue until you come all over these nice sheets."

Holy Mother of God. It was a struggle not to come on the spot there and then.

"Toiletries bag, on the nightstand," Mitch replied. "Lube in the top drawer."

Nikko chuckled and the bed dipped again. "Guess I know what you've been doing these past few nights." He heard the *snick* of a tube flipping open and then—*Christ, yes*—a cool finger sank inside him.

"Well, I had to do *something* to keep myself occupied," Mitch gasped, balancing on one arm as he reached down to wrap a hand around his aching dick.

"Hands off." The note of authority in Nikko's voice was a serious turn-on. "Tonight that cock is all mine, you got that?" Another finger stretching him, getting him ready for that long dick.

"Okay, who are you, and what have you done with Nikko?" Mitch joked, panting when Nikko nudged his gland. "Never—oh *fuck*, right there!—never knew you liked topping."

Nikko leaned over him, his heavy hair trailing over Mitch's back, and kissed between his shoulder blades. "I was the top in both my previous relationships," he whispered before planting more soft kisses down Mitch's spine until he reached his fingers wedged in Mitch's hole. "Never bottomed until New York."

Mitch's heart gave a jolt. "Oh, God, Nikko, I—"

"And before you become overwhelmed by guilt," Nikko added, placing a gentle kiss on each ass cheek, "you need to know something." He withdrew his fingers, and Mitch stilled at the feel of Nikko's cock against his entrance. "I loved it"—the head pressed slowly through the tight ring—"every single time"—inch by inch Nikko pushed gently, filling him, stretching him—"you were inside me." Nikko grabbed hold of his hips. "Like I'm all the way inside you now."

Mitch dug his fingers into the bedding and held on tight. "For the love of God, Nikko, fuck me."

Nikko's breathing sped up. "My pleasure," he whispered. He began to move, slowly at first but picking up speed with every thrust. "God, you're so tight."

"It's been a while, okay?" Mitch panted as lightning shot up his spine.

"I believe that was my line," Nikko said with a chuckle, sliding in faster. "I used to look at you, naked in the playroom, and every single time we fucked I wanted to bury my dick in your ass so badly." He was breathing harder now.

"Fuck, Nikko...." Mitch loved it when a lover talked dirty.

"You like that, huh?" Nikko laughed and punched his cock into Mitch, making him cry out. "The things I'm learning about you tonight...." He thrust harder, deeper, until Mitch was crying out with the need to come. "Your ass is gripping my cock so tightly." A pause. "Oh my God. Seeing my dick spreading your tight hole makes me want to come."

Mitch shoved back onto Nikko's cock. "Then come. Do it. I want to feel you come." He shoved back again, this time squeezing around Nikko's length.

Nikko groaned, tightening his grasp on Mitch's hips and pulling them together, the loud slap of flesh on flesh so fucking erotic. "Shit, I can feel you, feel your muscles gripping my shaft." He reached under Mitch's body and wrapped his fingers around the full, heavy cock, pumping it. "You're almost there, aren't you?"

"Fuck, yeah," Mitch growled into the sheets. He raised himself up on his arms and twisted to stare at Nikko over his shoulder. "Harder, fuck me harder." He cried out when the head of Nikko's dick grazed his gland. "There!"

Nikko's hips pistoned, rutting into Mitch. "What—here?" He thrust in hard. "It *was* here, right?" Again, only harder.

Mitch's cock pulsed, creaming over Nikko's hand, and he arched. "Fuck!"

"Oh, God, yes." Nikko bent over Mitch's back, his dick throbbing inside him. "God, Mitch, I feel you." He pressed his chest to Mitch's, his body shaking, his breathing harsh and loud, his cock twitching inside him.

Mitch pitched forward onto the bed, taking Nikko with him. He lay beneath his smaller lover, out of breath, out of come, and out of his mind with awe. "God, you know how to fuck a man's brains out." Minishocks jolted through him, the remnants of his orgasm.

Nikko's chuckle tickled his ear. "I can't have fucked that much out of you. You're still talking." Mitch held his breath as Nikko eased his cock out of him. He rolled over as Nikko dropped the tied-up condom onto the floor, and grinned. Nikko knelt up on the bed and grinned back at him, his chest still rising and falling rapidly. "Well-fucked is a good look on you."

Mitch laughed and grabbed Nikko, pulling him down onto his body, his hair falling over his shoulders, thick and heavy. He gazed at Nikko's face poised above his. "Is this what I have to look forward to from now on? Is this the new and improved Nikko?" Mitch reached up to run his fingers through Nikko's hair, loving how Nikko leaned into the touch.

Nikko smiled. "This is me, Mitch, the Nikko I always was. You just didn't get to see me." His smile faltered. "I hope he isn't that much different from the guy you fell in love with."

Mitch stroked his sweet face. "Baby, I love you—every part of you." He cupped Nikko's head and drew him down into a lingering kiss, their tongues tangling in a slow, erotic ballet. When they parted, he smiled. "There's just one thing."

"What?"

Mitch stared into those dark eyes. "Maybe we should sleep in your bed. Unless you want to fight over who gets the wet spot?"

Nikko laughed. "Good thinking." Then he bit his lip. "Maybe I should have been a little quieter?"

Mitch chuckled. "Trust me. That ship has most definitely sailed." *And if we're really unlucky, tomorrow morning my mom will get a lot of mileage out of this.*

Chapter Twenty-One

NIKKO OPENED his eyes. Something was different. He was still in Mitch's old room, with its pale blue walls and dormer windows, the sunlight just beginning to edge its way into the room. Then he realized what had changed. A warm, solid body was curled at his back, an arm draped over his waist, and a strong leg hooked over his. Mitch's breathing was even, his lover still fast asleep.

Nikko lay very still, unwilling to disturb Mitch from his slumber. He closed his eyes and let his mind play over the previous night. He still couldn't believe how boldly he'd behaved. For the first time since he and Mitch had met, Nikko had felt free to be himself. More importantly, he recalled the way he'd made love to Mitch with nothing short of relief. Gone was the numbness that had been so prevalent during his encounters at the club.

I have to stop thinking of it as a club and see it for what it was—a whorehouse. It may well have been an exclusive whorehouse, frequented by rich men who paid handsomely to fuck men in anonymity, but that didn't change what it had been in essence. But his fears that the joy he usually found in sex was lost to him had proved groundless. Nikko had exulted in the way Mitch made his body sing in ecstasy. *I felt so... alive.*

None of this altered his resolve, however. He'd come to a decision—he would wait until January to continue his studies. The intervening four months would be enough of a buffer zone to enable him to enter his master's degree program with renewed enthusiasm.

That only left one thing to be decided—Mitch.

There was no easy-fix solution to solve this issue. Mitch had his career. His life in New York. His family here in Maine. The only question in Nikko's mind was centered on the likelihood of making a long-distance relationship work. He didn't want to lose Mitch, not now. But the thought of spending long periods apart made his heart ache.

And I haven't given a thought to what Mitch might want. What if he doesn't want a relationship under those terms? What then?

Mitch stirred, his arm tightening to pull Nikko more firmly against him, making Nikko aware of the hard cock nestled in his crack. "Good morning," Mitch murmured, rocking gently, the motion allowing his dick to rub slowly over Nikko's hole. "God, you smell sexy first thing in the morning."

All contemplative reflections were put aside as Mitch's sensual movement awoke Nikko to the possibilities of a morning of intimacy. Nikko did his best to keep his breathing regular, but what was uppermost in his mind was the thought of maneuvering his body to give Mitch greater access. Judging from the way Mitch was rolling his hips, he had the same idea.

"Do you know how much I loved waking up in your arms last Sunday?" Nikko said in a low voice, giving himself up to the sensuality of the moment. He breathed in the warm, familiar musk that was Mitch, relishing the feel of Mitch's arm around him.

Mitch stilled and his breath stirred the hairs on the back of Nikko's neck. "Me too. I missed this, missed it a lot this week."

Nikko turned over in his arms to stare at Mitch. "Then why didn't you say something? *Do* something?"

Mitch studied his face in silence. Eventually he let out a heavy sigh. "I guess I was afraid."

"Of what?"

"Finding out you didn't feel the same." He gave a quick shrug. "And then there was that whole, 'not pushing you, giving you space' decision."

Nikko huffed. "Yeah, okay, I can understand that. All *I* can see, however, is four mornings when we might have been waking up like this. Four nights when we could have been going to sleep wrapped around each other." His sense of loss was so acute, it made his heart ache. *Maybe it's because I don't know how many times we'll get the opportunity to be together.* He hungered for as much time with Mitch as he could get.

Mitch chuckled. "Nikko Kurokawa, are you pouting?"

"No," Nikko said, more vehemently than he'd intended.

"Yeah? Tell that to your bottom lip." Mitch was definitely awake now and smirking.

"Oh shut up." He was *not* pouting. Not.

"Oh my God, you are." Mitch rubbed across Nikko's lip with the pad of his thumb. "Yep, definite pouting going on here." Another slow rub, dipping briefly between his lips.

That was *so* sexy.

Nikko tried to be pissed at him, but disconcertingly his dick was getting in on the act, jerking up toward his belly. *Just go with it.* He sucked on Mitch's thumb, loving the way Mitch's breath caught, how Mitch's eyes darkened with desire. When Mitch brought his mouth to Nikko's, however, he attempted to move away, muttering about morning breath.

"Don't care," Mitch said with an evil smile. "And there's a packet of mints in the nightstand if you're really bothered."

Nikko stared. "Mints?"

Mitch met his stare. "This is my room, remember? This is where I sleep when I come here for the weekend. And if I want to keep mints in my nightstand drawer, I will."

It was Nikko's turn to shrug. "Whatever." Then a wicked thought struck him. He stretched out an arm to yank open the drawer and felt around until he heard the crinkle of the bag. He removed a couple of peppermints from the bag and popped them into his mouth, allowing them to dissolve slowly on his tongue.

Mitch watched him with incredulous eyes. "Wow. You really do hate morning breath, don't you?"

Nikko ignored him and dove under the sheets to where the object of his attention awaited him, full and thick and pointing toward Mitch's navel. A second or two later, he knew the penny had dropped when he caught Mitch's softly uttered "fuck" as Nikko licked over the head of his cock. He chuckled and lifted the already solid dick with a couple of fingers, moving into a more comfortable position before sliding it between his lips and giving it a good, hard suck.

"Fucking *hell*."

There was nothing Nikko liked more than giving—or receiving—an enthusiastic morning blow job. The sheet completely covered him, bathing his view in a diffused light. He gave Mitch's beautiful cock his undivided attention, licking it from root to tip, taking it as deep as he could, wetting it thoroughly and then blowing softly over it, watching Mitch's balls tighten and the muscles in his abs jump. When he tasted precome, he prayed silently that Mitch's nightstand drawer held something more than a bag of mints.

Nikko crawled up Mitch's body and poked his head out from beneath the sheet. Mitch regarded him, his head propped up on thick pillows, his pupils huge, blown with desire, chest heaving. Nikko grinned. "Tell me there are condoms in your drawer."

"Well, I *could* tell you that, but I'd be lying," Mitch said, out of breath.

Damn it. Not that Nikko was averse to the alternatives, but he'd really wanted Mitch inside him. His hole clenched at the thought of Mitch taking him.

"But I don't suppose you'd be interested in the fact that I brought my toiletries bag with me last night when we changed rooms." Mitch's eyes held a mischievous glint.

Nikko gaped at him. "Oh, we want to be funny, do we? Someone wants to be a smartass? Two can play at that game, you know." Not that Nikko had any intention of changing course. He wanted, too.

Mitch grabbed hold of his arms and tugged him until Nikko was astride him. "Baby," he groaned. "For God's sake, I'm so hard it hurts. Glove me up and ride me."

Suddenly all the humor of the situation vanished and the air was charged with sexual energy.

Nikko leaned over to peer at the floor beside the bed and stretched his hand toward the bag, his fingertips just catching on the zipper. He pulled it up onto the bed, unzipped it, and tipped its contents onto the comforter. Mitch wasn't laughing. He was stroking his heavy, thick dick, smearing precome over the taut, shiny skin that covered the head, his gaze focused on Nikko, his breathing rapid.

His fingers trembling, Nikko tore open the packet and freed the rolled latex. He covered Mitch's hard-as-steel shaft and then dribbled lube over it. Nikko shifted forward and positioned himself above the head of that glorious cock.

Mitch stopped him from lowering himself onto it. "Wait a sec." He grabbed the lube, slicked up a couple of fingers and reached between Nikko's thighs to slide first one, then both fingers into him. "I won't hurt you by letting you take me unprepared," he said firmly, pushing deep and making Nikko groan.

His words sent a flood of warmth rushing through Nikko. *He's taking care of me.* Mitch didn't break eye contact as he gently moved his fingers in and out, his lips parted, his breathing shallow. When he crooked his fingers to connect with Nikko's gland, a whole-body shudder rippled through him. Mitch nodded and did it again and again, until all Nikko's attention was focused on the sensations in his ass, tingles shooting along his dick to where a thin strand of precome glistened in the morning light as it descended from his slit onto Mitch's belly.

It was one of the sexiest things Nikko had ever seen.

Mitch gave him a single nod. "Now, baby. Guide me into you."

Nikko grasped Mitch's cock around the base, holding it steady while he eased the head in. He sank down slowly, his breath escaping in a long, drawn-out sigh of pleasure as Mitch's dick spread him wide. "I'd forgotten how good that feels," he moaned softly, bracing himself on Mitch's chest and rolling his hips. He gazed into Mitch's eyes. "Love it when you're inside me."

Mitch planted his feet on the bed, and tilting his hips, he began to thrust in and out, taking his time, his hands on Nikko's waist. "I love feeling your body tight around my cock," he said with a sigh. "The heat of you, the way your ass pulls me deeper into you." He slipped his hands around Nikko to pull him down, their lips meeting in a fervent kiss, tongues plundering each other's mouths. Nikko groaned into the kiss as Mitch picked up speed, thrusting faster and with more force, until he was moaning constantly.

Mitch grabbed hold of him and flipped them so Nikko was on his back, Mitch's dick still buried to the hilt as he covered Nikko with his body. He hooked his arms under Nikko's knees and rolled his ass up off the bed.

Oh, God. Everything got that little bit tighter. The change of angle had the head of Mitch's cock nudging Nikko's prostate with every thrust, and Nikko began to lose it. He knew he was babbling incoherently, with only single words making any sense—*harder*, *fuck*, *yeah*, *deeper*, *love you*. Mitch kept right on interrupting his nonsensical murmurings with kisses, tongue sliding deep in time with his dick, and God, that was so *hot*.

Then everything changed again as Mitch slowed down the pace. He stroked his cock in and out of Nikko's hole, each long glide making Nikko sigh with pleasure. "Oh, God, that's perfect," he breathed.

Mitch's face hovered above his, eyes large and so much darker than usual, lips parted. "I want this to last." He pulled almost all the way out and then slowly filled Nikko until he was balls-deep in his ass. Nikko wanted to *purr*, it felt so good. Mitch kissed him, the kisses languid and thorough, the gentle pace heightening the intimacy of their coupling.

Mitch broke the kiss and stared down at him. "I love you." He pulled out and then all the air was punched from Nikko's lungs when he thrust powerfully into him, leaving him gasping.

"God, *yes*," Nikko croaked.

Mitch grinned. "You like that?" He repeated the action, slamming into Nikko, hard, deep thrusts that hit his gland every time. "Want to see you come from this," he panted. "You're gonna come without touching your dick." He snapped his hips forward. "Fuck, I feel you. Your ass is rippling around my cock."

Nikko pushed back, meeting Mitch's thrusts, rocking on that thick dick impaling him. He wasn't sure how much more he could take. Nikko shuddered, each pump into his body sending him higher, higher, until he felt like he was flying, soaring, every nerve in him sparking, alight with ecstasy.

Then he felt it, that familiar lightning that tingled up and down his spine, rocketing through him from his balls all along his cock. Nikko shot his load, his come spattering his chest and abs, his body arching up off the mattress, his thighs trembling with each jolt of his orgasm.

Mitch groaned. "Fuck, you're beautiful when you come." He continued to fuck Nikko through his climax, his rhythm erratic, his thrusts hard and fast, balls slapping against Nikko's ass.

Nikko reached for him and dragged him down to meet his heated kiss, their tongues colliding once more. He squeezed tight around Mitch's dick, feeling the shudders that coursed through his lover, and the soft cries and groans as he neared completion. Nikko did it again, wanting to see Mitch lose it, to feel that throb inside him when Mitch filled him with his come. He sucked on Mitch's lower lip, his hands holding that face he loved so much, and then plundered that sweet mouth. "Now, Mitch," he panted, pushing the words between Mitch's lips. "Come now. Come."

Mitch threw back his head with a loud cry and then buried his face in Nikko's neck, thrusting all the way inside him, body stiff above him. "Love you, baby," he gasped.

Nikko wrapped his legs and arms around Mitch's body, holding him close, feeling his cock twitch inside him. Mitch lay on top of him, his breathing loud in Nikko's ear, little tremors pulsing through him now and again as he came down. Nikko held him, loved him, told him how good this felt, how good Mitch made him feel. When Nikko's heartbeat had returned to its normal rhythm, he stroked Mitch's face and kissed him, leisurely, thoroughly, the two of them still connected.

Mitch lifted his chin. "I don't want to come out of you," he admitted quietly.

Nikko stilled. "Why not?"

"Because this feels perfect. We're joined, as intimately as it's possible to be. I don't want to lose this feeling."

His words sent Nikko's heart soaring. "I know. But it's not like this is the last time we'll make love, is it?" He smiled. "Because you're addictive, Mr. Jenkins. And any time you want me?" He leaned in closer and whispered into Mitch's ear. "You can have me."

Mitch shivered. "Fuck, the things you say." After a moment he chuckled. "Although I can see that raising a few eyebrows if we keep disappearing. Someone *will* make a comment, believe me."

The way Nikko was feeling right then, he felt like he could deal with anything.

"WE NEED to talk about sleeping arrangements." As always, Mom came straight to the point.

"Okay." Mitch knew he sounded cautious, but he had no idea what was about to come out of her mouth. Nikko paused, toast halfway to his lips, and met Mitch's gaze. Mitch had a feeling his lover was thinking the same thing.

Mom sat down at the table with them, a small notepad and pen in her hand. "It would make things a whole lot simpler if you two share a room. That way, I can put Deirdre and Eric in her old room, Monica and Shaun in hers, Gareth can have a room to himself and the grandchildren can sleep down in the basement on the sofa beds. Cal and Ben can share, as can Lisa and Debbie. It's not like they haven't done it before." She paused and regarded them. "That wouldn't be a problem, right?" Her eyes sparkled. "At least I'm assuming not after this morning. Or last night, for that matter."

Mitch heard the hitch in Nikko's breathing. He reached under the table and took Nikko's hand in his. Mitch smiled innocently at his mom. "I'm okay with that." He gave Nikko's hand an encouraging squeeze.

Nikko blinked. "Oh… sure, that's fine. Do you want help getting ready for your guests?"

Mom beamed. "Thank you, Nikko, that would be wonderful. I'm going to make up all the beds and put out fresh towels, and an extra pair of hands would be great."

He smiled. "No problem."

Mom rose to her feet, patted his arms and left the kitchen. Once she was out of earshot, Nikko sagged into his chair. "She heard us, didn't she?"

Mitch laughed. "Baby, I think the next-door neighbors heard us."

Nikko let out a sigh. "You know, this morning I felt like I could take on the world. Now?" He shivered. "I have twenty-four hours until your family arrives, and I'm shaking like a leaf. Not to mention I don't think I can ever look your mom in the face again." He stared glumly at the tabletop.

Mitch leaned closer. "And if I promised you that she's heard worse?"

Nikko's head shot up. "You?"

"Hell, no. I'm talking about my sisters."

Nikko's jaw dropped. "Seriously?" He shook his head and then smiled. "Okay, I don't feel so bad now."

Mitch laughed. He lifted Nikko's hand and kissed it. "Good. I wouldn't want you to feel bad about this morning. I loved every minute of it." He grabbed Nikko and pulled him from his chair onto Mitch's lap.

"What are you doing?" Nikko tried to climb off, but Mitch held on tight. "Your mom will be back in a minute."

Mitch cupped Nikko's face, looking him in the eye. "Let her look. If I want to hold you, cuddle, kiss you, I will, okay? And that goes for the rest of my family. I don't care if they see us. God, I had to put up with them canoodling with their boyfriends when I was growing up. This is just payback." He laughed quietly, his hands gentle on Nikko's bare arms, rubbing, stroking.

Nikko relaxed a little into his embrace. "Okay."

He tilted his head. "What's making you nervous, baby?" When Nikko remained silent, Mitch studied him for a moment. "Is it because of what happened to you? Do you think they'll look at you differently?"

"How could they not?" Nikko asked softly.

Mitch wasn't going to tell him about Monica's outburst. He put his arms around Nikko and held him, stroking up and down his back. "For one thing, I don't think they'd say anything, and for another, if they did? My mom and dad would be really pissed. I'm sure you've noticed, but they already think the world of you."

"Really?"

Mitch had to smile at that. "Where have you been this week? They adore you." He knew it was the truth. His parents had warmed to Nikko almost instantly; Mitch swore he heard the click. "I promise you, it really will be all right." *And if it shows signs of not being, I'm going to bust some heads.* Not that he was too concerned. He had every faith in his siblings.

Mitch released Nikko and then patted his backside. "Now go help my mom get the place ready."

Nikko must have been feeling more confident. He narrowed his gaze and gave Mitch a look that promised retribution before exiting the kitchen in search of Mom.

Mitch grinned. Bedtime was looking more promising by the second.

Chapter Twenty-Two

"ANYONE WANT more coffee?" Monica asked, the pot in her hand. As voices rose to demand more, she made her way around the dining table, pouring out the fragrant brew. "Okay, that's it. If you want any more, you know where the kitchen is," she said with a grin as she sat down next to her husband.

Nikko gazed around the table at Mitch's family. Twelve adults of varying ages, and after four days, he was starting to know them a little better. Gareth was so like Mitch, it was uncanny, both in appearance and personality. He'd quickly worked out that Deirdre had a great sense of humor. Monica was more difficult to decipher. She didn't talk much, but she'd been pleasant enough with him. Mitch's brothers-in-law were both kind and considerate. The younger members of the family were aged from their midtwenties down to eighteen. Cal was the youngest, about to go to college. They were friendly and outgoing, and Nikko had warmed to them immediately.

It had taken Nikko maybe a day to stop waiting for the shoe to drop. Mitch's family was adorable, and if they'd had any thoughts on his life during the last two months, nothing was mentioned, at least not in his hearing.

He'd come to look forward to dinnertime. No matter what people did during the day, when the evening came, everyone gathered around the rectangular dining table. Dinners were always loud, with lots of conversation and laughter. At first Nikko had been hesitant to join in, but Mitch had soon put a stop to that. And once Valerie had insisted that he play the piano for them, the tone had been set for subsequent evenings, with everyone taking turns to play. Nikko had deliberately chosen pieces that were popular and less challenging than the ones he'd played during his first days there.

It seemed the rule for these family summer get-togethers was that there were no rules. Everyone did their own thing, sometimes in a larger group, other times not. The young people tended to stick together, preferring their own company and spending most of the time on the beach or sunning themselves on the patio. What Nikko liked most was how everyone got on with each other. The atmosphere in the house was pleasant and positive.

Nikko's days were spent with Mitch. They'd take a car and drive inland to see a different side to Maine than the coastline he'd come to love. Although the quiet, sparsely inhabited rural areas were often pretty, Nikko's heart belonged to the ocean. There were some places that quickly became favorites—the picturesque Cape Porpoise with its fishing boats and white-clapboard houses; Ogunquit, where he soon discovered the gay beach and the quaint café that had once been a gas station; Kennebunkport with its antiques shops and tea rooms. He'd listen to Mitch recounting tales from his childhood, loving how the memories lit up his lover's face with happiness. He'd watch Mitch laughing and joking with his brother and sisters, interacting with his nephews and nieces, and each new encounter revealed a little more about the man he loved.

His nights were spent in Mitch's arms, and he had no complaints whatsoever about how their love life was progressing. As the evenings wore on, he would find himself eagerly anticipating the hour when Mitch would close their bedroom door and they would spend the rest of the night bringing each other pleasure. When they were around members of the family, Mitch didn't hesitate to show affection toward him, and it gladdened Nikko's heart to see the reaction of those who loved him.

"Where have you gone?" Mitch whispered in his ear, bringing him back from his thoughts.

Nikko smiled at him. "I was thinking about how happy I am with you," he said truthfully. Mitch's eyes lit up and he leaned closer to kiss Nikko on the mouth. Nikko melted into the kiss, no more than their lips pressed together, warm and soft, but also an intimate connection that made him yearn for when they'd be alone.

His kisses make me hungry.

"You know, watching you two is like being around a pair of horny teenagers," Deirdre remarked. "I always get the impression you're imagining each other naked." Her eyes twinkled.

"Mom!" Debbie, Deirdre's eldest daughter, stared at her mother with a scandalized expression.

Nikko knew his cheeks were flushed; he could feel them burning.

"And of course you *never* made out with Eric when you two were first going out together," Valerie commented dryly. She caught Nikko's gaze and winked before returning her attention to her eldest daughter. "For instance, there was that time your father and I went out for the evening to a concert, and when we returned, there was a—"

"And you can stop *right there*, Mom," Deirdre interjected, her face bright red. Beside her, Eric was chuckling. She turned on him, her eyes wide. "And you're supposed to be on *my* side, not laughing along with her!"

Eric was shaking with laughter and failing miserably to look contrite. "Your mom does have a point, babe. We weren't exactly angels, were we?"

"That is *not* something to be admitted in front of our children," she muttered, glaring at him. Her son Ben snorted in an effort to smother his laughter.

Mitch guffawed. "Why not? I think it's good for them to know their parents were young once." He got a hard stare for his efforts.

"*I* think it's great that Uncle Mitch and Nikko feel comfortable enough to be themselves around their family," Cal stated quietly. When the laughter died away and heads turned in his direction, he gave a sheepish smile. "I mean, it makes me feel good to know that if—when—I bring my first… boyfriend here for a summer visit, I don't have to be worried about him feeling awkward. I'll be able to tell him this is a safe place."

A hush fell over the group. All the hairs on Nikko's arms stood on end, and he looked around the table at the faces of those gathered there. All he saw were expressions of love, affection—and surprise.

"Is there someone you wanted to invite?" Monica asked him, almost shyly. "You could have, you know." There were murmurs of agreement from Valerie and Malcolm.

Cal blushed from the collar up. "No, Mom. There's no one—yet." He reached for his glass of water and drained half of it.

"Nikko, will you play something for us?" Valerie asked suddenly. A chorus of approval greeted her suggestion.

"What are you in the mood for?" he asked. He had the feeling Valerie was trying to save her grandson from further embarrassment by changing the subject.

"The way this evening is shaping up, maybe we should be requesting show tunes," Gareth remarked with a snicker.

"Behave." Valerie gave him a look that would curdle milk, and Gareth had the good grace to flush. She turned to Nikko. "Would you play one of my favorites, 'Clair de lune'?"

Nikko beamed. "I'd love to." He rose up, and after kissing Mitch on top of his head, he walked through into the piano room and sat on the bench. The others followed, and by the time the first clear notes rang out, the couches, armchairs, and floor cushions were all occupied and everyone was listening intently. Nikko poured his heart and soul into his playing, and when Mitch brought a chair from the dining room to sit with him at the piano, Nikko's happiness was complete. The look of love and pride in Mitch's eyes sent warmth radiating throughout his body.

Nikko brought the piece to a close amid applause. He was about to play another piece when a wicked idea struck him. He paused, his fingers poised above the keys, and then launched into the opening chords of *Cabaret*.

"Argh!" Gareth howled. "I was only kidding. I *hate* show tunes!" Laughter broke out and Nikko halted his playing. He caught Gareth's eye and grinned. Gareth wagged his finger. "You have an evil streak, don't you?" More laughter at that. Gareth glanced across at Mitch who was chuckling. "You're going to have your hands full with that one. You sure you know what you're letting yourself in for?"

Mitch focused on Nikko's face. "Oh, I know, all right." His eyes shone, and the emotion Nikko saw there made him catch his breath. Mitch's love for him was there for all to see.

"I'd like to play something," Monica said. "If Nikko's had enough of playing for a while?" Nikko stood to one side, and as she moved to the bench, she leaned forward and planted a quick peck on his cheek. "That was just beautiful, Nikko. Thank you."

Impulsively, Nikko hugged her. "Thanks," he whispered. Mitch took his hand and led him to the spot Monica had vacated on the couch. Nikko sat on the floor at Mitch's feet, leaning back against his legs.

Mitch bent over to whisper in his ear. "Welcome to the family." He kissed the top of Nikko's head and then sat back. Heat radiated through Nikko's chest and a lightness spread throughout his limbs.

He had a new family.

"THAT'S THE last of the glasses and mugs from the living room," Mitch told his mom as he deposited the tray next to the dishwasher and began loading it. The rest of the family had already dispersed, leaving only him and Mom in the kitchen. Nikko had gone up to their room to grab a shower before bed. The heated glance he'd given Mitch when no one was looking left Mitch with no doubt that their night wasn't finished, not by a long shot. While his mom's back was turned, he adjusted his dick, praying she didn't notice. He knew that was probably a lost cause—his mom noticed everything.

"I'm glad we've got a chance to talk." Mom was heating a cup of milk in the microwave, the tin of hot chocolate standing on the counter in front of her. "There's something I've been meaning to bring up for a few days now, but I haven't been able to catch you on your own." She smiled. "You and Nikko are kind of joined at the hip. Not that I'm complaining, you understand. It's good to see my baby so happy." She paused. "And it's your happiness that I want to discuss."

"Oh?" Mitch didn't have a clue what was coming. He closed the dishwasher door, switched it on, and came over to sit at the breakfast bar. "What's on your mind?"

Mom poured steaming milk over the powdered hot chocolate and stirred briskly, not looking at him. "Are you certain you want to go back to New York?" she asked quietly.

Mitch stared at her. "Excuse me? What brought this on?" The familiar tight feeling around his chest, the one he got every time the thought of being parted from Nikko came to mind, was back with a vengeance. Except it wasn't just leaving Nikko that sent him into a panic—he'd soon realized it was also the idea of going back to his life in the city. Try as he might, he couldn't get up any enthusiasm for living in New York.

"Your father and I wondered if you were ready for a change, that's all." Her tone was innocent enough, but Mitch knew better. He recalled his conversation the previous week with his dad.

"What's the alternative?" Wherever he lived, it was still thousands of miles away from Nikko.

Mom turned to face him. "We know you're going to miss him, honey. We just thought you'd be better off being nearer to those people who love you, instead of being in New York and miserable."

"Have you forgotten something? Gareth lives in upstate New York, remember? And we see each other fairly frequently."

"Pfft. Gareth thinks nothing of driving five hours to come here for the weekends. You'd still see him—if you lived here...."

Now she had his full attention. "What are you talking about?" Mitch narrowed his gaze. "What are you up to?"

She gave a nonchalant shrug and picked up a cloth to wipe the counter. "I was just talking with my friend, Rachel Devon. I used to teach with her, but she moved schools a few years ago. It seems her high school is having real problems recruiting a history teacher." She gave him a sideways glance. "Your minor is history, right?"

Mitch folded his arms across his chest. "You know perfectly well it is." He sighed. "Go on, what else did Rachel say? And which high school does she teach in?"

"Old Orchard Beach High School. It's not that big a school, to be honest. In fact, it's the smallest high school in southern Maine. It has three history teachers, but one of them has given notice that he'll be leaving them at Christmas, so the position wouldn't be available until January. I just thought it might be worth your while giving them a call, maybe sending them a copy of your résumé, to see if they wanted to interview you...." Mom stopped wiping and looked at him directly. "It was just a thought."

"Uh-huh," Mitch said dryly. He couldn't deny it piqued his interest. However, moving back to Maine would be a huge step, not to mention a scary one, and Mitch's last experience of stepping out of his comfort zone had led to....

He stopped that train of thought right there. It had led to Nikko.

"You'd have to hand in your notice," Mom continued, "especially if you wanted to make a clean break and not go back in September." He stared at her, dumbfounded, and she frowned. "What?"

"Oh no, please, continue. You've obviously been giving the matter some serious thought. So, according to your plan, I apply for this job and move back to Maine? That's assuming they give me the job, of course. How exactly am I meant to live if my new job doesn't start until January?

More importantly, where would I live?" He had the feeling he already knew what her answer to that one was going to be.

"Mitch, this house has five bedrooms. I'm sure we have enough space for you and all your belongings for a few months. Plus, if you wanted more independence, there's always the space above the garage. We could put you in there." Her eyes gleamed. "That way, when Nikko comes to visit, you'd have some privacy." She bit her lip.

Mitch laughed. "You've thought of everything, haven't you?"

Mom stuck out her chin. "Well, do you blame me? If there's even a remote possibility that you might move back here, I'll do whatever it takes to help you out." Her glance softened. "Like I said, I just want you to be happy, baby."

Damn. His mom was sneaky.

"Look, I'll think about it, all right?" He could do that much.

She walked over to him and caressed his cheek with her soft hand. "That's good enough for me." She slid her hand to the back of his neck and pulled him down to kiss his forehead. When she released him, she grinned. "It's a good start, at any rate." Before he could respond, she continued. "Good night, Mitch." With that she exited the kitchen.

He stared after her, shaking his head.

She always has to have the last word.

NIKKO WAS floating on a sea of sensual joy. His body curved around Mitch's, both of them on their sides, his chest pressed against damp skin while he slowly rocked in and out of Mitch's ass. Wave after wave of pleasure washed over him, as he brought both of them almost to the edge of orgasm, only to back off and take things down a notch. Then he did it all over again, until Mitch was whimpering with need, begging him to let him come. It didn't matter that it was the early hours of the morning. Time had lost all meaning.

The world had disappeared, and it was just him and Mitch, lost in each other, locked in a spiral of heat and desire. Each slow thrust of his dick into Mitch pushed Mitch's shaft through Nikko's slick fist. Mitch was shaking, and Nikko knew it was time.

"Now, love." He worked Mitch's cock and filled him to the hilt, rolling his hips and groaning at the softness and heat that surrounded his hard dick. Nikko kissed Mitch's shoulder and then bit gently, exulting in the shudders that rocked Mitch's body from head to foot.

Mitch pushed his head back, and with a long, drawn-out cry, he came, pulsing over Nikko's hand, full-body shivers coursing through him. His body clamped down on Nikko's cock, and the exquisite tightness pulled Nikko over the edge, tumbling into a blissful abyss. Nikko howled as Mitch's ass milked his dick, come pumping into the latex. He let go of Mitch's sticky shaft and held on to him, shuddering as he came down from his climax.

"I… didn't think it possible," Mitch gasped.

"Hmm?" Nikko murmured into his ear.

"You and me. Sex. It just keeps on getting better and better." Mitch turned his head, and Nikko didn't hesitate, joining their lips in a tender kiss. Thoroughly melted, he slowly eased out of Mitch's body and dealt with the condom before returning to lie in Mitch's arms. Mitch's breathing grew more even, and he held Nikko closely, the two of them kissing at intervals.

Nikko sighed happily. "No arguments here." He closed his eyes. He loved the blissed-out sensation that always followed their lovemaking. They lay in silence for a while, Nikko listening to his lover's heart beating strongly beneath him. He stroked Mitch's damp chest. "Mitch? About dinner tonight…."

"What about it?" Mitch murmured, kissing his hair.

"Cal's remark about his first boyfriend—that *was* him coming out, wasn't it? I mean, the way your family looked at him."

Mitch nodded. "I loved how no one made a big thing of it. He was braver than I was, I'll tell you."

"I love your family," Nikko said sleepily, fighting a yawn.

Mitch chuckled. "Do you want to grab a quick wash before we fall asleep?"

Nikko raised his head. "One sec." He leaned over Mitch and peered over the edge of the bed. Grinning, he grabbed Mitch's T-shirt from the floor where he'd dropped it and came back to his lover to swipe it over Mitch's belly, before wiping his hand and both their dicks. Nikko dropped the garment back onto the floor and collapsed into Mitch's arms. "There. No more stickiness. *Now* can we sleep?"

He was dimly aware of Mitch's chuckle rumbling through his chest. "Go to sleep, baby. I love you."

"Love you too," he mumbled, already half-asleep.

NIKKO EASED out of the bed and pulled on his robe. Dawn had arrived half an hour before, and Mitch was still sleeping soundly, gentle snores escaping him. Nikko stood by the bed and gazed at his lover with a wry smile. *I should still be asleep too, considering what time we finally finished making love.* Damn body clock.

Nikko left the bedroom and crept downstairs, the house silent around him. When he entered the kitchen, he surmised Malcolm wasn't awake yet—the coffee machine was empty, clean but cold. Nikko smiled to himself and set about making the coffee how Malcolm liked it, imagining his delight to find it ready and waiting for him when he got up. Once the dark, aromatic liquid was dribbling into the coffee pot, Nikko opened the back door and stepped out onto the deck. The air was already warm, and birdsong filled the yard. To his surprise, he was not alone. Cal was sitting on the patio, curled up in a garden chair, seemingly deep in thought, a glass of water standing on the table next to him.

Nikko walked over and cleared his throat. "Good morning."

Cal gave a start and jerked his head to look in Nikko's direction. "I thought I'd be the only one up at this time of the morning."

Nikko smiled. "You'd be surprised. I'm here at this time most mornings, and your grandfather is usually here before me. He must be taking it easy this morning." He gestured with his head toward the kitchen. "There's coffee on if you're interested. It'll be ready in a minute or two, only I should warn you—it's made to Malcolm's specifications."

Cal grinned. "That's okay. I like Grandad's coffee. Mom thinks I'm weird, though."

"Would you mind if I joined you?"

Cal shrugged. "I don't mind." He gazed at the yard. "I was just sitting here, enjoying the quiet, thinking...."

Nikko sat in the chair next to Cal's. "It's a good spot for that." He glanced at Cal. "I think you were very brave last night."

"Oh?" Cal looked puzzled, but then he flushed and his eyes widened. "Oh. Yeah." His ears turned bright red and he coughed. "Thanks. I still can't believe I said that, or that everyone just seemed to... accept it."

Nikko left it there, not wishing to embarrass him further.

"My mom told me what happened to you," Cal said quietly. "I think you're the brave one."

Nikko wasn't sure how to react. "Ugh, I don't know about that." In the days that had followed his impulsive decision, Nikko had come to the conclusion that he'd been rash, but there was no way he could have let Ichy go back to being Richards's delivery boy. "I just did what I felt was right." He watched the wisps of cloud on the horizon, tinged with color. *I wonder if Ichy is watching the sunrise, wherever he is.* There was a dullness in his chest.

"Have you heard from your brother?" Cal asked him.

Nikko shook his head. "And if he's gone into a witness protection program, I won't hear from him. No one can tell me anything about where he is, how he's doing…." He swallowed. He couldn't think about Ichy. Everything was still too raw, too sharp. Nikko cleared his throat. "So, Mitch tells me you're going to college."

Cal nodded. "I'm going to the University of Southern Maine." He smiled. "Not venturing too far from home, am I? Mom's pleased about that. I'll be able to come home on the weekends—if I want to," he added.

Nikko laughed. "Yeah, good luck with that. I remember when I first got to college. I had way too much fun to consider going home as often as that. My grandma used to complain that I only came home when I'd gone through my entire wardrobe and needed to do some laundry." He got up from his chair. "Let me go pour us some coffee. I'll be right back." He paused. "How do you take yours?"

"Cream and one sugar, please."

Nikko nodded and went into the house, returning after a minute with two mugs. He handed one to Cal and retook his seat. "You looking forward to going to college?"

"Sure. It's kinda scary, but I'm sure I'll make lots of friends." Cal's cheeks were pink again.

Nikko had an idea what was going through his mind. "I met my first boyfriend about two months after I started my studies. We were together about a year."

"What happened?"

Nikko gave a shrug. "We wanted different things. He wasn't happy being tied to one person, and I wasn't happy about the idea of an open relationship, so we went our separate ways. It was good while it lasted." He smiled. "For one thing, I learned how to give a good massage." The memory of Mitch stretched out beneath him, boneless and groaning as Nikko kneaded his flesh, rose up in his mind.

"There's a story there," Cal said with a grin. He held up his hand. "Relax, I don't want to know." He met Nikko's gaze. "What advice would you give me? About relationships, I mean."

Nikko considered the question. "Be honest. Don't be afraid to say if something's on your mind. And don't let anyone rush you. If you don't want things to progress to… a certain level, then say so. It's your body, okay?"

Cal bobbed his head quickly, his neck red. "Gotcha." He took a sip of coffee. "Man, I always forget how strong that first mouthful is." Nikko snickered at that. Cal tilted his head to one side. "Would you mind if we kept in touch while I'm away at college? I don't want to be a bother or anything, but we could e-mail each other, text, maybe FaceTime now and again?"

Nikko smiled. "I'd like that." Cal beamed and the sight warmed Nikko inside. They sat in a comfortable silence, disturbed only by the chirping of the birds in the trees. Nikko reflected on the words of wisdom he'd just given Cal.

Maybe I should follow my own advice. There were a few things that had been on his mind the last day or so, and he knew he shouldn't keep them to himself. Mitch deserved to know what was going on in his head. But talking with Cal had given him an idea, one that required a little research.

I'll do a little digging, then *I'll talk to Mitch.* Hot on the heels of that came another thought. *But I'd better make it soon.* They didn't have long left together, only a couple of weeks before Mitch would have to leave for New York.

Nikko closed his eyes as if that would stave off the pain he knew was coming.

Fat chance.

Chapter Twenty-Three

"THANKS, DETECTIVE Jamison." Nikko pushed down hard on the urge to sigh and did his best to sound positive. "And thanks for talking to me. I know you're busy."

"Hey, no problem. I'm sorry I couldn't give you more information, but—"

"It's okay, I get it." Well, part of him did, the logical part that knew the NYPD were acting in Ichy's best interests. The illogical part wanted to yell *But I'm his brother, damn it! Surely I can be told?*

"So, you and Mitch...." Detective Jamison paused. "You're together?"

"Yeah." *But not for much longer.* Time was definitely the enemy right then. "We're at his parents' place in Maine at the moment."

"I think that's great." Nikko heard the note of warmth in the detective's voice. "I wish you both all the luck. I really mean that." Voices in the background. "Oops, sorry, gotta go. Listen, you've got my number. Any time you need to talk about this, you call, okay?" He chuckled. "I'm not saying I'll always be available, you understand, but I'll get back to you."

"Thank you," Nikko said sincerely. "Good-bye." He disconnected the call and placed the phone on the table next to his chair. Nikko closed his eyes and sat still, taking in the sound of the gulls shrieking as they soared above him, the cheerful chirp of small birds in the trees, both in the yard and beyond the back fence. He'd kind of known before he called what the response would be, but having it confirmed just brought the whole situation home to him in a wave of sorrow. His chest ached and all his limbs were like lead.

I love you, Ichy. Wherever you are.

"Phone call finished?"

Nikko opened his eyes and gave Valerie a half smile. "All done." He spotted the glass of lemonade she held out for him. "Oh, thank you."

Valerie sat in the other chair and took a drink of her lemonade. After a moment she peered at him over her glasses. "Want to talk about it? You seem down, sweetheart."

Nikko drank deeply and then set his glass on the table. "I called the detective who interviewed me to see if there was anything he could tell me about Ichy. He was very honest. He told me that when someone is taken into witness protection, it's very intense. The US Marshals show up, you get your stuff. They don't tell you where you're going or who you're going to 'be.' They take you somewhere, give you a new identity and a list of rules. No calling, texting, e-mailing anyone from your old life. And you have to abide by their rules because it costs thousands of dollars for each person in the program."

"Is Ichy's evidence that vital to the case?" Valerie asked, her gaze focused on him.

Nikko nodded. "We're talking about drugs across state lines, not to mention international boundaries too, so it's not just the NYPD involved—it's the FBI and the DEA. So no one can know where he is—not even me." Hearing Detective Jamison state the stark truth had made Nikko want to curl up and cry.

I won't see Ichy again until this fucking *trial is done with.*

God, it hurt.

"Nikko, can I ask you something about your case? You don't have to answer if you don't want to." Valerie's voice was gentle.

"Sure." He braced himself for whatever was coming.

"How come they didn't arrest you? And what about the others who worked in the club? Were they free to go too?" Valerie's cheeks flushed. "Not that I'm complaining. I'm overjoyed they let you go." She reached across and grasped his hand, squeezing it tightly.

Nikko gazed at their joined hands and smiled before raising his head to look her in the eye. "I asked the detectives about this. They told me human trafficking is a *big* deal right now for law enforcement. Apparently, there's a movement to not charge unwilling prostitutes anymore—they're seen as abuse victims. And because I was held against my will—well, that's what it amounted to, with them holding Ichy, too—they're going to charge Richards and the others with kidnapping too." His chest tightened. *A day will come when I'll be able to think about what happened without wishing the earth would open up and swallow me whole*. No matter what Mitch said, Nikko found it difficult to get past that one irrefutable fact. He'd been a prostitute.

Valerie stroked his hand, making him aware of her presence. "I know this must be an awful time for you, but you have to do your best to put it behind you. You have your whole future in front of you. You have so much talent, Nikko, and I for one can't wait to see what you do with it." She smiled. "And then there's my son, who wants to build a life with you...."

"I want that too," Nikko said quietly. "It's just...." He paused, unsure of how to frame his thoughts.

"Go on." Valerie's fingers wrapped around his. "You can be honest."

"We're going to be so far apart."

Valerie chuckled. "That's just geography, sweetheart."

He nodded. "It's funny you should say that. A few days ago, I was talking with Cal, and a thought occurred to me. I'd already kind of decided that I'm going to defer my studies until January, but for the first time I considered looking at universities closer to New York." He paused. Saying it out loud made it more real.

"You'd transfer?" Valerie straightened.

He shrugged. "I don't see why not. I chose San Francisco primarily because of its location. Oh, it's a great program, don't get me wrong, but there was the added bonus that I'd be near Grandma." He swallowed. "And that was my second issue. If... if I did transfer to be closer to Mitch, I'd also be moving farther away from her."

Valerie smiled. "Honey, that's fixable too. Move her with you. I'm sure there'd be places for her wherever you choose to go. It's not like she's tied permanently to one place, right?"

Nikko stared at her. He loved how she looked at potential problems and came up with solutions.

Valerie laughed. "What? Of course I'm going to make suggestions if it means you and Mitch stay together and make this work." She leaned forward and cupped his cheek. "Nikko, you're family." Valerie sat back and gazed at him fondly. "I'll be honest. When I first found out how old you are, it did concern me. Not so much now—I was looking into the future and imagining when Mitch is seventy and you're still a spring chicken at forty-seven...."

He laughed too, but what raced through his head was the fact that Valerie still saw them together, twenty-five years into the future. *Us growing old together....* There was a fluttering deep in his belly, and he realized that the idea didn't scare him. "And now? Does it still concern you?" He waited anxiously for her response.

There was that fond smile again. "Not so much, no. Not now that I've seen you and Mitch, seen how you interact… how much he clearly loves you." She sighed. "It won't be easy, but, then, things that are worth fighting for never are." She tilted her head. "Can I give you some advice?"

"Of course."

"Don't go rushing into anything, with regard to looking at possible universities." She met his gaze. "And talk to Mitch."

His scalp was prickling. So was the back of his neck. Then it struck him. "Where is Mitch, by the way?" And now that he thought about it, the house was awfully quiet. "Where *is* everyone?"

Valerie got up from her chair, wincing. "Damn. You'd think my arthritis would ease off when it's warmer. Must be getting old." She grinned at him. "The grandchildren all headed for the beach—which beach, I have no idea—and their parents all went to Ogunquit for the day. Gareth is with his father in the garage, talking about Malcolm's plans to turn the space above it into a self-contained apartment. And Mitch? He went off somewhere, said he'd be back by lunchtime."

Somewhere sounded pretty vague. "He didn't say where he was going?" Mitch hadn't said a word to him, either, which wasn't like him.

Valerie regarded him with a frank stare. "No, he didn't."

The back of Nikko's neck was still prickling.

"I'm going into the kitchen to make some bread. Have you ever made bread before?" Nikko shook his head and she beamed. "Want to learn how?"

It was on the tip of his tongue to say *Sure, seeing as I've nothing else to do because my boyfriend has decided to go off somewhere and not say a word....* He bit back the retort. "Sure. That sounds great." He got to his feet and followed her into the house.

"Well, you know what they say," Valerie said as they came through the back door. "The way to a man's heart…."

That got a chuckle. "Yeah, but Mitch's stomach is a bottomless pit."

Valerie's eyes grew large. "Oh, I am *so* telling him that when he gets back."

"Tattletale."

She laughed. "No—Mom." He joined in with her laughter as they set about assembling all the ingredients. He tried not to think about Mitch.

I'll find out when he gets back. Even if I have to tickle him to get it out of him.

Nikko was already learning Mitch's weaknesses.

D*AYS DON'T get much better than this.*

The sun was setting behind them, the last rays casting long shadows of the rocks at their backs stretching out over the sand. Mitch leaned against the sun-warmed boulder, Nikko sitting between his legs, his back against Mitch's chest, his head resting on Mitch's shoulder. Mitch had his arms around Nikko's waist. The beach was emptying as people headed home for the evening.

Mitch didn't want to move. He was comfortable, he was warm, and Nikko in his arms was just perfect. Speaking of Nikko....

"Hey," he said softly. Nikko inclined his head in Mitch's direction, and Mitch kissed him, slow and easy, loving how Nikko just melted into the kiss, his arm coming up to loop around Mitch's head to pull him in deeper. When they parted, Nikko's eyes were shining. He let go of Mitch and brought his head back to its original position with a sigh. "That was a weighty sound," Mitch observed.

"I wish we could stay here forever," Nikko said simply. "I love it here."

"This beach?" Goose Rocks Beach was their favorite.

Nikko shook his head. "No, Maine. It's so beautiful here."

Mitch stilled. *Go on, you couldn't ask for a more perfect moment....* His heart pounded. "So, why don't we make it forever?"

"Huh?" Nikko turned to regard him, a frown creasing his forehead. "What do you mean?"

"Why don't we stay in Maine?"

Nikko chuckled. "You mean, besides your job in New York and my studies… wherever." He sighed and looked out toward the ocean. "Not that I don't love the idea. It's just a dream."

"But that's what I'm saying," Mitch pressed on. "It doesn't have to be." Fuck, his heart was hammering.

Nikko sat up and shifted until he was sitting cross-legged on the towel, facing Mitch. "Okay, what's going on?" He pulled his braid over his shoulder, fidgeting with the end of it.

Mitch took a deep breath and forged ahead. "I'm not going back to New York."

There was a stunned silence. Nikko sat still, his gaze locked on Mitch's face, lips parted.

Mitch took hold of Nikko's hands. "I e-mailed the principal my letter of resignation, and mailed him a hard copy this morning."

"You did that… without mentioning it to me first?" Mitch winced at the hurt in those dark eyes. "I'd have thought this would be something we should have discussed, if we're serious about each other." Nikko's Adam's apple bobbed. "I mean, I know I've been thinking about my future too, and I was going to talk to you about this before I did anything, but this… this is huge." His breathing grew more rapid. "What will you do for money?"

"Let me finish, please." Mitch's heart sank to see the worry etched on Nikko's face. It had seemed like a wonderful idea at the time, to sort it all out and then surprise Nikko with it, but seeing that expression on Nikko's face made him regret his decision. "I had an interview earlier today, at a school along the coast. Ordinarily they'd be closed for the summer, but when I e-mailed them about the vacancy and sent them my résumé…."

Nikko gave a slow nod. "Let me guess. They jumped at the chance to interview you while you were staying so close."

Mitch couldn't take his eyes off him. "Basically. They want me to start in January." Before Nikko could say another word, he surged on. "I know, I should've said something, but I didn't want to worry you with the whole, '*hey, baby, I'm thinking of quitting my job*' scenario until I was sure I had another one lined up. But when the principal at the school here e-mailed me and asked me to come in for an interview…." He swallowed. "It all moved so fast. When he offered me the job, I knew I had to let my school know as soon as possible." Mitch sighed heavily. "I was going to tell you tonight." He sagged against the boulder. "I just wanted to surprise you."

Nikko said nothing, and Mitch's heart sank even further. He gazed at the towel, unable to look Nikko in the eye.

"January, huh?"

Mitch jerked his head up. There was been just the faintest note of amusement in Nikko's tone. "Uh, yeah?"

Nikko nodded. "So me deciding to defer the start of my master's until January would be quite a coincidence, then?"

It was Mitch's turn to stare. "What?"

"That's what I was going to talk to you about," he said. "My head's not in the right place for studying right now. I've gone over and over it in my mind, and that seemed the obvious solution. And then I got to thinking that I could study anywhere." His eyes twinkled. "I was actually considering transferring to a university in New York so we'd be together."

"You were?"

"Uh-huh—until I spoke with your mom this morning." He narrowed his gaze. "She knew where you were this morning, didn't she?"

Mitch groaned. "What did she say?" *Damn her. She just couldn't resist meddling.*

Nikko chuckled, and the sound lightened Mitch's heart. "She just told me not to do anything rash and to talk to you." He stared meaningfully at Mitch. "Which was what I'd been intending to do all along."

"All right, all right, I get the message!" Nikko snickered. Mitch reached for his hands once more. "We okay? I never meant to hurt you," he said quietly.

Nikko sighed. "I'm sorry I reacted the way I did. It just felt like you'd made a huge decision without a thought for how I'd feel, or how it would affect me—"

Mitch stopped his words with a kiss. Nikko stiffened for all of a couple of seconds before surrendering, feeding soft noises of pleasure into Mitch's mouth. Mitch broke the kiss and pulled back slowly. "Baby, let's promise to make any future big decisions together, okay?"

Nikko smiled. "That works for me."

"Can we go back to how we were sitting before I spoiled everything? Because up until that point, I was really enjoying holding you."

Fuck, the light in Nikko's eyes…. "I'd love that." He turned and wriggled back until Mitch had his arms full once more. Nikko's head on his shoulder, his arms around Nikko's waist, Mitch's legs on either side of him—perfect.

As if he'd read Mitch's mind, Nikko exhaled. "This feels perfect."

"No argument here," Mitch murmured before kissing Nikko's temple. "Love you," he whispered.

Nikko's gaze met his. "I love you too." He settled back against Mitch. "You know I was talking with Cal a few days ago?" Nikko said after a moment.

"Uh-huh." Mitch was enjoying the peace.

"Well, I looked up the University of Southern Maine after our conversation, just out of curiosity, you understand. Did you know they have an excellent Master of Music program?"

Mitch started smiling. "Really?"

Nikko nodded. "So I was thinking...." He twisted to look at Mitch. "What if I transferred there? I'd be in the same state, I'd already know someone at the university.... All I'd have to do is look into finding a place for Grandma, and it'd be perfect."

"Wait—moving Grandma?"

Nikko grinned. "That was your mom's idea."

Mitch snorted. "She thinks of everything. She even suggested me moving back to the house, *if* I got the job."

Nikko sat upright. "Hey, that's a good point. Where will we live? I—"

"Whoa there." Mitch tugged Nikko until he was in Mitch's lap. "Don't think about that now, okay? Right now you have more important things to do, like contacting San Francisco and putting the wheels in motion for your transfer. Once that's done, we'll have four months to sort things out, all right?"

Nikko sighed. "I suppose so."

Mitch kissed him, letting his lips linger until he felt Nikko relax into his embrace. Nikko shifted once again until they were seated as before, Nikko cradled between his legs, in Mitch's arms. Nikko turned and nuzzled Mitch's neck, lifting his chin to kiss Mitch's cheek. Mitch rested his head against the warm boulder and lost himself in the moment—the tinge of purple at the horizon, the cries of gulls above their heads, the smell of the ocean air, and Nikko in his arms.

"So I guess it's official."

"Hmm?"

Nikko kissed his chin. "You and me. In love. Living together."

Mitch laughed. "Yeah, that sounds kind of official."

"I suppose we'd better tell everyone tonight. You know, make it *really* official."

God, Mitch loved him.

"Let's just enjoy the sunset, baby," he murmured. "With my mom on the case, that's all we need to think about right now."

Everything else could wait.

In the kingdom of Teruna, the red-cloaked Seruani teach the Terunans the art of love. Taken from their homes at seventeen to be trained, they are shunned as outcasts by society and considered the lowest of the low. So when Prince Tanish falls in love with the Seruan Feyar, the man who took his virginity and the only one to share his bed, he is not about to declare that love. No one can ever know, because the consequences would be too painful to consider for both of them.

When the king of Vancor visits Teruna, he promises that his son, Prince Sorran, will marry Prince Tanish to solidify the alliance between the two kingdoms, with the proviso that the virginal Sorran is instructed in the art of pleasing his husband-to-be. When Tanish's father chooses Feyar to be this instructor, the lovers decide Prince Sorran must be taught that this is to be a marriage in name only....

A resentful prince, unwilling to share his lover.

A resentful Seruan, unwilling to share his prince.

And the shy prince whose very nature sparks changes in the lives of all those around them.

Teruna is about to change forever.

www.dreamspinnerpress.com

FIRST
K.C. WELLS

It's taken Tommy Newsome a while to get his head around being gay.

Growing up in a small town in Georgia hasn't prepared him for the more liberal life of a student at the university in Athens. Add to that the teachings of his parents and his church, and you have one shy young man who feels out of his depth. Working on his daddy's farm hasn't given him any chance of a social life, certainly not one like the clubs of Atlanta have on offer. Not that Tommy feels comfortable when he gets to sample it—Momma's lectures still ring loudly inside his head.

All that changes when he goes to his first gay bar and sets eyes on Mike Scott.

When Mike's not behind the bar at Woofs, he's busy with his life as adult entertainer Scott Masters. Twenty years in the industry and the times, they are a-changing. Mike's not had much luck in the relationship department, but as his mom is fond of telling him, you keep fishing in the same pond, you're gonna reel in the same kind of fish. Maybe it's time for a change.

And then a beautiful young man asks Mike to be his first....

www.dreamspinnerpress.com

LEARNING TO LOVE: Michael & Sean

K.C. Wells

Learning to Love: Book 1

Sean and Michael are best friends from the minute they meet and become roommates. But after supporting Sean in the wake of his brother's death, Michael finds himself questioning his sexuality and thinking about his roommate in a totally unexpected light. After all, he and Sean are straight—or so he thought. Suddenly Michael's not so sure any more. He turns to their gay housemate, Evan, for advice. Little does he know he's not the only one seeking Evan's help.

Michael and Sean are both thrilled to explore their newly discovered feelings for each other, but not everyone shares their enthusiasm. When the reality of homophobia intrudes on their academic and personal lives and threatens their happiness, the adversity should draw them closer. Instead, it drives a dangerous wedge between them and puts their relationship, their futures, and their health at risk.

www.dreamspinnerpress.com

Love Lessons Learned

K.C. Wells

John Wainwright is having a momentous day. To start off, he lands his first teaching job. Then his brother, Evan, and Evan's husband, Daniel, take him out to celebrate in Manchester's gay village. An encounter with a sexy man forces John to admit what he's been denying for too long—he's gay. His coming out proves he's supported and loved by his family and roommates. What more could a man want? There's just one small problem: John's dishy Head Teacher, Brett Sanderson, and John's gigantic crush on him. Too bad Brett is straight.

Brett Sanderson leads a double life. At thirty-three, he is the Head Teacher of a primary school. But for seven years now, during every school holiday, Brett has fled to Brighton, where he becomes 'Rob,' a man who has a different guy in his bed every night but has never had a relationship.

Once he's back in school, Brett is firmly back in that closet, until his newest staff member starts prying open the door. When John pulls out all the stops to get Brett's attention, neither man is prepared for the consequences.

www.dreamspinnerpress.com

COLLARS & CUFFS

AN UNLOCKED HEART

K.C. WELLS

Collars & Cuffs: Book 1

Since the death of his submissive lover two years ago, Leo hasn't been living—merely existing. He focuses on making Collars & Cuffs, a BDSM club in Manchester's gay village, successful. That changes the night he and his business partner have their weekly meeting at Severinos. Leo can't keep his eyes off the new server. The shy man seems determined to avoid Leo's gaze, but that's like a red rag to a bull. Leo loves a challenge.

Alex Daniels works at Severinos to scrape together the money to move out on his own. He struggles with coming out, but he's drawn to Leo, the gorgeous guy with the icy-blue eyes who's been eating in his area nearly every night.

Leo won't let Alex's hesitance get in the way. He even keeps him away from the club so as not to scare him. And as for telling Alex that Leo is a Dom? Not a good idea. One date becomes two, but date two leads to Leo's bedroom… and Alex discovers things about himself he never realized—and never wanted anyone to see.

www.dreamspinnerpress.com

FOR **MORE** OF THE **BEST GAY ROMANCE**

DREAMSPINNER PRESS
dreamspinnerpress.com

Lightning Source UK Ltd.
Milton Keynes UK
UKOW06f1921200716

278883UK00014B/550/P